THE KILLING GROUND

"*The Killing Ground* mirrors Settle's steadily deepening interest in the past, an interest that has raised her panorama to a level of myth...Settle fans have watched this author spin a far larger terrain (in space and time) than Faulkner's Yoknapatawpha County."

—Doris Betts, *The Philadelphia Inquirer*

"One of the most powerful, eloquent writers we have. *The Killing Ground* is a classic novel of conscience. That is the American novel at its best."

—*Vogue*

"Every word rings true, every character is fully formed, and best of all is the sense running through it of time coexisting, the past richly evident in the present *The Killing Ground* is a real pleasure—the fitting culmination of her Beulah quintet."

—Anne Tyler

"A complex tale, complexly told—well worth the unraveling."
—*Los Angeles Times Book Review*

"She simply tells a story in a manner exquisitely suited to it, and in doing so manages somehow to bring the whole world into focus. One could hardly ask a writer for more."

—*Newsday*

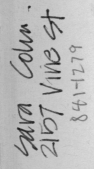

Bantam Windstone Books
Ask your bookseller for the books you have missed

THE LONG MARCH by William Styron
LOST IN THE FUNHOUSE by John Barth
THE MEMOIRS OF A SURVIVOR by Doris Lessing
THE MIDDLE GROUND by Margaret Drabble
MY LIFE AS A MAN by Philip Roth
MY MICHAEL by Amos Oz
NIGHT OF THE AUROCHS by Dalton Trumbo
THE NEEDLE'S EYE by Margaret Drabble
ONE DAY IN THE LIFE OF IVAN DENISOVICH by
    Alexander I. Solzhenitsyn
PORTNOY'S COMPLAINT by Philip Roth
THE REALMS OF GOLD by Margaret Drabble
SET THIS HOUSE ON FIRE by William Styron
THE SNOW LEOPARD by Peter Matthiessen
SOMETIMES A GREAT NOTION by Ken Kesey
THE STONE ANGEL by Margaret Laurence
THE SUMMER BEFORE THE DARK by Doris Lessing
AN UNKNOWN WOMAN by Alice Koller
V. by Thomas Pynchon
VISION QUEST by Terry Davis
A WEAVE OF WOMEN by E. M. Broner
WHEN SHE WAS GOOD by Philip Roth
WHERE THE JACKALS HOWL by Amos Oz
A WOMAN OF THE FUTURE by David Ireland
WRINKLES by Charles Simmons

The Killing Ground

Mary Lee Settle

BANTAM BOOKS
TORONTO · NEW YORK · LONDON · SYDNEY

THE KILLING GROUND

*A Bantam Book / published by arrangement with
Farrar. Straus & Giroux Inc.*

PRINTING HISTORY

*Farrar. Straus & Giroux edition published June 1982
Bantam Windstone edition / October 1983*

Windstone and accompanying logo of a stylized **W**
are trademarks of Bantam Books. Inc.

*Bantam Books are published by Bantam Books. Inc. Its trade-
mark. consisting of the words ''Bantam Books'' and the por-
trayal of a rooster. is Registered in U.S. Patent and Trademark
Office and in other countries. Marca Registrada. Bantam
Books. Inc., 666 Fifth Avenue. New York. New York 10103.*

PRINTED IN THE UNITED STATES OF AMERICA

H   0 9 8 7 6 5 4 3 2 1

Contents

*We are fighting, as always, the long
battalioned ghosts of old wrongs
and shames that each generation
of us both inherits and creates.*

WILLIAM FAULKNER

I

The Return
June 1978

IT is five o'clock in the morning, Daylight Saving Time. I have been sitting on the balcony of the downriver room on the second floor of the Howard Johnson's motel on Canona Boulevard almost all night. In other cities motels may be escape routes to anonymity, but not for me, not in Canona, and not this morning.

In the first twilight of dawn, the Canona River moves like a silver snake under a suspension of white mist. The still-unlit south hills, under their lush cover of trees, are primordial across the river. The hollow where my ancestor and namesake Hannah woke over two hundred years ago is a dark gash between them. But the tree she crawled in to sleep, on its mound of earth, is gone, covered by the retaining wall of the road to the suburbs.

In our white arrogance we have honored her as the discoverer of this valley when, mindless with panic, she fled across this bottomland. She was not the first. In a shift of time and light, Hannah's sycamore is not yet there, for even as huge as it was, it was seeded and grew on an abandoned burial mound.

It has taken three thousand years to build this city. If a city consists, not of old campsites, old fires, but of shelters, tombs, sacred forms, and places for murder, with the illusion of permanency so that in a lifetime it can be left and returned to, as I have done, then this city is three thousand years old. I can see, from the balcony of the motel, the confluence of two rivers, an ancient marriage, where wanderers ceased their nervous movement, became, for a while, constant;

3

built, buried, worshiped, and after fifteen hundred years shrank back from the valley and left their dead behind, without names, lost. Below me the Boulevard, that was in my lifetime River Street where the coal barons built their Gothic mansions, follows what the first white men, only two hundred years ago, thought was an Indian trail through virgin forest but was, instead, an overlay of trees hiding a sacred road, abandoned to animals, then to tribal Indians.

Why the unknown people came here, and why they left, no one knows. Did they come to mine for black flint, mica, steatite, to carve it into ornaments and weapons, denoting caste, and to trade it for copper, sea pearls, and shells, denoting riches? We do know this. There was a ruling caste who deserted the valley for the lines of hills, north and south of the river, built citadels of earth and dry stone walls that have left their traces. We know, too, that they worshiped a goddess, the grand mother, the earth her body and her temple. I see a child's hands, even then, learn that a bird can be caged with twigs, and I see her beaten by her mother for breaking a taboo. She runs away, and is afraid of being alone, and comes crying back. Did she leave with them? Did they mine out the steatite, flint, mica? Did their slaves refuse to work?

The sacred road below me leads to the killing ground at the confluence of the rivers from a great stone circle near the eastern mountains. In the first dawn, to placate the grand mother in the sacred circle so that she will release the sun from the ground where she has hidden it, a man pours the blood of his son on a stone column, a phallus in the center of the killing ground, conductor of lightning. He reads in the dawn shadows the copulation of earth and sky. No ram appears in the thicket, no covenant. As the ground soaks, the mother drinks and the sun rises over the eastern ridge. He has fooled her. It is the blood of a slave and not his own son. He has hopes that the lie will bring forgiveness.

The blood makes a snake track along the killing ground, and he lifts a live snake from a basket, labyrinthine coils around his arm, cold ripples of skin in his hands, and shows the people that the blood has come to life. He listens to the hiss and rattle of his mother goddess, hears her commandments out of the prevailing wind, and is certain that his faith has saved him.

Now, near the place where the stone stela stood, the spire

of All Saints, the Episcopal church, pierces the sky, and on Sundays the chalice is passed discreetly.

The mound tomb in the hollow is so old that Hannah's tree shelter has grown on it a thousand years after the desertion of the first city. Is it the tomb of a priest who has been bitten by a snake? When he was found, a steatite foot lay beside him, ritually killed, a mica bird-claw, a necklace of sea pearls, and his skeleton was painted life color with red ocher. There is evidence that the flesh was stripped from his bones. Was he exposed? Eaten out of respect? No one knows.

The grave was found when the new road to the south hills was being blasted. His skeleton measured seven feet, and my father said there sure were giants in the earth in those days. His wife lay under him, six feet tall, in her crushed ornaments of mica and copper and her gorget of hieroglyphic stones. Flint weapons too delicately carved to kill an earth creature accompanied their immortality, which is here, in the Howard Johnson's motel, in the limitless time-scape of my brain, and in my handbag on the bed behind me.

For eighteen years I have carried a black flint spearhead, as delicate as a jewel, that my father picked up from the grave before the final blasting to widen the road. He gave it then to my brother Johnny, and after his death I took it with me on a journey that has lasted for eighteen years, an exile, a search. Now, in this dawn, there is a cohesion of time in the shape and flow of the river and in the books I have written, discoveries turned into the hieroglyphs of words.

Those first ancestors, the unknowns, still exist within the cells that made us. The first white farmers, our forefathers, only two hundred years ago, found more than a thousand mounds in this valley, the detritus of a culture. They plowed up the skeletons with their plows. They were not wasted. The bones were burned for lime and spread across the fields to be eaten in the food of the first harvest, a thanksgiving. The circles were plowed level, and the stones founded another layer of the city. They burned the sacred snakes in the spring, and cracked the stone stela with fire. At night they, too, feared the vast dark, and formed it into heathen demons. Sometimes ghosts scratched at the log doors. Indians, in their tribal decadence, called this a cursed valley.

It has been a perilous wandering, perilous meaning circular, from this spot above the river, back to it from the depths of time, circumstances, questions that have led me two continents and three hundred years away, drawn always to some evocative source. But now I know that for me the source is here, alone in this dawn in my own city, in this font, this fountain filled with blood drawn from Emmanuel's veins. Emmanuel, indwelling and monstrous, a great hand, plunges into my heart where my brother's heart is, and the heart of this place for me.

To trace the spacious circle of my search, I, half asleep now, take a boat at the shore of the river, the water road below this motel balcony, and float in that element, ignorant of time, out of the mountains toward the west. It is the second oldest river in the world. I follow it to the great central artery of the Mississippi, through the Gulf of Mexico, into the Gulf Stream that leads on to the English Channel, on up the Thames. This water takes me up the gentle Windrush to Burford, where Johnny Church, soldier in Cromwell's army, watches dawn, too, at the window of Burford church, where the new sun, through the red glass robe of a saint, stains the stone floor. The church is his prison on the morning of April 14, 1649, and I know it as well as I know the room behind me.

I have asked for this room in the Howard Johnson's motel. It is near as I can be to the space where I slept for the most of my childhood until I was fourteen, before the house built by my great-grandfather, Senator Neill, was torn down. Below the window the elfin orange roof of the motel entrance covers the side lawn of the old Carver mansion. Anderson Carver, old Broker, burned it down with a cigarette when I was ten. I watched then from the window of my bedroom in this same place in air. The flames lit the night sky and danced on the river. I could see my father, Preston McKarkle, down below me, his face lit by the glow, watering the side lawn and the trees to douse the flying sparks, and hear my mother calling from their bedroom window behind me, "Mooney, for God's sake, the house! The house!" She only called him that when she was upset.

Now the twenty-story Coal Building obscures the view. I can see only into the darkened window of someone's office.

I have come to this place, on this day for a reason, and I have stayed awake most of the night for fear of missing the dawn. It was from this angle of vision, looking south as I am doing now, June 7, but sixty-six years ago, in 1912, that Lily Lacey, the sister of my Uncle Dan Neill's wife Althea, looked out of her window on the second floor of their house on Lacey

Creek, and dreamed of New York City. I am building that house, which I cannot know, from other people's memories, from such angles of vision as this one, a house of words. But there is not, for me, as there was for Lily, true darkness. There are always lights.

Below me on the Boulevard by the river the green fog lights are isolated in silence. A single traffic signal marks time, green yellow red green. I wait. Lily within me waits. All I have known about her are shards of fact, that she ran away, that she was killed in the First World War. Lily, death, war, and old photographs which I suspect of lying, are all I have to help me conjure her, those, and in the dawn, the understanding and imitation of her flight.

On the south hills opposite the Howard Johnson's motel, the ancient breastworks are gone, their stones incorporated into the gardens of the houses of the rich. I cannot see any houses. They are huddled behind the blanket of trees that give the illusion of virgin forest as the sky turns to lavender. The birds sing songs from the beginning, and in one of the houses a man has hanged himself and has not been found. He turns back and forth. The toes of his Bally shoes scrape the floor of his garden room, faintly. He has dressed himself carefully for this abandonment.

The dawn turns white. A great stain of smoke soils the southwestern sky, a long invasive trail. It is perpetual and marks the map of the city from above, a pillar of cloud the color of human waste by day. By night a pillar of flame will belch from the chimneys of the chemical plants. The buildings in the way of the prevailing wind are pocked deep with disease, and too many men here die of lung cancer.

The first car cuts through the illusion of silence without time. It is an old Ford, stopping at the light, its engine breathing. A foot zooms impatience with the light. It changes, bringing a growl from the Ford. Nothing is past. There are still voices out of the wind, the sounds of threat. The lost, fragmented signals are heard by the ignorant, who answer in tongues, or by family members like myself, who embarrass their kin. The man demanding change with his foot in the car below survives for a Cro-Magnon second in a surge of muscle and blind will.

This day begins to move. True dawn begins to color the white sky. The unknown giant, and Johnny Church, shot at Burford, my namesake Hannah, and lovely dangerous Lily are in lost graves, forgotten, except by me and a lone reader who has not been able to sleep either, who is bringing them to life from the books of my search. It has taken us both a long time to give them back their lives.

The sun rises above the eastern mountains; around the upriver bend to the east, the first coal barges of the morning are pushed slowly on the beginning of a journey to the Gulf of Mexico. I count ten of them, a black leviathan of barges. Morning obliterates the past. It drags me back into the confined circle of my own life, to this motel room over the river. To keep it at bay, I take out the black spearhead, smooth it with my fingers, hoping for the comfort of memory. Instead, I see the narrow single lifetime of myself, here and in this brutal century, about which the ladies who will pick me up to do my duty to this city as it is this morning are blessed with unawareness. I am bored with my dislike of them, their dangerous satisfactions.

They are, in one of the bloodiest centuries of the Christian era, women to whom nothing has happened that is not personal. Aging, dry, and complicated girls, they still call each other girls, weathered by years, unchanged. I hear playing cards snap, the chink of Mah-Jongg tiles, and their edged voices in other rooms sit with me, sit with me awhile.

Telephones dial and dial and dial; they reject silences. Now they exist on sufferance and rule kingdoms too small, clubs, gardens, their imitators. They are the prisoners of the welfare of their parents, their husbands, the habits of their privilege.

They have attended on every event of my life in this valley, on weddings and funerals, on my brother Johnny. Even my recall of him is attended by them. But they can tell me nothing of why I am really here, except in hints of memory to be matched and fitted. They do not know how to remember events, only where they were at the time, mistaking this for the events themselves. One brings back herself in tennis shorts, standing by the telephone too shocked, she said, to take a shower, and thinks that for me, too, this is Johnny.

They carry in themselves the residue of old needs and fears which have been composted into prejudice. The origins are buried in their minds as deeply as the spearhead was buried under the first Hannah's tree, for they fear the exposure of facts as I fear the isolation of illusion.

My Uncle Ephraim, my father's brother, tried to tell me this a long time ago, but I reject his voice for this day, and make instant coffee in a plastic cup to stop the drowsiness that comes now after my watch in the dawn.

I can foresee them, them and myself in the morning. Maria, the widow of John Boy Crane, who carried his child name to his grave, will drive her Cadillac Seville. Her little paws in the last pair of white gloves in the valley will clutch the wheel. She has picked me up at the airport in this car, and deposited me at the Howard Johnson's motel, protesting, "I don't for the life of me know why you have to stay in a motel in your own town," and she has sat in the dark with the engine still running to show she is annoyed. The seats are blue leather and the computer winks. Maria has explained that it is her "last" luxury and that she has bought it because it is American and she thinks people ought to buy American cars. She has confessed the extra cost of the leather seats, the computer, and astroroof. "I needed them," she has explained.

Beside her, in the front seat, Ann Randolph Potter will have the place of honor, being the oldest, which in this way they will not let her forget. There are rules here. What they call age groups carry on from childhood, as formal as innocence. She will be the only woman in the car who is not a widow, besides myself. Her daughter, Sally Bee, is long dead, and Ann Randolph seems to have forgotten her. Her husband, Plain George, has deserted her for his longtime mistress, and has been dropped socially. All of the women in the car have the habit of rallying around Ann Randolph as if she is ill. She, who is sixty-six, has had surgery to lift not only her face but her spirits.

The Cadillac door will close on me. It will fit with a slight puff, a lady fart.

Beside me in the back seat, where it smells of fine leather and there is no noise but the breathing and voices of women, there will be Daisy, widow of Lewis Cutright. Her son, Lewis Jr., who calls himself Beverley when he is out of the valley, lives with his friend in San Francisco on money left in trust by Lewis's mother, Miss Alida. Daisy reads books on homosexuality and says she doesn't know what went wrong. Her son and his friend visit once a year and demand that she assume the virtue of tolerance, which is hard for her. I can see her square-jawed profile. She wears her ugliness arrogantly, and has made me ashamed for years of being younger, prettier, and more talented. Daisy has, in her words, thrown her energies into the arts. Some way she connects this with her attempts to understand young Lewis. She is the chairman of the hanging committee of the new art gallery. This morning's rites are to raise money for it.

The fourth woman, Kitty Puss, is my cousin by marriage to Brandy Baseheart. She will bring me my brother Johnny as none of the others will and I fear seeing her. She will be what she calls frank. "Jesus," she will say, "I'm only being frank."

They represent, for me, my sister Melinda, ten years older than I am. I have seen them all grow, weather, and begin to shrink, almost as magic women. When I was growing up, they wore whispering evening dresses that made the rooms smell of tissue paper, silk, and flowers.

I see myself in the car, and it smells of leather, cigarettes, and linen. The red eye of the computer will wink as we cross the Mingo River that runs south into the Canona and begin the long drive up the holy road that leads to the sacred circle at the hilltop. The car will float upward through centuries of change. We will pass the cave that was a home, and in my childhood a place to dare.

Maria's shrill stream of complaint flows from her mouth. It is the only sound in the car except for the distant rich whisper of the engine. She, white-faced, black hair dyed dead-bitch color, guides us toward the safety of all our childhoods.

I try not to look at Kitty Puss, but then I do. Kitty Puss Baseheart, once the fastest girl in her crowd, graceful and dashing, is red from bourbon and the sun over a perpetual golf course she seems to have walked across all her life.

The road circles the high hidden valley where the golf course was before the Country Club moved to the southern hills. It is now a park. As we drive along it, I can look down at the hazards and traps that still form, faintly, fragments of the earthworks of the sacred circle at the end of the long rise from the valley.

The towers of the old Country Club rise still, but not for long, against the sky. It was at first the Slingsby mansion, built in 1900, before Mrs. Slingsby decided that Gothic architecture was what she called nova reesh, and built the Federal house on River Street. I can see the towers again as we turn into the drive, vine-covered to their pinnacles. The red tiles that Mr. Slingsby imported for the roof are snaggled, some askew, some fallen, broken on the terrace. Down from the western tower a broken gutter's tear stain divides the wall. There is mud now where the lawn was, a sink catching the rain, a hand lawn mower, its wheels half mooned by mud, half a tipped wheelbarrow, half a flagpole, and sunk to the waist, a marble statue of Aphrodite, no longer needing to hide her genitals with her pretty hand. She, half clothed with mud, cries too as the roof cries, her stone face streaked.

The broken terrace, where once ladies from Washington walked with their parasols while their husbands made coal deals in the library, is invaded by young trees. The almost transparent ladies, time-yellowed, like old newspaper, turn on their rich tracks along the broken stones. The coal boom at the beginning of the century made this tiny mountain kingdom. Now it destroys it, and the house sinks as Rome sank, but not in centuries. This destruction is counted in decades. The coal mine, started far up the north hollow fifty years ago, has tunneled under the house and it is unsafe.

At once I am eleven, and yellowed paper too, watching the ghosts at my sister Melinda's wedding. Then I am seventeen, up there at the hollow window of the ladies' room, staring out into the night in deadly fear that Johnny won't come to the dance and see that somebody dances with me. I am wearing green voile. Dark red lipstick is slashed across my mouth, and I am seductive and pure and unaware. Eleven and seventeen and forty-eight, still asking one single timeless question while houses rise and fall, fortunes are made and lost: "Where is my brother Johnny?"

For if obsession, siege, the hovering of a spirit demanding a central place, all the way into a darkness where I have not yet gone, is love, then I am in thrall, sunk in love, as I have always been in whatever guise I found him, with my brother Johnny—Brother Jonathan, Johnny Rebel, Johnny Dalton, Johnny the Kid, Johnny run the streets. For he, my brother Johnny, deep within me, has run away from the little old woman and has run away from the little old man, and run away from me too, he can, he can. I carry a perpetual longing to know what happened to him. I have lived a prayer against his betrayals and surprises. I have come back this time, once again, for I have failed before, to find him, bless him, release him, and bury him at last. I know, if anyone does, why Antigone had to bury the evasive Polynices. She buried an obsession so it would not haunt her. She had to bless him who was unblessed. At last, at last, she must have told herself, grief-stricken and relieved, I will know where he is.

So I am tracing Johnny's life from here and now to there and then and back again, a brother who, like Polynices, may not be worth all this, but that was never the question, with either of them.

So the house in front of us sinks slowly. A great rent down its façade tears apart the window of what was once the ladies' powder room, crashes the windows of the great hall, releasing small animals and birds. That room I have known in that coolness in summer against tennis-sweaty legs, or coming in from the sharp snow, a rich security of fathers, bourbon, pine, and holly. Gold Christmas tree lights were mirrored in the polished floor, and shone in the dark windows. A huge fire burned in the fireplace Mr. Slingsby brought back from Europe, reflected on what I called the scutcheon, and burnished the paneled walls.

Now, long fissures divide the red-dog sea, and the house begins to crumble so fast that I can watch time acting on it. It sinks down, down, dragging the wheelbarrow, the lawn mower, Aphrodite, the euonymus, tendrils of pachysandra, the broken windows, the towers, falling, and we, too close to its suction, sink with it, down, down through the red industrial mud. The ladies in the car do not move. They have been frozen there too long. We sink with the house, to be found among the trash of an age, studied as something once sacred, now unknown, a hint of a lost time in a tomb of steel, a sacred chariot called Cadillac. There will be skeletons, fragments of leather and linen, wedding rings, diamond watches, gold cigarette lighters. Are they priestesses, these upright skeletons of grandmothers in the insignia of their rank? I am one of them.

The telephone shrills on my bedside table in the Howard Johnson's motel and I am awake again. The coffee in the plastic cup is cold.

At nine-thirty it was already as hot as hell. The car windows were closed, the engine running to keep the air conditioning cool. Kitty Puss said so and Maria, from the front seat, told her it would be cooler up on the hill. It always was. Daisy went back to the car to wait. She said she wouldn't be caught dead hanging around some motel lobby.

After all, it wasn't as if Hannah had to be treated with kid gloves like a stranger even if she was well-known. Daisy giggled at the word. Besides, she wanted to impress on Hannah there wasn't much time.

"God. She was still asleep." She heaved her body into the back seat. As it was, they had to wait ten minutes.

"They can't start until we get there," Maria soothed.

"Oh, for heaven's sake." Daisy jabbed her elbow into Kitty Puss's hard fat, trying to make herself comfortable. She hadn't meant to. She said she was sorry, but Kitty Puss didn't even look around. Daisy never did know whether Kitty Puss was just rude or if she was getting as deaf as a post, or if she'd started again.

"On a morning like this, too," Daisy went on, fuming. "It's the only big fund-raiser for the new art gallery." She said what they all knew, so no one, for once, answered her. "I don't suppose she cares. She probably does things like this all the time."

"She came, didn't she?" Kitty Puss told the river.

"Well, after all, she ought to," Daisy told Kitty Puss's broad back.

Kitty Puss said that if she had to go to another damned meeting she'd shoot herself.

"It's not a meeting. It's a fund-raiser."

"Whatever," Kitty Puss told the river, and couldn't resist saying, "I didn't see you shelling out." Daisy felt tears behind her eyes.

"She gave in kind." Maria hated cruelty. She always said so. Daisy patted the mound of cloth in her lap and considered hours and hours of dedicated work. She had wrapped it so carefully because of Maria's dog hairs. She started to pick at them. Maria didn't feed her dog right and she told her so, not for the first time, leaning her arms on the front seat, so that Ann Randolph had to cringe into the corner against the closed window.

Hannah had not seen their faces outside of her mind and memory for ten years, and even those images were like cartoons. The women were shadowed by the car roof and she couldn't see them until she stooped to get in. She was suddenly a foot from the shocking face of Daisy, not the hard, tennis-playing girl of her dreams, but for her an old woman, a face imposed on the one she had known, found again, recognized, and said, "Daisy?" still not sure.

"Get in. We're late." That was Daisy, unforgettable, the voice still strident.

The women were in the same formal positions in the car that she knew they would be. "Why, honey, you look wonderful." Formal twittering. "Welcome home!" A network of voices that Daisy soon controlled. "Go on, Maria!"

"Now look to your left and you'll see the new art gallery. It's the only original house left on the riverbank. We saved it. The number of lovely old places that have been torn down...It's going to be for local artists." Hannah's clenched neural reaction to the woman made her do as she was told.

"We've all contributed. I do macramé." Daisy patted the tissue paper in her lap.

"Don't think she doesn't know the place." Kitty Puss laughed. "She misspent her youth there. My God, didn't we all?"

Ahead to their left, the old beer joint, the Wayfaring Stranger, looked like a doll's house, San Francisco style. The gingerbread-trimmed porch was new, painted gleaming white, the door bright red, the façade butter-yellow. "Slow down, Maria, she can't see a thing," Daisy commanded. "Of course" —she looked, too, as they passed it, slowly—"a lot of it had to be reconstructed. We did it from pictures of the houses of the correct period. It's all authentic," the word a little prayer.

It was gone, behind them, the old Wayfaring Stranger, shining and dead.

"It was filthy," Daisy told the car. "We voted to leave the riverside porch. You know, where the jukebox and the bar were. We made it into the main gallery. We needed one in this town, let me tell you. The state took over the museum," she said sadly. "At least, that's where the children all go now. It's awful. Professionals from out of state. You know, models of coal mines and a lot of stuff about early man. I wouldn't call that taste. We're the hanging committee, so we have control over taste."

"Truer words were never spoken," Kitty Puss told the river.

"Now, Kitty Puss," Maria said, by habit.

"I didn't say a goddamn thing. I'm on my good behavior."

"I don't know. All that's left to us is the arts..." Daisy mourned. "When I remember the clinic and all those dear little colored children. I've always said, children ought to be born black and then turn white. They're just dear when they're tiny . . . They took that away and then the museum, I don't know . . ."

"Who?" Hannah forgot not to ask.

"Why, the govment, honey, govment interference."

"Don't tell her. She's a damned radical anyway," Kitty Puss stated as if Hannah were not there.

"She is not. She's a Democrat." Daisy's back was turned to her while she argued.

"Oh, kiss my foot," Kitty Puss told her. She'd had enough of being on good behavior. She leaned around Daisy. "I thought I kicked your butt out of here . . ."

"Now, Kitty Puss," came faintly from the front seat.

Daisy laughed. "My God, I'd forgotten that. You were wearing your Dior dress . . ."

"And you kept yelling, 'Kitty Puss, you'll tear your Dior.'"

They were pleased with each other, remembering a funny story.

"She had to leave and then come back and lord it over us," Kitty Puss reminded them.

Daisy remembered Hannah. She patted her hand. "We're only teasing," she said, "we think it's just wonderful what you've done."

"Whatever that is." Kitty Puss hadn't finished.

Ann Randolph whispered, "You left, too, Kitty Puss."

"We went to Hilton Head. It's not the same."

"Anyway, Kitty Puss came back and opened the house again." Ann Randolph's whisper quieted the car.

Maria thought she had better change the subject before Kitty Puss got going again. "There will be a lot of new people there this morning. People who would never have been at the old club," she complained.

"She means Jews and rednecks." Kitty Puss was enjoying herself.

"I do not"—Maria's voice went up an octave—"you know I don't."

"We were able to keep *some* control over the guest list," Daisy assured them all.

Ann Randolph passed a bag of Jordan Almonds over to the back seat. Her hand was old, her fingernails like little pink shells.

"She always carries them." Daisy was solicitous of the bag, as if it contained a part of who Ann Randolph was. She passed them, yellow, green, pink, lavender, and white. There was only the sound of chewing like the crunch of tiny bones.

As they crossed the Mingo, there was, at last, a silence in the car. Hannah watched Maria's profile, now in daylight. Hannah would have known her anywhere, on cruise boats, on show planes, figuring the tip carefully at ladies' lunches, in all the brave and forlorn activities.

She was seeing them at last, freed from her dream. They were healthy and their teeth were straight, and nobody looked haunted. There were no threats, no cultural mountains. For a dangerous moment, forgetting, she sank into peace. The blue leather felt cool against her back. They were not fearsome. They were pathetic, redundant. She knew, seeing them that way, that she was taking some final revenge.

"You'll meet the new curator." Daisy couldn't bear the silence any longer.

"He's as queer as a three-dollar bill," Kitty Puss informed.

"He is not." Maria allowed herself a little spurt of anger. "He went to *Choate* with my *brother*."

"The perfect marriage. Widows and pansies." Kitty Puss had to have the last word. Daisy wouldn't let her.

"He plays an excellent game of bridge and he has taste. That doesn't make him . . ." She stopped. Honoring the embarrassment of Daisy's son, no one spoke for a minute. Hannah was left to wonder what she was going to say. She looked at a bit of bird dropping that had escaped the careful polishing of the car. They were driving in an event that never changed, as the houses changed, the streets, the landscape itself, rising and falling.

Kitty Puss wouldn't shut up. "We got *Deep Throat* for Charlie Bland's birthday. It was a riot. You should have seen us being tolerant."

"It was very interesting." Maria's mouth went smaller than ever. "After all, we have to keep up with things." She sounded sad.

"It made me want to fuck." Kitty Puss grinned.

"Now, that will be enough," Daisy used the curb. "I'm sure Hannah isn't interested. She probably does that kind of thing all the time. She's artistic. I for one thought it was disgusting," Daisy finished bravely, "no matter what you say."

They drove on, their images of Hannah as intact as hers had been of them. There was nothing more to say. She wondered if she was going to be sick on Maria's blue leather.

Kitty Puss was entirely alone. The other four women were as far away as continents. She sank back into grayness, mind just ticking over. There was always the question of what a rich, well-educated woman was to do with her life. She'd tried to talk to Charlie Bland about it, but he just said kneel down and thank God. He was no use at all. She had been well-educated too, she'd gone to Smith, which ought to have satisfied her, and she was better-informed than the rest of them. Good works? She hated them, hated the busy butt of Daisy when she was good-working. "It isn't *what* you say. You have to follow procedure," Daisy's chorus. Take a lover? God knows she'd done that, for what good it did her. She liked the phrase, though, even though she was damned sick and tired of the lover.

She and Charlie Bland had behaved so well that it disgusted her. No courage. No panache. She didn't fool herself about why. You don't give up a large slice of coal property to run off like a slut with somebody you've known all your life and not get invited anywhere. So they had waited, and waited longer, and when Brandy died she thought the waiting was over, the constant unfaithfulness of Charlie, the boring good behavior so that nobody was hurt. Discretion, another name for cowardice. But by then they both knew, knew without saying it, that it was too late. Too late. It rang in her mind. Drift. Too late. Shit. She knew too much. She always had. He was only good old Charlie Bland with the setter dog eyes that got all the women. Nothing more. Not a damned thing. Silence that she had once taken for depth was dumbness. Boredom that was the only calm she knew settled over her. She leaned back on the cool leather and watched Hannah. Hannah McKarkle. Good God. Who would have known? That goddamned nosy little brat. Kitty Puss had to admit she envied her. After all, she'd *done* something. What it was Kitty Puss didn't give a damn about. When her books were mentioned, and that seldom, it was usually because somebody had read a newspaper clipping, she always said, "Hell, don't talk to me. I haven't read anything since *Little Black Sambo*." It got a laugh anyway. Jesus, get a laugh, above all get a laugh. It wasn't true, but it was a good remark. She did read. She read *The Wall Street Journal* religiously, at the same time every day, with her first drink.

Hannah looked like she had been up all night. Kitty Puss didn't have to wonder why. Nobody stayed at a motel in her own town except for one reason. Lover was a fine word, but it ended up where it began, in a motel room. She and Charlie knew them all, not so much lately, but once in a while still. It surprised them both. She wondered who the man was. She knew Hannah was married, to some man she never brought back with her. That wasn't quite fair. She'd married after she left the last time. At least Kitty Puss thought so; she hadn't paid much attention. Nobody mentioned Hannah until they started reading about her. Being married wouldn't matter to an artist. They were notorious for their loose lives. She knew that much. Kitty Puss wished for a loose life. It would be something to do anyway. God, Hannah looked like her brother. The presence of Johnny flooded her mind. Sometimes she got them mixed up in her dreams, Johnny and Charlie Bland. Same kind of man. Same way of going. If it hadn't been for the war. If Johnny hadn't made her wait so long, not knowing...

The woman had that same aloof way of holding her head. She wasn't looking at them and after a few mutual blah-blahs she had hardly said a word. She was just sitting in the corner, her hands twisting together, staring at a drop of bird shit on the car window. Otherwise spotless. It always was. Except for the dog hair. Awful little lapdog. Kitty Puss needed another drink. It was the only way to get through the morning. I am bored and rich and sick to death of Charlie, she said, but not aloud. What the hell is he up to? As if I don't know. She'd seen the police car when they passed his house. No good fooling herself. All the times before. He'd either wrecked his car or gone on a bender. The number of times, oh why bother... Let him have his sweet dreams. Sweet dreams, Charlie Bland. Sweet dreams, Johnny McKarkle, sweet dreams all the feckless kindly careful brutal boys in their Argyle socks. She had been free of thinking about Johnny for a long time. He'd been dead twenty, no, eighteen years, and Charlie Bland had walked into the space he left. A paper imitation. Space in her soul. In the middle of her soul.

Now Hannah had to come back and call Johnny up to haunt her. They passed the cave near the bottom of Country Club

Hill. She saw him there four o'clock in the morning. Country Club dance. They hadn't been able to wait. Made love in the cave. The smell of his white shirt against her face. She had never been able to figure it out. Johnny and Charlie were as dangerous as twin snakes, but they exuded safety like those plants that exude a scent to catch flies. Venus-fly catchers. It will be all right, honey. Honey honey honey, choirs of bad boys singing honey honey honey.

Maria looked back and caught Kitty Puss's face in the rearview mirror. "What are you smiling about?" she asked, eyes back quickly on the road.

It was none of her damned business. My God, you couldn't even smile... A whole life in a fish tank watched by other people. But right there at the center they couldn't get to, she had dreamed for years of Johnny, then Charlie, then both, mixed up, Brandy right there beside her in the bed, faint sick traces of the cutest boy in town. She wondered if he'd ever known. No. Of course not. You don't notice other people very much, when your only claim to fame is one song that nearly got into the Princeton Triangle Show in 1940, and then you just keep on repeating yourself year after year, the cuteness waning, the mistakes growing at the perpetual piano when you were too drunk to play and thought you were still the life of a party that had long since gone home.

The last time she'd seen him... she had turned back at the living-room door and he was still playing Cole Porter in the empty room of their condominium at Hilton Head under the portrait of General Mosby he was supposed to be kin to. Old Bushwhacker. He hadn't inherited any of that, God knows. She had thought that night, she remembered later, he looks like a picked chicken. Poor bastard. But it was like so many nights, and she had gone on to bed, and when the music, Christ you couldn't call it music any more, stopped, she thought he'd gone to sleep on the sofa. She could have sworn she heard him open the refrigerator door after the music stopped.

But she found him at the piano, as dead as four o'clock. Heart attack. He'd wet his pants. He was half senile anyway, like an old dog. Too much mileage. He was only fifty when he died, the same age that Johnny would have been if he had lived and things had been different. Thank God for the wild boys. She didn't know how she could have borne life without them.

Of course there were the tame boys, her own boys. They and their wives came down to Hilton Head and saw to things and treated her like she didn't have good sense. She hadn't seen either of them in a long time and she didn't miss them. She loathed women who clung to their families, and the boys, frankly, bored her. Always had. Awful children. Carver had a high IQ and couldn't digest a bite. Said four words a year. Went around looking neglected no matter what she did for him. Solemn. No light touch like Brandy had had and he had played the piano like a professional when the boys were little, anything you asked, no matter how old. Tiptoe through the tulips, the wedding of the painted doll, every song Cole Porter and Noel Coward ever wrote, oh God.

As for Mosby, Mosby was a prude, no, a prick. Mosby was a prick and his wife was a prickess. Mosby was useful, though. New York law firm. He took things off her hands. Grabbed them out of her hands was a better way to say it, even if she knew a hell of a lot more about finances than he did. He was afraid she'd run through the money when he sold the mines to an oil company for three million dollars after Brandy died. Spud and Melinda were living it up in Aiken on their share. Hannah hadn't gotten a cent. It was only fair. After all, she had such a full life, what did she need with it? Her father had neglected to change his will before he died; he'd left her share in trust to her children if any. Well, she was forty years old when he died and there still weren't any. Spud got a court order. Hannah was off some fool place where they couldn't find her anyway. Tough titty. She had to go hightailing off in ways her father disapproved of. Anyway, what good did money do you? She had a pile of money, so did Maria, and so did Ann Randolph even if Daisy was as poor as a church mouse, whatever a church mouse was. There was, let's see, nearly ten million dollars riding in the car, and a fat lot of good it did any of them.

She felt for her handbag. It was all right. They were already halfway up the hill. Not long to wait.

Maria forgot Kitty Puss. She had too much on her mind, real worries. She had mulled it over, and talked to Daisy on the phone about it. She simply didn't know what to do with Hannah. I mean, she thought then, who do you ask to dinner with an author? The fact that she'd seen Hannah grow up didn't help, you know, all she'd done since. She couldn't remember who the people in Hannah's age group had been anyway. The new Episcopal minister? That was all right. He was a liberal. The women in the church liked him even if the men didn't. He dressed in a cassock, and smoked with a long holder, and once he called himself the bride of Christ. John Boy said he was a son-of-a-bitch, and she told him, she told him right then that Father Twiller was only making a joke and he said you don't make jokes around me about Jesus. Well, when John Boy died he preached a beautiful sermon. High church, even if John Boy was low if he was anything; twice-a-year low-church country-club Episcopal. She gave herself a little time of sadness about John Boy. She missed him more than she could tell anybody. Nobody to button her up. Having to go places alone. Those were her first thoughts of loss. Some others she didn't want to think about. Waking up like that from a dream that there was a little boy crying somewhere in the house. She thought it was Little Bit but it wasn't. The tears were just flooding down her own face. That awful birth. They'd examined her and they said she was so small they didn't see how she stood it. They said she had a virgin's womb if they ever saw one. After Little Bit had passed on, only six years old from just a simple case of flu, they said he just gave up, he had grown on inside her head, the way she knew he would have been, somebody to look after her when she got old, well, older.

Somebody to look after her; she'd thought for a while that Charlie Bland had shown an interest, you know, there were signs she was sure. She'd kept the house going of course even if it was too big. All that planting. She'd told Daisy about the crying. She didn't know why, just habit. But she only told her the first time it happened, Daisy of all people. Daisy didn't have a sympathetic bone in her body, after all she did for her, thoughtful little things, presents Daisy never could have afforded, the coat she'd bought in Italy that was practically new. It was way too big for her, big enough for Daisy. All Daisy said about the crying was, you'll have to pull yourself together, nobody can do it for you. Cold water. Cold comfort. She didn't really like Daisy very much. She never had, even if she didn't miss a day seeing her or one phoned the other. It was just the way things worked out.

Sometimes at night it was much worse than that, even if she did lock all the doors and check all the windows and turn on the burglar alarm and bolt the bedroom door. She had this terrible dream that she would never have told to a soul, she was so ashamed, and in this dream she would scream and scream. A man, you know, well a black man was standing right there so tall at the foot of her bed his face was hidden by the lace tester like a veil. He was stark naked, and she could see his you know huge hanging down, and she'd scream John Boy help me. Then the dream would change and she was a little girl before the Civil War and that same man was chasing her across a huge field but he never caught her and she never stopped running and she woke up screaming and crying in the empty house, and weeping for John Boy. She could feel the tears rise in her throat when she thought of that. Crybaby. The road ahead swam, and she slowed down, glanced at the swimming computer light, and then had to tip her head back and let the tears run down safely behind her nose so that Daisy wouldn't see them and insist on driving the car. She wouldn't let anybody drive her car, certainly not Daisy. She slammed. That's the kind of driver she was. A slammer.

She had been sensible about her widowhood, though. There were right ways to do even that. Don't push yourself on people, and start entertaining as soon as it was acceptable, to show you weren't going to be a burden in everybody's mind about what to do with you. It was her duty. Duty. She-crab soup, a tenderloin, salad, spoon bread only Daisy always said batter bread, spoon bread is country. She hadn't dared plan a soufflé even if it was Cora's specialty. You never could tell how long people would want to drink. Then strawberry shortcake, and after that, cheese. She'd forgotten what they called it but it was the right kind of dessert cheese. It was hard to find extra men. She wondered at the word "extra." They weren't extra at all. They were all that was available. Dear old dependable Charlie Bland, Father Twiller; then there was the new young man the League had hired to start the new art gallery. He was much younger but he was artistic and surely that was right for Hannah.

She and Daisy had discussed it at some length and they decided that as the co-chairmen of the hanging committee, she hated the word chairperson, even in her mind, they ought of course to be there, and one more couple, the Goldsteins. They were artistic too, Hannah's kind of people, even if they were, well, Jewish, but things had changed so radically that she could hardly keep up. They decided to have the younger League members who were working on the new project in for brandy and coffee later, my God she'd forgotten to pick up those good Swiss mints. That way there wouldn't be any hard feelings and Hannah seemed to be a real celebrity to the young ones. My God, somebody you'd seen grow up couldn't be that, but she was known, well, people really did write about her even in *The New York Times*, so Maria had some idea at least, enough to carry on a conversation, about what she did.

Maria felt as satisfied with her plans as she ever felt at anything. She could hear Daisy tapping her big foot and could feel it vibrate against the back of the seat. She tried to read what that meant.

Then she heard Daisy say "Far be it from me to interfere," about to stomp in where angels fear to tread. "You have to understand Hannah that this audience is not really intellectual or literary like you're used to." She sounded like the words were a little shameful. "They just want a few interesting anecdotes, and something amusing, you know how it is." But Maria didn't hear Hannah say anything. Her mind dissolved into fragments of worries she couldn't name, flowed to the faint tick of the computer as the car changed gears on the hill rise.

Daisy had waited all the way across the river and up the old Country Club road and past the cave to say a word. As a matter of fact, she was surprised at how far they had driven. That damned girl beside her hadn't been one bit more artistic than she had, growing up. Artistic. It was nothing but a curse. A quality you had in families that you couldn't let get out of hand. It reminded her of Maria. She looked at her silly hair she spent a fortune on. It made her smile. When Maria and John Boy took their Little Bit, damned stupid name for a child even if it was only a nickname, took him to a psychiatrist, she went with them of course. Maria always needed somebody standing by. He said the child might be autistic and Maria said it runs in the family. He takes after his grandmother. We've still got a lot of the things she made. When the boy died, he never did have much life in him anyway, that crisis went on for a whole year. Daisy couldn't call her life her own. She had to be on hand at all times. You couldn't do a thing with Maria and then one day the crisis stopped just like that and she never mentioned the boy again. It was very unhealthy.

Daisy tried not to look at the streetcar bed they were

passing, a wide grass verge now but she could still see if nobody else could where the tracks had been, right in front of the porch of her mother's house and Lewis's mother's next door, Miss Alida's, twin houses. New people lived in them. People she didn't know. Her mother. Going off like that, said her grandson needed her in San Francisco as if he ever needed anybody but Daisy. She and Lewis had to go and get her after that awful marriage broke up. She was all of seventy-six years old and the boy had run through every cent she had and then walked out leaving her high and dry. Things like that happened in California. California didn't have any backbone, just a fault instead, a great big fault running right down the middle of it, the San Andreas Fault. They just packed her up in that awful apartment and brought her back East where she belonged. She had kicked like a steer. She seemed to resent them more than she did the boy who'd left her like that. But what were you to do when your duty was staring you right in the face? She'd lived with them ever since, bitching and complaining, worse after Lewis died and Daisy had the awful shock of his will. Last will and testament after all they'd been led to expect. Here she was, riding in a car she couldn't dream of affording. She needed both of the Social Security checks and her mother never let her forget it. But it wasn't like those colored people on food stamps and relief wouldn't do a lick of work if you paid them, she had to cut the grass herself, after all John Boy had paid in no matter what her mother said. She was ashamed of needing the checks but then she had to keep the house going. There was no question of moving. Her son, she never used his name in her mind, and sometimes she was aware of that and wondered why. She knew of course. He'd changed his name as if Lewis Jr. wasn't good enough. He called himself Beverley and used to drop Beverley, old family Virginia name he said right in front of her. Well, you could get by with anything in San Francisco, they were so naïve. He needed the stability of the house even if he did come back just once a year with his friend and then he sighed all the time until she wanted to knock him in the head, except when he and his friend and her mother laughed at things she didn't understand and preferred not to. My son, my mother, my husband, my friend Maria, she recited the litany. What happened? Then there were the dogs, they'd never get used to anyplace else. They were too old.

When Maria bragged about paying her bill at Saks with her Social Security check, it made her absolutely furious. Maria sent off for everything in *The New Yorker*. But when she mentioned the matter all Maria said was, I pay it back in taxes. That put her in her place, a reminder that John Boy had been a better provider than Lewis and that just wasn't true, what with all the responsibilities they had, his mother living forever with all that expense, then her mother, God knows what her son had cost them.

She found herself staring at the streetcar tracks when she'd tried not to. Some of the girls in her age group actually rode the streetcar down from the club when they were growing up, but she wouldn't be caught dead in it. Maria's mother always came and got her in the car, but her mother never came and got her, not once. When she couldn't catch a ride she would walk the whole mile, down across the bowl of the golf course, down the hill, she said it was good for her tennis legs, and up on the porch where nine times out of ten her mother would be sitting there still in her jodhpurs drinking with Bobby Slingsby.

Artistic! She was just as artistic as the damned girl beside her, coming back, sitting there not saying a word, acting like if she did say anything they couldn't possibly understand her references. She just hadn't had the same chance, what with everybody looking to her. She had a perfect color sense, everybody said so, and she knew about Picasso long before any of the rest of them had ever heard of him. Nobody needed to tell her what was on Hannah's mind.

She'd come back ten years ago like the prodigal daughter, a lot of dangerous ideas, and making friends with Lord knows who, even negras. Daisy could take pride in the fact that she had led the pack to take her down a notch, if ever anybody needed it Hannah did, decimating a lot of liberal ideas and not volunteering like all the other women of her, Daisy didn't like the word class and she never said it aloud but she could think, couldn't she? Something she had done brought the whole thing to a head and they decided they had just about had enough. What did the girl expect? She was nothing but a traitor to everything she'd been taught. Daisy had made Maria call her up, she told Maria her voice was like so many other people's Hannah would never know. She couldn't remember why that time and not another time, after all it had been ten years, God how time passed. 1968. Of course. It had to do with war, and doves. Maria did call, she had the guts to do what she was told for once. She could still see Maria with that silly grin, looking over the phone at her the way she used to when they would call people and say do you live on the streetcar track well you better get off the streetcar's coming, and then Maria would giggle just the way she did when she hung up the phone after telling Hannah where to get off. Now here Hannah was again, turning up like the bad penny. Daisy had to admit though she had voted to ask her. After all, she was the only famous personality they knew and they had to have a famous personality. They had decided after a lot of meetings on the subject to go the whole hog and invite a black-woman-writer but none of them would come so they had to settle for Hannah. Daisy had worried ever since about what Hannah would say. If the past was any guide it would be any damn thing that popped into her head.

If her son had taught her anything it was tolerance. Daisy prided herself on that. She had said that to Maria before she suggested how Maria should vote on the black question. She'd voted nay anyway against her express wishes. Maria said there were a lot of things she would do for cultural activities but entertaining a negra socially was just not one of them. One of the younger members jumped in and volunteered when it was really Maria's turn. When Daisy told her not to speak until she had been given the floor by the chairman there was a titter from the younger age group. It hurt both their feelings after all they'd done, but neither of them showed it. Thank God they had some pride.

The whole thing had fizzled out anyway. There were only three black-women-writers they had ever heard of and none of them cared to come not for their travel expenses and no honorarium even though they had explained what the proceeds were going to. No, it was thank you very much after all that upheaval and carrying on. Give them an inch.

You just couldn't tell what Hannah would say.

Ann Randolph Potter, Mrs. Ann Randolph Potter, which was correct after the divorce, folded her lily-white hands. She inspected them with pride, lying there in her lime linen lap, such a good color with her hair. Not a mark on them. Of course the veins showed a little. Cream and gloves couldn't help that. The others danced attendance on her as if she were some valuable frail treasure because she was supposed to be brokenhearted. That was nonsense. She wasn't brokenhearted at all, but she did like the attention. Frankly, she was happier than she'd been in simply years. She had the whole house to herself at last after all the concern about Plain George and having to keep an eagle eye on Sally Bee so she wouldn't get into trouble and humiliate them all.

Of course, Sally Bee's death was the tragedy of both their lives, hers and Plain George's, everybody knew that. It had brought them closer for a while, everybody noticed; oh yes, closer and closer and giving in because of Plain George's feelings, and bored to death. Bored with death was more to the point. He had just let himself go as if nobody had ever died before. It wasn't as if they were the only ones to lose a child, one way or another, death or just going off and neglecting the parents, look at Maria and Daisy and Kitty Puss. You did everything in the world for them and what did you get in return? Plain George had let himself go terribly, not her, she prided herself on having outside interests to sustain her.

Ann Randolph loved having time and the house to herself at last. After all, it was her money. The only thing she had resented was Plain George going off with some tacky manicurist he'd been carrying on with for twenty years and she'd had no idea until the whole thing just burst in on her; everybody in town had known about the woman except her and they all said they wanted to spare her feelings; talked behind her back all those years. The woman wasn't even their own kind. But she had to admit to her pretty hands that that would have been even more embarrassing because she would have had to see them at parties and as it was everybody was on her side and all the compliments she got after her surgery were as sweet as they could be. At least Plain George didn't get a damned cent off her. He lived in some tacky little apartment, going to seed.

She caught a glimpse of Kitty Puss in the rearview mirror when she was trying to steal a glance at herself to see if her hair was still in place. Kitty Puss could use surgery too, that old square golf-sun rawhide face. No excuse for letting yourself go like that. She better watch out. Charlie Bland paid her attention too, never missed a compliment. She settled into a short dream of marrying Charlie Bland. She could, too, she knew that. She didn't look a day over thirty-five except for her hands, and she had kept her figure religiously, stayed in bed and let every muscle relax in the yoga dead man while she read the theatrical section of *The New York Times* and then did the crossword and thought from time to time that it still wasn't too late to have the career in the theater she'd always known was hers for the asking. After all, she'd had a lot of experience locally, and nobody would know, not up there, that she'd had surgery. All the famous people did it, they owed it to their public. She wondered about Hannah, and glanced back to check. Oh God, obviously not, not with those sun lines and crow's-feet; she supposed Hannah was too eccentric to care, people like that were.

She would achieve, after one of those mornings, a kind of grace she called grace of self, suspended in her body as in girlhood. Sometimes she got out her collection of theatrical programs; she had seen practically everything there was to see in New York, on every show plane that took off, and when she looked at the programs, Martin Beck, Shubert, Helen Hayes, she was back in those theaters every time, thrilling.

Then sometimes she tried on her evening dresses. She had kept every one of them. She could still get into dresses she had worn when she was eighteen and she looked lovely, just as lovely as ever—the peach silk with the beads, short in front with a train to the floor, long skirts were coming back and she was eighteen and was cut in on fifty times before intermission, girls nowadays didn't know what they missed, a prom-trotter, counting the cuts, one two three four, smiling and counting and whirling, she had her own personal stag line. The first long white satin with the rhinestone straps made her look like she had just risen out of water and cut to the waist in the back to show her tan, the bouffant lace, the cinched-in taffeta, the black moiré cocktail dress with the enchanting little hat with the ostrich-feather plume that framed her face, the flowing chiffon, I married an angel, it always reminded her of that one song. She put them on one after another and the boys came back like shadows, madly in love with her, six special-delivery letters every Sunday morning, class rings, fraternity pins, orchids, gardenias in green waxed paper, and roses, all the roses, and she had to throw away her life on Plain George that s.o.b.

She could feel the seat belt across her flat stomach. Daisy interrupted her. She said, "What on earth are you humming?"

"I Married an Angel."

"Well, for God's sake stop it you're driving me crazy."

Ann Randolph was sure she hadn't been humming, not aloud. Daisy could reach right into your mind and grab on it.

Hannah went on watching the bird dropping on the window and waited for it to be over. They were doing to her what they had always done, arousing compassion that made her impotent. They were pathetic, not monuments, not formidable, only frozen. With the pure courage of women without imagination, they traveled in a small pack, upholding each other, forming a circle like the wagons in Western movies, protecting themselves and each other when there was nothing out there. They roused in her, not love, that would have been a choice she could make, but loyalty, deep, deep loyalty, and she fell into it, as into the past and the rhythm of the car, and the familiar road, nearly asleep. Age and her own sameness, all the times she had gone up the same hill, caught her, and it caught Maria, who said the obvious, "I always feel like I'm a girl going up to the club again," and then, "no matter what," and fell back into silence with the rest.

Far away around the wide curve they could hear the cry of thousands of birds, settled on the distant roof and the broken towers, but when the car drew up in front of the terrace, it was not birds, but women, hundreds of them.

Hannah felt panic as in deep woods. She couldn't move. There were no young trees on the terrace, there were no cracks in the walls, there was no mud. There were swings and a monolith of modern sculpture designed for children to crawl on, through, under. But the children had gone. A colony of bulldozers and cranes was parked where the old tennis courts had been, waiting for the last meeting to be over. Workmen leaned against them, smoking and watching without interest.

"Come *on*," Daisy commanded.

Haley Potter was taking tickets at the door, awkward and eager to please as ever. She was saying "thank you thank you" and sometimes a special "oh thanks," to people she knew. "There's a huge crowd," she told Daisy, and then, "Hannah, welcome to our city. You're quite a draw," surprised.

They pushed their way through sound beyond noise, a persistent treble whine of women's voices, sharp against Hannah's body, a physical pain, toward darkness. Darkness in the great hall, and then deep twilight as she began to see again, at first only the shapes of women, crowded toward the doorway to peer at the speaker, then their eyes, and then at last the twilight lifted into the summer shade she remembered in the room she had grown up in.

The floor was dull, bare wood. The smell and shine of polish was gone, the scent of summer flowers. There was only the frail dust of age, neglect, women's powder, and dry heat. There was not a familiar face. Daisy had, as she had said, had some control. A full strength of white women suitably dressed parted to let them through, on parade. Hannah escaped the polite and avid staring by looking above their heads, searching for anything that had been left intact.

The fireplace had been boarded up. It and the paneling were covered with murals, made by nice children to please grownups. No monsters, no witches, no back-yard fights, no secret signs, only four-foot bunnies, ballet dancers, star wars, and spacemen. Faded blue prize ribbons hung at their corners.

She could see, behind the women, dirty six-foot-high glass display cases, standing askew, ready to be moved out.

"I wish you could have seen it..." Daisy was saying something more, but they were being pushed by the crowd slowly into one of the display cases. "Watch out," Daisy said instead. She sounded scared. The glass in the front had been broken. Only sharp fragments were left along the frame. Dust and trash had filtered in. It had been the women's idea of an 1860 room, a green-black horsehair sofa that looked like it had spent too much time in someone's attic, life-size wax ladies in 1880 hats and gray-black bombazine served a perpetual dry tea. A child's toy lay on the floor, an old wooden top with a string. A black shawl had fallen from the bent shoulders of an old woman. It lay like a rag by one buttoned shoe. The other shoe had rotted off and left a wax foot with no toes. A blackened silver haft had been put on the tray with the tarnished tea service. Daisy explained that the tea service was not valuable, just a copy, and then, watching Hannah, who stared at the haft: "Oh, that. It was a gift from the old Catlett family. I guess they forgot it when they moved the valuable things. You have to watch volunteers. They overlook things."

"I've seen it before." Hannah still stared at it, a clue in her treasure hunt.

"It's the Catlett coat of arms." Daisy was proud of that. "De Châtelet."

"No, it's not." Hannah forgot not to speak. "It's the handle of a riding crop, Cockburn arms."

"Oh of course you know better than the direct family." Daisy turned away and Hannah held her sleeve. "Please. What's going to happen to all this?"

"Experts!" Daisy let out a tiny burst of anger. "We are presenting it all to the state museum, absolutely free. They'll just put it in the basement and forget it. They said everything had to be authenticated. As if coming down through the families wasn't good enough for them. Coal-mine models and arrowheads, that's all they think about. The government always thinks it knows it all."

"May I have that?"

"Sure. Take it if you want to. Anything you like. I don't know why not."

Daisy plunged again into the crowd.

Hannah leaned into the case and picked up the handle, and followed Daisy. Behind her she heard a woman say, "What was that? A souvenir?"

A woman's voice above the polite murmurs, edged with excitement. "Are they giving things away? Come on!"

Hannah looked back. Two women were already undressing the old lady. "Watch the glass."

A call: "You ought not to . . ."

Imperious voice: "It's all right. We're volunteers."

Women clotted the wide stairway to the ballroom, whispering to each other as Hannah passed by. Daisy pushed them to the stair rail. "It's the speaker," she kept saying. Behind them Hannah could hear Ann Randolph calling "Wait for me." Someone touched Hannah's arm, but when she looked around, she saw no one she recognized.

In the old ballroom, women were murmuring "Excuse me," and clearing their throats, as they stumbled into the frail gold chairs that Hannah knew would still be there, old Mr. Slingsby's legacy to teach the women of his valley to sit like ladies. She followed Daisy to the podium set up in front of the french windows at the end of the room. Out beyond them she caught a glimpse, over the balcony edge, of the swimming pool, half filled with gravel. She turned around and faced them at last; her heart lurched. Upturned expectant faces were white in the sun from the windows behind her. They crowded the room; they stood against the walls. They overflowed onto the stairs. She had expected them to be sitting in judgment but they weren't. It was worse. They were waiting with the naïveté of birds to be fed, trusting her because they had read her name in the paper. They were doing what was right to do to pass a summer morning. What they saw as fame insulated her from judgment. They sat in rows and regiments of age. There were old women who must have once gone in the same way to hear Billy Sunday, there were rows of seventy-year-olds wearing hats who had come to the same room sometime in the twenties, she was sure, to start a little theater because it was the thing you did that year.

She wondered, "What do you want of me?" and heard the answer, "Nothing," as a swish of summer skirts as faint as leaves in the wind. She could see Maria's mother, her own mother's closest friend, waving little fingers discreetly at the level of her shoulder, survived into that late plump virginity, white cotton hair, and facial wit that Southern old women came to with deep relief that showed in their whole bodies, and made them seem like girls again. Beside her, as thin as a cracker, Daisy's mother looked like there was nothing anyone could say she hadn't heard a thousand times. She wore indifference like a sign, that and a printed chiffon scarf that flowed around her.

Hannah scanned the faces behind them, looking, as she always had, for Candy, whose father had named her Candida after his favorite play, Candy who would sustain her in the valley as she always had. If Candy had come, she knew, as she had always known since they were best friends from the second grade on, that things would be all right, that the sight of her calm face would cleanse her perception, jog her out of the blindness of her dislike, fear, or defeated compassion into, Candy's words, things as they were.

She searched through the rows, reading their ages by their hair, forties girls with their short, groomed caps, fifties girls, their worried plumping faces framed with discreetly teased sweeps to give them height, sixties girls, dull patience under hanging hair, looking as if they were considering divorce.

Candy sat six rows back, as if she had waited for Hannah to find her, with the neat containment and the heart-face that seemed not to have changed since she was a girl, the same wise cold-eyed kindness, missing and judging nothing, the same smile of complicity that lifted Hannah's spirits. Candy made a small sign toward the stairs and mouthed, "See you later."

At the back of the room where she was sure Hannah couldn't pick her out and have the satisfaction of knowing she couldn't stay away, Tel Leftwich whispered to her Aunt Lydia, "There they are in all their glory. The sacred circle." She had gotten off work to come. She wouldn't have missed it for the world. Her Aunt Lydia, who had never married either, patted her arm, knowing it was hard for her, delicate as she was. Tel watched Hannah through the distance part of her bifocals. She looked, to her, familiar to the bone. She'd gone from thin to skinny, Tel was glad to see. There she was, already forty-eight years old or was it -nine, time passed too quickly, and she was the image of Johnny who had never reached forty-eight thank God thank God thank God.

In the distance, that woman Daisy who Tel couldn't stand got up and flicked the microphone to see if it was on. Tel could hear the click of her fingernail behind her from the loudspeakers on the floor. She said, "Can you hear me back there?" She sounded like a radio in someone else's house.

"Yes," a woman called behind her. There was always one, wasn't there?

Daisy's canned voice behind Tel said, "It is both a sad and happy occasion." Tel could see she was reading from a bit of paper, didn't even bother to memorize. Tel believed in doing things right if you were going to do them at all. If the woman in the distance had ever had to do a lick of paid work in her life she'd have learned that. Tel could see her getting fired from job after job.

"Sad, because it is the last time we will meet in this lovely old house which has meant so much to so many of us." Not all of course, she would point that out. The voice from the speakers was separate from Daisy herself, who seemed from where Tel was sitting to be miming silently. It made her look like a damned fool.

"But not really sad any more because continuity goes on." Continuity goes on, what a phrase. "The new quarters will house local art instead of children's activities, and they will need your support just as this has over the years. I call the quarters new but they are not. They are in the beautiful old Cutright house, the last house left on the riverside, which we have saved from wanton destruction."

Tel wanted to laugh, all the time she'd spent in the

Wayfaring Stranger. She'd only gone there to see if Johnny was all right, that's the way she preferred to remember it. Aunt Lydia mistook that slight rictus of a suppressed grin for pain and patted her arm again.

The canned voice kept on. "Now youall visit there and volunteer to work, you hear? You will find pledge cards at your seat to give to the ladies at the door when you leave. Just mark time or money or both."

Tel could hear Daisy's throat rumble, and the crackle of paper, then: "I want to introduce our speaker, who needs no introduction."

"That won't stop you," Tel whispered to Aunt Lydia and somebody said "Shhh!" Down below in the empty great hall a telephone rang and went on ringing. "What on earth did I do with it?" Daisy, in the distance, was finding her place. "Oh, scuse me," girl-like, and read, "Hannah McKarkle was born in Canona West Virginia she attended Sweet Briar College and the Pratt Institute." Daisy's voice took on life. "I thought you might be interested to know that Pratt had numerous holdings right here in this valley..." She found the place in the publisher's hand-out again. "Uh, she is the author of numerous works of fiction including *Prison* I mean *Prisons O Beulah Land Know Nothing.* She is working on a novel about the coal business in 1912 called *The Scapegoat*." She turned to Hannah. "Isn't that right?" Daisy flirted, "We sure do hope you tell the real story, you know, our side, don't we, girls?"

The telephone had stopped ringing, or somebody had answered it. Tel couldn't decide.

Hannah had been trying not to listen. Daisy seemed to be talking about someone else. She might have been one of the paper ladies on the ruined terrace of her dream. She looked up beyond Daisy's head. The ceiling had been painted night-blue, and pasted with silver stars like the stars in the grade-school notebooks. The Big Dipper, Cassiopeia, the North Star, the Pleiades, dim and forgotten when they got tired of astronomy. All along one wall, slightly turning in the breeze from the low windows, a line of little bodies seemed to be hanging by the neck as if they had been executed and left there as a warning. Only the stability of no imagination could have created so grotesque a display for the children. They must have loved it. She recognized a garroted Pinocchio, Alice in Wonderland, the White Rabbit, the Little Tin Soldier, a policeman, Punch and Judy.

Daisy, having gotten through quickly what was, from her voice, an uninteresting necessity, said, "Hannah's mother was a Neill, the Senator's granddaughter." Her voice gained comfort. "Her father was one of the leading lawyers and coal owners in this valley, Preston McKarkle, from a lovely old place in Greenbrier county. She is descended on her mother's side from the first member of the House of Burgesses from this county and from the first white woman ever to see the Canona River, and is named after her in honor of the first Hannah. Her mother told me that. Hannah's family was on the Southern side of the Civil War. So, no matter where she's been or what she's done, she is one of us and always will be, she can't escape that."

Daisy didn't end. She stopped, and lowered herself from the platform.

Polite applause rose and died.

Maria and Ann Randolph sat in the front row, almost against the podium, in seats that had been saved for them. Daisy sat down beside them, and moved the soft parcel she had left in her chair into her lap. She looked as if she expected the worst. Beside her Kitty Puss lolled, not giving, as she would have said, a shit. Hannah could no longer avoid looking directly at them, Maria, shrunk, every hair in place, her hands folded in her lap like a little girl, waiting for the next hour to pass. Ann Randolph's vacant doll's face with its weather-beaten eyes was too tight against her skull to show anything; her bouffant cloud of hair was so thin that Hannah could see through it. Daisy, rock-jawed, had changed least. She had simply eroded. Kitty Puss had evolved through wind, sun, bourbon, and boredom to red clay. They sat close to each other for strength, a tiny minority of judgment, aging and half forgotten, having only a little power over a few of the naïve women behind them. They were as still as the dusty wax figures in the broken display case, demanding that she rise and entertain, flower for them acceptably without offense, flower for them acceptably for a little while on a Wednesday morning in June.

Their hands were old, the last pre-revolutionary hands, with risen veins, brown spots, and shiny manicured nails. Hannah spoke silently to their eyes, knowing she would never say it, in a dark nostalgia for their old brutality that had once hated her out of the valley with a force as primitive as the mountain women who were their ancestors. She made a silent accusation to them that she knew was no longer important, old and dry as they had become, lifeless as the puppets hanging in the breeze. "You are not even cruel any more, you are your residue, your own ashes." They were willing her to get up. Row on row of women waited.

The low windows were veiled with vines; the women sat in silence and morning darkness in blouses and shirtwaist dresses, predominantly blue, under a dark veiling with old stars as dim as dust specks, a rank-and-file of women, the League to the front, the forlorn hope, with the main body of troops behind them, and no way out.

Daisy whispered, "Start." She had waited long enough.

There was no longer anything else she could do. Hannah told herself in her mother's dead voice, as she got up and smoothed the skirt of the nice blue linen she had chosen as camouflage, that she mustn't make a mountain out of a molehill. On the long few steps to the microphone her mother's voice added: "Remember, don't talk topics." She tried to ignore the voice in her head, but what she said directly to Candy, surprising herself, was "I am so glad to be home again," meaning it for the time being, and launched, as Daisy had told her to, into an interesting anecdote. "The search for who we are started in England," she began, knowing they liked things English. "I found it in Burford, in a churchyard. It is April 1649."

Tel Leftwich settled back to wait for her to make a fool of herself. The voice behind her on the floor was muffled in the loudspeakers and the women's skirts. Tel could hear the electric murmur and hum against the diaphragms. ". . . a true story told by Johnny Church, a soldier in Cromwell's army. His regiment is riding toward Burford across the plain from Salisbury. He dreams, as soldiers do, of home. So *Prisons* begins, 'I am twenty today. There is only Thankful Perkins to tell it to, but Thankful is asleep . . .'"

That reminded Tel that she was worried sick about one of her boys. He was like a beautiful animal pacing a cage. He had talent, too, she was sure of that. She could always tell. He could fix anything. Her hi-fi, her car; just because he was not a scholar in the formal sense. Her Aunt Lydia said, one of those trashy kids is going to knock you in the head, Tel. Something about him reminded her of Johnny, only the language was different. He talked about a need for his space and Johnny always said let's get out of here, it was the same thing, the same sense of being trapped he couldn't articulate and only she understood he told her so.

The persistent electric voice intruded: ". . . so Johnny Church and Thankful Perkins are shot in Burford churchyard on the morning of April 14, 1649, for their beliefs—free speech, free elections, democratic ideas—for what we, this morning, take for granted as our right, never question, often neglect. They are buried in unknown graves, but Johnny leaves a legacy, a warning: 'If we honor each other this democracy of men will work, but courtship will kill it . . .'"

Guidance, that's what they needed. There had been boy after boy like that, deeply needing Tel. It kept her dedicated to teaching. She saw them fixing a series of cars and hi-fis through the years, tinkering with the television until she had to call the man. She always paid them for whatever they did. They appreciated that.

She heard a woman running up the stairs, and turned to see who it was, first her head, then half her body twisting north and south, searching for somebody. It was that awful awkward Haley Potter. She looked like somebody had slapped her at last. Hannah's voice, from the floor beside the woman, interfered with Tel's staring. She dragged herself around toward the shadow of the woman standing in the distance against the sun.

"So in 1649, and then in *O Beulah Land*, which is the eighteenth-century novel of what will be the Beulah Quintet, the first Hannah in her mindless fearful crossing of the Endless Mountains that we called the Alleghenies sees a valley from across the river, shaped like a hand flung down among the mountains. Jonathan Lacey crosses Virginia, and settles it and calls it Beulah, here in our own valley. I found clues to the story all over the world, a kind of archaeology of time and place: the dreams and habits and language our ancestors brought with them, even the nightmare fears of hierarchy and poverty. These things met, I hope, and married what we found already in Virginia, a new focus, new necessities."

Oh God, she would bring up the fact she'd been all over the world, slip it in like that. Well, she could, couldn't she, now that her parents had died. Tel wondered about the man she married; she never brought him back, not that she'd been back herself for years. ". . . and then in *Know Nothing*, the third book, in the first half of the nineteenth century, a family has become entrenched at Beulah and what has been a land-hungry dream becomes, for the third Johnny, a prison of responsibility and rising Civil War . . ."

There wasn't all that much of Johnny in her, not really, oh, something about the set of her head, maybe. They both got that look from their mother. Their father had liked Tel. He'd made a point of being nice to her, he really had. She retreated from the incisive voice, Eastern accent she'd picked up, God, into the bleak safety of old wounds, old slights, invited to family things but not to parties, where they just had their crowd. It was all the mother's fault. She still hated her, still hated the girl up there, still saw her as a girl and told her, I never had your chances. If your god-damn mother had let Johnny and me marry, things would have been different and he'd be alive today.

Hannah had read her mind. She heard her say "Johnny" as if she were calling him, "named for Brother Jonathan, the eighteenth-century archetype of the revolutionary soldier. Brother Jonathan, Johnny Reb, Johnny Appleseed, a charac-ter once as familiar as Uncle Sam, fades in and out of our history . . ."

Haley Potter was whispering to somebody. Tel could hear the whisper begin to spread like a small wind.

". . . to trace the clues to both the failure of a dream and its persistence in our innate dissatisfaction with things as they are, that is our constant undercurrent, and breaks sometimes into revolt, as we saw in the late fifties and early sixties."

The voice in the loudspeakers was tangled in whispers. Somebody leaned close to Aunt Lydia. "Good grief," she sputtered into Tel's ear, "Charlie Bland has committed sui-cide." Tel could feel Aunt Lydia's spit.

The whispers were spreading toward the front. Somebody, she thought it was Daisy, it usually was, hissed, "Shhush." There was silence, only the mechanical voice. The whispers spread again. The voice tried to rise above them.

"Sometimes I had to manufacture clues. In *O Beulah Land*, which I wrote in the British Museum, the first Hannah, starving, sees two bears fighting across a hundred-foot-wide place in the New River. Now I was far from the New River, so I had to construct it. And that is part of what a novelist does, takes the material at hand, translates, reconnects, conjures.

And to write about the past, 1649, 1774, 1860, 1912, I must create a memory through research, become, if I can, one who does not know the present, to start over, become contemporary with the time, find out, not what was happening—but what people thought was happening—a self-hypnosis, an empathy. When it succeeds it lives in timeless moments which are always present. A hand feels the texture of a glass. A dirt road feels like an old corduroy road under my car wheels. I hear the animals again. I see residues of inherited prejudice left over from real fears. I watch who we pick as our heroes, our parodies of lost hopes..."

Tel could see awful Daisy shake her big head, which sat up like a knob above the others. Obviously she was giving some instructions to Hannah, because she seemed to pause and stumble back to the story... "Uh... I had to measure the North Library of the British Museum Reading Room... It was ninety feet long..."

The whisper was spreading again; it must have reached Hannah. She raised her voice again. "... I measured part of the hall outside so that I could stand one hundred feet from the far wall. I was waiting for someone, well, bear-size, to pass across the other end of the room, so I could study how much detail of a bear Hannah could have seen across the New River. Now you have to understand; there are a lot of eccentrics working in the British Museum." She tried to shout through a wind of whispering. "As I stood there one of the attendants came up beside me and asked what I was looking at. 'I'm trying to see how much detail of a bear'... I could feel him freeze beside me. 'Yes, my dear, I see a bear. Of course I see a bear. Don't you think you've been working a bit too hard?'"

There was a faint titter up near the podium. Tel watched Haley Potter working her way to the front, spreading the news like a dark stain in the room. She leaned down to somebody in the front row. Kitty Puss Wilson staggered to her feet and started to run against the current of women. Daisy ran after her. They passed by Tel as if somebody had stolen Charlie Bland from them. It had been that way always, owning everybody's death, didn't even invite her to be at the house when Johnny died, not that she would have set foot in the place, even though she was a cousin by marriage, which was closer than any of them, except socially, of course.

In the lost space of the morning Hannah went on trying to retrieve attention, through anecdote after anecdote, making a nice story for nice women out of eighteen years of work, poverty, and exile, the persistent demand that had flogged her on, fighting the preoccupied whispers, the turned heads, the swelling of some event, a counterpoint of fascination that was spreading from nerve to nerve.

At last she could sit down. Daisy was back in place. She looked stricken, but she got up to do her duty, engulfed in the pile of cloth she held, and the mild applause.

"We want to thank Hannah McKarkle for her interesting talk. Since she would not accept an honorarium, we have a gift that we hope will be suitable." She untangled the tan cloth and shook it out. It fell, a large slab of macramé, four feet square. She had to hold it high. Knots and fringes dropped into place. There was another faint sound of applause. People were already getting up at the back. "On behalf of the Canona chapter of the Junior League we present this macramé plaque." She whispered to Hannah as she handed it to her. "We've got to leave right away. Something has happened." She pulled Hannah off the podium. She was trying to keep from stumbling over four feet of macramé, trying to roll it back up. Daisy grabbed it and said, "Here, let me do it. You'll ruin it."

Bird sounds rose and filled the room. Women flowed toward the stairs, propelled by news and questions. Someone picked at Hannah's sleeve and said, "That was interesting. My, you've been a lot of places. In England we saw forty-three cathedrals."

Daisy pulled her away. "Kitty Puss is in the car. We've got to get her home."

Candy stepped out into the aisle and hugged Hannah. She whispered, "Motel or mastodon cave?"

"Howard Johnson's."

"See you there in an hour."

"What's all the fuss?"

"Charlie Bland is dead."

"Come on." Daisy thrust Hannah ahead of her.

"I'll take her back," Candy called.

They were already too far away behind a wall of bodies to hear her.

The death of Charlie Bland had spread among the women. The dark nostalgia was back. Hannah could hear again the whispered questions at the death of her brother Johnny. Nothing had changed, nothing at all. The new death, as the old, fed them, gave them a direction toward vicarious bereavement. She heard Maria say behind her, "Should I cancel dinner? Do you think I ought to?"

"You certainly should," Ann Randolph told her.

"What am I going to do with all that cheese?" Maria thought aloud.

Daisy still had Hannah by the arm. "We'll have to be with Kitty Puss. I'm sorry this has happened. Cancellations." She lowered her voice at the door of the car, so that Kitty Puss, huddled against the back seat, couldn't hear. "He didn't have a soul," and then, "We'll have to make all the arrangements," the imperial "we" from the time when such women had torn the flesh from the sacred corpses with their fingernails, to Daisy, who would call Carver's Funeral Home. Daisy moved down against the window to stare at Kitty Puss to see how she was "taking it."

"We know what to do. Don't worry." She tapped the window. Kitty Puss ignored her. Daisy climbed into the front seat. Maria couldn't find her keys. "Stop fumbling," Daisy ordered her. "I'm in a state of shock," Maria fussed.

There was a sharp giggle from Kitty Puss. Ann Randolph, who had climbed in beside her, and was patting her with one hand and holding her handkerchief to her eyes with the other so no tears would streak her makeup, caught the giggle. Daisy told her she ought to be ashamed. "I can't help it." Ann Randolph stopped.

As they drove back around the wide curve, Daisy leaned on the back of her seat and started to talk, as if she were in a race with her own story, "You ought to know the background," but it wasn't about Charlie Bland. It was as habitual a story as if she were keening. "So I said to the mayor what do you mean telling me what I can and can't do let me tell you my family helped to found this town when you were a redneck from some hollow . . . I just told him I said you'd better know who you're talking to he didn't say one word then I went straight to the planning commission, political appointees suburban housewives nobody knows and I said you are not to tear down that house..."

"Shut up, Daisy," Kitty Puss ordered.

"What?"

"I said shut up. She usually tells how she told everybody off when she's three sheets to the wind." Kitty Puss censed the car with the smell of bourbon. Nobody said a word until they were passing the cave again. Then it was Maria, who questioned the road ahead. "Do you think the balance of his mind was disturbed?"

"Of course," Daisy told the road. "It always is. I firmly believe that in cases like this... He had everything to live for; why, I just saw him *yesterday*..." Kitty Puss and Hannah were aware of each other listening to the flow of clichés. Kitty Puss held her breath and shut her eyes.

Hannah had come back on her search for Johnny's death and been caught in a repetition. They were going slowly up the south road, almost to the identical Tudor houses that Hannah's parents and her sister Melinda had built, high on the hill, a secure citadel against the valley below. Now, thirty-six years later, the trees were old and spread their shade across deep lawns that Hannah had remembered first as raw ridges. She wanted to call out as the car stopped in front of her parents' house: "Don't leave me here." She thought Maria had slipped in time and had driven back into the mourning for Johnny. She wanted to run back to the Howard Johnson's motel, to Candy, who would set it all straight. But it was Kitty Puss who got out of the car, staggered a little, and then knocked on the car window beside Maria. When she opened it, warm sulfur-laden wind flowed in against the air conditioning.

Kitty Puss had obviously rehearsed, all the way down the hill, across the river, and up the south road, what she was going to say. She leaned her elbows on the windowsill. She was completely calm. "Maria and Daisy, I'm going in there and lock my door. Don't call me on the phone. Don't ring the doorbell. Don't bang the fucking door knocker that Brandy brought back from Bermuda. Got that?" Maria and Daisy stared straight ahead. "Now fuck off." She ran away over the carpet of pachysandra through the tunnel of shade from the ragged trees.

"She got some someplace. I could smell it." Daisy watched

after her. "How she gets it, I don't know. We watch her like hawks."

"She's been that way ever since Brandy died. She just never got over it. Now this . . ." Maria said.

"She and Brandy were so close," Ann Randolph explained to Hannah, and began to cry.

The car sat there.

Ann Randolph had had her cry. "They bought the house after your mother died. Kitty Puss couldn't wait to get into it," she told Hannah. "We thought you knew."

"Didn't Melinda tell you?" Daisy asked from the front seat.

Hannah could only shake her head.

"We forget when you've been here and when you haven't." Daisy inspected the property. "I don't know. They wanted to be near Melinda and Spud. Then they moved to Aiken and now there are new people. Kitty Puss hasn't a thing in common with them. Do you think she'll sell? She ought to clear out some of those trees. Too much shade, acid soil."

"Brandy never would let her"—Maria sounded sad—"even when they went to Hilton Head they just rented."

There was only the whisper of the air conditioner and Ann Randolph's renewed tiny sobs.

"There's too much heartworm in Aiken," Daisy told the trees. "I *told* them." And then she, too, burst into tears. Maria put her head down on the steering wheel.

/

I left them there in what had been my parents' driveway. I knew I was, once again, in the way of the formality of their tears. I made a murmured excuse, but I think they hardly heard me. Cultural activities were over, and mourning had begun.

I walked slowly down the narrow road among the fortresses of houses, Daisy's that had once been Bobby Slingsby's, a lookout over the valley, and on the rise of hill above it, Maria's mother's square Federal pile, with its three-story-high stone columns. It was the first house on the hill to have a swimming pool. Anderson Carver, old Broker, was her brother.

Every year she would clear it of friends and family and invite Broker to dinner. We, who had been taught as children to call her Aunt though she wasn't kin, would find out and hide in the bushes to watch Broker shamble up the walk across her glossy lawn to see how drunk he was. One night he fell into the pool, and Johnny fished him out and took him to the door. When Johnny saw Aunt Mamie's face he switched to a hatred of her which never left him but which he hid from her, as he hid his hatred from most people, under a mask of politeness. Aunt Mamie said he was "gal-ahnt." The contemptuous ridicule he already carried as protection was accepted as wit. She said he was just like Jeb Stuart.

As it had happened in all my growing up after we went to the hill, my brother Johnny walked beside me, a boy again, as if he had waited to meet me, too deep within me, too alive to mourn any more. We passed by Maria's twenty-year-old Queen Anne imitation, with its correct landscaping that looked like it was shaved every morning, then Ann Randolph's colonial nest, with its Mount Vernon columns, and its thirties green-and-white-striped awnings. The trees that had once been spindled plants with wrought-iron rails around them to keep the pure-bred colony of dogs from peeing on them met across the road, a deep, rich, green shade. The police car was still at Charlie Bland's bachelor retreat, the most public retreat in town. I could see people beyond the windows of the garden room, where indoor plants, presented by a series of women, climbed the glass. Johnny was gone, as fleetingly as he had come to haunt me, as if he had nothing to say about the matter. I was relieved. I wanted to walk for a little while, alone, without the deception of his irony. I had walked for half a mile.

I saw Maria's car turn into Charlie Bland's drive.

Up on the hillside beyond the wide space where his lawn met Aunt Mamie's, I passed Uncle Sugar Baseheart's great yellow-brick banker's Edwardian mansion, with its spacious verandas on three sides, where I had spent so much time draped over the wicker furniture, sunk in summer afternoons. The grass had grown high. A line of grooming defined the division of the property. There was, for the first time I ever saw one on the hill, a For Sale board tipped halfway over in deep grass, more than a sign, a warning. When Kitty Puss said she wouldn't be caught dead in such a mausoleum, it had been sold, as other houses there were, simply by letting the word out among the families. That had passed. Now it was for sale again, this time to the highest bidder, as their coal lands had been, opened to the invasion of strangers.

Beyond the veil of trees, beyond the citadel, I walked into the main road down the hill, and stood above the buried ancient mound. The city lay below me, spread from the downriver factories, across the river, up into the opposite north hills. The river was defined by the Coal Building, the motel entrance a tiny orange roof, Carver's Funeral Home beside it, from that distance, as it had always been, Jim and Martha Dodd's coal-baron Gothic shrine. The whole city was dotted with church spires and it was as quiet for a little while as it had been at dawn. I could have been a stranger with new eyes for it; it seemed as pleasing as a small city in Europe, mapped by water and hills.

I passed the C&O station, now nearly deserted, that had been the main release from the city, faced with excitement and sometimes dread. Under me, below the road, a long freight train of coal cars rumbled east. I found myself saying the old chant L and N, C and O, N and W, Lackawanna!

On the bridge over the Canona, the cars, the endless train, the noise of the city, drowned the sound of the river. Downriver, almost under the bridge, the old Wayfaring Stranger in its new paint was reflected in the water. Beyond it the city pier, where Lily, Althea, Mary Rose, my mother, my Aunt Annie, all of them in their leghorn hats and their dotted-swiss dresses, embarked for moonlight rides on the old paddle-wheel boat, the *Spirit of Canona*, was covered with parked cars, small rectangles of industrial colors, blue, maroon, red, orange, black, side by side by side.

Then, for the only kind of pause I have ever sensed as holy, I was not listening, not looking, but poised above the river between escape and commitment as I had been sometimes in the rare times when I was alone there, as a child, an unknown part of my city. Some pivot within me was grave as gravity, as light and shining as the Fool's whirling center. Once my mother had called out to me out of a nightmare of her own: "No matter where you go or what you do, *I'll* always know you're a damned fool." I thanked God for the Fool. It had taken a long time to know I was not damned.

As much as I cared for Candy, even she, waiting for me in the restaurant of the Howard Johnson's motel, was a duty I turned toward, walking down the bridge into Mosby Street where the traffic flowed, and even the corner at the foot of the bridge, as I had glimpsed him once, was haunted by Johnny, completely alone, lost and hung over. He seemed to be wondering which way to go.

Candy's mother was the most genteel woman I have ever known. She was compacted in it. She made mine and Maria's mothers look like gypsy queens. She imitated so far beyond them that she parodied everything they took for granted. Until Candy and I were ten, my mother always introduced her as my "little friend from school," but after her father won a Pulitzer Prize for his reporting of a mine disaster, Candy was invited to the parties planned by the parents. That was all the honor meant to Candy's mother, that and the move to the mecca on the hill.

I can see now that she was in a perpetual light-blue panic of fear, a fear of people who were not worth the salt in Roland Pentacost's bread. The only part of his newspaper she ever read was the Society Page, while she commented, not expecting to be heard, "Do tell! I didn't know they had the money." Mr. Pentacost had hired Haley Potter's aunt to write it under the inevitable pressure of the women. She needed a job, as she said, in keeping. My mother pointed out that if you didn't get into Miss Lisa's page when you went away, or had a visitor, you were "totally ostracized."

Little of this seemed to touch Candy and her father. When Candy ran for the legislature, in 1968, her mother followed her swearing in with little moans of "Why is she *doing* this?" and "What does she *see* in these people?" while her father and I watched Candy, below in the great chamber, taking her oath to the chorus of her mother's "We don't know a soul here." Candy's father, of course, knew them all. After the ceremony we passed through a corridor of his friends. Candy's mother looked neither left nor right.

I think that Candy's father, like the twelve teachers in the Hasidic tales that you are given in many disguises, was the most profound of my guides, because he was the first person I ever knew to see me separated from anybody else's life. I had written my first story. I was fifteen. Of course I showed it to Candy, but I never would have shown it to anyone at home, except Johnny, and he had gone to war. We both thought it was wonderful. It was set in an Italy I found in Edgar Allan Poe. Candy persuaded me to let her show it to her father.

He called me into his office, like a grownup. I remember being scared to death as I climbed the stairs, and stopped at the door that read ROLAND PENTACOST, EDITOR in big black letters. I thought then that they were black for his politics. He called himself a black Republican, the last extant, I remembered the word, member of Lincoln's party. He said too many Republicans, he called them new people in the same tone my mother used for invaders on the hill, were to the right of Andy Mellon. When Candy began to work in Democratic politics, he only said, "So be it, honey. I'm too old to change."

I had no way of knowing then that almost every Southern writer finds a Mr. Pentacost in growing up. They come in all sorts of motley, and they bring, as gifts, glimpses of possibility beyond the noisy, ever-present demands of social life in Southern cities, the demands that are their comfort, their kindness and ease, their hard-bought security, and their weapon against those who can't conform. Such Hasidic guides, undefined even to themselves, provide a provincial oasis, where the tendrils of a wider culture extend from outside and whisper a hope that makes the inner isolation bearable, a haven of music and conversation away from the stultifying atmosphere of demanded imitation, claustrophobic blood ties, "good ole boy" ridicule. Candy's home, at least on the front porch away from her mother, was my oasis. It was there I first heard Mozart on the Victrola, there I listened to her father read Tolstoy and his favorite writer, George Bernard Shaw, aloud. He always called him that, all three names, and he would stop, and say, "Tarnation!"—it was the only swear-word he allowed himself—"Did you hear that!" and read the line again. I don't think I envied Candy, but sometimes I wanted to crawl inside and be her more than anyone else in the world.

Finally I had the guts to open his office door. He sat, formally, behind his desk, in the turn-of-the-century winged collar he affected all his life, his gray hair long and flowing. He looked like a back-country preacher. Candy said he dressed like a parody of one of his own cartoons. One wall was covered with a map of Europe and Africa, stuck with red pins. The wall beside his desk was Asia and the Pacific, floor to ceiling. In some conceit of his own he had found thumbtacks with heads that were little gray shops. I knew them all, for I followed Johnny through atlases and Mr. Pentacost's newspaper. And he, surrounded by war, right in the middle of it, was taking the time to see me. On his desk, in the center of the world, lay my story. He put his big square hand on it and kept it there, holding the paper down.

"Sit down," he said. I felt like a stranger.

Then he began. "You have picked a good model, 'The Cask of Amontillado.' Good story. One of Poe's best. But you learned from his weaknesses and not his strengths. You haven't been in Italy. Neither had he. There was plenty of revenge right in his own back yard." He cleared his throat. "The essence of good writing is not necessarily to write what you know. That is stupid. How can you ever learn if you do that? It is to see what you know as if it were new. Child's eye. Alas, I don't have it, never did. But I know it when I see it. That's why I'm an editor." He took his hand from the story. I thought he was going to give it back to me, and I could feel tears of failure gather like a cold in my nose. But he went to his window instead. "Come here." He snapped his fingers. "Now look down there. Street you take for granted. Mosby Street. Known it all your life." Across the street the Masonic Temple was white marble in the sun, carved in pinnacles, balconies, secret signs. "Thoreau once said that he was born in Concord just in the nick of time. What in tarnation was Concord? A one-horse town in Massachusetts. This," he said, he seemed to forget me, "is my Concord. He made a silk purse out of a sow's ear. That's what you do when you write well, make a silk purse out of a sow's ear. Look at that building. All the magic of old Araby right here in your own town."

He pushed me back to my chair and then he sat down again. "You might go to Italy sometime, and even Araby, oh, all sorts of places, but go from here and now, your own Concord. Don't skip." He closed his eyes. "It was not corn I hoed, nor I who hoed corn. Ain't that something? Thoreau's little old corn patch. Not worth a red cent. You read, read everything you can find. Now you go on, honey, I got work to do." He handed me the story, and guided me to the door with his hand on my back.

"I like the fact that you typed it and you spelled right, took trouble. It shows promise." He smiled. "Write me another story."

I was alone, outside the closed door. I wanted to be brokenhearted, but I couldn't be. He had treated me completely seriously and that was worth anything else he had to say, even the last, Write me another story.

I passed the Masonic Temple on the way to Candy. There it was, old Araby, still shining in the sun.

There was a Volvo station wagon parked in front of the motel. A bumper sticker read *Art is In*, a motto made up by somebody over forty. I knew that some of the ladies of the morning had invaded the sanctum. Somebody had edited the sticker with purple marker to *Fart is Out*. I wondered if whoever it was knew that Whistler had spelled art the same way.

It would have been easier if on that June day I had kept the clarity of love-free vision, but there was Candy.

She sat in a corner booth in the half-dark restaurant, watching the door. Behind her head were the brown-and-yellow stripes of national-chain wallpaper, in the American substitute for home, easy familiarity at every stop on the highway. Between the windows hung a jigsaw puzzle print of a painting of an overturned skiff on some Maine shore. I stopped, waited to go toward her as into cold water. I looked beyond the boat, cowardly as if I hadn't seen her yet, pretended to scan the room for her, past the paintings of an Iowa barn, a doggie, a still-life with bananas, a painted window reflecting a mirror reflecting a window with a snowy landscape, not one reminder of the town we were in. We could have been anyplace. It was, for a minute, a relief.

She was not fooled, I knew, by my pause. She had a terrible sameness about her, as if nothing had happened, or ever would, or if it had it didn't matter. She had sat there ten years or ten minutes, leaning back against the high booth, dwarfed by it. Candy had not grown since she was fifteen, and I, as she said, shot past her. She was still five feet two,

still with her hands folded together without any sign of
tension, in a clean round-collared shirt, her arms straight out
along the wood-grained vinyl of the tabletop. For the time of
crossing the floor I let myself think that I no longer cared for
her rightness, her calm that was too near complacence. I
wanted to ruffle it with facts, but there were so few she didn't
already know, accept, and live with.

I slid into the booth and saw her close, her heart-face, her
clean short neat dark hair flecked with gray, her blue eyes
winged with deep lines, Irish as Paddy's pig, her father said,
from the Irish kings her mother swore were their inheritance,
loved her as much as ever, and leaned, as I always had,
forward, toward her ease, my shoes tipped back as once my
saddle shoes had been, started in the middle, girl again.

"Did you know . . . ?" We both laughed.

"You come back for the damnedest reasons. Why?"

A skinny, towheaded waitress with lank hair held back with
a barrette came and pushed menus between us. Even in the
brown Howard Johnson's uniform, her face, her voice, her
name Juanita pinned to a sign on her flat chest, were as local
as the river. She said, "Y'all take your time." She leaned on
her hands, her arms stiff, as at home as if she were in her own
kitchen and we were company, read the menu too, and told
us not to order the turkey club. "We ain't got no turkey left.
Hit wadn't no good nohow." She relaxed onto one hip and
found something in a tooth with her tongue. She made the
national anonymity of Howard Johnson's restaurant as local as
the town drugstore where Candy and I had sat, after school,
she leaning back, me forward, urgent, the marble table cool
under our bare arms.

"Let's have a glass of white wine."

"All right, honey. You want one too, Miz Tennant?"

"Sure, Juanita. How's your boy?"

"He's still on probation. He's got him a job loadin' trucks."

I looked after her, all the way to the kitchen, a relief for a
minute from Candy's incisive watch, the interrupted "Why?"
She was back almost at once, with two delicate stemmed
wineglasses. "Y'all take your time," she said again as she set
them down.

"I just walked down from the hill," I told the wine. "It's all
the same."

"That's the way you see it." Candy reached across the table
and touched my hand. "Oh, Hannah, I miss your being here.

Tell me everything. Tell me about George, how you spend your days..."

Juanita waited by the table to hear, too.

I couldn't say a word. "Why don't you come and see us?" I finally asked Candy. Juanita moved over to the next booth. I heard her say, "All right, ladies, made up your minds?"

I heard them order, listened carefully while they asked for separate checks.

"Are you happy?" Candy touched my hand again.

I could sense attention on us from the next booth.

"Yes," I told them all.

"Does it hurt your work?"

"No. It makes it possible... Why don't you come?"

"I will sometime." We both knew she wouldn't. "Hannah, you know I won't get out, and you can't get back. That's the way it is... I envy you, though." She turned her half-empty glass. She didn't envy me at all, and we both knew it. She was the only woman I had seen that morning who didn't, one way or another. There was a giggle from the next booth, a whisper. "Go on!" I could hear someone getting up, a creak.

A voice over us, "Hi, Candy." I had to look up. She stood there, a young, bright-looking girl, and smiled. "We're so proud of you..." She shoved the Howard Johnson's menu in front of me. "Can you sign this?" She handed me a pen. I signed in the space between hamburger and bacon burger. She took the menu back and inspected it. "I've read all your books." Dead silence. "Candy, I'll be down to work this afternoon."

"I'm running again," Candy said. "This is Nancy Carver, one of my best workers."

"I'm learning to be a ward heeler," Nancy Carver explained. "Well, thanks for this. I certainly will treasure it." She was already on her way. Behind us, a twitter of voices, the passing of the menu, Nancy Carver, "I *told* you I'd do it."

"I was thinking about Roland. How is he?"

"The same, looks like an old rooster, still pontificating. I used to be so ashamed of Pop because he wasn't like everybody else. You used to come and see him when you didn't have anything better to do." She had always been too self-protected to sound so bitter. My memories of Candy, peaceful, too, listening to him reading Bernard Shaw to us on their porch, were wrong. I saw for the first time that we had wanted to change places with each other. I wanted to say, "Candy, I didn't know."

As if I had said it, she answered, "I got over it, but then, I don't know. There was that longing..." She brushed it aside. "I know I was lucky. There was nothing to fear, no unearned inheritance. I never had to suck up to my parents, or feel like a burden. No—" She stopped whatever answer I had. "Unearned is wrong. God, you earned it—you didn't even get paid. No," she answered again, something I hadn't said. "The best thing that happened to this valley was when your family threw you out on your ass. Let me tell you something. I still dream about you. Once I dreamed about a coal truck. You and I were sitting in it watching a building burning. I tried to get out and run and you held me back. You said No you don't. No you don't, that was what you said, and you called me Johnny. The next day I voted for the strip-mining law—the coal lobby—Jesus, the pressure... you don't know. I think half the women you were with this morning called me up to pressure me... Most of them don't own an acre of coal property any more. They've sold out to the oil and chemical companies." She had missed me. She wanted to tell, not ask. She seemed to want to set me straight about something. I waited for it.

"Those pathetic bitches..." She was still caught by them, as I was. I was ashamed for both of us, our lingering adolescent knee jerks.

"The two most dangerous groups in our society"—she was retreating into abstractions as if she'd touched a live nerve— "are rich old women and unemployed boys on relief. All that unused energy. They have that in common. I escaped it. I work. I get up in the morning and I join the city." Then, a little shyly: "When the legislature is in session I'm so busy. There's a lot I can't do." Sudden switch. "What are you trying to find out, Hannah? Same old thing? Just what is it you're trying to do? Still chasing Johnny while the world goes to hell in a handcart? You think we're disintegrating? What did you call it once, the senility of the century?" She had slipped back to the safe harbor of being my critic, my little neat judge. I was too furious not to answer.

"No. If I said that, I was wrong. We're shedding, like snakes when their skin is too old. The danger... you retire behind abstractions. To hell with the century. I'm trying to find out what lay behind one act of violence, the fist of one man hitting a man he didn't know. You say it doesn't have anything to do with what's going on. It's the goddamn center of it, one fist, one man, one act. If you think that, try walking down a city street at midnight dressed as Johnny was."

I had hurt her. She was as furious as I was. "I was only trying to get you to define it. You think I don't know. What do you think *I've* been doing all this time. Twenty years ago, while you were hightailing it around New York and Paris and God knows where, I was teaching school up Lacey Creek. I did it for ten years. I saw the IQs of my kids go down by ten percent because they weren't getting enough to eat, while you useless unweaned Eisenhower bitches were giving parties. I had kids who walked three miles over the mountains in the rain to go to school. While your lot were wrecking cars and being unhappy, I was working my way through law school with the help of a husband and two kids. It was the only way I knew to do what I had to. I wanted to be sure of what that bunch of lawyers at the State House were up to. Let me tell you something. I'm glad about what happened when you came back. It got your ass in gear at long last."

I had stripped away a layer of her I didn't know she had. She took a deep breath.

"You don't even know who Johnny is *yet*. My God, and you've followed him through three centuries. He's as much you as your hands or your face." She had waited so long to say all this to me that I didn't stop her. I couldn't. Maybe I'd been waiting to hear it.

"At least you used yourself as a guinea pig. Most artists don't. They keep a sadistic watch. They suffer vicariously, like women at somebody else's funeral."

We had both run down. We stared at each other like enemies. Then we relaxed into a peace at the other side of both our necessary outbursts. We had given each other the gift of our anger, as we always had, a never-ending complicity of trust.

"Well, what do you know? Look who's here! Honey, I'm so glad to see you. Move over, let an old man in." He shoved me over, and sat down beside us. He put his heavy arm around me and squeezed. It was Plain George, twenty pounds heavier than I had seen him last and bald as an onion. "I've lost some and I've gained some," he said, touching his head and his belly. "Wawnita, come on over here and give these

ladies a drink. What is it?" He smelled my empty glass.
"White wine, what are you trying to do, rust your gut?"

"I talked to Irene this morning..." Candy and Plain George
were taking up a conversation I had no part in. Irene?
Oh—Sigsbie, who had given me my first manicure when I
was sixteen. I could still hear her, "Bite your nails. Quit that.
Tell your mamma you got worms."

"Yeah. She told me. She's got the sixth ward sewed up
pretty tight. Of course, you can't count on nothing till the last
dog's dead."

"How is Irene?" It was awkward, but I wanted him to know
I remembered. He wasn't fooled.

"Sigsbie? You never called her Irene in your life, honey.
Marriage had ruined my old girl." He grinned. "Goddamned
woman lost weight, joined a garden club, and started using
them little old doilies on the table. Made me get all four feet
out of the bottle." He sounded proud.

Juanita plunked two large iced-tea glasses full of wine in
front of us. "We run out of them fancy glasses. I didn't want
ye to have to wait."

Plain George said, "Where the hell's mine?"

"You don't get none." Juanita grinned.

"All the women are against me." He held my hand. "Honey, you know about Charlie Bland, don't you?"

That was what had bothered me. Plain George had been
the ever-present strength in time of trouble all my life, the
first to offer solace, a car, a drink, the first to know that words
didn't mean much. He should have been the first man at
Charlie Bland's door. He should have been the one to cut
him down. He would have done it tenderly.

He spoke then, but not to me; it seemed to be to Charlie
himself. "It wouldn't do Charlie any good if I went up there.
All those women milling around." The door to his best
friend's death had been closed to him by the women. "I don't
know. It didn't even surprise me. Everybody's going to ask
why." I hadn't, but I had been ready to. "Charlie got tired of
being the star in all their bad movies. I don't know...it
brings Johnny back. I'm damned if I know why...I got to go.
Y'all stay here and get drunk. Irene won't let me..." I
watched him lumber over to Juanita to pay her for the wine,
and heard her say, "Ain't you going to eat nothin'?" He just
shook his head, and went out of the door.

Juanita came over to the table. "He's real upset."

"A friend of his died this morning," Candy told her.

"Yeah. I know about that. Wha'd he do it for? He had plenty of money..."

A man called, "Juanita, come here. We ain't got all day."

"Oh, shut up," she called back. "Can't you see I'm taking these ladies' orders? Here." She got out her order pad. "Eat the seafood."

When she had gone, Candy told me about Plain George.

"If you think the old women are dangerous now, you should have seen them carve up Plain George. Daisy's in her art phase now. You should have seen her in her Christian phase. She took in everybody else's sins. She insisted on Plain George confessing to Ann Randolph something she'd known for years and hadn't faced. Old Sigsbie. Ann Randolph had no choice but to go through the motions. She went through them all. The overdose, the divorce, getting Plain George fired. Ann Randolph owned the company. They treated him like a dog. Plain George is a lot younger than Ann Randolph"—she went on telling me what I knew—"he was only twenty when they had to get married. She was years older and had all the money..." Candy had lapsed into the language of old gossip. "Did you know that she was fat as a pig until she was sixteen? Somebody that knew her in Virginia told me that."

"What's he doing now?"

Juanita answered, as she put the plates in front of us. "He ran for Justice of the Peace. He was mighty good to my boy. He never done nothin' but steal some tars. He said he didn't have nuthin' else to do on Satidy night. Now y'all enjoy that, you hear?" She was off again.

"I got him to run." Candy smiled. "He's good. I think he's happier than he's ever been. He ran clean. Wouldn't take a cent. He said he'd been bought on the hill, damned if he was going to be bought in the valley."

It was two o'clock. She put me in my car, and leaned over and kissed my temple. "You *tell*, honey. Tell everything. We're counting on you. What are you going to do now?"

The question was larger than I was prepared to answer. "I'm going to see Aunt Althea," I said instead. "Family..."

"Don't forget how much I miss you."

"It won't be so long this time..."

"Oh yes it will. You left us all way back there." She walked away before I found an answer.

I drove down the Boulevard, still with Candy. It wasn't

true. I hadn't left them and I told her so. I also promised her that I would tell, tell everything, keep on mining all the strata of us as I had been doing for eighteen years. When I drove up to Aunt Althea's Spanish house, she was standing, waiting at the door. She screeched like an old bird before I was out of the car, "Where the hell have you been? You promised to take me to the picture show," as if she had last seen me yesterday instead of ten years ago.

"It doesn't start until six o'clock." I got out of the car. "I checked the paper."

"You're lying. An old woman has to pay for her pleasure. Come on in the house. I know what you want. Nebbiest youngin' I ever saw."

Althea was mad as hell, but she wasn't going to give the girl the satisfaction. She turned on the car radio, switched it off, and said, "For God's sake, turn that thing off." She had been promised the picture show, and the promise was receding behind them. There was one thing left to do—not tell the girl a goddamned thing.

She clicked her fingers. "You're goddamn right," she told Hannah, "if you want to get anything out of me, you'll take me to the picture show," and laughed.

Althea was eighty-three years old, and she had, locked in herself, freckled, faded clues to something imperative. She knew it, and enjoyed the power to withhold it. She had teased the girl and her own memory all afternoon, stretching out a visit the only way she knew how, querulous and evocative. She had spread an album on her coffee table, moving the china Spanish dancer aside, while she accused, "You said you were going to take me to the picture show," and pretended not to remember people in the old snapshots while she had watched Hannah turn the broken and black pages.

Called from the photographs, through the dark glass of her forgetfulness, she had glimpsed rooms, faint echoes, corridors, gestures, old, dried, cracked loves and hates, bones of desire.

There was the machine gun crouched on the porch faint as a shadow. There were frail brown vines. The smiles were false, the faces frozen from having to pose for too long. She laughed. "Your daddy took that picture. He couldn't work the Kodak." She pointed and explained, "*That* was Broker Carver. Him—" and slammed the book shut and said, "I'm tired of this."

"Come for a ride before we go to the movies," Hannah said. She knew she would. "There's something I want to see."

"I'll just bet you do." She settled herself in the car, pleased, but determined not to show it. She had on her best low-waisted dress and Mary Jane slippers, and going through the hall she had paused at the mirror. "Won't find a thing. Bullheaded. Poke your nose in—" In her mind, she mixed and judged the dead and the living without sentiment, fragmented faces called up, confused by time. She sang a little bit, sometimes television commercials, once chanting, "Maize, what you call corn." She turned the car radio on and off and said, again, "Shut that damned thing off. I don't know—" and went on snapping her fingers. She kept up a dribble of talk to herself between the snatches of slogans and old tunes. Mind lulled, Hannah drove on up the river, but once she snapped into attention at her brother Johnny's name.

"Johnny used to come and sit with me, not that the rest of you took the time or the trouble, too busy going to the Country Club. He came with his bottle and he talked to it more than he ever did to me. He'd look at it and say, 'Holy shit, I could drink it all,' and I'd interrupt that love affair and tell him it wouldn't do a particle of good, I'd tried that, God knows.

"Afterwards, when it happened and you gallivanted off someplace and left us to pick up the pieces, your mother went the way she always expected me to but I never did, anyway not after I was on to her. She went downright tacky. You know—spiritual—she was a mark for every shirttail fortune-teller that came down the pike. Called that boy back from the beyond, speaking language he wouldn't have been caught dead using—messages through some trashy Indian. She'd come sit with me then, oh yes, stripped down to size at long last, and tell me she was a happy mother do not grieve; she'd found peace. Messages like that, I am at peace it's beautiful here. Johnny! Good God! He never would have deigned. Just some pap to ease her conscience which was no hard task. You're a chip off the old block. You won't leave well enough alone, either."

She grabbed Hannah's arm and made her jerk the wheel. "You weren't even here. What do *you* know?"

Hannah steadied the wheel.

"Anyway, your mother always said you didn't bother." She began to laugh. "You don't even know how it happened."

She couldn't make Hannah answer.

She tried again. "He fell down the stairs. That's what your mother said. A household accident. She believed it, too."

She had finally tricked Hannah into speaking. "Whatever happened to the man?"

"What man?" She was intent on paying Hannah back for the picture show. "Go on. What man?" Daring her, damned if she'd tell. "It was, after all, only a family matter." She began to hum again.

When they turned through the underpass of the railroad to go up Lacey Creek, she said, "I might have known."

The road was paved and wide. It followed blasted cliffs close enough to touch. On one side Lacey Creek lay deep among the trees. For the first mile they caught glimpses of clear water. It was so quiet they could hear its flow.

"What you want to come up here for, I don't know. You've been all over hell's half-acre." Althea remembered something that had happened to her in Rome. She had told the story before and she knew it, but it amused her to see the girl prick up her ears. Girl, hell. She was fifty if she was a day. Now she changed and censored the story. She did mention the Spanish Steps and the Borghese Gardens. Then, with a sudden little spurt of malice, "You're not the only one who's been places and seen things."

"You won't find a damned thing," she said when Hannah pulled the car off the road where the valley widened out in front of them. She stopped against the first mountain that formed the bowl, once called Seven Stars. There had been an old streetcar diner and filling station against the bare rock. Now only a paved platform and one rusty pump were left.

On both sides of Lacey Creek houses spread out through the bottomland. The shapes were left of the old Jenny Lind company shacks, and a few of the older miners' houses with their stone foundations. Now they were painted pink, yellow, lavender, the colors of birds' eggs and spring flowers. The board-and-batten church was white, with a small tower like a needle to the sky. The company store was gone. The trees were whitewashed halfway up their trunks. The white wood porches looked new. There were porch swings and gliders from Sears, covered with bright prints. One thing had not changed. No one sitting on the porches in the distance seemed to take notice of the strange car. Althea knew they saw them, and it made her grin at the girl, who said, not meaning to, "It is clean and calm and I am not prepared for this."

"Why not? What the hell did you expect?"

The little yards were fenced. There were flowers in carefully etched beds cut into the grass. Some of the houses had been covered with aluminum siding, and asphalt tile stamped to look like brick, not the dead dirt yards Althea remembered in another spring in 1960 when she had taken the bull by the horns. Then there were stringy hopeless creepers, sagging front stoops, swings made of old tires, porch furniture of old car seats, the whole place a crying shame and she said so at the time.

In one of the slumps in the coal business, Imperial had sold the company houses to the miners, some for fifty dollars. Houses too rickety to sell had been torn down; where they had stood, there were house-shaped vegetable gardens.

"Your mother always said the important things happened on the north side of the river. She lived and breathed Beulah Beulah Beulah. When you started this fool thing I wondered how ong it would take you to come over here." Aunt Althea smiled at her sister-in-law, the girl's dead mother. "I told her lies were to no avail. I said so, Sally Brandon." She spoke directly to her in an old complaint.

She was suddenly tired of the girl sitting beside her. She said, "You go ahead, honey. I'm perfectly satisfied." She went on smiling, folded away into a place and time the girl couldn't know. It wasn't any of her business. She watched her get out of the car alone, not knowing where to go, lost. She looked back at the car from across the road where the dirt side road crossed a wooden bridge and beyond it the railroad spur up Lacey Creek.

Althea sat, still smiling, watching something the place had brought to her mind. She came back to the girl standing there so forlorn, and waved for her to come back.

"It's too far to walk," she said. "You drive on across the creek. The back road runs by the graveyard and right past the house." Her smile turned into a grin.

They followed the dirt road and then the deep-rutted back

path until they had to stop. Only the erosion of rain had kept it in the shape and position of a road at all. Even the shale from old mines had long since washed downhill.

Even so, Althea didn't get out of the car. "You gwan up there," she pushed at Hannah. "Gwan. I'm going to smoke a cigarette."

The back road still struggled up through the trees. At the hill's crest Hannah had to push her way through a thicket of honeysuckle under the dim green afternoon. There was no house. Old lilac bushes were tangled with the underbrush. Formed by trees, some fallen, a space of weeds and daisies hinted at the old lawn. There was nothing else. A rain-dimmed sign on a tree read PRIVATE NO TRESPASSING DANGER.

"No," Althea called. Some way, eighty-three years old, she had climbed the hill road and had found her way through the thicket. She looked large against the honeysuckle. She was still grinning. She stood gnarled and time-carved, refusing to die. She had survived them all, her family, her house, even some of the trees. Her eyes gathered it in, the weeds, the neglect. She touched her fine white hair as the hot wind tugged it.

"Here's the walk, not there," she instructed. "You can feel the brick with your foot. My God, the mighty brought down." And she looked around, not giving a damn. No. She did give a damn. There was in her a triumph. She knew she had won some battle the girl hadn't yet fought.

She walked toward her along the hidden path, sure-footed, completely at home. "I always thought they burned it down for the insurance." She stood, judging the space where the house had been. "Hunh! Watch out, the foundations are still here. Sit here on the porch—" Ignoring Hannah, she said, "There was a green sunlight through the vines." She looked at her accusingly. "It's all gone. I told you. Are you satisfied?"

Now, as she pointed, Hannah wondered how she had missed the blueprint of square-cut stones hidden in the weeds. She knew it had been a big house, but the shape bordered and crossed by the foundation stones was small under the high trees.

"Go right ahead. Be my guest. You look like a dying calf. If you can't stand the heat. What was said that?" Althea sat down on porch steps that went nowhere. She fumbled in her bag and found her cigarettes. She sat, anonymous and patient. Hannah stood in the center of one of the room-size squares made by the stones and watched her. From the back she looked like a parody of a young girl. She had clasped her knees and tilted her body back a little, her small head with its thin cap of white hair, still in what she called a boyish bob, was tilted, too, her gnarled hands hidden, her shrunken face that Hannah remembered always as plump, almost swollen, hidden. She had let her body relax into some old way of sitting. She was totally still, and then her arm moved and she blew out a cloud of cigarette smoke and watched it dissipate into the air.

Behind her a few rambler roses had survived in the weedy meadow grass.

She looked around then and the illusion still held, a litheness in her. "You're standing in Papa's library," she said. "Now, over there"—she pointed—"there would be a chimney. There was the living-room fireplace and the dining room and it went right up into Mother's room. Companies do that, have you noticed? They won't leave the chimney to mourn where the house has been. Oh no. They don't want people crawling over it collecting insurance, that's why. Private burning they leave the chimney to remember. This is company burning."

Hannah couldn't move. She was in thrall, caught by what was no longer there, as if it held her. Althea had settled down in the sun and she and the emptiness held Hannah back. She sensed it.

"You were bound and determined to come up here. Well?" She took another drag of her cigarette. "You asked for it, you're going to get it. I *told* you take me to the picture show."

"Wasn't there a cellar?" Hannah was afraid to move inside the foundations, a fear of hidden caves, of falling.

"No. Papa said Grandfather didn't believe in them. They brought damp, he said. Now, how can you believe in cellars? The way he said it, it was like believing in God. Papa had a wine cellar, though, back there against the hill. It had pictures in it from the Indian times. Don't go over there, though. It's full of snakes. Professors come up here and poke around. They say it's been in use for something like three thousand years. Did you ever hear tell? No fool like an educated fool. Papa used to say it was a gentleman's duty to keep good wine. We always thought he had a fortune in wine but when he died it was as empty as his bank account. That was the way he talked. I *liked* Papa, but I didn't have all that much use for him. There's a difference. Mother?"

Hannah hadn't asked her.

"I was scared to death of Mother. Your mother was of her mother, over to Beulah. *That* we had in common. Old Mrs. Neill never let me forget her damned Virginia connections. She treated me like your sainted Uncle Dan, the Golden Boy, the son-of-a-bitch had married beneath him. The Brandons. Oh God. The Cutrights, the Laceys, the Kreggs, the god-damn Senator. Your mother was named for the Brandons. Hell's fire, your uncle got so low you couldn't get beneath him, and I mean sex, too. You spoiled kids don't know what mother-in-law trouble could be."

Hannah remembered her grandmother from Beulah, but that was so much later, after she had turned away from all of them, her mother, her Uncle Dan Neill, even Uncle Sugar with his rich clothes and his rich walk, coming up to the porch on River Street. It seemed to her then that they were asking for something, attending on her, paying court to get her attention, but they never did.

They hadn't sold the house on River Street until she died. The property, they said, had risen in value, so it came down, broken and swept away, the Lancelot hallway, the mullioned windows, the heavy dark woodwork, the electrolier over the Duncan Phyfe dining table from Beulah, the Delft tile, the portraits of Great-grandmother Melinda Kregg from Albion, with one rosebud in her hand, and of Great-grandfather Senator Neill, all sold or flung over a whole valley, a table here, a silver teapot there, wherever what was left of the family lived.

It was from that house on River Street that Hannah, born in 1930, had picked up fragments, an archaeology of memory and curiosity, that went all the way back to "Before the War," trunks in the attic, old letters, neglected clothes, a ball gown that Great-grandmother Melinda had worn, rolled strips of ivory silk, wedding pictures freckled like old hands, all the things thought worth keeping when Beulah fell.

But it was from the old woman in front of her that she learned about what are called the Twenties. Because of her the decade left over in her house meant darkness, and blinds drawn in Spanish rooms, dark carved furniture, lamps with fringe and the faint shape of an undusted Spanish galleon with parchment sails that sat above her head on the Crosley radio she was not allowed to touch.

She never went upstairs. Her mother wouldn't let her. They only went there when Sally Brandon thought they "needed" her. She went up to the door that was left unlocked, and marched in, making more noise with her feet than she usually did. Once they went in April and the house was a neglected tomb, its stillness defying the noise of her shoes. She flung open the dirty french doors to let in the sun, and it lit the skeleton of a Christmas tree that had sagged against the wall.

Hannah was afraid they would find them dead.

She didn't know then that that was the way alcoholic houses looked and felt. She only knew she wanted to run.

And her Aunt Althea, who had lived like that, had survived them all, in the same house.

She turned and looked at Hannah. Something in her face set her off, she talked in a spate, as the old do or people who have been alone too long. The face she saw was changing in her furious eyes to her hated sister-in-law's, then to her sister Lily's, then to all her enemies pinned there in the foundations among the weeds. She attacked what she saw. The concerns that lodged in her were long gone, but to her they were as alive as the afternoon they were caught in together. They had kept her from ripening into age. She was not old. She was used and weathered and cynical but the girl in her still raged.

"Nobody told me. Why didn't they tell me?" She shrieked like a bird whose nest had been fouled. "They knew. Your mother knew, all the time, but she and her high-hat sister were too goddamned ladylike to talk about such things. She only told me later, too late." She stopped, and when she spoke again, her voice was quiet and young.

"My God, I thought those girls, Sally Brandon and your Aunt Annie Neill from Beulah, were the goddamned cat's pajamas. First thing we moved down to River Street, the center of the world after Papa died, center, hell it was where they put the nozzle for the world's enema far as I'm concerned, was your mother and your aunt hightailing it down River Street in their white gloves and I remember one in dove-gray silk and one in taupe, taupe they called it, taupe georgette, in their big hats. I thought they were just wonderful, those girls. How was I to know they'd tripped and fallen lower than we ever did and that it was all pride and one-dress poorhouse Tory? Your mother never did know except with her mind and what the hell is *that* that they were poor. Broke we were, poor we were not she used to say like that kind of fooling people was something to take pride in. We had, she would say, owned a great deal of the valley, and that gave us strength.

"We never became friends until there wasn't anybody else and she came home to roost and there wasn't any use hiding every last thing any more. We'd take a little nip together and she'd spread her knees like anybody else and goddamn admit what was true when it was too late."

Her voice took on an old fury, and she talked to the Sally Brandon she saw within the girl, standing in the weeds.

"Why didn't you tell me then? Why didn't you tell me in time?" she asked her, blind-eyed, little bird head turned; all that was left were bones held together by fury and parchment skin like the galleon sails.

Hannah wanted to run away from it as she always had. She could smell the empty space and the dead color of her hair.

"*She* wasn't the only one with what she called background." Althea's voice was soft again. "Let me tell you something. I have never in my life felt as *real* anyplace else as I do right here, whatever's happened since. Everybody has their kingdom." She was quiet, her knees clasped, looking down an old lawn toward ghosts of lilacs and cedar trees, across a valley that was no longer what she saw. Down to the right there was a tangle of wire and a patch of almost weedless grass.

"Papa put in a tennis court. Lily was the best player. I'd try but Mother would interfere and say Lily's the best player, pushing her forward like that, pushing her all the time. She was Mother's favorite. I never would have looked at your Uncle Dan but for that. I just got damned sick and tired of being outdone—

"Why didn't your side of the family tell me?" Her voice stabbed at Hannah again. She had heard it all before. It was called Aunt Althea's chorus, but not in that empty place, not with the fury that made it a new song instead of an almost unheard habit whine.

"Do you know where they were going, in their buttoned shoes with their tip-tap prance, in dove-gray silk and the taupe georgette, the only visiting dresses they *owned*? They were going to the picture show at the old Canona Opera House. They called themselves the picture-show brigade.

"Because he, Captain Dan, the Golden Boy, the *Senator's* grandson, the pride of the family, was on a screaming bender in the back of that house on River Street and nobody could go near him but his mother and she would say girls, it's time to go to the picture show and then, gentlemen get like this sometimes. At least he does it in private, he's got that much pride. Coal and licker, licker and coal, goddamn licker and coal!"

She raged up from the stone steps and stumbled toward Hannah, seeing her mother, the obsession that had kept her alive so long made her face pink. She bared a set of big new Medicare teeth.

"He didn't go to Thurmond like we thought when he was up here in 1912 so high and mighty and you knew it. He came right down to River Street. Oh Miss Rule the Roost, you didn't deign to tell me that until he was dead and gone, how he came home from New York, tragic Dan the City Man, with his tail between his legs, like he was the only one that crashed, and under the taupe georgette your underwear was more patch than lace, and you and Annie could tell when he was there by the pall over everything when you walked in the front door. He ruled the roost then, didn't he, didn't he, though? Will he start again? Has he started again? And the threats! His crisis was always bigger than yours. Will he commit suicide? Will he cash checks this time? Keep him hidden, keep him penned up, Mother's Golden Boy. Wash the vomit off his clothes with your own hands and send him back upriver to us like he stepped out of a bandbox."

She was so close that spit sprayed Hannah's face. She saw her at last.

"Well," she said, and she was calm. "You wanted to know, didn't you? They married him off to me and put me in a living hell, and all to get his hands on Seven Stars. Well, he wasn't Dapper Dan for long, let me tell you. They think all fearsome things are up some alley or down some tenderloin street. I tell you they's just as many dark things caught in the dimity curtains or in the drawers behind the sachets. You talk about fearsome things! It isn't all blood and other kinds of people let me tell you."

Hannah knew that. Her Uncle Dan Neill had been a

shadow over them; he had haunted her mother, as her brother Johnny still haunted her. She remembered her Uncle Dan in an old coat with the sleeves frayed, his ankles swollen over sloppy shoes, his belt below his fat stomach. He was a parody of a good ole boy, a Knight of the White Camellia, blaming it all on the Jews and the unions, and hollering in the back of the house on River Street that Hitler was right, with her mother's eyes on the front door praying she'd get rid of him before anybody came in. She said he dressed and talked like that just to get her goat.

"Now get the hell out of here," Aunt Althea commanded her as if the house still existed. "Let me sit here by myself a little while." Then, sweet old lady: "You come back and get me, you hear, honey? My!" She turned and turned in the weeds. "We had the best times here. I just want to sit and think about it."

Hannah wanted to leave and she had released her. She had to pull herself together and do what she had come to do, safe objective archaeology, still shaking from the attack that her mother had borne. It was only when she got back through the brambles to the old road that she wiped the spray of her Aunt Althea's fury from her face.

She stumbled among the wooden crosses fallen in the old graveyard, read the faded names almost hidden in the weeds: Escew, Catlett, Tremble, and in a plot apart from the others, Lacey, the black Laceys. Some of the graves were sunk below the ground. "Spissus," she said, "heavy soil," and wondered why. She looked beyond the graveyard toward the deep gash between the hills where the little rill had flowed down past Seven Stars into Lacey Creek, where in her mind, as real as the memories of her own life, Lily still read Montaigne to Eduardo. The hollow was gone. The tops of two mountains had been thrown into it, smoothed over, connected by a high unnatural dam, newly sewn with grass. There was a pool below her of opaque blue water. Beside it an old man stood, his head thrust forward as if he had been listening for something for a long time.

Every day Old Man Tremble got him his stick even if he didn't need it. She'd holler out of the kitchen and she'd say,

"Don't forget your stick," she'd say, "Where ye goin'?" and he'd say, "Up to see the pond," and she'd say, "Yes you go on," she'd say in that molasses voice they used for old fellers she'd say, "oh yes you go right ahead that's good for ye," like she was a goddamned registered nurse.

He figured he had to go on up to the pool. His grandson Hapgood he said it was because he didn't have nothin else to do, he said the old man was a bassackwards one-arm sombitch and he said it right there in front of him like he couldn't hear or didn't have all his marbles, Hapgood and his motorcycle and his pimples and his beer belly and his hair hanging down to his heinie even if he did make sixty-eight dollars a day. Hapgood said Old Man Tremble's pension and his Social Security come out of his pocket and don't you forget it Grandpa and it never done nothin of the kind.

Old Man Tremble was setting on the porch when he seen that car come up there. He never told her. She'd say, "Who do you think that is?" and lean her big belly on the porch rail and shade her eyes with her hand. She'd say, "I don't know," she'd say, "Now I wonder," and he didn't care to hear her go on. So that's when he got his stick and just happened to be walking up the road when that fancy car come up there and damned near stalled on the railroad crossing. He took care not to seem to take no notice but he never missed a thing; it made him grin. It wasn't no state car. It didn't have no white papers piled in the back. That's how you could tell the state. Besides, it had a foreign license—Virginia license. Woman driving had the shape of one of them women come up there from the state ask you all kinds of questions act like they had a right coming up there, my God ask you anything private, set on the porch rail ask you when you got your teeth and why didn't you wear them. Ask you if your prosterate was bothering you right in front of her, ask you how much you spent on food. He told them, he said hit wasn't none of their damned business he wasn't on relief he was on the John L. Lewis pension paid him for his arm and the Social Security and he didn't have nothin to do with no state or no govment.

He couldn't see the women's faces, nothing but their shapes when the car passed him. He couldn't see up close but far away he didn't miss nothin. They's bad times back then. Wasn't hardly anybody living up there. Wasn't mor'n three four families still on Lacey Creek in them days. Bottom dropped out of the coal business he'd saw that many a time in a long life God knows.

Old women broke quicker than old men. He was not broke at all. One of them state women come up there in her big car, she said the old woman was depressed, hell's fire who wouldn't be depressed at that time wasn't a mine opened and they had to live on state mollygrub. That was before he got on the pension. She give the old woman some pills but they wasn't worth a hill of beans. She come up there one day and she said to the old woman, "I been thinking about you," act like talking to some little baby, and the old woman never looked up. She told her, she said, "I sure as hell ain't been thinking about you." Wasn't long after that she died and she said she didn't give a damn she was glad to, they wasn't nobody left.

He could see that foreign woman in the car craning her neck like she was staring at him through the rearview mirror and he turned his back on her and acted like he had something to look at way over other side of the valley. My God, he used to go on up there when he was a boy, and they wasn't a thing left. Old Catlett place. Look at them now.

Them Catlett boys was as selfish as a bunch of hawgs. No sooner had they got their hands on the property than they sold out to the first wildcat operator come along. How they got old man Catlett to sign he never knowed. But he done it. He reckoned it was because they's thowed out of work too by the automation.

No sooner had he signed than that stripper come up, stripped up behind them and thowed trees and hard pan down and clogged the creek and when the rain come they was a flash flood and the barn and the house stood there since before the Civil War wasn't nothin but match wood. The least one, he wasn't no more than twenty-four then, he took and moved them out of Lacey Creek. That was before he come back up there and worked that little old dog-hole mine.

That was the thing. They wasn't no work for nobody, but the newspaper said they's running more coal out of there than they ever done.

Bunch of new fellers with high school diplomas and motor-cycles come up there working the machines. Fixed up them houses like Hapgood done, and stood around shootin their mouths off and drinking beer. Wouldn't let him tell them a damned thing. Why he knowed more about the coal business than they ever would. Long-haired Communis bastards not dry behind the ears. Know-it-all. Hapgood!

The car had turned up the old track by the graveyard when he turned around again. They's going to get stuck up there, damned-fool women, and they'd have to go on up there and take and haul them out. That pleased him. They's going up to the graveyard. Women was always doing that. Couldn't leave you alone even then.

Now what he done was he looked down at the water of the pond. He could see himself in it, his shape anyhow. He liked to look at himself. He looked like he was made out of rawhide. He looked like one of them Civil War sodjers with his sleeve in his pocket. That sure used to get the women but it didn't any more. If he couldn't see much more than the shape of his head leaning over the water that was nobody's business but his own. He knowed what he looked like even if he couldn't see airy a thing. He looked mean as a snake. He was made out of steel-reinforced concrete and he had four thousand lines of meanness on his face, especially when he took out his teeth. He didn't care for them anyhow. He could feel the dander rise. That's what he always waited for up there by the pond, for the dander to rise.

When that woman from the car come down there and stood across the water from him, watching him, he never looked up. She didn't say nothin. He respected that. He could see her face in the water too, looking down into it. It wasn't no more than ten feet across. He waited and she waited too. She outstared him. That wasn't because he couldn't outstare her, but he decided he wanted to talk. It wasn't that she won. He just changed his mind. It wasn't none of her damned business. He ground his gums together, chewing on his dander. If she asked him about his prosterate, he knowed what he'd do. He'd take and thuow her in the pond. He could see her disappearing under the water.

"What can I do for ye?" He said as mean as he could, but it come out polite. He couldn't help that.

"Mind if I ask you something?" Foreign kind of voice, like on the T and V, or them young fellers come up there that day in 1960. He knowed it was 1960. He never forgot an election year. John F. Kennedy come up there, and he talked to him personally. John F. Kennedy hollered at him right across the road and he had Franklin Delano Roosevelt with him, and Old Man Tremble come down off that stoop and he was right up close enough to touch them. They had on tennis shoes. That wasn't no kind of shoe for a politician to have on. She said it wasn't Franklin Delano Roosevelt with him, it was his boy. It was not; he went right up there and shook hands with him so he remembered like it was yesterday. They took their picture and they said they'd send him one but they never done it so he couldn't show her when she shot her mouth off. You couldn't tell her nothin, know-it-all. John F. Kennedy asked him what he thought and he said what he thought about what? He had that same kind of foreign way of talking that woman had across the pond from him. He voted for John F. Kennedy because he figured he was rich enough to be honest. He said a lot of stuff but he never done nothin.

You take your coal leases and your politicians and your union men and your govment all you want. In the end it was some one feller acting like you and him kicked the end out of the same cradle, or some damned woman wanting to butt into your prosterate.

Big talkee and little dooey.

That woman couldn't keep her mouth shut.

She said again, "Do you mind if I ask you something?"

Oh boy! Here come the prosterate!

But she never said nothing like that.

She said, "What's this for?"

He told her. He said, "The govment done that." Then he said, "You'd a thought they wasn't no more coal to run out of them mountains. But they come up here with them big bulldozers and they flang the mountain right down. Shoot and shove. Shoot the top with dynamite, shove it over. I never seen nuthin like it. They shipped out everything that was black. Old gypsy mine. That was before the govment. You can still see what gypsy mines was like over acrost the holler."

He told her then: "I'm eighty years old. You wouldn't know that, would ye?"

She said she wouldn't know that. His voice began to tune up. He had found a new face to tell it all to, whatever it was, and he didn't have nothing else to do.

"I used to work the real mine, Seven Stars. People by the name of Lacey owned it, owned everything around here. They lived on the hawg's front tit. That was before Imperial bought it. I worked Godley and Number 9, and I don't know what-all. Back when I was making coal we had five grades.

We's particular about how we done, put that coal through a shaker and lay it in them cars like it was a baby to keep it from breakin up. They was slack coal, and pea coal and egg coal and nut coal and lump. They don't run nuthin but slack these days. Machines! Even up to Number 8 they don't use more'n two three hundred men why when I was up there we had a thousand to twelve hundred men working—all muscle power. It was skilled work. You had to know how a top sounds when it's workin, gettin ready to fall. A-poppin and a-crackin. What hit me was a kettle—one them petrified wood roots fifty million years old they tell me. Our preacher says that ain't right according to the Bible. Anyhow it sets up there in the sandstone ceiling and don't give no warning, just drops on ye. Number-one killer.

"They taken and put them machines in because of the union. John L. Lewis went along with that. He seen the handwriting on the wall Minny Minny tickle your farson. But the coal ain't nuthin but slack we called it run-of-mine. I been a union man all my life. I get a pension. John L. Lewis give it to me."

She had to bust in and ask some fool question. "Do you remember Mother Jones?"

"Yep." He wasn't going to tell her a damned thing, interrupting his train of thought like that.

But she waited, a long time, so he finally told her. "I'se fourteen years old when I joined the Mother Jones Union we called it then. She give me a pair of shoes onct. Little tiny woman, cussed like a section foreman." But he wasn't interested in Mother Jones. He wanted to tell about himself. "I got mashed in the mine. They tell me I see everthing bassackwards. I don't do nuthin of the kind. UMW doctors! I got the workman's compensation."

He cleared his throat. "Now that there." He poked his head down once at the water. "*They* done that. When you'd a thought they wasn't nuthin left up there, they come in and stripped again. The govment made them build that high-wall, made them do right. This here is overflow. Pretty, ain't it?" He didn't give her a chance to bust in again. "They come up here in their big cars and taken pictures. They don't take no pictures of what's behind that high-wall, let me tell you. One of these days"—he was pleased—"the whole damn thing's gonna come right down and drown this here valley. Lemme tell you"—he stopped to take a breath, and went on, full of glee—"one of these nights a great storm's gonna come and lo and behold that there high-wall is going to come right down I don't care how many out-of-state engineers they hire with the taxpayer's money. Boondoggle. Lemme tell you something. The earth fights back. I seen it many a time. You kin gouge it and pick it and poke it and shoot it with all the black powder you want to. Sooner or later, it gits mad. It'll come back in time and git ye. Now I ain' talkin bassackwards. I seen it plenty of times. You take that there creek. Why I seen it black as ink and you couldn't put a foot in it. Sludge. It's all gone, washed clean. I caught me a big trout just two miles upcreek. Now you take a piddling pond like this here. Come a big storm that acid sediment will flush out like a indoor toilet. We'll all be dead. This will all be gone and forgotten." He blotted out the pastel houses and the gardens with one contemptuous wave of his hand. "The mountains will rise and the valleys will call out. Now you take this here pond. This here's as no count as a hawg waller. I told them that when they come up here. I said it ain't gonna hold I said you creating a hazard I said.

"I said they won't no grass hold on no hard pan. I told them that." He squinted up at the steep slope of the high-wall, six hundred feet above them.

"Is it as clear as it looks? Are there fish in it?" She was plumb full of jackass questions.

"Hell, lady, they don't nuthin *live* in that." He was masculine and patient. "Some surface mines they got fish but there's too much mine acid here. One seam's full of acid waste, another one ain't," he explained. "Ain't no mine the same. They got personalities same as us. It looks prettier'n it used to, though, I'll say that for it."

He spat, and his spit troubled the water and destroyed her face. "They ain't got no real water that color. Television water maybe." He grinned. "We got the color T and V.

"Lemme tell you something. These young folks don't know nuthin. I just want to put them back there two three days. I shot me a man in the strike." He tried to look as mean as he could, folded his mouth so his nose damn near touched his chin. He hadn't shot nobody but that was his affair and none of her own. He'd shot at plenty, though. That's what they done, shot at. Scared the pants off them fellers. "That's what I done." His little mean eyes squinted, a gunsight squint, full of pleasure.

He heard a yoo hoo! from the hill behind them, a young girl's voice. They both looked up. A woman danced in the distance, waving from the edge of the hill meadow.

"Why if it ain't Althea Lacey," he said. "She ain't broke atall. She's still pretty as a picture. Lord I seen them girls hightailing it around here like they owned the place which they did. I thought she was dead. I got the long sight. It come with age."

That woman said she was coming back and bring Althea so he could pass some time with her; she said she had to go on up the hill. He didn't give a goddamn if she come back or not. He wasn't about to answer no more fool questions. He was already setting on his porch when they come back, but he never waved. He was sure he had not told that goddamn foreign woman a goddamned thing.

I took Aunt Althea to see *Close Encounters of the Third Kind* after we'd stopped at her house so she could go to the bathroom. She said it was a piece of foolishness, and added, "Thank you."

I took her to dinner at the Pizza Hut; she said it was her favorite place. She played the jukebox and she ate silently, like a child. When it was over, her face still streaked with melted cheese, she said, "You get the hell down here to my funeral. I'm not about to be buried with nobody here but that bunch of poormouth Leftwiches."

I drove her back up the Mingo River, where she had lived for so long. Her house was dark.

"You come with me. I got something for you." She grabbed me, talon claws, and dragged me to the door. "You wait right here. I'm not going to invite you in. You won't know when to go home." She was gone, deep into the house. She hadn't needed to turn on a light. She knew it too well. I could hear her, slowly climbing the stairs.

There were night sounds of traffic in the distance, the shrubs had grown to cover the first-floor windows. I felt the deep uncut grass under my feet. It was pitch-dark until the light from an upstairs window cut across the yard.

She was standing behind me. "Here." She thrust something into my hand that felt like a stone. I knew what it was.

"You ought to have the damned thing. Keep the Leftwiches from grabbing it when I'm gone. Now go on home." She slammed the door and left me in the dark.

In the dashboard light I looked at the family ruby ring that went to the wife of the eldest son. I sat there in the dark, with the red stone that the first Hannah had found in the creek. It had come full circle, from her to me now that there was no eldest son.

Aunt Althea yelled out the upstairs window, "Go on home."

Slow, slow, as if I had climbed a lifetime of a mountain to the top, and had seen ahead an endless stretch to go, like a series of giant furrows in some field the Lord had given me, I got out of my car, an aging woman who had dragged the young girl within her into too many places she wanted to forget. I had promised myself to be alone again on the lookout balcony of my room; they had all, I hoped, forgotten I was there. But at the desk there were invitations to dinner from the children of people I knew, a new breed, but not one from "one of us." They were, I knew, all in at Charlie's kill, Haley Potter at the funeral home, Daisy at the house, sad clinking of ice in glasses, voices subdued in Charlie's living room, the garden room ignored, except for tiny thrilled peeks from time to time. I looked up at the motel clock—nine o'clock. It was too late to answer the invitations, and I was exhausted from too much exposure, from all the rituals.

There was one ritual that hadn't happened, and I think I went into a light sleep, half expecting it. It came at eleven o'clock, and I turned on the bedside light and picked up the phone. It was the drunken, abusive, friendly call in the night, Canona's genteel version of the fiery cross. I think, if it hadn't come, I would have missed it.

It was, of course, Kitty Puss. I thought I could see her, propped up on the pillows of her bed in what had been my parents' room, staring out into the darkness, full of resolution to lay down the drunken law. She took for granted I would know her voice, and she plunged into the middle of a long monologue she had already told me in her mind, and maybe aloud in the empty house.

"What the hell you keep coming back here for I don't

know. My God, we got rid of you once." She took a deep breath. I could hear the ice in her glass. "I don't blame them." What for she didn't say. "Why don't you write about nice people, my God, there are plenty of nice things to write about. Dirty books. Not that I would read them. I haven't read anything since *Little Black Sambo*." She paused. I think she expected me to laugh at her old joke. "What do *you* know? Let me tell you something. He didn't have anything to live for. He wasn't allowed to breathe. You didn't know him like I did. Boy, did I know him. If it hadn't been for your goddamn mother we would have married and things would have been different. He'd still be alive." She wasn't talking about Charlie Bland. She was talking about my brother. She had stripped away the death of Charlie down to the essential killing, for her, of Johnny, as if the drinking had floated her through time, and wrecked her there.

"I didn't want you to come back, but they had to do it. Every one of those damned women forgot what you'd done." What had I done? What was she talking about? She answered me as if I'd spoken aloud. "Coming back, acting like we didn't know what you were doing. Running around with a lot of people nobody knew. If you were going to live here, why didn't you behave yourself, peeking and prying around? We thought if we stopped asking you to parties you'd get the hint, but oh no, not you . . ."

I knew then, oh God, I knew. Five years after Johnny's death I had come back, carrying with me some hope, as we all have, that "things would be different." I see now that it was the kind of nostalgia that soldiers have, that things will be the same, but only the same as the simple dream of calm they carry with them for a place that has never been on any earth but the landscape of their hope. I had had battles, too, had been too poor, too far from home. I was bored with my own courage.

So I had turned my back on everything I had learned for what I took for granted, as familiar as my bones, for a clutch of loyalties that were more clinging than love because I thought then that there was no more choice than in the flow of the river. I was coaxed home like a runaway dog. What happened then had been my grievous fault, as a fault in marble weakens it, and grievously had I nearly broken on it. "It was all your fault," Kitty Puss told me, and I said, "I know," to myself and not to her.

I had told myself that my search for Johnny's life had led me home, and at first, after my traveling, I had gone there as if I were in love, broke, drawn to a safety I knew was false, refusing to believe it. I had told myself I could live there and work. I even took an apartment in the free city below the citadel to show my independence. After all, a hundred thousand people that we didn't know lived in the city, not caring whether we existed or not. Practically, there were clues I had to trace. I had already found that there were roots of Johnny's death that stretched back to what I thought then was the beginning, the first Hannah's mindless discovery of the valley. I had been wrong. The roots ran deeper than that, how deep I couldn't know then.

The women had taken my search to be a threat, my long hours in the library, my new friends in the town, the places I found, the people I saw, even the courtship of Charlie Bland, his "nigger" jokes, his acceptable anti-Semitism. He was a genteel whore, and a minority of women who thought they were a city would mourn for him. He had seduced me because he had been a model for Johnny, his sense of freedom, his exploiting of women that they took as a compliment, that they took as the light of his attention. It was his notice of me that infuriated them, even though they had been through it before—the Charlie joke was that he met all the trains. It hadn't lasted long. I saw in time that the real man behind the role Charlie played was Johnny.

The final excuse for what mountain people call "hating out," and in that they had been as primitive as tribal women, which they were, was over Vietnam, a war that hadn't touched them, except in opinions and a rise of the Dow Jones Average.

I had marched, in a small procession along Mosby Street, with a ragged group of anti-war protesters. They had read about the protests in New York and Washington, and their own march was a pathetic imitation, twenty or so of them, kids straggling down a nearly empty street, with me and Candy, two local ministers, the town librarian, and two reporters from the local paper. I know now that part of my impotent little fury then was at the hills, where the sons of people I had known all my life stayed in their colleges, while the boys from the hollows went in droves to war as they had always done, accepting as gospel the war cries of a class they had no part in. They went dumbly, except for a few, my little

snaggled group, and they came back less dumbly. I wondere
as I heard Kitty Puss light a cigarette, where they were.
Were they the old man's Communisses? His grandson Hapgood?
Kitty Puss called me back to her: "Well, what have you got to
say for yourself?"

I didn't answer. I was listening to another phone call, ten
years before. I had had no idea anyone had seen me marching
until the telephone rang that night in my apartment, the
ritual phone call, as on this night, an anonymous white-gloves
voice saying, "You better leave town. We don't want you
here . . ." and hanging up after a nervous giggle. I had never
known which of the women I knew had done it. It was a
generic voice, as the manners were generic, the white gloves,
the sense that I had betrayed their evasions. With the
perception that a drunk can have, and the patience to sustain
it, Kitty Puss had waited for it all to come back.

Then she said calmly, "If I had your chances . . . It was *me*
he came to when you weren't around. He hated it when you
went away." She had gone back to Johnny, and made him as
alive as if he were standing on the lawn below, when we lived
in the Neill house, long before the Howard Johnson's motel,
whispering while I waited, awake for him, "Sis, honey, come
and let me in. Dad's locked the door."

But it was Kitty Puss saying, "I'd hear his car and I'd say
Brandy we can't turn Johnny away. Where had he got to go at
this hour of the night? Me, huddled in my bathrobe to keep
warm at the kitchen table. Sometimes he would cry, he had a
tragic something about him always even when we . . ." Her
mind evaded something. She circled in memory, caught still
as I was with the question, "Why?" She called through the
phone, "Why couldn't he go home?" Then, a swerve: "You
know. You always knew. But, Christ, did you have to tell?"
And then, a final cry, the most dangerous from her cornered
species: "You embarrassed us!" And she hung up as if she'd
said it all, which she had.

I knew she would call back, think up more to say in her
drunken grieving. I rang the desk and told them not to put
any calls through, and tried to sleep again. It was no use. I
went out onto the balcony where I had begun the long day,
and sat staring at the black river, and watched the lights go
out, one by one, on the hill opposite, until the street by the
river was empty, and the town had drifted back into a sleep as
ancient as the valley.

...ad called up an old trial and I was back within ... in the morning paper: "Local writer leads ... father was striking the paper against his hand ... stood at the door of my apartment at seven o'clock in the morning. He strode into the room without looking at me. How did he begin? I only heard again ". . . Some consideration for our place in the community . . . under no circumstances are you ever to humiliate us again . . ." as if I were sixteen instead of thirty-eight years old. It was the fall of 1968, and everyone I had grown up with voted for Richard Nixon, all except Candy. I remember my father, sitting on an old horsehair sofa Mother had lent me from the attic. "You've broken your mother's heart," he said, his head in his hands.

He left me there, in an apartment I had tried to live in for three years, where I had come as near to real hunger as I ever had come in my life, where I had gone to their cocktail parties to eat the hors d'oeuvres. I had a hundred and twenty-seven dollars left after paying my rent. Neither my mother nor my father had asked if I needed money. They were waiting for me to be starved into the house on the hill. I sat in the place on the sofa and thought then: "To save my soul, I don't know what I am going to do."

I sat there most of the day while thin November snow slid past the window.

That night I packed everything a 1960 two-toned Ford would hold. I think my father and I were both awake until morning. He was at my door again at seven o'clock. The first thing he said was, "Have you seen your way clear?" but he had seen the car, and knew that I was leaving. I can't remember that he said another word. He wandered around the apartment, touching things, and then he left. When he told me goodbye he was crying, and I had never seen him cry before in my life.

I stopped for breakfast at McDonald's. When I opened my bag there was an envelope. Some way he had prepared it and put it there in his wandering. His deceptively strong handwriting he was so proud of . . . "We don't see eye to eye over this, but blood is thicker than water . . ." Reverberation of clichés as deeply meant as a litany. I wondered, is it blood and not this strong river of time and circumstance that is carrying me toward what I have to do? He had written, "We have a charge account at Altman's. If you have to use it, don't let your mother know. Send the bill to my office," and later,

"If I could see the reason for this." He had added a post-script, "If you are sick you know I'm here. Or"—the writing fainter—"if you ever see your way clear..." and hadn't finished the sentence. He had enclosed three hundred dollars in cash to bless me with.

A boy and a girl sat in the next booth, facing me. Where did they come from? A brother and a sister, twins? Their hair was red, their skin white. They had medieval Anglo-Saxon faces, and long slim necks, a natural elegance, throwbacks to some English ancestry that could have been aristocratic. They looked as frail as gossamer. They seemed to move within and around each other. I could see that they were, in the true meaning of the phrase, "not all there." They had, together, a poised innocence, half-minded and sad. They were solicitous of each other.

They were waiting, too, waiting to move, and they had been there a long time. A slat-bodied waitress came up to their table and said, "I tole you before. Now you-all go and set on the library steps. Your mama won't be long."

In the insulting space of McDonald's, the girl stood in her high heels and jeans and cried, her brother comforting. She said, "Ma'm, we're lost, as lost as anybody else. What would you know from up there you old bitch?" pure mountain voice.

They wandered, as my father had, out of the door into a cold sun.

"They're in here every morning," the waitress explained when she saw me watching. "It's the same thing every morning. Their mama leaves them when she goes to work. I tole her..."

I never saw my father or mother again. When she died in 1970 I was in England, and when my father died two years later I was in France. I had begun to teach, to earn enough to sustain me while I worked. Spud and Melinda didn't consider sending for me. I mourned the words of cables signed with Haley Potter's name.

How much had I drawn from that night, that third going forth? Could such small seeds of personal life grow into such perceptions, flights, and such returns? Did Lily use the account from Altman's? Outside the motel room in the space where my own bedroom had been, I listened to the downriver wind. Did Johnny Church refuse to doff his hat in 1645 because of a father, still carrying the scars of Mooney McKarkle, who yearned to "get someplace" and an adolescent girl near middle-age who had, once again, to leave home? Did revolution come from being hated out by small-town genteel women with expensive teeth and little hands? I didn't know, and yet I did. It was not a circle, but a spiral, an eternal return, a double helix like the DNA factor.

I turned on the light and set the ring, the spearhead, the blackened silver haft of Ensign Cockburn's riding crop side by side. They had come back to me, and I had earned them. I took the haft into the bathroom and rubbed it with toothpaste until it was as shining as it had been in Ensign Cockburn's hand.

I left the next morning early to get a last look at the dawn over the river. On the upriver side of the Howard Johnson's motel, Jim and Martha Dodd's house looked tiny, huddled in its shadow. A discreet brass sign on one side of the door read CARVER'S FUNERAL HOME. I knew that Charlie Bland lay there at last, after what my McKarkle grandmother called "the perils of this wicked world."

Under the chemical-laden air, I could smell the river mist. I passed the coal-baron Federal Slingsby mansion that had become the headquarters of the United Mine Workers District 17. Now, inside, it was painted cream and green. The rooms had been partitioned into offices. I remembered the bank-president portrait of John L. Lewis, hung over the fireplace in Mrs. Slingsby's old drawing room where I had gone to tea, sitting on the edge of a French gilt chair. Mrs. Slingsby wore a collar of pearls and spent her summers at the Savoy Hotel in London. In the same room I had talked to a man with a crew cut, who lay back and put his feet on the desk and told me he had been in his first miners' march when he was six months old, in his mother's arms. "Mother Jones led it. She called it a prayer meeting, the old devil," he told me. He fed on the vision of the old days. Bullets flew through Mrs. Slingsby's drawing room as he talked. Bullets as long past as Mrs. Slingsby's pearl collar.

I drove again up the south side of the river, past the road to Lacey Creek, with the ring on my finger, my haft and my spearhead, a back seat full of notes on white paper, and a

memory of shut-away faces, Aunt Althea's and the ol̶
and the high green retaining wall that shut out the ̶
Lacey Creek.

I crossed the river again, to the north side, toward Beulah,
into Neill country. I knew I couldn't come this far and not go
all the way. I had spent eighteen years searching for something—
oh, an answer that I knew already I wasn't going to find
questioning a stranger across a pond, or trying to see with my
Aunt Althea's mocking eyes. But I was driving toward it, east
across the endless mountains, and there were last stops to
make, genuflections to places I had known.

But I took with me what I had seen, my own face, reflected
in their eyes—a stranger, shut out. Oh, I knew that "Tell
nobody nothing" look, that extreme you-go-to-hell politeness.
All the way up through the narrows toward Beulah I fed on
that blank lack of trust; goddamn mountain paranoids, behind
a barrier of childish cynicism as high as the green wall. Once
through that barrier, with a little sweet talk, the remembering
of a name, and you could have the teeth out of their mouths.
I'd seen, and had, that happen often enough.

Swept by the great Goddamn of the morning, I was so alive
with a fury that I had thought long past that I missed the exit
to the mansion at Beulah, now almost under the four-laned
ramp that passed high over the town.

I was already at the little church before I stopped.

It seemed sunk into the ground with age. It, too, had been
deserted by my family. Most of them lay in perpetual care on
Sycamore Hill, the cemetery in Canona, with Johnny and my
parents.

Deep below the marks of the places I had traveled, all I
had learned, in a linen dress that cost a hundred dollars, I
stood there in the graveyard under the trees. Below me
stretched the valley of Beulah, as it had been when the first
Hannah had gazed on it from across the river, like Moses at
the Promised Land, and then had finally reached it to find
her death. The first log fort had stood on the same knoll,
overlooking the bottomland. The illusion that it was unchanged
stayed for a minute in the silence. Not even a car passed on
the highway behind me.

The valley was so small, less than a mile from hill to hill, hill to river. There was no longer any crop but people, no space that was not filled. Train tracks from the upcreek spurs that led to long-worked-out mines crisscrossed the bottomland. Down by the river I could see gardens, and neat small houses, but along the creek bank the trailers were so close together that the people must have breathed their neighbors' sighs. It had all been put into production. For this, this little pride of ownership and greed, the firstborn of the Egyptians had been smitten, and it was my own brother.

The creek below ran as clean as it had when old Hannah's husband, Jeremiah, had lain in it, scalped, with his blood threading the water weeds. I had seen it clogged to the banks with mine waste, an open industrial sewer. Now it was as clear as its first dawn. Along the banks, weeds and even flowers covered the trash thrown down from the trailers. Two small, towheaded boys waded slowly, concentrated on the water. One of them reached down, careful as a hunter. The crawdads were back, too, as if they had waited for men to finish with the creek to return.

Under the traffic dust and the rambler roses I could barely read the stones of the only family graves left when the highway was built. They lay exposed to the road gravel, a few feet from the berm. I found James Fitzgerald Neill, 1810–1858, and an inscription that was so worn I could make out only "he . . . Jesus." Next to him, his wife, Anne Brandon Kregg Neill, with all her pedigree, 1805–1885, Aunt Annie, who my grandmother said was a Presbyterian saint, as hard to live with as having God for a boarder. Beside them at last, Lewis Catlett, 1827–1900, had come back to Beulah with Sara Lacey Catlett, 1832–1907, beloved wife as in Life so in Death, easier to read.

In my childhood the road had run through trees in a wide curve around the property. Grandmother still called it the Jeems–Kanawha turnpike. She refused to sell it to the state so long, as she said, as she had breath in her body, but while her body still lay in the upstairs bedroom on her blue satin bed that had been a wedding present from Chester A. Arthur, Uncle Dan got the condemnation rights through he had been pushing for so long. "For God's sake, Dan, she's still *warm*," I heard my mother yell in the upstairs hall of the Neill house on River Street. The church and the graveyard, and the creekside lots, were all that were left to the family of

Beulah by then, but they still called it "Mother's estate," that and the house on River Street. As the stones from ancient forts had been hidden in the foundations of the houses on the south hill in Canona, the graveyard and the house on River Street were lodged in the English Tudor houses that Mother and Melinda began as soon as the will was probated and the property sold. "Oh, Preston, at last we can have a place of our own," my mother had sighed, as happy then as Uncle Dan.

In the truncated churchyard I knew that I was reaching into caves of memory, recognitions that could be rung against what I had learned for the adultery of nostalgia or shame or pride, burn off the rust of all the evasions, and see that what had happened rang true. I sat down on Annie Neill's tombstone and let it happen, without what my grandmother would have called fear or favor. It was, after all, why I had come back.

I was stripped down beyond language, the protection of time, the discrimination of memory, into the reality of a returned day. The blood-red rambler roses that had spilled then over the graves, the voices, the Fords, the people wandering under the trees, the scent of moss and angel-food cake, were all there as I had first seen it, not to pass by, but to stop, really stop, for the first time, although Mother said it was simply no place for a sensitive child. My grandmother set her foot down. She said so.

She said, "Anne Brandon, I am setting my foot down once and for all," and when she talked to my mother that way, even if she was on my side, I wanted to kick her legs and tell her, "Don't you talk to my mamma that way, she's sensitive, too," because I knew she was, and I had to protect her or she'd come apart and her skin would get all white and papery and she would squeeze the top of her nose with her fingers. I was more afraid of that than I was of some graveyard. She had simply appalling headaches brought on by worry. Sometimes it was my fault and sometimes it was Johnny's.

I knew why my grandmother set her foot down.

It was the centenary of the church, Miss Leah's Chapel, and, as my grandmother pointed out, it was, after all, the only church in the valley that could celebrate a centenary in the original building in 1938, and there was some argument even about that. She always held it was earlier. "Let's see, Grandmother Leah Cutright was married to Grandfather

Peregrine Catlett in let's see," and I was all ears because she was dipping deep into the olden days like a bucket in a well.

Mama said Grandma Liddy told her it was 1826 and my grandmother said, "You were too young to remember when the Senator's wife died." She never called her Grandma Liddy like Mamma did. She didn't call at all. She referred instead to the Senator's wife or Miss Lydia. Mamma said she had been a burden on her shoulders, but my brother Johnny told a different tale when he wanted to scare me.

Mamma said she was *sure* she remembered her.

"You could not have done so and that's my last word..." I was sitting on the floor listening; as my grandmother said, drinking it all in. I didn't see why Mamma couldn't remember. She was ten years old when her grandmother died. I could remember when I was three. I wet my pants at a party because I got too excited and Mamma hurt my hand when she grabbed it to get me to the bathroom too late and she wore a white fichu on a gray dress which brought out her lovely head of hair.

Of course it wasn't Grandma's last word, not by a long shot. It never was. She said what she had to say, and then, "I will hold my peace," which meant we were all to do exactly as she ordered.

Mamma drove Grandmother up there every Decoration Day, but I never had gotten to go before because Mamma said it was no place for children. Only this was a special one and I couldn't wait to see a place that was no place for children.

So there I was, one hundred years, or maybe one hundred and some more years after Miss Leah's Chapel was dedicated. I sat in the middle of the back seat of my daddy's black Buick between my brother Johnny and Grandmother. It was hot as hell. I had on my blue silk dress that was smocked by the nuns and my white socks and my Sunday patent-leather shoes but it wasn't Sunday it was Decoration Day and my lace gloves that came in my Easter basket. I could feel the sweat under my naturally curly hair. I could hear my petticoat when I moved, and my feet wouldn't reach the floor of the car.

I was mad because I didn't get to sit on the flip-up seat and my sister Melinda was mad because she had to. I knew that because every time my feet jogged too near she would slap them away and say, "You're getting my skirt dirty." Grandmother said Melinda took up too much room. She was grown up. She was eighteen and went to dances when anybody asked her. Sometimes they didn't and Mamma would say, "There are other things in life," and she would say, "What?" and Mamma would say, "Don't talk back to me."

I was wedged close to the smell of Grandmother's age, old pee-pee, dusty violet sachet, and smoky black georgette. We passed the salt licks and the big sign for the Ring-a-ling Brothers with the Siamese twins on it, and the bridge where a man had been lynched, and all the way up the river she kept saying who lived here and who lived there when she was a girl. "A gel," she said, and I thought my God! only I didn't say it or she would have tanned my hide. Was she ever a gel? That old solid smelly body.

But I knew she had been. I heard Mamma discuss it with Uncle Dan when they didn't know I was listening. She said Grandmother was Lacey Kregg from Albion on the James and Aunt Toey told her—I always listened when they talked about Aunt Toey, who was borned into slavery. Aunt Toey said she wasn't the only one bought and sold in the olden days. She said Lacey Kregg was sold by her papa to Senator Neill's son, Peregrine Lacey Neill, like she was a prize filly and they had this wonderful wedding in Washington, D.C., and Chester A. Arthur was there. I knew all that was true because Mamma kept the picture on her dressing table. It was as freckled as my grandmother's hands. They all had on old-fashioned costumes.

But Uncle Dan always said the most interesting part. He said Aunt Toey had told him not once but many times that Grandmother was a bastard and that their *real* grandfather was Major Johnny Catlett, who was killed at Manassas. She said their Grandmother Melinda had died of a broken heart.

"There's not an *iota* of truth in that statement," my mother would say every time. "You just say that to get my goat..."

Aunt Toey was buried at Beulah, too, in the old slave section. Her granddaughter Delilah worked for us after her husband John was mashed in the mine. Her little boy Toey was Johnny's same age. They lived out back of the Neill house on River Street. But they didn't come to the centenary. Mamma said it was out of the question, they wouldn't be happy. Delilah slammed the breakfast biscuits on the table so I knew she was mad as hell, but nobody else noticed. Her name wasn't really Delilah, it was Gertrude, but Mamma said she couldn't get used to that, all our cooks had been called

Delilah. We all called her boy, Jack, Toey because Mamma said to. She said Jack was too much like John.

We were driving up the river to Beulah, where everything had been lost when the bottom dropped out of the coal business. It was always doing that. I could see ahead through the trees around the big curve to where a line of cars were parked, Fords and Chevies. Some of them were so old they were like those cars I used to see broken-down on River Street with mattresses and chicken coops on top of them in the Depression when nobody had a red cent. I couldn't have been more than three years old then. Johnny said they were Model T's, and the newer ones were Model A's. He knew all about cars. Uncle Sugar Baseheart was already there. We could see his Cadillac. Grandmother said it stuck out like a sore thumb. Mamma said it was thoughtful of him to bring our cousin Brandy and Grandmother said it was the least he could do. Cousin Brandy was the envy of us all. His mother, that was my mamma's sister Annie, had died in childbirth. So he got to go away to school before anybody else. He went to Fessenden and he and my brother Johnny were going to Andover in the fall and he said he'd look after Johnny when they were the same age and Johnny told him don't lord it over me, Brandy. I used to look at Brandy and wonder what it was like to be the son of somebody who Mamma said was just a name on everybody's lips.

As if anybody could lord it over my brother Johnny. He just sat on my other side as aloof from it all as if he were someplace else. I could see him watching his face in the car window. I could see his reflection with the trees whipping past behind it. He paid a lot more attention to me than Melinda did, though. He was fourteen and Melinda was eighteen and she said I was underfoot all the time. Melinda was as lovelorn that June as the Lady of Shalott but dear Lord knows she didn't look it. She was trying to look like a Pond's lady but she only succeeded in looking as healthy as a Postum ad.

It was lovely and damp and shady and I was the littlest one there by far. The highest monument was the Senator's. It reached up into the trees. From the road it looked noble, at least that was the word Mamma used, but from almost under it, looking up, it was scary. I could see the big beak of the American eagle. The stone bird seemed to be ready to take off through the sky, with the draped stone flag clutched in its talons. The stone ladies, Minerva and Justice, mourned against the big black marble column, with moss and dirt all down their bodies. The base was covered with moss, too. Mamma, behind me, said it was covered with neglect, her voice way up above me. Uncle Sugar patted my head and said, "Here's my pretty little onion," and said he bet I didn't know who the ladies were. I told him they were Minerva who came out of her father's head and Justice who was blind and he said I was precocious and Mamma said huh too big for her britches, reads everything she can get her hands on. I'd already read the *Thousand and One Nights* and *Great Myths and Legends* and *King Arthur* a long time before, and I was in the middle of Pierre Louÿs's *Aphrodite*, which I found in Johnny's closet. He always had good books, better than old *Ivanhoe* Mamma made me read because her beloved papa had read it to her. I hated it. Ivanhoe was sick all the time. I loved Uncle Sugar's smell, tobacco and tweed. I connected that smell with money.

Maybe the monument dominated the churchyard and all the dead, but my grandmother certainly dominated the living. Even when they were talking to each other in those murmuring muttering voices grownups used when they were in solemn places, they seemed always to be turned toward her. That day she was every inch Lacey Kregg from Albion on the James no matter what had happened in the interim. The voices above me broke up like the dappled sunlight through the trees.

I heard Uncle Sugar say, "Justice would have to be blind to stay on the Senator's tomb." There were a lot of people milling around, trying to keep from walking on the graves. All over the graveyard, people had put white wicker baskets full of rambler roses. Mamma said in one of her delicate voices, "I can't stand them." She had another delicate voice for reading poetry out loud. She kept looking around through the crowd for somebody. She said, "It's the least they could do."

Ladies in those sun-dried fresh-ironed summer dresses in company-store gingham colors kept coming up to my grandmother and remembering themselves to her as if she still lived in the big house when she hadn't set foot in it for thirty-two years. They stepped around Major John Catlett, CSA, and left a space around Lewis Catlett and Sara Lacey Catlett, and Anne Brandon Baseheart. I wondered what it was like for Brandy to have to step around his own mother.

But he wasn't paying any attention. He and Johnny were standing apart from everybody, watching in the kind of lordly way Andover boys had. Daddy said they looked like they were just changing trains. But they hadn't even gone to Andover yet; they were just copying off Charlie Bland and his crowd, who were already in the middle of Princeton.

I couldn't find my grandfather. The ladies, Mamma said they were Methodists and never neglected a chance to eat, had put a huge table up with a white cloth that rested at one end on the family vault where he was. There weren't any names, but I knew who was in there: Leah Cutright Catlett, and Peregrine Catlett and Senator Neill's body and Lydia Catlett Neill beloved wife, and Grandfather Peregrine and a space waiting for my grandmother. The vault was only for direct heirs and their spouses Johnny told me that. He said that Miss Leah had been buried in the family ring that ought to have come to Grandmother. She said she wouldn't touch it with a ten-foot pole, but when the vault was opened to put Miss Liddy in, he said Uncle Dan told him that Grandfather pulled it right off Miss Leah's skeleton and handed it to my grandmother and said, "There, Lacey, I've heard enough . . ." I had to crawl under the picnic table to read who they were, but nobody saw me do it. I peeked out from under the white tablecloth and could see the ring on my grandmother's hand. She'd taken off her glove to shake hands, because a lady never shook hands with her gloves on. It was demeaning to the recipient. She taught me that and the Bible and a lot of other manners I was supposed to remember that Mamma said were totally out of date, no, passé, but not in front of Grandmother. Uncle Dan said it wasn't a ruby at all but just a garnet but Grandmother said it was a ruby because it came down through the family and always had been no matter what Uncle Dan said. I stayed there awhile, under the table where it was cool and damp and like a white tent, and watched shoes go by and listened to voices. They were, from there, disembodied voices. I'd just read about disembodied voices. They could have been all my ancestors instead of Methodist ladies and Methodist men. I could see the women's big crumpled legs above their rolled stockings. Mamma disliked Methodists because Daddy's mother was rock-ribbed. Every time I showed emotion she said it was the Methodist in me coming out. Grandmother McKarkle was mean to Mamma.

She said that Mamma thought strait is the way and narrow the gate led to the Canona Country Club.

I heard Mamma say, "Well, there they are at last it's about time."

I crawled out from under the table and went to watch my Uncle Dan and my Aunt Althea get out of their Model-A Ford to see if they were drunk. Mamma was wondering the same thing. I knew, because she clutched my hand tight and said, "Where on earth have you been you've ruined your dress," in a not-caring voice.

They weren't. They were sober and solemn. There was a girl with them. She was all dressed in deep mourning so I knew who it was and I knew why she was dressed like that on a hot day in nearly June. It was Aunt Althea's niece, Thelma Leftwich, her sister Mary Rose's daughter. She had only been an orphan for one month. Her parents had been killed in a car wreck. I thought she was the prettiest thing I ever saw. The black suited her. It made her really look like the Lady of Shalott. She walked in a special way, like she knew she was the center of attention. I watched Johnny and Brandy sidle around acting like they didn't notice her, but they ended up talking to her. She wasn't exactly a cousin, a cousin-in-law I guessed; Mamma said a connection. You invited them to family gatherings, but not to parties, because they wouldn't be happy.

The preacher announced the first hymn. He said it was the song of the valley, "O Beulah land, sweet Beulah land, as on the highest mount I stand," and I sang Mamma's favorite hymn, the song of the valley, the beautiful song of the valley, with the Methodist ladies to the pump organ and could hardly finish because I was crying. Mamma and Grandmother just moved their mouths. When it was over, I cried in Mamma's lap, it was so beautiful, and she whispered over my head to Grandmother, "I told you we shouldn't have exposed her to this sort of thing."

I could hear the preacher start in that kind of voice that gets stronger and stronger and then begins to lilt. "I will take my text from Isaiah 62, verses 4 and 5." I looked it up later and learned it by heart, because it was where the song of the valley came from. "Thou shalt no more be termed Forsaken; neither shall thy land any more be termed Desolate: but thou shalt be called Hephzi-bah, and thy land Beulah: for the Lord delighteth in thee, and thy land shall be married. For as a

young man marrieth a virgin, so shall thy sons marry thee." I
forgot exactly where it was, only that it was Isaiah, so I had to
read the whole damned thing.

Then that preacher started yelling out things and thumping
the Bible that made Mamma and Grandmother go stiff with
scorn. I was not surprised. I knew all about different reli-
gions. When I cried, Mamma said that was the Methodist in
me coming out, and when Melinda went into training for the
Tennis tournament, she said it was the Presbyterian in her
coming out, too, like Grandmother, but the Episcopalian
didn't come out in anybody. It just stayed inside. That was
the difference.

He hollered that there was more than one kind of divorce
that was a sin and to sell the place God gave you to strangers
and go into exile in the land of Egypt and take your ill-gotten
gain was divorce, too. His name was Mr. Carver. What he
said wasn't fair. I wanted to stand up and bear witness and tell
him that the Neills had lost everything in the Tennessee Coal
and Land Company in oh-seven. We didn't drive all the way
up there to be insulted by some backwoods preacher. I wasn't
crying any more. I was furious. Somebody said "Amen," and
then somebody else did. I started looking around to see who
said that, but I couldn't tell. Uncle Dan and Aunt Althea
were sitting with some hillbillies. They had a boy with them
who looked like Ichabod Crane. Everybody in the chapel
except Johnny and Brandy and the Lady of Shalott and me
and Ichabod Crane was old. Most of the women had wide
bodies, grandmother bodies, and gray hair under their straw
hats, and they were fanning themselves with paper fans that
said Jesus Saves on one side and Stanback for Pain on the
other, or fans made out of straw. I hoped I'd get to take one
home, but fat chance with Mamma poking me with that
eyes-front poke. So I looked over the preacher's head at the
vaulted ceiling and then at the big painting of Jesus with his
flock behind him. It wasn't like a painting in a real church.
He was carrying something that looked like a puppy but I
knew it was supposed to be a lamb. Under the painting
somebody had printed: Feed my flock. It was cool and still
and kind of holy in the chapel except for the preacher
carrying on and I ignored him.

When Uncle Dan came over at the picnic and introduced
Mr. and Mrs. Catlett and their boy to Mamma, she said,
"How do you do?" in her frozen voice. She was still suffering

from the sermon. But the man didn't pay any attention. He said, "Why, you're Perry's girl. I haven't saw you since you were in a middy blouse." Then he went over and spoke to my grandmother like he had every right. He said, "Don't let that bother you, Miss Lacey." I guessed he meant the sermon. "They just want somebody in the big house. Somebody to go to in time of trouble."

"I know," Grandmother told him and she sounded softer and more peaceful than I'd ever heard her. What he said reminded me of something I had promised myself to do no matter what the cost as soon as I could get away without anybody seeing me. I fully intended to go right up to the big house. After all, it was my inheritance even if Mamma said wild horses wouldn't make her set foot.

His wife and Aunt Althea were acting like they kicked the end out of the same cradle. "Cousin Perry was mighty good to me," I heard the man tell my grandmother, as if she didn't know that. Then I knew who it was. Jake Catlett from across the river. Mamma said when she was a girl he used to come over and sit on the porch with her papa and talk by the hour. They were first cousins. She said her papa insisted over Grandmother's objections that Jake's daddy Lewis Catlett be buried in the family plot. "Plot yes, vault no," she'd told him. So they buried him beside his brother John Catlett CSA. Sometimes on the front porch on River Street, they told the story like it was still happening. There were a lot of stories like that, like when Jake Catlett brought Mamma's papa's body downriver from Beulah on a shutter from the big house after the tragedy. He had been twined like ivy into all those stories so I had to get up close and see him.

He was just a rake-skinny tall old hillbilly in a Stetson hat and one of those shirts with a tight separate collar nobody else had worn since the year dot. Aunt Althea called his wife Essie and said, "Dear Lord, it's been a long time." Essie called Ichabod Crane her least one. "Last shot out of the barrel," Jake Catlett told Grandmother, and, I don't know, she didn't even freeze up even if that was a vulgar remark. "I don't know what we'd do without him," Essie told Althea.

People were lining up for the picnic, so I left them to it, and lined up, too. There was a wonderful smell of glorious fried chicken and early corn on the cob and potato salad and citron cake and angel-food cake and lemonade all mixed with the leaves and the moss and the rambler roses and the sun-dried cotton dresses and the men's sweat. Uncle Dan lined up behind me and patted my head as usual. I wished he wouldn't do that, like I was just a child. He said, "Honey, it's a real groaning board." For once he had on a suit and a collar and tie and a straw hat instead of the pants down under his belly that looked like he slept in them. Mamma said he used to look like he stepped out of a bandbox, but he certainly never had since I remembered. She seemed to worry about him all the time.

Aunt Althea was plump that year. She wore off-the-face hats and lace jabots. Mamma said she looked like a floozie. I thought she looked pretty for somebody her age. I guess she was relieved to be at the picnic. Her mother had just moved in with them after her sister Mary Rose was killed in the car wreck and I heard Mamma say she wouldn't allow a drop in the house. She was a holy terror. Uncle Dan had to go to the hotel.

He did that a lot. Once, hearing a car stop and thinking it was company, I ran out of the house. It was a taxi. Uncle Dan was sprawled across the back seat with both his eyes closed. They were black as old meat. He looked foul and scary. He smelled like rotten food. I ran and hid behind the Dodds' boxwood trees next door, and saw Mamma, green dollar bills flapping in her hand, walk out, thrust bills into his hand, and slam the taxi door. I watched her walk back up to our door slowly, her head down, exhausted, her tweed jacket drooping from her shoulders.

Sometimes when the telephone rang, Mamma would answer it, and say so little that I couldn't tell who called. Then she would say to Daddy, "You'll have to go get him. Nobody else can handle him," and trudge up the stairs as if her room were at the top of a steep hill. But that day he was as sober as a judge.

They were all sitting around on the tombstones, careful not to put their feet on the graves, busy feeding their faces, so I finished mine quickly and it was time if it was ever going to be, besides I wanted to be by myself for a little while. Mamma was staring into space, and Daddy was deep in conversation with Jake Catlett. I heard him call Daddy Mooney, and he didn't even look down his nose the way he did when Uncle Dan called him that, so I knew he was relaxed. They were all spread around so relaxed I thought the rambler roses would grow up from the dead bodies and wind around their legs and hold them there forever.

Nobody saw me go. I walked down the road under the trees, fast at first to get out of sight around the big curve, and then slowly, strolling, so if anybody did see me they would know who I was. Who I was at that point was all the ladies who had strolled down that road in the olden days monarch of all we surveyed. I was Great-grandmother Melinda in her portrait dressed in her ball gown with the red rosebuds, and her broken heart, and I was Grandmother in her wedding dress when she was married in Washington, D.C., and I was Mamma when she was eight. I knew all about that. I always asked her to tell me about when she was a little girl before her papa died and she always ended with, "the world just came to an end," meaning the Tennessee Coal and Land Company thrust them out of the land of Beulah.

Up ahead of me I could see part of the big house. I half expected avenging angels with swords at the gate, but there was nothing like that. There was a huge road sign right in the yard with a Chevrolet coupé and a twenty-foot-long blond girl in a bathing suit and tacky high heels. Potter Chevrolet. Part of the sign had come loose and flapped down like a hat over the bathing beauty's face.

The gate hung on a rusty hinge. I knew every inch of it in my mind's eye, and in Mamma's and Grandmother's voices, the spacious front porch Grandmother had built across the front, the perfectly beautiful front door with its arched fanlight and its woodwork they didn't make like that any more, and the Italian marble fireplaces with the ornate ironwork that the Senator had put in that weren't in keeping with the period of the mansion, the fine brick made by slaves and the eight- not six-paned windows with the swags of pure silk bought in Richmond.

It didn't look like that at all. I just stood on the brick walk, afraid to go nearer. The cupola at one end of the porch was still there, deep in grass, but the swing where Jake Catlett had talked by the hour with Grandfather was gone, and the rest of the porch was all sagged. The front door had a plain lock nailed on it, the kind you hang on a hook. I didn't dare look down toward the bottom of the garden for fear I'd see Grandfather. That was where he had done it. Johnny told me that. I couldn't have seen anything anyway. It was too deep in weeds and straggly bushes. The house didn't look like a mansion at all. It looked empty and frail and sunk. I made myself go up on the porch to peek in the window. I had to watch out where I stepped. The wood was rotted. It all was so small behind that big sign, small and dark. I couldn't see much through the window. It was too dirty, just a vague empty room that had been the parlor. I went on around the house with my heart beating like a trip-hammer, whatever that was. It was what Daddy called that condition. I never felt so lonesome and little in my life, but I had to do it. I had no choice. It was my only chance.

The corncrib was tipped over into the creek, and the chicken-house just looked like an old shed, but the worst disappointment was Mamma's playhouse. Oh, it was there all right, but it just looked like a saggy outhouse not like the perfect replica of a Southern mansion she always said her papa built only for her. The old well was still there on the back porch. I got a wooden crate that said Carnation Milk and I put it by the well wall so I could look down. Mamma said that when she was a little girl she stared down into it and saw the fairies although she never explained why fairies chose to live down a well. I didn't believe in fairies any more anyway, but I just thought I'd look. I leaned over and sure enough there was a face down there but it was just me; then I realized something in a flash. I wasn't, for that minute, Mamma's little girl or Daddy's daughter, or Johnny's kid sister or Melinda's cross to bear, or a little bit of Lacey and a little bit of Kregg and a McKarkle temper, and Neill weaknesses, and Catlett bones, or one part Methodist, two parts Presbyterian, and one part Episcopalian. For once in my life I was the only person ever in the world to stand on that Carnation Milk box and look down that well at that time on that day. But I didn't stay that way. I remembered what happened to Narcissus. It wasn't that he looked. Anybody would do that. It was that he looked too long. So I climbed down off of the box and brushed the moss off of my dress so I wouldn't fall in love with my own self.

The kitchen door had been broken open, and I made myself go on in. Mamma said Aunt Toey had sat by the kitchen fireplace for years until her grandson came and got her and moved her across the river to Lacey Creek against Grandmother's orders. She'd been Great-grandmother Melinda's personal slave and Uncle Dan said Grandmother thought she still owned her. I was afraid to turn my back on the fireplace.

Johnny told me that at night Aunt Toey walked back from the graveyard where they'd buried her in the colored section with her people and sat right back down there. I didn't know how he knew that. He didn't know the big house except from hearing them go over it again and again, any more than I did. It was just a story he made up, but I still didn't want to turn my back for fear I'd hear her behind me rocking and rocking. There were still some thick dirty cups on the drainboard, left over from when the house was a clubhouse before the upcreek mine closed.

I backed out of the kitchen door into the dining room and it kept on swinging and creaking, just like somebody rocking. That was where everybody and his brother came to dinner. Empty. It wasn't even scary. Everything was empty, the back hall, the front hall, the dusty parlor where Mamma said when she was little Grandmother sat with Great-grandmother Liddy and every night at eight o'clock she would help her upstairs like she was a burden sent by the Lord. She said ladies of a certain age then moved into black bombazine as if it were a country. I knew they were behind me. I felt their eyes on my back when I went into the hall. The wallpaper was the same as they all said. Nobody had bothered to change it when the mansion was turned into the clubhouse for the mine. But it was dim and brown and hung down in places and there were leak stains on it. I could hear all the sounds and smells of emptiness, birds in the attic, things lost and not forgotten.

I kept away from the stairwell. Johnny said that the Confederate soldier who had died in the attic was still up there moaning and if you got right under the stairwell he would reach down a long skinny arm like a vine, and grab your hair. I did hear moaning but it was only birds. I kept telling myself that. The only piece of furniture left in the downstairs bedroom was Great-great-grandmother Leah's bed she'd brought all the way from Cincinnati on a barge. Grandmother said that when they moved down to River Street they left it there because it was too big to move and she hated it anyway; they'd moved it down from upstairs to the men's parlor because she said she wanted to die there to be near her son Johnny who'd been killed in what Mamma called the War Between the States and Daddy called the Civil War. She said it was because his family was different from hers. That bed was where Mamma had hidden when she was eight years old after she'd sneaked out at night by herself to see the infamous

Mother Jones and Grandmother dragged her out and whaled
the tar out of her. She said Mother Jones sounded like a
holy-roller preacher. Miss Leah had lost her mind and they
could hear her in there talking to Johnny Catlett, giving him
express orders.

I wanted it all still to be alive to me but it wasn't. It was
nothing, nothing but dust and cobwebs. I even knelt down in
front of the dirty marble fireplace and looked at the Medusa
head in the iron back that Mamma said used to scare her, it
was so alive when the flames leaped in front of it, but nothing
happened. There was only a skin that a snake had shed, and a
little hard dead mouse. I poked around in the closet. I only
found a celluloid collar and a bone stud and an old cuff-link
with some squiggly initials I couldn't read. I put it in my
beaded bag.

I just couldn't make myself climb the stairs. I told myself
I'd seen enough. So I went along the wall to the back hall to
go back before anyone missed me and worried themselves to
death.

Then I just froze. I thought I was going to die. Another girl
in a dirty blue dress all faded and musty was staring straight
at me. It was my mother, a little girl but my mother, looking
as scared as I was. I knew if I stood there I would see
Grandmother when she was young and Miss Melinda, and
Miss Leah, and Miss Annie. If I ran she would run too, away
from the whispers, the cold grownup faces with things on
their minds. I backed up, and so did she. It was only me in
an old freckled mirror but for a minute it had been her. It
really had. I could swear to that. I ran through the dining
room and out the kitchen door and around the house and out
the gate. Somebody was following me. I swear.

I ran until I got to the bridge across the creek and the
button came off my shoe so I had to walk. At least I wasn't
sweaty when I got back to the churchyard. They were still in
the same positions. Nobody even looked up. Grandmother
was holding court under the trees, and Mamma and Uncle
Dan and Aunt Althea were at it again.

"You've got to see your way clear," Uncle Dan told her.

"Once and for all I will not let Preston push through the
condemnation rights while my mother is alive." Mamma had
little beads of sweat under her leghorn hat.

I knew they were talking about the very churchyard they
sat in, and the new road and the WPA or the PWA. They

were always fighting over condemnation rights. I looked it up. Condemn. It meant to find guilty or convict. I didn't see how in the world they could make a churchyard guilty and convict it to be torn up. It was simply beyond my imagination.

"It is not recumbent upon me," Mamma told them.

"That's all very well..." Aunt Althea was steaming up to raising her voice. "Make Mooney pull some strings."

Mamma stopped that. "Althea, you're only an in-law. You have no say in the matter."

"God help me," Aunt Althea muttered. Mamma was always calling Aunt Althea an in-law, but not Uncle Sugar. He was rich.

"You don't need the money. You've got Mooney." Aunt Althea's voice sounded mean.

Mamma looked up and said, "Where on earth have you been. You're as dirty as a pig," but she only said it by habit and they went right back to condemnation rights. Uncle Dan and Aunt Althea had been hit by the Depression like being hit by a car I supposed, but we hadn't. I heard Uncle Dan say, "So be it. The drop will fall..." Johnny explained that that meant when you were hung the trap door opened under your feet and it wrang your neck. It was Uncle Dan's favorite expression. It was like when the bottom dropped out of the coal business. Anyway, I connected them.

I looked around for somebody to at least see me after all I'd been through. Was that asking too much?

Johnny and Brandy were showing off in front of Thelma Leftwich. "Sissy," Johnny said, "you're standing on Aunt Toey. She'll reach out and get you." He wouldn't have done that to me except in front of Brandy. I jumped and he and Brandy laughed and Thelma smiled an ethereal smile because her parents had just been killed in a car wreck and she couldn't laugh yet. I wanted to smash her jaw.

We drove back down the river in that kind of new darkness that looks purple for a little while; then it melts into black. It was dark in the back seat. I wanted to ride on forever, not get home, there with my head in Johnny's lap. He comforted me. He always did when we were by ourselves or nobody noticed. I rode suspended there in safety, nearly asleep, but not quite. I didn't want to miss the sweet darkness. I let Beulah come back, but it was the Beulah that had been put into my mind all my life, parties and servants and lovely furniture and wide lawns, and Grandfather's manners and light touch. It was not what I had seen but what I had been taught, it was what Johnny called happy smiling nigger Beulah, but not in front of Mamma. He never said things like that in front of her.

I thought my grandmother was asleep. She hadn't said a word since we got in the car. I could hear her creak once in a while. But when we passed another car, its headlights caught her eyes. They looked like pebbles. She was just sitting there staring at nothing. It was scary.

Up in front, Daddy was listening to Jack Benny on the car radio. Mamma was pinching the top of her nose. I knew she was getting one of her appalling headaches and when we got home we all have to concentrate on that. But not yet.

"I *hate* them. I'm deeply allergic to rambler roses," I heard her say.

"Neb mind, honey, we'll be home soon and get you to bed," my daddy said in that special voice he kept for her ears alone.

A car passed on the new road behind me. I sat on for a while on the tombstone turning and turning the ruby ring Aunt Althea had given me. I got up and smoothed my linen dress as if I were girding my loins. I had seen the little girl who was then my mother that day as through a glass darkly, a dirty freckled glass in the center of my memory. And now I was going to have to see her and Johnny and all of them face to face. It was not enough to know. I had to go there again with the same terrible eyes, the eyes of the child I had been, strengthened and protected by the woman I had become. I turned the Volvo around and went down under the four-lane ramp on the old road to the big house at Beulah.

The big house was protected from red dog and road dust by a veil of newly planted small cedar trees and a white horse fence, and against the fence a border of three-year-old lilac bushes. The Chevrolet sign was long gone, the lawn was tended. I stopped at the gate. Beulah had been restored, as it never was in life. The wide porch had been torn away from its façade. Now a small entry with wooden columns led to the old door. Its fanlight had new glass. Beside the steps, a plaster black-face statue with bright blue eyes, dressed like a jockey, held up a perpetual tray in its hands. On it someone had carefully painted ESCEW. I hesitated before I knocked. I could hear a soap opera, or a family argument, going on inside. It was suddenly turned off. I could hear footsteps coming to the door.

Mrs. Escew saw one of those women coming up the walk. They all looked alike. It wasn't anything you could put your finger on. She sighed. She'd been up since six and had fixed breakfast for Harlow, so he could get on upcreek to the mine, like she always did. She liked doing that. She'd done it every day for forty years. Good God, the time passed. They sat there across the old table and respected each other's silence and read the paper. She liked the smell of the morning and coffee and bacon. It made her feel peaceful.

Now, at ten o'clock, she had run the mop around, picked the peas—late ones; she found out how to grow them in the shade under the Althea hedge. She'd put two loads in the washer, and she could hear the comforting hum of the last load in the dryer when she took her colander of peas into the library—library hell, he just called it that—and felt like she'd earned the right to sit down for a little while and watch "Alice Love Career Woman" on the color TV and shell peas, and try to forget the tomatoes. "Let me tell you," she told Alice, "if you let your tomatoes get on top of you, you've got yourself a real problem."

She felt sorry for Alice, out there among strangers in the corporate structure away from her own people. Alice was a fool about men, she could have told her that, but the divorce was inevitable, she could see that, too. He never had understood Alice, how empty her success was. Yesterday Alice had told him so, and he just walked out and slammed the door and it was time to pick peas again. The garden was about to drive her crazy, keeping up with it.

Alice was still standing there, all by herself in that nice split-level house that was in her own name, and that was when Mrs. Escew saw one of those women hightailing it up the walk like she owned the damn house and was going to change it.

Mrs. Escew hadn't wanted the Big House anyhow, but Harlow said they had to, it was their duty. She wanted a nice modern split-level like Alice had, without her troubles, not the old barn of a place with the pigeons hooting in the attic and a thousand miles to walk every day to keep it up. Harlow said it was a landmark and she ought to have some feeling for it, the Neills didn't give a damn.

That wasn't the reason and she knew it, but she never said so to Harlow. He just wanted the Big House, he still called it that. He said he had watched it deteriorate ever since he was a boy, and they never had a pot to pee in.

She turned the television sound off and left the picture on and hoped the woman would take the hint.

The woman knocked again; well, she was just going to have to wait a minute. Mrs. Escew wished she didn't have her curlers in. She looked back once and Alice was still standing there. Her face filled the screen and tears were just a running down her face, the damned fool. That man wasn't worth it. Secretly Mrs. Escew thought there wasn't a man alive worth that kind of carrying-on, even Harlow.

She opened the door and waited for the woman, woman about forty or maybe older. That was another thing. You couldn't tell with these women. They didn't spread out. They had some secret.

She waited the woman out, and finally she said, "Mrs. Escew?" like she already knew her, and then, "My mother was a Neill."

She might have known. Never had a bit of interest in the old place until she and Harlow worked their tails off fixing it up, and got their pictures in the papers, and then one after another, they came up there and sniffed around and talked about the Senator, the Senator, that old bastard, and acted like they knew the Big House better than she did and she'd scrubbed every inch of it down on her hands and knees.

"Why, come right in and look around," Mrs. Escew told the woman. "Any member of the family." People around Beulah still called it the old Neill place after all they had done. It made her fly red.

"This is the library," she told the woman. They stood at the door, and then went on in. Alice was saying something to her neighbor, Mrs. she forgot her name, didn't like her anyway. And that woman was patting her shoulder, just like she hadn't gone off to a motel with that son-of-a-bitch not two episodes ago.

She hadn't had time to move the colander of peas, or the morning paper piled with the green shells. "You just got to set down once in a while," she said as she passed the chair.

She had shown so many of those women around that she could almost do it without thinking.

"They used to call this the library." The only books were a Bible and a series of Reader's Digest condensed novels. She'd read them all, and she planned to send off for some more when she had time.

The green ivy tendrils of the wallpaper were covered with a history in photographs, a large color print of the New River Bridge, a log cabin, Harlow and her at their wedding, Harlow in the army, holding up a tarpon in Florida, his face growing larger from his gaunt boyhood, to a "portrait" on the table. He had filled out and prospered. He looked like a Rotary Club member. One wall was covered with framed eight-by-ten glossies of the house before, the house after, the house in snow, in spring. "They wrote it up in the paper," she explained. "They give us those."

Old Miz Escew from across the river was tinted a faint pink. She stared down from over the fireplace. She looked as if she didn't own the place and didn't care to. Mrs. Escew hadn't liked the old woman, but sometimes she had to agree with her.

"That's Mr. Escew's mother," she said when she saw the woman peering around the room as if something had been misplaced. The pastel of Jesus looked down from over the sofa; beside him an old signed picture of John L. Lewis. Harlow was proud of that. He said John L. Lewis looked like the president of a bank. Over the rolltop desk Mrs. Escew glanced at two framed degrees her and Harlow had earned but she wasn't about to tell the woman about that.

"This is the dining room," she motioned from the door. She always had felt a stranger in that room. They only used it twice a year.

"My husband and me restored it," she told her own shoulder. She always said that, at the same place, she didn't know why. "We found authentic fireplaces." She always said that, too. She took the woman right to the attic, and hoped she was counting the steps. She had to say one thing, though, the woman wasn't talking Senator. She was asking real nice things like, "Where did you find the mantels?" and "It must have been a lot of work. I saw this place when a cat couldn't live in it." Mrs. Escew liked that. She decided she liked the woman all right.

She paused on the stairs, turned back, and grinned at her.

"We're a historical monument," she said. "Good God and the Pittston Coal Company! Us!" The bedrock of her, unchanged, saw it all with a poker-faced amusement. Her voice poked fun up at the surface. She never would have done that in front of Harlow, proud as he was. It was only for a second; she went on down the stairs, back to words she had said too many times.

The tour ended in the kitchen. Now, there wasn't any historical foolishness about the kitchen. It was hers, all hers. Without a single reproduction of anything. It was full of sunlight, the smell of coffee, a new white glossy stove, cabinets, freezers.

"You wanta cup of coffee." It was a statement. She didn't wait for an answer.

They sat opposite each other at the kitchen table, nursing two strawberry-covered mugs. Mrs. Escew had put strawberries all over the room, wherever she could find a place. The red spots cheered things up—prints on the newly ironed tablecloth, falling down the curtains, in decals on the doors of the white cabinets. Two large freezers filled the wall under the window to the back porch that ran along the side of the kitchen wall. On the stove a large canning kettle sat with clean jars ready in it. The rest of the peas were on the kitchen counter, a bushel basket full. She hoped the woman would see how many there were still, but she looked like she'd never shelled a pea in her life.

She lit a cigarette and drew the smoke down into her gaunt chest. "Mr. Escew wanted the place." She blew smoke and words around the kitchen; that explanation was enough. It suited her. "He said it was a shame."

She let a silence fall, then, "What do you do?" It was only polite to ask.

The woman seemed to search for an answer. "I teach." She wasn't giving anything away either. In Mrs. Escew's opinion, that was right.

"Oh, a schoolteacher..."

Mrs. Escew let another nice comfortable silence fall, sat in it, sipping her coffee.

Then: "Shame we didn't do all this before your mother died. She would have liked it." She always said that when a Neill turned up. Another demanded silence.

Mrs. Escew had had enough silence. She apologized for

something, and was mad at herself for doing it. "Of course, we can't run it like you Neills could."

"It was a boardinghouse." She couldn't believe it. A Neill saying things like that about her own family.

She wanted her to leave.

"Oh no. A senator and all..." She looked beyond the woman's head at the big vegetable garden. "Good grief!"

"I have to go upriver." The woman seemed to know she had gone too far some way.

"You might as well come on out this way." Mrs. Escew glanced at the kitchen clock. There was still ten minutes of Alice. She opened the kitchen door.

The dogs ran up, barking. One was the old mongrel, Chip, with a gray muzzle, they had brought from the upcreek house, the other an American Kennel Club registered collie, too damned dumb to house-train, but Harlow had bought it to go with the Big House and named it some fool thing like Princess Holly of Beulah. It wouldn't do a thing you told it to.

Chip headed for the woman's leg. He always did that.

"Kick the bastard," Mrs. Escew called out, not looking around. "Ain't nothing but a cross 'tween a feist and a cur."

The woman kicked, missed, and both of the dogs ran off.

They walked around the back of the ell where the smoke-house and the milk house had been. They had been made into a garage. Steel beams held up the roof where the brick wall had been taken out. In the garage sat Harlow's new Mercedes-Benz he wouldn't drive up to the mine.

"They used to keep horses and all." Mrs. Escew looked at the car. She had to set the fool woman straight about her own people.

"It's a beautiful car," damned woman sounded enthusiastic. It made Mrs. Escew want to spit.

The woman said some fool thing. Her voice was drowned by a coal train passing from up the creek. The sound filled the air, shook the ground. Before the caboose passed, she had started to talk again. She didn't realize that Mrs. Escew couldn't hear a damned word she said.

She just heard, "Are any mines opened?"

"Mr. Escew is stripping, up to Hanna, that old pillar-mining left a lot of good coal. Surface mining," she explained. "Used to call it shoot-and-shove until the govment stepped in. He's made a lot of money." They were around the house at last.

"You come back see us sometime. You hear?" she said to the woman's back, hardly knowing she said it. Before the woman got down the walk, she was back in the library, watching the last precious minutes of Alice. Alice had found out about the motel while she was showing that fool woman round. She was hollering at that Mrs. Something. She never would know how Alice found out.

I could still see Mrs. Escew through the front window. I heard a woman yell, "It wasn't love; it was sex. Don't you understand, Alice?" electric voice from California to Beulah.

It was strawberries, those unashamed strawberries. I sat in the car and the tears ran down onto my dress. I didn't want anybody to laugh at her strawberries. I cried for the second time in eighteen years for the wasting of my brother Johnny, and my mother, ten years old in that kitchen.

All the time that blank-faced woman in her sprigged cotton apron had trudged around the house, and I followed her low monotonous lecture that she didn't want to give, I had been in another house that was no longer there. It had been swept clean of whatever blood, birth, death, or change there had been. We had been thrown out, like old newspapers. It wasn't tragic; it was only sad.

I didn't follow Mrs. Escew. I followed my mother, a little girl in the years before 1907 when they "lost" the house. They spoke of it through the years as if it had been misplaced and would someday be found again. I saw the kitchen we sat in crowded with people. I had been raised on the road to my mother's Mecca; she peopled it with dreams of her own. Sitting in the silence nursing the strawberry mug, I had gone back to my dead mother, but what I heard again was not a dream, but one of those rare rifts in the golden haze of memory.

"Every night"—she told the story bitterly—"it was the same. I was only a little girl but you couldn't fool me. Already I couldn't wait to get out of the place where everything was the same and nothing happened. Time ruled those rooms with an iron hand. Old Aunt Toey sat by the kitchen fire. That was before her boy took her over to Lacey Creek. She'd been born into slavery. Mother said she was the same age as my Grandmother Melinda who married Crawford Kregg from Albion on the James. Aunt Toey said she was eighty-two but Mother said she was seventy-seven and not to believe a word she said. Mother acted like she still owned her, but when we lost Beulah she shipped her over to her grandson on Lacey Creek like she was a piece of furniture we couldn't fit into the house on River Street. She always said it was against her orders, but that was a downright *lie*.

"Aunt Toey slept all the time like an old dog. Every night the same. Mother sat in the living room in the big chair and Grandmother Liddy, who was a Catlett before she married Senator Neill, sat in the rocker and they didn't say one word to each other. Mother sat like a statue. She'd given up. She'd even stopped talking about how she and Papa were married in Washington and President Chester A. Arthur came to the wedding and how Papa was a catch and cut a swath through Washington society, the bon ton." I heard the hard sound of my mother's old anger. "Bon ton. Shit." I had seldom in my life heard her use that word before. What trigger had released her? I couldn't remember. "After the Senator ran through ever last thing we didn't have a pot to pee in. Now that's the hard truth of the matter.

"Promptly, when the old clock in the hall struck eight, it was like a knell, she hauled Grandmother Liddy up the stairs with the expression on her face how long oh Lord how long. I'll tell you one thing. *I'll* never let you children haul me around like a sack of potatoes with that oh Lord how long look. You remember that, you hear?

"Sister Annie entertained in the parlor like Mr. J. D. Cutright and Mr. Anderson Carver and Mr. Baseheart had come to court her. She played I'll be calling you . . . ooo . . . ooo . . . ooo on the player piano, singing along. I loved that piano, and I loved the parlor. My Grandmother Melinda looked down from the mantel from Before the War, with a rosebud in her hand, and over the sofa the Senator reminded them all just exactly who we were even if Mr. Cutright did go to Princeton and so did Anderson Carver. So did your Uncle Dan. Fat lot of good that did. But oh Lord God, J. D. Cutright then; he came from Cincinnati and he took actresses out to dinner and he rode a big black horse. He and Dan sat there like they'd had dinner instead of eating supper and they smoked their cigars and their white Arrow collars gleamed and they talked about who all they knew in the East and

Annie was going Cockadoodledoo at the piano. You'd have thought the coal mines were a thousand miles away. Now J.D. is coal-operator fat and as for Dan . . . I would stand at the door and dream of the East and downriver and a time at Beulah that would have made even J.D. sit up and take notice." Hard truth hadn't lasted long. She had slipped into nostalgia again, the tremulous voice she used for saying poetry, or telling fairy tales.

"Then Grandmother Melinda seemed so alive to me. Her still patrician face moved in the light of the lamp when somebody crossed the room and made a draft; white face, night-black hair, oh she must have been lovely. Aunt Toey said she died of a broken heart, but Mother said it was nothing of the kind. She died of the flu." Her voice was hard again, haunting the car. "Mother only inherited her pride and not her looks. She'd say, 'I married money!'" The words were sour and made her mouth pucker. "We were haunted by money. Money money money! The drains said money, don't run out of money. Money makes the mare go, don't marry for money but marry where money is; pride and patches and no money. That's what I lived with. I would climb up the pear tree and think about money when I wanted to be thinking of higher things. Your generation! Are you listening? You don't know. Once I stole tomatoes—we called them love apples— and tried to sell them and give Papa the money. He laughed at me. He said country people thought love apples were poison.

"Annie was nothing but a damned fool, acting that way in the parlor when I wanted to go in and play the piano my own self. I would watch the notes pouring down, all lacelike, you could see the melody, just pouring down. They weren't courting Annie. They paid to stay there when they came up from Canona to the mines. Mother called them paying guests in her poorhouse Tory way. They were not. They were boarders. She ran a boardinghouse, right up until we lost most of Beulah and moved down to the only property we had left, the Senator's house on River Street. He'd had the foresight to put that in Mother's name."

Somebody was leaning against the side of my car.

"Can I get anything for you, honey?" Mrs. Escew reached in and patted my shoulder. "Another cup of coffee?"

"No, honey." I found Kleenex and scrubbed it over my face. "I don't know what came over me."

"Come on in. You oughtn't to be driving."

"I can't. I've got a long way to go," I told her.

I did. I had thought the years of searching were over, but they weren't. Like the first Hannah, I had to cross a hundred miles of "pleasing though dreadful mountains and hills as if piled one on top of the other." I had found that eighteenth-century description of the Alleghenies in the British Museum, three thousand miles from the land of Beulah.

"You come back now, you hear?" Mrs. Escew stepped away from the car. All the way to where the road's turn shut Beulah from sight, I could see her standing there beside the gate to her Big House, and could still feel the touch of her hand on my shoulder.

From the riverbank to the road in what had been the upriver field of the old Beulah, a huge factory covered the bottomland. The air above it shimmered with heat. All the way up the river valley, I passed an almost unbroken sprawl that cluttered the bottomland from mountain to mountain and crowded the steep hollows: tipples, beer halls, poolrooms, gas stations, roadside signs, factories, greasy elbows, slag heaps. Here and there it was broken by a cared-for town that had once been a coal camp. The whole space was filled wherever a man could find footing to make a little money. Some had failed, and had left sagging, empty stores, burned-out one-story shacks that nobody bothered to clear away.

It looked like a place too many people had passed through, ignored, or had to leave, as I had. It had its oases, like any desert. A wild narrow waterfall rushed from high on a hill down to a culvert under the road. A house in the mouth of a hollow had been newly painted. A vegetable garden was terraced on the steep slope. I passed a fine stone Catholic church, a baseball field, new company houses faintly imitating garden suburbs. The old mines had left only their town names, Coaltown, Peabody, Triumph. The new names that occupied the valley were Union Carbide, Monsanto, Du Pont.

The mountains rose higher and the valley murmured. The last factory smokestacks were as tall as cathedral spires throwing out dark-red flashes like pentecostal fire.

Beyond the last factory the air cleared as if it had been freed. After the heat it was a bright summer morning. The road broke toward the river. Beyond me the great falls fanned, throwing swaths of spray into the clean hunter's day.

The water above the falls formed a wide, deep lake where huge island rocks rode like proud keeled ships. Around it the mountains stood, sheer rock cliffs, impassable until the rock was blasted to expose the graves of great forests that made black coal seams shining in the sun.

The lake reflected the surrounding mountains. I saw the same calm water where Johnny had thrown me from a rowboat to make me swim, the same willows reflected on the banks. A cool wind from the mountains touched my face. Indian Rock, like a castle in the middle of the lake, surrounded by a moat, was as it had been when the settlers had lived on it for six months under siege from the Shawnee.

Then I saw that someone had floated an old rusty trailer halfway across the lake, and parked it on top of Indian Rock.

I began the climb up the most western mountain. It was as if my father met me, as he always did, at the first curve—at least all of him I can remember as a man, the gesture of his hands, the cringing of the lower eyelids in his still face against small, distracting blows, the training which isolated him and made him seem, with a little fear under his measure of success, perpetually preoccupied with my mother. He had a kind of mountain watchfulness underneath the golf tan and the well-cut clothes Mother insisted on, prepared always to follow her if she walked or catch her if she fell. He would sum it up by saying, "We better get Mother to bed," not as a man of his wife but as a father of a constantly ailing child. I don't think she demanded his love, but part of her did live on his almost singular concern.

"You leave the Neills in the valley, Hannah. Now you're in McKarkle country." He said it so many times by habit; as a child I remember my mother twitching beside me, as she did when he repeated things. He didn't seem to say it to me, although he used my name.

The road was a series of hairpin curves, climbing higher and higher. I caught glimpses of the river, down the steep drops, as I climbed, on the way to Lookout Rock, the next station for me on the old Hannah's escape. It had taken her forty days and forty nights to get to where I would drive in three hours.

I stopped in the parking space where a state landscape architect had made an oasis surrounded by the rough stone wall "in keeping" with the wild cliffs. Cars from California and Ohio were parked side by side, piled high with baggage as if they, too, were on some odyssey. On top of the packed back seat of the car from Ohio lay a peacock-patterned mountain quilt from a roadside stand. I had seen, and not seen them, all the way up the mountain, signs saying Authentic Quilts, Tamed Bear, Rattlesnake Pit.

When I got out of the car, my legs were shaking. Rustic arrows, designed by the state, pointed along a path with a log railing. Lookout Rock was poised over a thousand feet of space above the river. I stood where it was said that George Washington had once stood, a young surveyor, and looked westward toward the hope of bottomland beyond, where he, a poor man, could lay first claim to Western acres and make his fortune.

There was no one else there. It was one o'clock. I could hear people hidden by the trees beyond the signs that pointed to the picnic tables.

The flat rock over the deep circling gorge was etched with wind that seemed as old as the world's beginning, bending the young trees downriver and fanning my face. As far as I could see upriver, the mountains rolled, green and endless walls.

Far below, a miniature freight train traveled east around the great curve of the opposite mountain. I judged as easily as breathing a hundred or so coal cars, open-topped and black. That far away, I heard a diesel whistle around the curve through wave after wave of air eddies. Across the river and a mountain away from the gorge, the top had been stripped to dead rock and the trees below it had been burned out by some old fire. My face felt damp and cleansed by the healing wind.

Down below in the gorge the table rock where the first Hannah had been driven by hunger to eat raw bear meat was as small as a pebble. When I was a child, face pressed against the window of the train, I saw the great rock, its prow splitting the wild river in a perpetual shower of foam. It was only a glimpse; the train ran fast through the gorge. Then, in the only widened place against the steep mountain, I saw a fairy castle, all of stone, with towers and stone walls, and a garden gone to ruin. The windows were hollow. There were shards of broken glass on the wide terrace. Beyond it a line of coke ovens made the air above them shimmer from their heat. All that was stamped in memory as the train passed, mingled with the stories I was learning to read alone. Now there was no Pullman in the daylight, only the coal cars passing. The tiny train below me disappeared around the curve of the mountain.

I was on my way to Uncle Ephraim McKarkle's farm and I feared that stop more than any of the rest. When I dreamed about home it was not the house on River Street, or the "new" house in the southern hills above Canona. It was my Grandmother McKarkle's farm where I still had the illusion of the end of things, and that form of peace which is always sought for and always remembered, something unquestioned, and I didn't want it, too, changed, made alien by time.

Two hours later I reached the high savannah of Greenbrier, and turned south on the country road. I had to slow down. The road was narrow, but that was not the only reason. I was almost to Fairy Land Cave, where the first Hannah had climbed, all day long, up the face of the cliff. I had hiked in a long line of Girl Scouts, along a concrete walk into the cave mouth. There was a line of naked electric lights along the path. Everything had names. There was the organ, and Jesus with his Flock, and Snow White and the Seven Dwarfs. The cave was clammy inside. There was nothing left to fear. But when the guide turned off the line of electric lights, it had been, for a minute, ancient and blind, a black pressure against my eyes, as heavy as death, as it had been the first time I had entered it, a wild black tunnel. My brother Johnny told me it was Dead Man's Cave. A man had been lost in it and starved to death. I was seven years old. Johnny, already thirteen, whispered to me, as we rode toward the huge grinning rock mouth, that the man still haunted it, calling "Find me, Mother, find me." He said you could hear his voice, carried by the wind through the black tunnels. He said, "You listen. You'll hear it."

My Uncle Ephraim walked in ahead of us. I had clung to the broad back of my pony, and smelled its sweat. Inside, in the dark, they called, "Come on, come on, you're safe with us," and I could hear the cave wind beyond them moaning, "Find me, Mother, find me."

I made myself tether the pony and follow them. I always did. Columns of icy stone sprang out on the beam of Uncle

Ephraim's flashlight, and then were in the dark behind us. It was cold.

I passed the sign *Fairy Land Cave*, then the entrance to its little park in a grove of trees with picnic tables, where a few campers were parked. Children were playing on the swings. A Frisbee flew across in front of the car.

The June afternoon buzzed in the sun. Ranch houses with station wagons parked among the flowering shrubs were strung along the road where there had, when I went there as a child, been pickup trucks, and instead of lawns, fields tilled almost up to the doors of farmhouses. Some of the old houses were still there, but they, too, had changed from farms to what my mother would have called "places." I passed tax-shelter fields where Angus grazed.

The entrance to the farm I still thought of as my long-dead grandmother's was exactly the same, except for the wrought-iron sign on a post that read *Green Acres*. The mailbox below it was glossy with carriage paint, but it still read *McKarkle*, and I felt a lurch of relief and found myself letting it be the same as it had been, my father's birthplace. Now it belonged to Uncle Ephraim, my father's baby brother, sixteen years older than Johnny, but more brother than uncle. Johnny once said that Uncle Ephraim taught him everything he knew. It was the only time I ever saw Uncle Ephraim mad at Johnny. But he didn't say anything. He just got up and replaced his chair at the kitchen table. His movements seemed to take an hour. Johnny was seventeen. He got up too without saying anything and stayed out all night long. Uncle Ephraim sat on the porch until he heard Johnny's new car coming back at six o'clock in the morning. When he knew that Johnny was all right, he went out to do his chores.

Johnny and I had always fought in the back seat of my father's Buick not to be the one to open the farm gate. There was no gate. There were cattle rails laid in the driveway. I felt the car lurch over them and thought of miles of corduroy road with logs laid across that must have made the carriages lurch and sink in the same way.

When I turned the curve so that the old McKarkle farm came into view on the rise above, I had to stop. No matter how far I had traveled, or what had happened, or how deeply my life was lived in other places, the sense of ensconcement, of taproots down, was no place else.

It was the seventh sense. It had nothing to do with

happiness or liking, or even caring. It was as organic as the
two oak trees that stood, and always had, on either side of the
old farm road that was now a graveled drive. It was the color
of blood and it moved slowly through my body, deeper than
decision, as unquestioned and instinctive as the sigh that
released my fatigue. It was not peace as peace is sought, but
a flowing, a direction. I had known it before, every time,
even when I had hated coming back, but now I knew what I
had not known then. It was an illusion, too, like the illusion
of sameness in the house in the distance, up the rolled
blue-green lawn.

I sank into the silence, which was not silence but a breeze
high in the oaks, a sigh of leaves, and far away the faint buzz
of a tractor. I could see a man getting up from a chair on the
porch and knew it was Uncle Ephraim, and that he had been
waiting for me, for that unearned surge of welcome I knew
was flowing toward me.

Across the lawn, past the rhododendron and the June
borders of flowers, it could have been my mother in the
shadow of the porch between the new colonial columns. I saw
the same crossed legs, the printed blouse with its round
collar, Lady Hathaway in a khaki-colored skirt, contained in
neatness, still girlish. She waited, too. She had been waiting,
and would wait like that always, a shadow reflecting the
shadow in my mind of a woman who had been dead eight
years.

The woman who sprang up as I drove nearer, and followed
Uncle Ephraim onto the lawn, moved out of my memory and
became another woman, my Aunt Rose, yielding in her walk
to her pleasure. She was not like my mother at all, except for
the careful uniform. It still looked alien to her lithe body. She
was thinner and her hair was snow-white, her face smooth
and young and tanned, a woman who had grown into bone-
deep beauty. Two bird dogs careened toward the car. Uncle
Ephraim clicked his fingers, and they stopped and lay down,
their tails swishing across the grass.

Rose and I clung to each other under the oaks. She smelled
of shade and cologne. She called over my shoulder, "Oh,
leave it," to Uncle Ephraim, who was leaning toward the car
to get my bag. He stopped, bent over, turned, and grinned, a
happy man, carved by time and sun, brown and secure.

In her touch, the feel of her fresh clothes, her skin, and
beyond her, the sameness of the house, I was caught in the

enchantment of security without responsibility that was child love. Then I was within both of their arms, cared for, in an instant of a dream as selfish as pre-puberty and fed with recognitions, self-centered, pure and sexless, the promise of blessing so long as I didn't rock the boat.

It passed almost at once.

A man sat in a neat containment, an old dandy in an elegant tailored summer suit, on a green-and-white chintz-covered glider, not moving, waiting for me to come to him. It was Rose's father, my Eddie Pagano, who my father had always referred to as a bastard, although he seldom swore.

"Papa lives with us now," Rose said, sensing the pause. She went ahead of us to the porch. Uncle Ephraim and I followed. I fell in with his slow pace, his abiding scent of tobacco, sun, man sweat. Rose leaned over and kissed her father's temple, let her kiss draw him into the welcome. But he held out his hand to me, rejecting easy polite affection. He did not smile. He was too dignified for that. I felt his hand in mine, narrow and small.

"Rosie, go get the girl a glass of wine." His voice was as commanding and quiet as his body, as imperious as my grandmother's had been, on the same porch, laying down the law to my father, scorching my mother with words so that she always seemed smaller when we left.

"Yes, Papa," Rose McKarkle, once Rose Pagano, said, as she always had to him.

Mr. Pagano broke the silence she left on the porch behind her. "I remember you." There was only a faint hint of the mountains in his neat voice. He was not one of those old people who controlled by talk that couldn't be interrupted. He controlled by a silence that was stronger. I saw Uncle Ephraim relax in the demands of age he had been used to all his life and had never fought against, saw that he had not aged but had weathered instead, year after year in the land and summers and winters, always at home, always honoring age. He had the face still of a boy, unchanged, quiet, and kinder to the world around him than it had ever asked for or noticed.

I sat in the wicker rocker, tired from my drive. I sank, ten years old again, to the floor at the corner of the old porch in the vine shadow, back when there were no columns, only posts, and the cupolas at either end of it held swings on chains that went scrank scrung when I swung.

My grandmother had summoned the churn out into the fresh morning. She said nobody made butter right but her. She called Uncle Ephraim and my father to her as if they were still boys and laid down the law to them, but what it was about that morning was lost from my mind. I saw my father, stripped of authority, that powerful man I feared and didn't know, as awkward as a boy again. I could almost hear again the thunk of the churn my grandmother used so well to punctuate what she had to say.

She still called my father Mooney, even when he was forty-eight years old, paying no attention when my mother, with a slight dry cough to draw attention away from the churn, "broke the news," as she put it, that he had just been elected president of the Canona Country Club. My grandmother received that news with a noisy thrust of the clapper and banished Mother from the porch. She said, "Love of God, Sally Brandon, go find something to do. We have property to discuss." Then she looked down at me and told me little pitchers had big ears, and to go find Johnny.

But when I ran into the house I saw my mother standing at the window, so lost I wanted to draw her to me as if I were her mother instead. She looked like she hadn't been invited to the human race. She didn't see me. I tiptoed away, embarrassed for her. That girl she hid behind her camouflage followed me, haunted me, turned up in the places I ran to. In London, Paris, I would wake up trembling for the pain of that virgin girl who betrayed my mother when she thought she was alone.

It was the lost girl I saw that morning behind the armor of her rigid body who had held my brother Johnny in what he called durance vile. He had been caught in a lust for her presence and her notice—no matter what form it took—which he mistook for love. It was evasive flirtation. She learned to use it with all of us, her head turned aside like the Virgin trying to ignore the Angel Gabriel. We called it her Rossetti look, trying to exorcise it with a joke, always and forever trying to tiptoe away from its insistence, I all over that Uncle Ephraim would call hell's half-acre, Johnny into secrets.

A bee buzzed around Rose's geraniums; it was so quiet on the porch that the bee seemed an interruption.

Mr. Pagano decided to speak. He took up with his voice

exactly where he had left off in his own mind. "Smartest foolish woman I ever knew. She saved my life once."

"My mother?" I was confused. I was sure I hadn't spoken.

"No, honey, Lily," he said. "Lily Lacey from Seven Stars." I had heard the story so many times before from him. He had always told it when he saw me. Unlike so many of the others, Mr. Pagano had been honored by my questions, and I was grateful for that. He told me as much truth as he could, a man who'd gone far beyond feeling he had anything to lose. He let the glider move a little; it droned as he droned, same words, same pictures, changed by lacunae of forgetfulness and the censorship of memory.

But his Lily Lacey was faded and worn. I knew Lily within me, realer than a faded memory in an old man's mind. I wondered, as I always had, how the fictions of the questing mind stayed so alive. Two fictions met in me, one of his dimmed memory, one risen clue on clue, from myself who had called a Lily from my own dreams.

I watched his face, hoping he would think that I was still listening, looking for the boy I had fashioned of him. There was nothing there but an old man. The Eduardo he had been was mine now, born in my search.

He said, "First time I ever saw a grapefruit. I've hated the damned things ever since," as if that were as important as the way his Lily had taken him on the train out of the state to escape a lynching during what he called the mine wars. He smiled, as if it were no more nor less important than the grapefruit. "After that I made a fortune. All you need is a train ticket, a good suit, and a hundred dollars."

The old war, the grapefruit, the woman, were as alien to the columned porch as coal in Greenbrier county, an intrusion.

Ephraim McKarkle let the old man's voice mingle with the sounds of afternoon. He knew the story, all the stories. It wasn't rudeness or retreat; he didn't see it that way. He was listening to the tractor in the south field, hoping it wouldn't stop so he'd have to pick himself up and go up there and see what was the matter. The boys ran it too fast. "A tractor ain't a hot rod," he told them. "Dammit, you got to listen to the engine, feel it."

He hadn't said a damned thing since he'd sat down because he didn't have a damned thing to say. He wished Rose would come back. She knew how to deal with her father, soft touch, quiet, "Papa?" turn him off like quieting one of her dogs, way she smiled. He looked at Hannah. My God, still had that girl look, oh but old around the chin and eyes like she'd been places and seen things—too many places and too many things. She had gone a little stringy, beginning to look more like her mother; tapped her foot the same way, not knowing she was doing it. Skinny women. He mistrusted them. They had no idea of the kind of peace you could feel in your body after hard work.

He knew she was poised to disturb, stick her damned nose in, make them remember, dog on scent. She wouldn't stop until she'd stirred up all the horseshit. She'd done it before. She said she was trying to find out something. She couldn't let her brother die in peace. She was one of those people that had to know why—the only question there wasn't any answer to. He could have told her that, but he knew it wasn't any use. He remembered trying to comfort her, to shut her up, but he couldn't do it any more. It was too late. "I got troubles of my own," he told himself.

He was sorry she had come. He wouldn't have said so, even to Rose. The girl was alien. Her mind was someplace else, a place he had no desire to go. One foot over the mountains, you were in limbo. Rose had gone to all that trouble, fresh flowers, like the little old thing he'd taught as much as she'd take was the goddamn Queen of England. Standing there at the door of the guest room with her hand to her mouth, Rose had had that look he hated, as if she were a thousand miles away.

He'd spent twenty years trying to wipe that look off her face. The girl brought it back, he knew that. He didn't want her to stir Rose up and he didn't know what to do about it. Rose still cried in her sleep once in a great while, but she always swore afterwards she didn't remember what she'd dreamed. Goddamn, a hurt woman never did get over it no matter what you did for her—like a horse, shy in the same place every time, spooked. It seemed like the memory stayed in their bodies, women and horses.

The old man was saying something. Oh, he had gotten to

that part of the story. "I owe no man. I sent the Englishman's suit back, too." He always seemed to take more pride in that than in his goddamn coal fortune. As if he'd heard the thought, the old man said, "Hardest hundred dollars I ever made . . . I never set foot on Lacey Creek again." He harped on that.

Why you wanted to go hightailing all over hell's half-acre, Ephraim didn't know. That girl sitting there tapping her foot, her eyes gone blank like people's do when they are caught in old stories, there and not there. Didn't she know that the only way to get a bit of peace was to be unconscious of all the questions, let dreams stay in the dark where God intended them, live and let live, day after day? Things in the world were bad enough without that, but what the things were he preferred to leave alone.

The sense of ensconcement had gone. I was free of them all for a little while. I wondered why the passing of that illusion of home was a relief and a loss at the same time. They had asked me nothing yet of where I had been. I knew they wouldn't. I was piercing the circle of their day, or it had pierced me. From such porches, such afternoons, you disappeared, you reappeared. I was a ghost from a past they shared with me.

I watched my uncle, the one man in my family who had helped me escape. He had given me, once, a greater illusion of safety than anyone I had ever known. He had an air of waitfulness, of having more time to be generous. Good poker players had it, a sense of being in control, and not yet ready. Johnny had had it.

I wanted to burst the illusion, harrow the afternoon with language. "For one last time"—echo of a phrase of my mother's—"I want to know who killed my brother. Oh, we all know a name, but beyond the hand that did it I want to know why and I still intend to find out." I was conscious of tapping my foot, and I made myself stop. I had fallen into my mother's language and the tapping of her foot. I felt weightless and insubstantial. I wanted to run away from the danger of their kindness. Beyond that I yearned to explain, to hear my own voice telling them, and myself, how and why it had happened. I wanted to tell the past self within me, unsatisfied still with the old blindness of "That's just the way things are, honey." I could hear them saying that, mild, bland, happier than I could ever be. I envied that with my whole tired questing self.

"Don't try to fool me," I told them all, quite silently, "the answer lies under all this lush green. I have a right to know."

And then I wasn't sure. "Muddying the water," I remembered Uncle Ephraim telling me, "bad animals." I didn't want to be his bad animal. I wanted to hug him as I always had. I wanted to be stupid and daily, anonymous and taken for granted. I smiled and Uncle Ephraim smiled back, conspiring beyond Mr. Pagano's talk.

I was as relieved as I could see he was when we heard Rose's steps across the creaking boards of the hall. We both looked up. The old man inspected the tray Rose brought. She served him first.

"Rosie, you didn't bring any tomatoes."

"Papa gets the first tomatoes of the year," Rose explained, not to me, but to him. She teased gently, "Find an Italian you find a garden."

He folded back into his containment and sipped the wine she had brought out, and let us sink into the fine lethargy of the late afternoon, that eased the long drive, and time, and any sense of arrival, and we were simply there, and forgetfulness and the wine warmed us, quieted questions, let us live in peace.

I knew later, lying in my fresh bed on the near-dark, listening to the wind that had risen in the night, that my dear Rose had taken her kind of trouble. The flower arrangement on the table near the window was a shadow against the moonlight. The last thing I had seen when I turned out the light had been a picture of my father at twenty-two, a solemn graduate, his hair parted in the middle and plastered to his head, his eyes so vulnerable I was surprised at tears behind my own eyes.

When they had seen me to my room, Uncle Ephraim had picked it up. "I haven't looked at this for so long," he said, wondering. "I've seen it, but I haven't looked at it." But it was himself he recalled, not his brother. "I wasn't more'n seven years old. Ma took me to his graduation. Never wanted to get out of a place so much. Couldn't even squirm. My pants were too tight." Then, remembering his brother, he said, "He had all the ambition. Worked his way through college. I didn't have to. There was cash money. Ma never let me forget that but she wouldn't have shown him how proud she was for a farm in Georgia."

Then he put the picture down again and said, "I wonder why we say that. Georgia land ain't no damned good. Good night, honey, I'm glad you're here."

In all the house there had not been one relic, one memory of Johnny. They had wiped themselves clean of him. In the night, hoping for sleep, I longed for my own life, the one they would have called my "outside" life, George's easy grace, his humor, my own bed, the place I called home. They had not asked one question. During the whole evening, the walk around the farm, the improvements, the new show barn that Uncle Ephraim called the Angus Hilton, the garden, the redecorated living room, the little swimming pool, the new horse stalls, they had strolled with me, presenting what they had become. At dinner Uncle Ephraim said above the candles, "Rose, turn on the goddamn light, I can't see to carve," echoing my father when my mother, as he said, put on the dog.

I praised the new peas, and "Papa's" tomatoes, and asked about the horses.

Far away in the dark dining room, the clock chimed twice. The sound died.

Rose was afraid to go to sleep again. In her first dream in seven months—she always knew how long the relief from him lasted—she had been with Johnny. The dream wasn't good or bad; it didn't even explain anything as some dreams did. She had been walking with Johnny down River Street in Canona under the trees that weren't there any more. She couldn't remember that they spoke or looked at each other. They had simply been together walking down a street in her mind.

She was drenched with sweat. She didn't want to move and wake up Eph, dear Eph who worried so when she was like that. He would feel the heat of her and stroke her hair back from her forehead. She told him it was natural, that you went through that at her age, but he would go on stroking her hair, staying awake when he needed his sleep so, with all the work he did. He said when a horse sweated like that he called the vet.

She had to get up and change her gown. She didn't like to admit, even to herself, the other reason. She was so ashamed of it. She had waked with an old insistence Johnny brought back, even though they were just walking down a street, nothing else, she was sure.

Deep in her, she pulsed with an urgent surge, down there. She had never felt that way with Eph and it made her sorry, and relieved at the same time. He would have hated that in her, behaving like an animal in heat. She would have disgusted him.

Sometimes in the night, when the house was empty of the children, she got up and went into the guest room and made love to herself, letting all the pictures rise and engulf her. She would never have called what she did then, in her shame, any other word, not that word.

She had to see if Eph was asleep.

She whispered, "Honey?" testing.

He didn't answer. He was a healthy sleeper, all that air and sun every day. He said a healthy man didn't take his worries to bed with him.

She got up slowly, as quietly as she could. Eph's old setter, Jubal, turned and muttered in the corner. He had always called his male dogs Jubal.

Eph said behind her, "Honey?"

"You're snoring, honey. I'm going in John's room." It was the lie she always told when she had to, as he called it, night-walk. He respected the lie. Loving lies were frail and shattered easily. They had to be protected. She eased the door shut.

They were so careful, always had been, not to call their first son Johnny.

She wandered for a little while through the dark house, and listened to night sounds. The rooms were as familiar as her own body, yet, at night, she still felt like a visitor after twenty years.

She could feel their presence in the darkness, their sleep; Eph, Papa, now Hannah. She didn't have to do it, and she was glad. Shame filtered lust out of her and left her exhausted. She leaned against the door of the living room, and let the wind from the opened window begin to dry her gown. It swung around her, a relief of a breeze.

Hannah had brought it all back. Rose had made herself look forward to her coming after so long. She felt she owed the girl something, but she couldn't for the life of her think what it could be. She wished in the night, as ashamed of that as of her lust, that the girl would go away. She thought if she could talk to her in private, maybe she would satisfy whatever it was, and free her and all of it from her mind at last.

She waited at Hannah's door, trying to sense wakefulness, hoping for it, feeling selfish about that. She released her hair from the sweat of her forehead.

"Honey?" she whispered when she opened the door.

"I'm awake." Voice from the darkness.

Oh yes, Hannah was waiting. She would be.

Rose went to the window and pulled back the curtains. "It's hot. I thought you might be hot," she excused herself to the night outside. She went on looking out across the lawn. A white animal, one of the cats, ran across the dark grass.

"I have to talk to you. There are things you don't understand," she told the cat, and the woman behind her she thought of as a girl, and herself; a spate of words, as if she were half dreaming. She let all the images come back which had come to her while she had lain coiled, wide awake to anything that waited to enter her.

"We were close. Closer than you ever knew. I was the kind you people played with but you didn't marry." She was lancing a memory, letting it flow clean. "Goddamn son-of-a-bitch. One night in one of those places he took me to, some fellow insulted me, called me a Dago whore. He was drunk. Johnny just laughed. He didn't protect me. He said consider the source. Afterwards, he told me he hadn't picked a fight because he had five hundred dollars cash on him. We sat on the steps of the Owls Club with no place to go, and he said that while the drunks stepped around us."

She was still for a minute, at the window, and on the steps of the Owls Club. That wasn't what she had meant to say. It had just come out.

She waited at the window, and she waited in her new white dress, while her papa and her mother watched from the living room. Her papa had been proud when she told him who had asked her to go to the movies. He said, "McKarkle?

Nice people. His father was a fool when I first knew him, but he turned into a right smart man, power in the community."

When Johnny came to the door, her papa said, "I used to know your father," to show that he approved of the boy. He made it seem as if they had met the right way, in a parents' house, and not in the drugstore.

They didn't go to the movies.

Later, in Johnny's roadster, he had taken her virginity with a strength so furious, so sudden that it woke in her an animal, she thought of it that way, an animal she had been proud of once because he said he loved it. For twenty years she had wanted to cut it out of herself like an abortion nobody wanted. She had known at once that he wouldn't have done that to one of the nice girls.

In that first night she had sneaked upstairs, feeling for the first time like the Dago whore the man had called her years later. She had hidden her creased bloodstained dress and tried not to cry. But she must have cried because her papa heard her. He came to her door, and said, "I'll kill him."

She told him not to talk like that, that nothing had happened.

"We've got as much money as they have," he told her when she had calmed him. "Don't you forget it." As if that made any difference.

But she told none of this to the girl behind her, Johnny's sister. It wasn't any of her damned business. She was still for so long her mind veered at last to other things, things that were a damned sight more important, and let those words loose in the night instead.

"I'm worried about him"—who it was, she didn't say. "He held back his beef for a higher price last year. This year it's lower. He didn't used to do that. Now that Papa's here, he wants to show him he can make money, too. Papa built the new barn and the swimming pool." She made herself laugh. "Papa was just trying to pay his way but I know Eph doesn't see it that way. He's worried about John, afraid he'll take drugs. I told him he wouldn't do that, he's a good boy." Pride crept into her voice. "He got straight A's or whatever they call it at Lawrenceville. He's been accepted at Princeton. Ed is a junior. He's bright."

She flicked at the curtain and leaned her head against the window frame. "Oh hell, I don't know what to do. Get these night sweats. Menopause. I wonder why it's a pause. It's not, it's a race, a race through your body. I've got to hold everything together. Papa"—she flicked back in time—"he used to slap the polenta stick on the table in the kitchen. When he did that, every soul in the house stopped dead in their tracks. Italian houses always had a polenta stick—you know, great big thing like a club. One slap of it on the table and you couldn't hear a sound but the clocks ticking."

She pulled the bedroom chair to the window and sank into it, still watching the night. "Those Italian hints. I got them all the time when I was a girl. Make me homesick for something I hadn't known. All of them"—she didn't say who.

She shifted her body, making the chair creak.

"Eph took me abroad last year. Boy, was that a mistake! We went to Perugia. That's where Papa was born. I don't know what I expected, but I sure as God know what I found. Nothing. As Grandma would say, 'Niente!' We went up a little side street and saw the house where he was born. It was pathetic. A little boy came out the door and stared at the American tourists. I tried to tell myself it could have been him, you know how you do. He asked us for chewing gum, only English he knew, I guess. Eph hated the whole thing.

"Papa never said much. He wanted to forget it, be American. When Grandma came to live with us, she talked sometimes. Papa said not to pay too much attention. She got things wrong." Rose laughed, once. "She didn't want to live with us. Her four grandsons carried her out of her house up Lacey Creek on the last chair. They had to move the furniture from right around her."

Then, as if she remembered the girl behind her, she said what she had convinced herself she had come to say. "Maybe she was right. It's better to put things behind you, let the dead bury their dead." She sighed away the last of her sorrow. She reminded herself, "I'm sorry the boys aren't here. They've gone cave-exploring. Spelunking. Terrible word. It worries me to death. We've got two wonderful boys. The stories I could tell you. When they're home the house is full of their friends. All nice kids from good homes, the Cutrights, the Carver boys, you know. We invite them up from Canona for weekends in the summer." She looked out at the silent swimming pool. "Half the night. I look out. Boys and girls swimming and splashing in the moonlight, prettiest thing you ever saw. Sometimes it is all I can do to keep from joining them, but it would embarrass the children." She chanted a litany. "They're going to get somewhere. Oh, honey—" She couldn't remember what she was going to say. She felt sleepy and peaceful. "Oh . . . this is your home, you know that." She tried not to sound preoccupied. She tried again. "How long can you stay?" She wanted to keep any fear out of her voice. She tried to show she loved the girl.

"I have to leave in the morning." The voice came from behind her. "Rose?"

She got up, sensing questions she wasn't prepared to answer.

"I'm sorry," she said to the dark form in the bed. "I'm sorry," she repeated, covering many things. "God, it's good to have somebody to talk to. Good night, honey." She escaped and closed the door behind her.

She hadn't let me speak. She left me stranded in the dark with all that she hadn't told me. I lay there in the bed I'd slept in as a child, summer after summer, and summer now came through the window, touched me, released the scent of Rose's flowers. She seemed to be still at the window, crying some cry I could barely hear. What had happened to her?

Not only age. That was too easy. The laughter she had had once, always ready in her, was part of my memory of her, the joyful gusts of it, a laughter without fear. Johnny had always said she had—what was the phrase?—a zest for life. He never brought her home. He told me Mother wouldn't understand her qualities. When he made excuses like that, his words sounded tired and trite.

Rose's ebullience, her riches, her easy manners, had been stropped down by what she had demanded of herself. Her social fear had shamed her in the face of the merciless gentility of women. She had camouflaged herself, even her honesty, to the bone. She didn't want to embarrass the children! Good Christ! I was suddenly furious at that damned needless self-destruction. I had seen it all my life, a disease to which we never became immune, we mountain people. I wanted to sleep it away, go back to my good life where it could not touch me, escape its sadness. In our shy pride we had, without knowing, imitated the strangers who took our land, aped the rapists. What did we call them—the outside interests. Why the hell were we so vulnerable? And coming

back released it in me when I thought I had fo(r)
was caught in seeing what it was in the night,
between the knowledge I had learned and the w
self-consciousness. What had they, the ever-prese
our souls, done but ignore us or mistake our ma...ers for
naïveté? We had succumbed to the careful gesture, genteel
mirror images of each other.

My brother Johnny. I could see that ruined face in the
dark. Once he and I and Rose had sat in the Wayfaring
Stranger and my older sister Melinda had caught us. What
was she doing there? I couldn't remember. One of her
slumming amusements, I suppose. Johnny had suddenly
pretended to be drunker than he was. Rose had sensed it and
had tried to cover it by being friendly. I could hear her voice
to Melinda, "Come see me sometime," easy mountain hospitality. Later Melinda had made a joke of it. "She asked me to
'come see her' sometime. Sometime. Imagine!"

There was a voice among the memories that were flooding
back, and that I wanted to escape by getting up and getting
in my car and racing away from it all, over the mountains to
the kinder world I lived in. Who was it? Somebody I couldn't
remember, but it was there. "Genteel murder is the slowest
form of murder. It leaves no sign of guilt."

"Oh, but it does in the victim," I wanted to answer at last,
"a long long guilt, a deep sense of loss." We had let ourselves
be seduced by the least seductive people in the world,
sexless, brittle, and unkind.

There was no hope of sleep. The room was full of what I
had come back to find and understand, armed so naïvely with
nothing but my search into the past. I had to go through to
the end of it if there was an end, a cure, a returned pride.

Somewhere outside a cat screamed and deep in the house
the clock struck three.

I wanted to laugh and I couldn't. I wanted to escape the
residue of Rose's mistaken grief, her choices, but I couldn't
do that either. I could only see that strong, deluded woman,
surrounded by love if ever a woman was, and still haunted in
the night by the dark lust she had been taught all the way to
her genes to call "being in love."

"He has been accepted at Princeton." Jesus. Was that
unworthy "acceptance" all that was left? My mother spoke in
the night. "All the nice boys went to Princeton. Mother called

rem coal princes, going off on Number 6 to Princeton. New people, she called them."

Somewhere in the road out beyond the farm, I heard a whish of car tires. I got up and sat at the window where Rose had left the pretty bedroom chair. I leaned on the sill. It was still damp from her night sweat. Out beyond the shadow of the porch, and the empty glider where Mr. Pagano had sat, the lawn lay under moonlight. The trees whispered. Far away the pool's still water was an illusion of a natural pond. An animal moved out of the trees, stopped and listened, moved into the moonlight, a young doe, stopped and listened again, slowly lowered her head to drink. Behind me the room, and the house beyond it, were as empty as the night, sunk in silence.

I hoped Rose was asleep at last.

In her struggle at the window to find happy images, Rose had hit upon the young as she was expected to see them. I could see them, too, all drinking Pepsis, dancing and splashing, chasing away the deer.

The wind was rising. It made dead branches clatter. It caught the curtains and billowed them out as if the dark room floated. They brushed my body like ghosts. If I had been a child and the wind had caught me in the live curtains I would have cried out "Mamma! Mamma!" but it would have been my grandmother who came in and shut the window and then led me back to bed and tucked me in and said, "Now you hush, honey." It was only the organdy curtains. Organdy. It sounded pretty, like new dresses. My grandmother always touched my head before she left. She was softened by the night, not like she was in the daytime, stern and huge in all her ways. I wouldn't have told on Johnny, that he had assured me there were white ghosts all over the house, and that they reached behind the doors to catch you if you had to get up and go to the bathroom; the Indian brave, the headless woman, the big black slave. I wet my bed, the same bed, when I had long since stopped at home, and my mother said that coming here got me too riled up.

I wanted—what?—to go to sleep, to find Rose's sadness boring and banal.

But she had made me a night gift of her sorrow, all unknowing. What had she done to Rose, my bright Rose, as stable in my mind as one of the trees?

In those child mornings, "keeping up" with Johnny and

Uncle Ephraim around the farm, I forgot the ghosts, ran after them to the call, "Come on, come on," from Johnny, far ahead. He still ran, as illusive in death, through all our memories, the demands of his haunting as ephemeral as the demands of his life.

The wind had blown the deer back into the shelter of the trees. As it is in the night, thoughts skittered, as if they too were blown about. The people in this house were, to me, realer than any other people I have known since. It was not love, not hate, it was commitment. They had no connection with how I lived, or what I had learned, or what I prayed for, but that deep claim. They neither knew nor cared anything about me but what I had left behind. I, in coming, had dredged their past, they mine. Their attic fragments, censored stories, pale watercolor sweet recalls were their protection from what I had to know.

I tried to keep on thinking of this, but I was floating in fragments, too, nearly asleep, and as aware as the deer somewhere outside. I saw Rose, as in the distance, shadowed by the trees, and lurched into staring, thinking that she was really there. It was only another ghost of a tree against the scudding clouds that chased the moonlight, swift across the lawn. Realer than that, I sensed Rose's deep love for the man she married, that she didn't know she had, sensed it dissolved in the dark pool of remembered lust. The vision faded even as it formed. It was too late. I yearned for sleep.

And he, that safe image of what a man was, my kind Uncle Ephraim, Owen Wister's Virginian with the straw showing. He never did an evil thing. He was honored by everyone who had ever known him, mild anti-Semite, racist; he stood for everything I hated. I was at war with the love I bore him. He was considerate of feelings he neither understood nor wanted to. His imitators, the wild peripheral men we bred, in their pickup trucks and with their gun racks, who were our own distant blood, acted out dreams for him he didn't know he had. He made jokes. They acted on them. I saw too clearly for my own good, layer on layer, stratum on stratum, of imitation as cruel as the women's. He used jokes, they used guns. He drove a Buick, they followed him in their trucks and did his dirty work. What was it Rose had told me, that he held back his beef to help drive the price up? Gibbon said that when the man who was later St. George of England held back his grain the starving people of Alexandria dragged him to death in the streets. My Uncle Ephraim would not have harmed a living soul.

"The devil," I told the mist that was beginning to rise from the pool, forecast of dawn, "hath power to assume a pleasing shape." I thought myself a fool, there in the window, to see that dear man like that.

I watched the mist. I sensed underneath the old farm the miles of limestone caverns. I went into the dark, deeper, deeper, past the pools that never saw light, through the narrow body-sized tunnels that opened into rooms bigger than cathedrals, all pressing black. I saw us all, and a million dollars' worth of high savannah that was the farm, on a thin shell resting on that primordial black space. I saw our imitations receding as far into the past, down, down to a genetic sense of loss that came, for all of us, from someone who had had to leave home. I had been Johnny Church, hallowed by the unblessing of his father, and Hannah Bridewell crossing the lawn. I watched, mindless with fear and survival. I saw Johnny Catlett, trying to escape and caught again to die at Manassas, and Lily, dreaming across the same mountains. I saw my brother, caged by his lovers, hated by his imitators, diminished by my mother's strict possession. Against them, shy, rigid, uncompromising, I saw what we stood for. We, more Anglo than the angels, were models of decorum, we strutted before the apers; we, apers and aped in turn, destroying, not by force but by something more evasive, a turning away, an indifference. There was no violence. There was not a voice raised, not a blow struck in the death we dealt and suffered.

The birds shrieked. A cock crowed down by the old barn. Tiresias could understand the language of the birds, but no one else could. That was his curse.

The lawn began to lighten. Rose and Ephraim's sons would be or would produce arrogant sons-of-a-bitches who would marry girls who said, "Imagine!" They would, finally, become their own oppressors, and that was what they had been led to believe they wanted.

There wasn't a goddam thing I could do about it. We were no different from anyone else. We, caught by mountains, were only more so, distilled into parody. The imitation of an oppressor who had thrown out our ancestors was the dark reflection of America.

I told Johnny Church that we would always fail and always win. That, as in a dream solution, satisfied me for the time being. I was sensible enough to know that I would go back to facts and figures in the light of day, escape and go on searching. I also knew, as I lay again in my bed, slowly drifting toward sleep, that I would take Rose and Uncle Ephraim with me in my heart and know them better when I was alone than ever when I was with them. This seemed sage and became the beginning of a dream that I forgot when Rose, dear Rose, bright as if the night had not happened, brought me a white tray with one of her roses, and the Wedgwood my mother had given my grandmother one Christmas because she "needed" it. I called her Grandma at the farm, Grandmother McKarkle at home.

Mother, with a tiny clearing of her throat that usually forecast a story that was more hope than truth, said my Grandmother McKarkle was a Middleburg from Virginia, and added, "You know, Middleburg in Fah'keer county," pronouncing it with care.

But my grandmother said there wasn't a word of truth in that. She said she was of German extraction. "My grandma always said we come down the Shenandoah and across to Dunkard's Valley where the Scotch on the river and the Irish in Irish Trace were more parilous than the Indians. Now she was borned in 1810 and she knowed."

She would say this and my mother would breathe, "knew," faintly. Later she would say that my grandmother's memory was not what it had been.

Late in the morning, Uncle Ephraim and Rose stood on the porch, waving my car away down the slope of the lawn, growing smaller and smaller until the last glimpse of them was as familiar, as unchanged, as the oak trees that finally hid them.

I high-rolled along the Greenbrier levels, past smaller hills, with the sun ahead of me. I drove on into the high savannah where my unsung ancestor Jeremiah Catlett had built his lean-to cabin. It had been called Dunkard's Valley, then Egeria Springs. It lay, surrounded by mountains, like a little Eden.

On both sides of the road, perpetually blue-green golf courses lay under the June sun. Walker's Creek ran out from the mountains, as groomed in the valley as the grass. It no longer swept past high crowded rocks where golf balls could be lost, but purled over a pretty sand and white-pebble bottom, widened into still pools of water, tunneled under pretty rustic bridges, curled around the smooth green mound which was said to be an Indian grave that had hidden the body of Squire Raglan, and now was a hazard making a dog-leg fairway on the sixteenth hole. Over the green fairways, clumps and pairs of figures strolled, at first glance as if they had been there since the last time I saw Egeria, as perpetual as the carpet-soft emerald greens with their bright flags, white-linen people stopping here and there, even the body arc of their drives and their huddled putts slowed down and formal as I passed. It looked as green as luxury.

I had left some wreckage behind me. I knew that, a cruelty of simply being there, a pierced innocence. I also knew that they knew better than I how to heal it. They always had.

It wasn't enough to find out that my brother had behaved like a son-of-a-bitch. Oh no. I had to find out why. I wanted to know how much of a man was what had been done to him, how much was choice, how much was imitation of some old way of living that had lost its force, and I was bound, damned, and determined to find out.

My God, I had traced us through four books, and still it wasn't over, paid my dues, and had been charged again. And I was back where it all began. Surely to God I was ready at last to face the living. I told myself this as I drove. I had come full circle to begin to shake the single event that had started it all, the smash of an unknown fist against an unknown face; as I had told Candy, one man, one fist, one act—an anger all the way to the source.

I raced along the highway, watched for State Police, and sucked lemon drops. I sang with the radio, making more rhymes. "Take a new name, Mame, Never go back, Mac, Go on the lam, Sam." What American, driving alone in a good car on a straightaway, passing two semis, is a forty-eight-year-old woman? Oh no, mean sixteen. "Run run as fast as you can, you can't catch me, I'm the Gingerbread Man. Come on, Johnny, come on, Gingerbread Man, let's get out of here!"

It didn't do any good.

I was finding it harder already to discover what I knew than it had been for eighteen years to seek out what I didn't know. I opened the window wide to the noise of the tires and the hot wind. I made myself slow down and look at the cuts where the road ran between man-blasted cliffs exposing a calendar of fifty million years of raw strata, tier on tier.

High on one of the cliffs someone had whitewashed PREPARE TO MEET THY GOD. It was as faded as hope under a spray-painted, Day-Glow red FUCK THE SYSTEM. Below it the signature *Boogie Head Mama* bled down into the shrubs, planted by the state.

II

Before the Revolution
1960

AUNT Althea, Rose, Uncle Ephraim, Mr. Pagano, the old man at the pool, had told me less than I sought and more than they had intended, all but Candy, who had given me my marching orders. To the women, I had come back as a stranger, to turn over rocks and find out where the body was buried that they had tried to forget, as they would try to forget Charlie Bland, and the loss of houses, and what had been taken away. I had to leave again to see them all clearly, beyond their still, shut faces, beyond the white papers I had thrown into the back seat of the car, Daisy's lumpy, dun-colored macramé, the haft, the notes, speech patterns divorced from air: slack, pea, nut coal, lump coal, rotten top, so much a ton, and my aunt's fury and Rosie's lust left over from old wars. The macramé lay across the papers, looking like a pile of rags. The ruby ring was on my finger. It glinted in the sun as I drove.

I crossed the Virginia border into a decision I knew I had to make. Thankful Perkins had called the road I was traveling the long road to Paradise. If his road had ended in the genes of people in Beulah valley, for me it had begun there, too. I had, at last, to go back to the event, the act that had begun my search, the fury of one unknown fist hitting an unknown face.

I dreaded breaking the news to George as much as he dreaded the results of what he called my "going over the mountains." Sometimes they were physical, self-inflicted atonements of pain, sometimes nightmares that would suddenly cripple me, or what seemed to him a long, sustained self-demanded violence of process. Work on the world I had left behind, but not yet escaped, made me vulnerable to terrors about money, fear of any vestige of the viciously correct manners of arrogant, genteel women that would leave me shaking as in a recurrent fever. I saw those little cruelties as weapons that hurt children and diminished spirit. I had, innocently, carried into my marriage the baggage of old wounds I hardly knew I had. That was what I, and George, who watched me, would have to pay if I sat down and counted the cost of the final and beginning burial of my brother Johnny.

I saw ahead the preoccupation, the self-demand for fountains filled with energy and truth that is the hardest part of writing and the least understood. Few who love books love the process that makes them. Raw, stumbling, obsessed, so fearful of that exchange of energy which is the kiss of social life, so self-protected against the ever-present devil of exhaustion, it can seem as naked and indecent as the larva and pupa stages of the butterfly, with far less certainty that the butterfly will be rare, beautiful, or even complete. I prayed for George's patience and his love; that he would understand that I had no choice but to bury Johnny, my suburban Polynices. I prayed that he would honor the courage it was going to take, and give me once again, as he had before, silence as a gift.

We had both hoped before this last crossing that it was over, but it was not, and I think we both knew that. Within the kindly, protective ignorant bourgeois day, hidden from those who still thought that a woman's work was somehow less important than a man's, I was going to have to shut myself away from all that was most dear and most dearly earned, and study the causes of a man's murder.

It was time to begin again, before the event. I had to go back to 1960, the year that *Town and Country* called the Year of the Poodle. I hoped that I would be able at last to see it as clearly as those other conjured centuries made free for me by time. After all, 1960 was as far from me in June of 1978 as that know-nothing girl I was schooled so carefully to be. I was going to have to try to relive her longings without contempt, and her fashionable unease without judgment, as I had tried to be Peregrine Catlett, slave owner in 1850, wear Lily's disguises in 1912, or face Johnny Church's death in 1649. I knew that I would have more trouble finding compassion with her than I had all the rest, since she was more obviously, though no less truly, myself.

I have no pride in what I was, but I had then. I was, in Aunt Althea's words, the cat's pajamas.

I lived, of course, in New York, a socialist in Bonnie Cashin leather, a radical with a guest list that consisted always of one or two understanding friends from Sweet Briar and their husbands, one black Ph.D. from Columbia, two beats, a junkie somebody from the UN, the publishing children of publishing parents, a few critics, once in a while a writer, and if I was lucky, a jazz musician; oh, and of course, the friends who mirrored what I was, thirty-year-old, carefully brought-up rebellious children. It was understood, looking at us, that we had not a lot of money, but "enough." What it was enough for remained unsaid, but it had to do with recognitions. We knew each other by signs, the way the men used their knees, and the women their shoulders, by our sleek hair and careful eyes, by the people we knew who had committed suicide, by our addresses and our underwear and the causes we supported. We drank a lot for art's sake and were prepared to follow Jack Kerouac all the way to the suburbs. I thought all this was individual at the time. Now I see we were a crop fertilized with money. In my case it came, by devious routes, from a coal-face in West Virginia.

We were the almost married, or some of us had been, but weren't any more. We shared angst in long conversations on telephones. I, too, was brokenhearted. That was understood. It had been my excuse for seven years of drifting. I, too, had been engaged, one of those incestuously approved-of engagements, longed for deep within to assuage a vague demand I hardly questioned then. He had the same name as my father and the same habits as my brother. He disappeared toward the Mohave Desert and exploded himself at a hundred and thirty miles an hour in a 236A Porsche that cost twelve hundred tons of metallurgical coal. He was drunk. It was what we called an accident. It was, then, the most respectable way to die, suicide by accident, preferably in an imported sports car. Everybody, including me, behaved well about it.

Six months after he smashed, he was gone forever from my

not from my excuses. I did then the next expected went to East 65th Street. I had a vague impulse he history of art. I went to lectures at the Pratt Institute and collected notes for a book I never wrote. I would change and refile the notes in box after box, thinking that I was working. It made a décor for my desk.

I wonder if anyone in 1960 knew that an era was at an end. We didn't think of it. The whole complacent world was a wall to bounce opinions against while we lived in its glow. We were the Eisenhower children who stamped their feet at Daddy. We had no way to imagine lives free of that benign confinement. But what we did not bother to imagine had already begun. Quietly in the South, nice black boys with crew cuts sat at Woolworth counters in their best sports jackets while we read novels about alienation or power, and went to Martha's Vineyard. We knew people who knew the Kennedys. Our politics that year were sexual. Angry intelligence, talent rising out of poverty, and being Jewish, were tickets to our beds. We had, to them, some evasive scent of power. We practiced that subtlest form of anti-Semitism. We "loved" Jews because they were Jews, we "loved" poor artists because they were poor. We knocked at their beds, trying to get in. We told about our lovers in the words of their breeds, and we bought their paintings, their magazines, and their fury whenever they would let us, and nobody, but nobody, teased their hair.

Looking back, I have to find some tenderness for that perpetual girl.

We wore black jeans and sloppy black sweaters from Bloomingdale's. Our hair drooped like Juliette Greco's. We were Antonioni's bored black-on-stark-white. We saw ourselves as "white niggers" until it came to the push.

My Petit Trianon that year was the apartment on East 65th Street that I called, echoing the fashionable poor whom I saw as somehow freer than I was, a "walk-up." The stairs were thickly carpeted to keep sound away from the duplex on the first two floors. I had been lucky to find it through a contact at a New York law firm who worked with my father on coal leases.

I remember the living room that had once been a master bedroom. It looked out over the quiet trees of the gardens between 64th and 65th Street. I see now that the carefully disarranged desk, the typewriter I kept free of dust, the low sofas, the black walls, the glass coffee table, the *Paris Review*, *Dissent*, *Commentary*, *Vogue*, and *The New York Times*, the poetry of Allen Ginsberg, were as impersonal a fashion for me that year as the Davidow suits my mother wore like armor, or my older sister Melinda's Bermuda shorts of bleeding madras, her socks to knobby tennis-hard knees, her pink Hathaway shirt, the off-the-forehead height and the flipped ends of her hair.

When I gave my "beat" parties—there seems now to have been a lot of them—I still hear noise in that room of broken glass, and of myself, using the word fuck with a slight pause. It was rumored that Norman Mailer hit somebody there. The word was spread. More people came to my parties after that. They waited, like the Second Coming, for it to happen again.

So two people lived in those three rooms on 65th Street, and they wore two camouflages. One talked the language, slept around a bit but didn't call it that. The other would have stepped over the body of my best friend to obey like a trained rat the demands of any female tyrant who roused in me a reaction to the timbre of my mother's voice. I called it being polite. When she came to New York on the show plane, she stayed at the Plaza. I hid *Howl* in case she popped in, and went into what I called purdah for the time she was there.

Sometimes I hid my diffuse anger under evening dresses and went to the kind of dinner parties my mother told her friends about. I had two, always ready, with cinched waists, one of lace and one of Thai silk.

Sometimes, too often, the two of us got confused. Once, at the party, the one long party in my black living room, a man I didn't know flipped *Vogue* onto the flokati rug from Greece, muttered, "Shiksa!" and advised me to "go down under a Spade." He said it would do me good. I managed a weak, "Imagine!" in my sister Melinda's voice. Once at one of those dinners full of industrial aristocrats with factory names, I found myself defending the UMW, about which I knew almost nothing, except with my furious heart. And it was furious. I'll give it that. But it had reasons that did not communicate to my head except in someone else's words. Afterwards, going home, I whispered, "Meatballs," to the taxi driver's greasy ducktailed hair.

I thought myself aware, and was aware of that, and of a vague yearning for a cause that would invite me in.

That spring I was invited, and it was by my brother

Johnny. If I had a rat's reaction to my mother and my sister in whatever form or echo I found them, I had something else then, the obsession of two rebels in a secret cell, for my brother Johnny. Johnny, I thought, had raised me, bought me my freedom, the freedom of daring places beyond the narrow lit street of our training. I see, when I think of it, discreet and dirty doorways, steps always going down, secret friends, bourbon in dirty glasses, the Wayfaring Stranger, the alley beside it down to the water where the river rats chittered or ran over our feet. It was my careless brother Johnny who told me to come back to West Virginia and work for John Kennedy. "The Kennedys," he said, "are out to buy the state. Senator Kennedy wants to be President. It ought to be a ball." So I went back, knowing as little as Kennedy's advance men about what local politicians called "the road to Mullins."

Oh, I knew facts. I read them in the paper. At Christmastime that year, there had been two parties that each cost five thousand dollars at the new Country Club. I remember oases of bare shoulders, beehive hair, girdled waists, and evening dresses with huge whispering skirts, dinner jackets with narrow black ties, and a fountain of champagne. Outside the city limits of Canona, beyond the high walls of hills and money, the county had just been declared a depressed area. The news made my father and Uncle Sugar Baseheart furious. They said it gave the state a bad name. They stood near the fifteen-foot Christmas tree with its gold ornaments and Uncle Sugar said, under the music, "We're running more coal out of the state than we ever did." I heard him. I was near them, teaching my cousin Brandy to boogie.

When John Kennedy was due at Canona airport in April, we met him with every sports car we could muster to show him we were not a backward state. I drove the Sunbeam Alpine, Melinda and Spud's second car. Johnny drove his Porsche. We didn't get near the airport. The hillbillies in their two-toned Fords and pickup trucks had been there since dawn. I didn't know until later that the crowd was planned. I stood up on the seat and caught a glimpse of a close-packed group of men, struggling through a crowd that surged forward among the television cameras. I saw one of them waving. It must have been John Kennedy.

It was all as chaotic as that. We, Democrat ladies, hung around the headquarters as avid as the "jumpers" in their curlers and their Dacron pants, to get near the Candidate, address envelopes, telephone, and when we were chosen, drive cars in motorcades. My sister Melinda worked beside me. It had become the thing to do. She said the Kennedys would bring style to the White House at last. She said it was all right once again to be a Democrat because John Kennedy was one of us. It was all heady and unthinking and exhausting.

Johnny, having lured me home, laughed at the whole thing. I told him it was the first time I had felt at home there in years. "I thought you would," he told me.

"Imagine me working with a bunch of silk-stocking Democrats!" I wanted him to laugh at that too, but he said it was better to be a silk-stocking Democrat and be guilty than to not be and be envious. Then, having got me there, he went, as usual, to his secret places, and left me to it.

We discussed the campaign as if we were running it. We laughed at the "Four F's" of the campaign plan—"The Flag, Food, Family, and Franklin D. Roosevelt." We knew things about the Kennedys that weren't made public. I, like the rest, had a heady crush on John F. Kennedy. Around me, in the crowded, yelling headquarters, the women began to wear their hair like Jackie's, and tight belts that had cinched waists for all the feminine years of Eisenhower disappeared behind over blouses and boxed jackets as if they had been suddenly declared illegal. It had all the atmosphere of getting ready for the Junior League Follies. Decisions drifted over me. I felt the taste of glue in my mouth, and faced the Catholic issue head-on, as we were instructed to.

The kind of young men I was used to walked fast through the mailroom in their white shirts and new slightly longer hair, talking to each other about unemployment and the Candidate.

Somebody brought in a copy of *Maria Monk* that he said had been mailed around to the coal towns. Somebody else found a letter that said that Catholics split open the bellies of Protestant women. Flurries of rumor, "they" were tearing down Kennedy posters, "they" were telling people the Pope would be in the White House. Rumor looks big at the center. We knew what was "out there." Out there were houses with pictures of Jesus, John L. Lewis, and Franklin Delano Roosevelt, and hillbillies who hated the Whore of Babylon, the Catholic Church. Somebody got the bright idea of bringing in the Roosevelt who looked most like his father and riding him around the coal towns. We were advised to wear sneakers and old clothes so we wouldn't look too rich. We spread the word that anybody who voted against Kennedy was a bigot.

None of it mattered.

The only chance I had to be a driver in a motorcade was on a Wednesday in mid-April. I couldn't sleep the night before. I was afraid of not waking at six o'clock.

At six-thirty in the morning, four convertibles, lent by Potter Chevrolet, started slowly up the south side of the river. I drove the fourth car. I remember mist on the water that morning and mountains that were the new yellow-green of spring. Two reporters from somewhere in the Midwest sat in the front seat beside me. They had come to report on the Catholic issue. I don't even remember their faces. In the back seat four more reporters were packed in; they smelled of nylon shirts washed out in hotel bathrooms, whiffs of cynicism and cigarettes. Morning lingered over us. We went slowly up the empty road. I could see the back of the Candidate's head. He sat beside his brother in the first car. In the second car Franklin Roosevelt, Jr., sat with a man who somebody in the back seat said was a columnist from *The New York Times*.

All the way up the river we stopped on a hand signal from the Candidate's car. I remember an old man standing beside the road. He was waiting to cross. The Candidate jumped out and shook hands with him. A photographer from the front car took a picture. We passed a stultified face I don't forget, a man in overalls, seventy years old or more. He looked shocked. He had had a dinner bucket in his hand, but he put it on the ground to have his picture taken and shake hands. When I glanced back through the rearview mirror, he was still standing there watching after us, the dinner bucket tipped over in the weeds.

We turned up a creek road, through a railroad underpass. I could hear the creek whispering. The mountains were so close to each other that we passed through a tunnel of trees and cliffs. On one side the blasted rock showed a faint seam of coal. For two miles we went, as slowly as we had on the highway, but this time it was to avoid potholes in the old blacktop. The motorcade went deeper, deeper into the narrow corridor. There wasn't a soul about.

Up ahead I saw a break in the trees. The first car stopped beside the road. We parked behind it. I had been told to stay near my car so there would be no time lost. "No time lost" was repeated, over and over. So the first time I saw the Lacey Creek of Aunt Althea's stories, it was from a distance. The creek, with a deserted railroad spur built high above it, crossed a bowl of a valley. On the opposite hill I saw a house that had been white sometime. There was no glass in its windows. Its broken porch roof sagged under wild vines. Near the creek there were Jenny Lind shacks, some half-fallen in, a few with washing hanging on lines. All of it seemed sunk in an undertow of desertion. The roads were black with old coal dust. Over the door of a dead cinder-block building with no roof, across the road, was a dim sign, *Odd Fellows Hall*. Someone had written on the wall, THIS WAY TO THE RAT-HOLE, with a black arrow, pointing down.

One of the reporters said, "Jesus!"

It was a valley of winter-desiccated shit, rusting cars, bare gray boards, and dusty weeds. Windows were boarded with cut up cardboard packing cases. I read GENERAL ELECTRIC on one of them. At the few houses that were still lived in, chickens scratched the hard ground. It was a graveyard of old car parts, a half-tire swing on a tree branch, sprung back seats on the stoops. Behind the nearest house a failed shed sagged, made from scrap wood, unfinished, as if whoever had begun it had lost the will to go on. Against the hill beside us, an old streetcar sank in weeds, walled up with tin signs, Imperial Ice Cream, Royal Crown Cola, Stanback for Pain, Chesterfield, Philip Morris, Ringling Brothers Circus, Red Man, Bull Durham.

Over the long-gone door hung Escew's Diner Coca-Cola, and a small round Public Telephone. On the broken pavement beside it there was a gas pump with a faded Esso sign. It seemed to be where American companies came to die.

Down the dirt road in the distance I could see them, walking slowly, John Kennedy and his brother Robert and Franklin Roosevelt, Jr., all in clean white sneakers, looking isolated and small under an empty April sky.

Fifteen minutes must have passed before a few people came slowly out of the houses that were still alive. They lingered on the stoops as shy as animals. All this was tiny in the distance. I saw one man come down to his fence, then another, and another. It took half an hour for the Candidate to gather enough people to make a speech to. I heard a reporter say, "Boy, somebody goofed."

I wondered, even at the time, if they had. I have never

been more ashamed than I was at that moment. I hadn't known. Oh, I had passed by people like them sometimes, walking along Mosby Street on Saturday afternoons. Maybe, for us, a sense of shame that stirs what is left of our old Puritan genes is the beginning of wisdom. I don't know. I only know I was ashamed for strangers to see us like that. I am aware now that I had never said "us" before, even to myself.

One of the reporters from the front seat had been following the little group. He ran back down the road, and told his photographer, "Don't bother. No speech. He's just talking and listening and he looks mad as hell. He's calling them Jim and Joe and you've got all that. One thing he said that was new." The reporter looked at his notebook, and read, "'This is as distressed an area as I have ever seen.' Come on," he said. "Let's go. Kennedy didn't even mention the Catholic issue."

In the distance I saw the Candidate standing beside a one-armed miner, having his picture taken. That was as near as I ever got to them, the only time I drove. We went that morning for twenty miles up Lacey Creek, stopping, starting, stopping.

"He ain't going to win," one of the men in the back seat prophesied.

It was not like that later. By late April the Candidate had caught on. There were triumphal processions. He was treated like a movie star. He rode past the quiet, cragged faces of men in white shirts, work pants, and Stetson hats, and their wives and daughters who jumped for the television cameras and screamed their Elvis Presley screams and tried to touch him. That I only saw on television, and I knew from the gossip at headquarters that much of it had been choreographed—small halls, little streets—packed so that five hundred people overflowed the space and looked, on television, like a mob.

But I still see the two brothers, with a simulacrum of Franklin Delano Roosevelt, walking along a dirt road alone on Lacey Creek, under an empty April sky.

Kennedy won the primary by a landslide. At the victory party we saw him step up on the platform in front of the microphone while we watched Jackie's hat. The back-slapping and the noise stopped. We stood packed body to body. He read a statement: "West Virginia has tonight given me a major boost toward the Democratic nomination for President." He thanked Jackie, and his brothers, "and all my cousins," and we laughed and slapped and cheered and didn't for that little while feel like single people. The sweat ran down my arms and I hugged Melinda. Johnny wasn't there. I kept looking for him, as I always had.

In mid-May I went back to New York. It was there that I heard that Kennedy's father had sent him a telegram that read, "I promised to buy you a state not a landslide." There were other versions, other jokes about the primary in West Virginia. I laughed at them all. It seemed important, in 1960, to laugh at the right time.

That's how Johnny got me to come back, whenever he demanded it, and usually the return itself assuaged a loneliness that I prided myself that only I could touch. From this far away I see, alas, that that too had an element of fashion, a princely sense of Anglo-Saxon sadness. We were rebels in red convertibles seeking inexpensive causes, a sleeping princess, a wounded Ivanhoe.

It had not occurred to anyone that year, least of all to us, that Johnny, at thirty-six, and I, at thirty, were too old for this; rebellion had set into habit. So I, too, was caught in the legend, and the protective dream of the brother as wounded in some secret war, as incomplete. When he snapped his fingers I ran to help complete him.

If rebellion and rescue had set into old habits, so had sex. Johnny said that our mother spelled sex with an "H." He was wrong. She didn't spell it at all. Sex was never very important to Johnny and me, except as a weapon. We had been taught to use that weapon to "marry well," or, in secret, to use the illusion of loss to take what we wanted. I see now that we were both sexual raiders, bushwhackers. Desire we saw as weakness, and that weakness had been leached out of us by long taboo. Such feelings were for darkness, strangers to our family, secret rooms, and into those secret rooms we took people who, as my mother pointed out, didn't have our background. We were taught by deletion never never to discuss or act on sex at home unless, of course, it was used to win more money. That was called love, and it was for sunny afternoons, and nice people, and plans, and what we saw as traps. Neither Johnny nor I ever made love to anybody at our parents' house, anyway not when we were sober. It would have been unthinkable.

But if Johnny and I were not good at sex—except that we were evocative as sin to those who tried to "wake" us and wipe the sadness away—we made a profession of post-coital tristesse. If I am cruel to the memory of us, we had one redemption. We didn't know. We were people who took themselves for granted.

All that summer I would hear from Johnny out of whatever night he thought of me, but it wasn't until Labor Day weekend that he said the magic words again: "Come on down here, Sissy, I need you."

When the telephone rang in my bedroom in New York at one o'clock in the morning on the Saturday night before Labor Day, I knew at once who it was. I didn't want to answer it. Carlo Tarmino. I haven't thought of him in years, and I have trouble remembering what he looked like. Oh, yes, I see him, as that night with the light of 65th Street across his sleeping face, and then, his eyes flying open. Carlo was from Brooklyn, and beat as he was, a one o'clock phone call still triggered disaster. Carlo had moved in with me during the summer, and had turned the end of my living room into a studio. His paintings were abstract and very large. As soon as Carlo was awake, he, too, seemed to know who it was.

It was embarrassing to lie there listening to that intruding ring. I let it ring five times, while we both watched the reflection from the streetlamp below my apartment washing the ceiling, and wished Johnny would give up. Carlo held my hand as if that could stop me, held it harder until he hurt me, but I finally drew it away and turned on the lamp, as we both knew I would.

Even then, just for a second, I wasn't going to answer. The phone kept on ringing, insistent, demanding. I stopped it with my hand and then was against its receiver, drawing a sheet around me to hide myself from Carlo and the light.

I heard the quarters tolling. Johnny called, "Hello there, fellah," sounding far away, turned away from the telephone, wherever he was, on his Saturday-night joy ride, taking the fact that it was I for granted. As I sank back on my pillow into that trance no one could break, Johnny's voice engulfed me from five hundred miles away over the mountains and in the nest of Canona.

Carlo said, "Oh, for Christ's sake, Hannah."

I held the telephone in my palm to protect it from his intruding noise and whispered, "Shut up."

He got up from beside me. I heard his bare feet shuffling across the floor. I didn't see him go into the living room, but I heard him put on a record of Erik Satie. It sounded thin and pure and out of place.

Johnny said, "Hannah, are you asleep?"

I asked first, as we all had a thousand times, "Are you all right, Johnny?" I had been asking that since I was six and had already begun the mother-worry of a trusted little sister. Even at twelve years old, Johnny was as elusive as a grouse.

He just laughed and answered, "Come on down here, Sissy, I need you," but he said it as if it were a casual invitation to be received in sense and memory, needing no space or time, or decision. Five hundred miles away in West Virginia, Johnny was commanding me from a telephone booth. When I knew which one, I would know how far he had gone in his night, that hot night where between the rich brownstones of 65th Street no air moved and the stillness inside the room was fetid with city breath.

"Where are you?" I asked softly, partly to keep my voice away from Carlo's disapproval. I heard him go into the kitchen. I could hear ice rattling, whether from Johnny's drink in the booth or from Carlo's I neither knew nor cared. The sounds met in my head.

Now, in the kitchen, I knew I was becoming "us," rolling in Carlo's angry mind toward "they." At such times he hated us. I knew he was feeding one of his dark red furies by sleeping with "an upper-class American bitch." I had no quarrel with that. My politics were sexual, too.

The door to the refrigerator shut.

"You should have seen me in my bunny suit. I was yum-yum . . . !" Johnny was at the time of night when he broke into the middle or the distillation of a story, expecting me to see the rest for myself. Usually I did. We had traveled for so long through the same past. But this story of the bunny suit he would have to be drawn to earth to tell.

"What bunny suit?"

"Hell, honey, you know." It annoyed him to be reminded that I was not always there, like an imp on his shoulder, watching and whispering, as he was imp on mine. I sensed in his voice the wit at the edge of despair that showed he had reached a stage of urgency in his drinking.

There was a long silence. The connection sang a single, thin note. I waited.

"I have"—his thin voice at my ear was factual—"a hat full of quarters. A goddam Chipp straw hat full of quarters."

"The bunny suit?" The bedroom door opened. Carlo tried to catch my eye. The music was a tinkle of falling glass in the room.

"What the hell is that?" my brother demanded. "It sounds like crap to me."

"Oh, don't go into your good ole boy act, Johnny. You know it's Satie. You gave me the record for Christmas for Christ's sake. Come on—the bunny suit." I wanted Carlo to hear me say that, not, at that night minute in the heat and being drawn back toward Johnny, knowing or considering why.

Carlo closed the door, carefully. Now I see his face, intelligent and thin, with hard blue eyes lighter than his skin. He had picked up a deep tan with me on the Vineyard.

"Hey, you know how I spent the goddamn morning?" Johnny was getting ready to tell me, share his hatful of quarters and his Saturday night—religious holiday over America, "Irish" night, "fun" night, the night for a man to fight free to the surface of his life, not caring how he did it or what he dragged up and let fly.

"Your three minutes are up," the soft mountain twang of the operator interrupted.

"Wait a minute, honey," Johnny told her, forgetting me. There were more bells of quarters. "Now for God's sake don't interrupt me," he commanded coldly.

"You know what today is, Hannah? It's Operation Spaceman. We all had to wear space helmets to talk on the goddamn telephone. Cover a lot of space through space. Telephone—get it? At nine o'clock this morning I was sitting in the goddam office in a goddam baby helmet, so help me, made out of blue sateen with a couple of wire rabbits' ears for antennae with little red knobs on the goddam ends."

I laughed, obedient.

"Ten of us on the telephone with these little old red balls bobbing every time we got in there butting our heads against some guy in a company store didn't have any customers left anyway. Special sale today. Jesus, Hannah, ten grown men hooked up like that to make us get in there. Sell. Get in there..."

His voice faded as he leaned away from the mouthpiece. "Charley!"

I knew where he was then. He had reached the Wayfaring Stranger, that juke joint crouched under Canona bridge where you could get sour bourbon in small dirty glasses and Custer's Last Stand was on the wall, courtesy of Budweiser. Charley, the fat ex-GI owner, tended his own bar and listened to all of us. He told me one night how at forty-five he was going through college in the daytime because his schoolteacher wife from upriver kept calling him a slob every time she got mad. "Man, does that dry hillbilly bitch get in my thirsty craw!" he had ended his story. "Man, did she loosen up when the war was on. Fooled the hell out of me."

Johnny wasn't drunk enough yet to call him "student," which Charley took from him with professional goodwill.

"Hannah, you still there?" Johnny came back, knowing I was. "So there I was this morning talking to this guy to keep him from hanging up on me. I could hear my voice and see myself and it wasn't my voice and it wasn't myself in the goddam cheap obscene blue sateen. I could see myself... oh, hell, goodbye, honey."

He hung up, ignoring the time he had paid for. I sank the telephone into its cradle in the pool of light under my bedside lamp. Heat lay over me like an incubus.

From the living room the nervous little control of Satie still twinkled from my hi-fi. I could hear Carlo set a glass down. I knew that any movement would be toward quarreling of one kind or another. The heat and then the telephone had set a charge. We both waited, I so near asleep, so not caring that I won the waiting, and Carlo came in, swimming through the heaviness, his face blanked of intelligence by the aphrodisiac of fury.

Out of heat and need he said, "Don't answer it again."

"I won't," I told him, but we both knew I would. Then I said, "Come here to me," a good sport, with that habit phrase women use to call all hurt children to be petted, all bad children to be whipped, a phrase for children out of a woman's mouth, but a woman disguised in a thin boy's body, a 1960 body—still providing the demanded bone and flesh. In another time I would have had larger breasts, great thighs,

the pink bite wounds of whalebone stays. Carlo caught my
pale honey-dyed hair as if it were waterweeds.

He dived down, holding my hair, his head rose from my
neck to breathe once, and reflect the light in his dry hard
eyes. He struggled against me, heavy and impersonal, then
back into the killing safety of my water, at the erect point of
fear, striking out, not giving a damn for that minute that I
wasn't there.

One night in my parents' house set sentinel on the hill
above Canona, at the persistently polite time of dinner, that
daily acted scene with the family where no one spoke the
truth at table, it being, by the rules of my mother's whip-run
house, a "peaceful, pleasant interlude" for all of us, Johnny
and I had watched each other through the yellow candlelight,
and I knew he wanted to get over the genteel wall, away from
the faces we assumed as if there were a disapproving guest
watching us all. I knew he wanted me to tag along, saying
nothing. I never knew when he would go. He had been down
the talking mouths of easy men and women when he wandered,
down to jukebox chapels below the main street of Canona, up
long narrow stairs to bars unrecognized during his blue-plate,
white-goods salesman days or in my mother's house.

I think now he kept that job instead of "going into"
insurance or banking as most of his friends did who were of
that carefully chosen array of privileged men without profes-
sions and obsession, to pay my mother back for her demands
on him. Any hint of his leaving her house, even his boyhood
bed, brought on a siege of brokenhearted silence.

But those accepting, yawning, secret dens, the Raccoon
Club, the Wildcat, the Wayfaring Stranger, drew him in,
becalmed him, as more intense men with less laughter are
becalmed by easy sex. He was away, with me tagging along
after him as I had done all my life, a little sister as trained as
one of the dogs. The loveless dry people we saw in the light
at the dinner table, their lips pinched, then closed, as if even
a childish yawn let the devil in, made him feel dirty, depraved. This I caught from him, how they fouled and hurt the
angel in us; he never knew, as I would have to learn, that it
was his own evasiveness which had long since dried their
mouths. He would slip secretly toward freedom, diver too,
quick killer, deep, not a free man, only a rebel.

"Oh, Jesus, oh, Christ," Carlo whispered.

He reached his climax as the telephone rang.

I sobbed with laughter.

It rang again. Carlo couldn't stop. He swore in gouts of words. It rang again. Carlo ran naked to the living room and slammed the door as if the telephone had questing eyes.

Of course I picked it up, and heard the quarters plunk, Johnny knowing I would be there and answer, dependable.

"Hey, fellah." The thin, faraway voice of Johnny was as close as my ear. "I've got a friend of ours here. Wai' minute." He turned from the telephone and I could hear a swish of a late-night car passing and knew he had wandered by now into the booth under the green fog lights of the Boulevard.

"Broker!"

I could hear them arguing.

To find Anderson Carver, he would have been down to the river. By this time Johnny's movements through the town of Canona were as formal as a ballet. He would have gone up on the bridge to watch the black water shining between the city lights on its banks, where long snakes of mirrored light in the water wriggled away in the distance toward high mountains he could not see but only sense by the cool breath that came down from the eastern gorge even on still, hot nights. He would trace the river from the fog lights, all the way up to its great bend above Canona where they turned, hidden by rising hills. From his center on the bridge the pinpoint glow of Canona's night houses splayed out through the valley and up the hills to either side of him. In the town behind the Boulevard that had been River Street, the flood-lit white thin tower of the Methodist church thrust up above the black roofscape. Beside the river loomed the dark monolith of the Coal Banking and Trust Building where Johnny had sat that morning, trying to sell televisions, or dishwashers, or what electric dreams he could, in his blue bunny suit. At Christmas the twenty stories of its windows were lit to form a gold cross that dominated the winter sky above the valley and swam huge in the flowing water. In summer the building was a dull shadow moved by the current.

But after he stood there for a while, the river always drew him nearer, down the long steps beside the Wayfaring Stranger, where if he lurched and fell the black water would claim him. It was as if for a priceless minute the shadows, the neglected beer cans, even the river, could suspend their meaning and be there, to be watched with the same unfearing love and as deliberately as when he was a child, ready to swim in the dirty water against our father's express command. At the times of his wanderings when I wasn't with him, I would wake in the night, at school, abroad, shut in my bedroom, dreaming as vividly as if I were awake that he had fallen, seeing the water close over him, and dream myself under it, drawn down, downriver, through a tunnel of darkness. I would wake up, tears bursting from my eyes; wherever I was, I would wake up and be back there with him on those steep concrete stairs.

Once at their base he stooped down, where the water was no longer black but rich undulating purple and blue, heavy with coal wash and chemicals from the upriver factories. He forgot me and watched his face, so like mine we could have been in that darkness reflections of twins. He was intent on his face forming and re-forming in the water, now dancing, a grotesque parody, now destroyed by a floating beer can; once a catfish surfaced the water into his reflected eyes. My face was mirrored, high over his shoulder, smaller, worried, waiting for his mood to bring him back away from the bank.

On that Saturday he had already been there if Broker was with him. I could hear them arguing. Broker's voice called out: "Hell, she don't want to talk to me, son."

Anderson Carver had gotten the name Broker in the twenties when, riding high, wide, and handsome on the Carvers' war profits, he gambled on wildcat gas wells, as if it took too long to mine the black gold for his needs. Those quick strong geysers of fortune the killing country offered to men who would take flyers let him down time after time. Where luckier men had tapped gas, Broker had tapped salt water—brine, once the fortune of the valley, now a disaster. He had turned from gas to the stock market, his money had swelled, grown huge, burst in 1929 when he was staying at the Biltmore after a Princeton football game. He had gotten off the C&O train at Canona station four days later, drunk. He never was sober again, but suicide by alcohol lasts for years. His gaunt, frail frame still carried life and hard-earned prejudice Johnny and I thought of as wisdom. At least Aunt Mamie Wilson recognized his existence, if only for once a year. His other Carver sister ran the library and didn't speak to him. She lived in the Carver house on River Street, next door to us before it burned. On the wall of her bedroom was a framed yellow letter from Carrie Chapman Catt.

Until the knowledge of Canona's one door-slamming sin was brought in on us by experience, we didn't know what it was that made Broker like a man already dead, shut out of people's minds. Money disaster had a phrase: You ran through every last cent. I could see people fleeing down Mosby Street, running through it, shoveling money, until they threw the last cent, and having committed the unpardonable sin, they were stripped as if they had shed their clothes, left naked, turned away from, cut from the minds, except in moral stories or in late-night memories. Money could be joked about, as sex was, but if mentioned seriously—a breach of form all the way to the soul—it was in low tones of awe or crisis or disaster, sending the room temperature down as once the admonition of Jehovah had, or the defeats of war in the same houses. But on the whole we were taught that money, like sex, its twin taboo, was something far below the more important things in life. What those things were we were left to find out for ourselves.

I could hear Johnny still arguing with Broker.

Carlo started the Satie record again in the living room. He turned it up. I held both sounds and was with Broker and Johnny, when I was eighteen, Johnny and I in evening clothes, lolling on the pissed-on weeds of the riverbank under Canona bridge, where Broker and his friends drank wine and threw the bottles at imaginary fish in the strong, dirty river. He told us the belly side of the whole town's history with that incisive bitterness of a man with no more to lose. He wore a suit of Johnny's—what we called a cad check from Brooks Brothers. Wine stains and dry snot decorated its curled lapels.

"Now, here's what they ought to do." He looked at Johnny, and the fog lights caught the deep runnels of his face. "They ought to bring the National Guard in here and take over. Just take over, lock, stock, and barrel. They ought to drain the coal out of this river. There's a fortune in this river—a goddam fortune. They ought to just string a hydraulic net across, up around Beulah, easy as taking candy from a baby. Nobody knows how to run this damn valley." He hawked and spat in the river.

"I sound like a Red. Goddamit, I am a Red. They ought to just march in and take over." His dull eyes glistened, and he looked up at Aunt Mamie Wilson's house against the sky in the distance on the opposite hill, shining with the lights of a party Johnny and I had run away from. "Bunch of Wop rednecks, union bastards." He forgot he was a Red. "I told 'em so at Princeton in oh-eight . . ."

"And about these flying saucers." He dropped into the language he had spoken for thirty years below the bridge. "They ought to . . . You believe in flying saucers? By God, I do. Them little green fellers are goin' to land right on this here river and take over."

I could see Broker and Johnny there in the dark, with the reflective water casting a sliding light across their faces.

Now the music of Satie was louder. Carlo had opened the door and looked into the bedroom. I started to hang up but he slammed the door again.

"Broker can't come to the phone. He has to pee," Johnny told me.

"Aw, don't tell Hannah that, you son-of-a-bitch, that's dirty." Broker's graveled voice was hollow in space beyond the telephone.

"Johnny, where have you been?" I wanted to know what had started the drunken search through Saturday night, which would end as blankly as it always did—what flick of yearning, which wrong memory, the clanging of what doors against his yearned-for freedom.

"It's Labor Day weekend, honey, and we're all in labor. Old Dan Tucker he got drunk, fell in the far, and he kicked out a hunk . . ." Johnny deflated. "Hell, *you* know where I've been. Goddamn club dance."

When mines beyond the north hills of Canona opened, five miles from the old Slingsby mansion, which had been the Country Club as long as I could remember, the members began to complain of the sulfur fumes from the growing slag heap away down one of the hollows, which by some ironic trick of prevailing wind would send its smell to permeate the terrace and the ballroom. Every morning the black servants would wipe red dog off the white windowsills and the gilt chairs, muttering to themselves.

So, two years before, the Country Club had been moved across the river to what the women called, with bright-eyed garden-club excitement, the unspoiled section of the southern hills. I always wondered if the women knew what they were saying.

Now the new golf course stretched in long fingers across the hogback ridges. In the center, at the head of a long hollow with a running creek which emptied into the river, a new clubhouse had been built. It was the first "modern" building in Canona. Looking out of its huge glass front, across the wide terrace, you could see in the distance a vague star cluster of Canona's lights between the dark hills.

Everything was brought over—oh, not the gilt chairs or the fine marble and mahogany bar, or the stone fireplace or the paneling in the great hall. The women were already blackmailing money out of the city to make the mansion into a children's museum, where, until the house was condemned, the children would suffer a long line of cute, historically invalid, exhibitions.

No, what was brought to the new clubhouse were the table arrangements for dinner, for dances, the mark of people, sets, crowds, adding, fusing, subtracting sometimes out of a quarrel or a marriage unsanctioned by the women, but with a still unchanging center made by accepted barriers of age and kinship.

That never altered. Years should mean growth, the marring and reordering of change, but the face of Canona Country Club, like the faces of some of its women, seemed only to weather and shrink.

It is hard now, from so far away, to remember any single night; they meld together under the terrace trees, the guttering of candles in the night wind, the tables covered with setups, melted ice, dirty glasses, baskets with scraps of potato chips, Camels and Chesterfields and Philip Morris. There is dancing, that would never have changed if I hadn't stopped, left for too long, and returned, so that I noticed the marks of time. They were Melinda's "crowd," women who had begun as slim and lovely and ten years older than me. They were twenty and I was ten and I looked up, accepting their wildness and their wit, tinged with the influence of sophisticated comedies, the elegance of more riches someplace else, and the end of Prohibition.

Then I was twenty and they were thirty and we sat at the same table under a sliver of moon that slid behind the tall pines and the same candles flickered and they were beginning to strain toward a recapture of delight. The women wore the same tight helmets of hair, the same flow and scent of evening clothes, but there was more bourbon and late at night the voices were edged, and the men had come back from war withdrawn and patient with the women. Then I was twenty-nine, the year 1959, and some of the women were in their forties and their necks showed tendons of strain and the men had slipped into a mutual solace. I heard a woman say, "Sensational!"

They had grown into a habitual kindness with each other, but they did not know it; they only would have agreed, if anyone said anything, which they didn't of course, that, outside of some nameless disappointment, nothing had changed at all.

"Jesus, just like last year..." Johnny's voice called me back now to the bedroom on 65th Street, beyond it to Labor Day of the year before. It is urgent that I recall it.

My sister Melinda Cutright, and her best friend Haley Potter, whose closeness was made up not of a meeting of minds but of wills, had arranged the table as usual and everyone around it. No one had ever cared or fought. Anyone who had fought Melinda had long since stopped. Certainly we had. On weekends she and Spud, her husband, entertained friends—whom Johnny and I always called "important people from Ohio." I never knew Melinda and Spud to entertain anyone without some reason. Their guests were always important, and we were always briefed ahead of time, as my mother had briefed us as children, on who to "be nice to."

On that night the year before, Melinda had told me to sit at their table for a while, saying, "You can join your own age group later." My skin had crawled. I had come back to be with Johnny and I had no intention of being shunted off.

The men moved easily in white jackets and the women in the expensive wide-skirted dresses they had bought so carefully for the last dance of summer. We swept in a noisy phalanx across the wide terrace, where the tables were lit with huge candles protected by glass cylinders. Our table overlooked the hollow to the valley and the flood-lit pool below the terrace. It was all so familiar that it hypnotized me for a while; we were lulled by the lovely night and the formal banter of the party where over and over the men at the table were chanting, "Sweeten your cup? You can't fly on one wing," while Sambo Johnson's aging band played "Slow Boat to China." They looked so bland, well fed, the men. Then I was shocked awake to the real time again. In the candlelight Kitty Puss lurched against my shoulder and whispered, "See, Hannah, we're still committing suicide in a cultural Sahara Desert"—and laughed. She followed Maria toward the ladies' room.

By the time I turned around to the table again there was perpetual Brandy, looking over the valley without seeing it, John Boy pouring a drink, and beyond him Plain George Potter—flirting heavily with the important wife from Ohio, a form of hospitality for all female visitors. The remark had isolated me. I suspected that some of them knew what was happening. In a conspiracy of silence they were letting the pretenses of the night flower to satisfy the women. They seemed not to give a damn. Charlie Bland asked the wife from Ohio to dance, leaned down to her as if it were a sweeter proposition. She got up and stumbled against her chair.

At the end of the table Melinda; her forehead reflecting candlelight was wet with whiskey she could drink all evening without losing control. She was instructing Haley Potter about Picasso. She was conquering Picasso that year, between golf and Goren, with much the same drive and cold correctness. Daisy kept trying to interrupt.

"Of course you wouldn't want him in the *house*," I heard her say, staring through the candlelight at Melinda. "I mean you wouldn't want to *live* with him." Tall, awkward Haley listened to them both and nodded, agreeing seriously.

Across the table my brother-in-law, Spud Cutright, was talking earnestly to the man from Ohio, who had sunk easily into his chair as if all the country clubs were the same in the same dull, groomed world.

There was a sense of something wrong, of demands stirring in the pines. Johnny had been put beside a new divorcée Melinda had picked up on Nantucket. He was being gallant, obedient to Melinda, who had whispered to me, "I think he's interested . . . Cornstalk Collieries." On that aging, drunken head, the floodlights from the pool below catching her weathered skin, lay Cornstalk Collieries. I wanted to laugh—or run from her ravaged face, her pink cotton-candy hair. She looked a living proof that you can be too rich and too thin.

As if he sensed it, Johnny caught my eye again, begging me to be still. He went on listening to her, wearing his expected face, teasing with his tender, sadistic watchfulness, hearing nothing she said.

Later in the night there were the usual gusts of quarreling between Plain George and his wife, Ann Randolph. Melinda's voice had a steel edge as she began to arrange where we would go. A fat man I didn't know took me aside and told me a dirty story about an impotent man and a whore in a motel. He told me because I had been away and so "would get this one," as if the world beyond the hills were compounded of easy sex and glittering free beds. It was a barbershop joke, the kind he wouldn't have told his wife. Under the lovely bowl of night in the candlelight under the dark trees, I felt sick.

Johnny rescued me. "Melinda says we're going there," he said. His eyes were haggard with boredom. I started to turn away but he caught my arm. "Oh, for God's sake, Sissy, don't rock the boat," he ordered me. Behind him the latest of Melinda's chosen women sat watching his back. She had dropped into hopeful, childish sadness and let her thighs yawn with need.

I knew I would go and not complain. Later I remember holding the divorcée's head while she was sick and moaning. In between retchings she told me about the "loss" of her husband; the whiskey had made her too soft, too vulnerable, for any reserve. In a tired language none of the others spoke, she was trusting me.

As if Melinda sensed it, although I said nothing (we never *said* anything), she pulled me out of her frail bedroom, leaving the woman alone, and muttered, "Every time you come back you get Johnny all upset."

Things, I could see, were not moving according to her plan. They never quite had, but she had tried for years. "If you had listened to me," she would say when anything went wrong. Melinda was right. She was always right. I thought of Broker, who would end his stories, "It's not right, Johnny, but it's true."

I looked at the clock on my Japanese chest—one-thirty on Sunday morning—suddenly realizing that the record had stopped in the living room and that I could not hear Johnny.

"Johnny?"

"I'm here, Hannah." His voice was as soft and calm as morning, as if he had been sitting cold-sober in the booth, waiting for me to speak.

"What are you doing?" I asked him.

"Oh, thinking. There's a twelve-barge stern-wheeler going by. Why didn't you come down, honey? I needed you—" He tried to capture the freedom of the night again. He sang. "Let's get stinkin like old Abe Lincoln," and then, "Goddammit, Hannah, what are you doing up there?"

Then it *had* ended with the need turning into begging from Melinda's trapped widow, that one or another one. There had been so many trotted before Johnny, with one thing in common, the smell of money. I had seen that supplication on the faces of wives, the yearning for the uncaught man, the demand of his secret.

I had seen Charlie Bland depraved by the same incessant attention, but it seemed then not to hurt Johnny; I thought then that he escaped it on his night routes that no one had followed except me. Now I know that impotent rebellion is a form of slavery. At least it was with Johnny.

"Sissy—you came down last year."

"Was it bad tonight?"

"Jesus, the usual . . . Important . . ."

"People from Ohio." I helped him finish.

"I start out in a goddam bunny suit and end up a call boy." Suddenly he was drunk again. "Why the hell didn't you come? Up there with that bunch of perverts."

"Oh, for God's sake, Johnny, not chauvinism from you!"

"Wait a minute! That's a Monday-morning word, this here's Saturday night. Sweet, sweet Saturday, not a woman in sight. Can't *nobody* find me. Mother and Father are at Egeria Springs."

"Why?"

"Mother needed the rest." His voice was dutiful as if he were saying his catechism.

I wanted to yell at him, "You told me, Johnny, you told me yourself. 'Little Sissy,' you said, 'run for it. Get in a little convertible prairie schooner and go West'"—as if he had known something he couldn't tell me without having to tell himself—but I said nothing. He had been trained to be "needed at home," and I could not break that hard diminishing charm.

I had been eleven when he told me to run for it. I was dressed in white organdy with a yellow sash for Melinda's wedding. Johnny at seventeen, in rented morning clothes, had already sneaked several drinks. I could smell Sen-Sen on his breath. He had lurched up to me, where I stood owl-eyed with pleasure and fear, waiting for the car to come for Melinda, and whispered that. He pointed to the new car Mother had made Father give him for his birthday because Uncle Sugar had given our cousin Brandy one, and because

Johnny would "need" it to drive to Princeton in the fall. It was the first MG in Johnny's "crowd."

It was my first wedding and I was willing it to be beautiful. Even at eleven I had to will it, and I wanted Johnny to shut up for once and let me do it, let me forget that the Cutright mines and Baseheart—McKarkle Collieries were fusing in blood as they had long ago in business, as if Melinda and Spud were to meet and couple at the end of miles of rich black tunnel under the hills, married by oily spirits Johnny and I had named coal trolls. I wanted only to see the wedding, the reception in the caressing summer sun on the manicured lawn of the old Country Club.

Johnny ran off before I could answer. Upstairs Melinda and Mother were still looking together into Mother's mirror. I no longer was allowed to call her Mamma. Melinda said it wasn't correct usage. They had let me watch Melinda dress, hear the huge white taffeta skirt whisper as it settled over her dark, muscular body and her legs, stringy from tennis. I stood in the corner of the room, out of the way, fidgeting in organdy which scratched, dressed an hour ahead. Mother's dress—a yellow chiffon she still called georgette—looked as dry as her skin and sagged too much over her little taut body. It is strange, since she has haunted my memory, that this is the first time I can *see* her, not as a ghost, but as she really looked that summer day in 1941. She was wearing a small, tipsy hat; a white ostrich plume tickled at her neck. She kept swatting at it as if it were a fly in her nervousness to get Melinda dressed. Out of the window of our house on River Street, through the frail, billowing white curtains, I could see our neighbor, Jim Dodd, sitting on the porch, waiting for Martha, his wife, to finish dressing for the wedding. I had a crush on Martha that year because she had given me my first silk stockings for my birthday.

Finally Melinda stood before the mirror, Mother beside her. Fear or excitement had stripped Melinda's face of that ever-present tension in her jaw, and for a minute she looked so lovely that my nose tickled with tears. It was as if just for a minute the fantasy would work.

"Oh, Linda, it's all so *right*. Melinda Neill McKarkle to James Donald Cutright," Mother chanted, awed, looking at her in the mirror. She hugged Melinda's arm so she wouldn't disturb the froth of her veil and the sprig of orange blossoms in her black hair, then Mother's eyes went far away and filled with tears, and I, at the time, thought she was trying to remember if she had forgotten something.

"Something old, something new, something borrowed, something blue," I reminded her, cold inside at the thought of walking down the church aisle.

"Oh, Hannah, run on, dear. You're in the way," Mother said, remembering me. She went on staring into the mirror.

From somewhere deep in Mother's dreams, which I sensed and feared with my skin but didn't understand, she had constructed a Melinda and a Johnny for herself. She had wanted to train one hard one to make up for the devil of a shyness she could never shake, land ghosts which she had carried from upriver at Beulah to the house on River Street. Melinda, with the silent Puritan will and the dark look of the Kreggs—at least that was where Mother said she got it—had taken on those bitterer dreams. Once she would have run a church, or managed the mores of hard sons and dim daughters, morally incisive and cold. Now she played games hard and well, managed, as Mother trained her to, perpetual cocktail parties with an eye to the business of "keeping up standards." Even her engagement to Spud Cutright had the air of a game well played. I, sneaking around, spying for romance, had heard of none. They had known each other too long.

With the same narrow zeal, she and Mother had planned and furnished the houses on the hill. Since 1939 the nice people of Canona had been worried about the war, so when the new houses began to follow the cleaner air across the river, they were as English as they could be. The women sought out worm-eaten pine. I remembered the day the old sycamore was dragged from its ground like an enormous snake. The trunk was hollow and bedded with leaves. Johnny and I had hidden in it when we sneaked across the river to play at running away. That was where they found the skeleton and my father picked up the flint spearhead which Johnny kept in his pocket as a good-luck piece.

When the road was built, English houses, Tudor, Georgian, and Queen Anne, sprang up like expensive mushrooms. Mother told Johnny and me she was putting some of the land they had bought "by" for us. The two largest hill crests with a view of the distant water she saved for herself and for Melinda. It was the same arrangement that we had in the family burial plot in the cemetery, which, on clear days in winter, we could see across the hills north of Canona. The steeple of All Saints seemed to point to the acres of white stone dots.

That year, because of the English, we worked for Bundles for Britain. Christmas presents all carried the British Royal Crest in gilt paper, and Mother bought the *Illustrated London News* and started using Pears' soap, which reminded me of locker rooms at camp. When the cake was thin you could see your fingers through amber, Mother made us save the little pieces and put them in a wire basket to swish through the bath water, practicing at war.

Of course, when the twin houses were being built, the mountain wood was shaped into exposed beams, the roofs rose steep, and the downstairs libraries were paneled, with holes bored into the fleshy new wood by a surly carpenter before they were stained. The houses had not been finished for Melinda's wedding. From the front window, as Melinda inspected her face for a last time in the house on River Street, I could see the two slate roofs.

I had watched Mother and Melinda go through the agonies of choice and then end with a bedroom for Melinda's new home that was a replica of my mother's—the same kind of mahogany bed with a tester, the "lovely old" chests, the billowing curtains, the bright slip rugs.

But if Melinda was cast into a hard dream mold, Johnny was cast as a rake. Out of a fear as deep and unquestioned as taboo, a fear of hurting Mother which they both thought of as love, he developed an insolent charm to please her and make her smile and say he was like her father, that ghostly dandy, Mother's model of a gentleman, who, she said, could have charmed the birds from the trees, and who had gone back to a Beulah he no longer owned in 1908, and blown his brains into the grass, and left Mother fourteen forever, inside the armor of her rigid body. On that point, as long as I can remember, had been her tears. Touching it had brought a nameless twinge of panic to all of us. She seemed always poised on the edge of another minute like it, and we were taught to respect that wariness like a cocked pistol. Trailing his bloody shirt—"He wore the *finest* linen always," she would say—she had solicited our tenderness.

Behind her, as she and Melinda stood in front of the mirror, was the picture of the only other wedding I ever heard Mother say was "so right." About her own she never said anything. The picture sat among the Waterford scent bottles—which never held any scent because it gave her hives—and the ormolu boxes for her jewels. I could see it that day reflected in the closet mirror, framed in gold and aged to sepia. There was President Chester A. Arthur, and my great-grandfather Senator Daniel Neill looking as rich as God, with his heavy black, well-fed beard, standing beside a beautiful, straight, sad-looking young girl, my Grandmother Lacey Kregg from Albion on the James, as if he had married her instead of the pale young man beside her with his silk mustaches, standing as languidly as he could before the long exposure of the camera. Mother would point to old General Crawford Kregg, who stood behind his daughter, and tell us he had taken her to Washington in clothes he'd borrowed money for, on the last useless land at Albion in Virginia, after the War had ruined him, going after Neill money as if the Neills had stolen it from him. I wished then that Melinda could look a little sad, like my grandmother. It seemed more fitting.

It was the only picture in the house of Mother's beloved "Papa," Peregrine Lacey Neill, who had driven a four-in-hand through the streets of Washington. She made us see him whipping the horses down Massachusetts Avenue, chased by a longing bevy of eligible virgins of good family. He had the look of high heartlessness Mother admired so. He seemed amused at the wedding, which had begun so richly the slow journey of his married life, ending at Beulah at the family mine, in a time of trouble no charm could stop. A year before his death, Mother's family had moved "downriver" to the house we still lived in the day of Melinda's wedding. In that narrow valley no Rubicon of decision was crossed. It was floated down, rather, to Canona, the center. "Downriver" had a finality about it which still exists. People were carried by the river to a more fertile promise, usually dislodged by two extremes, need and hope.

But Mother brought the ghost of her father with her and lodged it with Johnny. For me, she didn't have much of a plan. I think that I, like a wood's colt, was a surprise not provided for in dreams. For years I couldn't imagine my parents performing the necessary act to conceive me. But having done it, Mother had to find a place for me. She decided that I was the "artistic one of the family," and, having done that, she thought about me in guilty fidgets as if she had forgotten me before I was born and was trying out of duty to recall me. Johnny had been left to bring me up. We, bayheaded brats, saw Melinda being groomed over the years and ourselves fitted carefully into what a family should be, split so early to please her, into perceiving one life and acting another at the same time.

On the day of the wedding I stole a last look at Melinda in the mirror as I ran by to get out of Mother's way. I held the picture in my head, as I still do, thinking I would never again see my sister so lovely. If wanting to love and loving ever are the same thing, I loved Melinda that day, so pretty and unprotected by her will for once in her safe, planned life.

That was why Johnny's remark about running for it jarred my pleasure at Melinda's wedding, and made me mad at him. On the way to church in the family car, I squnched away from him when he dug me in the ribs to make me speak, and leaned my head like a dog out of the window all the way to All Saints. Later, at the reception, I had a wave of remorse, as I always did when I ignored him, feeling that I had let him down in front of the others. I ran through the crowd on the old Country Club lawn. Polite noise hummed over my head. I passed Mother and Father standing with the rest of the bridal party and slipped behind the pink ruffled bulk of Aunt Althea. Her voice in the air above me was going on as if she'd said it before and was running down. "It was simply beautiful." She looked down and caught me. "Wasn't it simply beautiful?" She asked me, I guess, because I was the only one of the wedding party who had sneaked away from the line and she'd already said it to everyone else.

I wandered down the long rope of people shaking hands as if they hadn't known each other all their lives. They stood in a line as though they were still having their pictures taken in front of the big stone columns of the Country Club porch. Father was standing beside Mother, watching her with that concerned look he had which had creased his face into deep lines that never tanned even when he'd been playing golf all summer. You could see the lighter streaks when you caught him alone, his face relaxed. Mother kept talking to the moving line of people as if she were dragging her mind back to their outstretched hands.

"Thank you. Thank you," she kept saying. Once she said it to empty air in front of her.

As I watched, the line swayed, broke, and they were lost

among the scattered guests. I couldn't see Melinda and Spud for the crowd around them, but Johnny and Kitty Puss Wilson were meandering across the lawn together to the big table with white tablecloths, made into a bar. Everything was white and glass and froth except Brandon's face, black above his laundered white jacket. Brandon was the best waiter in town. He knew what everybody drank. Delilah stood in a new white uniform waving flies off the five-tiered wedding cake.

I knew what I could do to make up with Johnny. I had been saving my money, as I always did, in that effort to wake Mother's and Melinda's attention with Christmas presents. Money was hard to get your hands on. Johnny never had any. We had all the things we needed, but money in its virgin form was dangerous.

I knew what Johnny wanted more than anything in the world that June of 1941. He had a picture of Douglas Bader in his room and he snatched the papers in the evenings and closed himself in there with them. Once I went in and he was standing in front of the mirror. It scared me for a minute.

He was not singing as he usually did, but speaking...

> "'A lonely impulse of delight
> Drove to this tumult in the clouds.'"

He caught me watching him, and instead of chasing me out he told me it was a poem he had learned at Andover.
"Hey, Sissy, listen to this. It's a poem by Yeats:

> 'I know that I shall meet my fate
> Somewhere among the stars above;
> Those that I fight I do not hate,
> Those that I guard I do not love.'"

He buried his head in his arms among the silver cups and the kind of Christmas presents seventeen-year-old boys get and don't use. I couldn't make out the rest, but he was crying when he finished. I pretended not to notice.
"Sissy," he almost whispered into the telephone.
"I'm here," I said, but we didn't say any more. We could sit for an hour in contact through that night wire as if we were sitting in the same room or the same bar, without

speaking, just letting the hatful of quarters tick away, thinking together silently like two mountain women on a party line.

We sang the poem to a hymn tune afterwards, and neither of us could finish it without our throats hurting. We sang it to "When I Survey the Wondrous Cross..." sitting together on his bed with the door shut. He told me how to fly a Spitfire. Then he made me promise not to tell what he was going to do. As soon as he was eighteen and had saved enough money he was going to leave Princeton and go to Canada to join the Royal Canadian Air Force.

Johnny and Kitty Puss had their champagne and were already going toward the hidden side porch of the club when I caught up with them. I pulled at the tail of Johnny's rented morning coat. He turned around with that insolent look he had when he was with Kitty Puss.

"Johnny, I'll lend you the money." I stood on tiptoe and whispered at the air.

He didn't change his face. "Okay, Sissy, okay," he said. Kitty Puss Wilson's face was already radiant, the way sweat is radiant when there isn't much of it. When she saw me she yelled, "Why, honey, I meant to tell you all the time, you look just gorgeous in that dress."

"It scratches like hell," I told her. I hated the word "gorgeous" coming out of her round red lips.

I thought Johnny hadn't heard me. Later, after I'd gotten into my bathing suit and was at the pool watching the people all bright across the grass, the ushers broke away and came pounding over the lawn, pulling Spud with them. I could hear Mother calling, "Don't, boys," but she was laughing. She laughed at expected things. Spud acted as though he were pulling back but he was loving being the center of that wildness for once.

Johnny saw me and yelled, "Sit still, Sissy!" I sat still, feeling scared of the way they looked in those cutaway coats and striped trousers, running toward the pool, ruthless with joy.

"Clear her head. She'll sit still," Johnny called to the others as if they weren't running right beside him. They grabbed Spud up into the air and threw him over my head into the pool. Brandy Baseheart went in after him and then Johnny; they splashed the scared children who clung to the pool edges and watched.

Kitty Puss Wilson stood like a figurehead on the diving

board, letting them cheer her from the water. Her dress caught the breeze and flattened against her body, swinging out behind her like the Victory of Samothrace. Then she made a neat swan dive into the water.

I did think Johnny had forgotten about my promise and I slipped to his room the next evening after dinner to tell him again. The door was shut and inside I could hear my mother. She was talking in her cold voice, the one we called her money-and-virginity voice.

"I want to exact a solemn promise from you, son," she was saying.

I couldn't hear Johnny answer.

"I know what's on your mind," she went on. "*I always know,* son. Now, your father and I have made every sacrifice for you to go to Princeton. We are *not rich people...*"

I knew that mood. She said it about the Pears' soap too.

I mooched on down the stairs to steal the paper and read "Boots and Her Buddies." I'd heard all about the sacrifices, so I didn't bother to listen any more. She and my father talked about sacrifice when they were laying down the law. It was like can afford and can't afford. There were lists—I knew them all—the Country Club, Andover, Princeton, cars, Egeria Springs, Nelson-Page where Melinda went to college, the correct clothes from *Town and Country* were can afford. Money in its virgin state, clothes we chose ourselves, uncensored books, too many picture shows were can't afford.

The next day the picture of Bader was gone, and Johnny acted as if he'd forgotten about Yeats. He borrowed the money, though, and promised he'd pay it back when he got his allowance, but he didn't spend it on going to Canada. He had the craziest summer he ever had in his new car with Kitty Puss Wilson. He spent the money on beer at the Wayfaring Stranger.

He got arrested for the first time a month before he went to Princeton. Father went down and got him out. Nobody said a word at dinner for about a week. Mother finally wrapped her mind around the fact and healed it for herself. She said she was sure Johnny had been made the scapegoat; the word "scapegoat" seemed to please her. The temperature of the house lifted and the summer gathered speed again. One night late I went downstairs, barefooted in my pajamas, to raid the icebox. I heard Johnny and Kitty Puss murmuring in the dark sun-room. They must have heard me because by the time I came back they had gone and the sun-room still smelled faintly of chestnuts. When I was twenty-one I cried at the same sweet chestnut scent, my mind's eye slashed open at last to that night, unable to tell a scared boy why I cried.

Mother was set on Johnny's marrying Kitty Puss. "I think those children are made for each other," she said one evening to Aunt Althea as they sat in the porch swing, watching them drive away down River Street in the car. Aunt Althea didn't seem to be "invited" to things, she just turned up from time to time and sat on the porch and watched the river and complained about Uncle Dan. It was the only time she wore the ruby ring that Mother said by rights should have come to her. She said she'd found it once just lying in the kitchen sink among the dirty dishes.

"I wonder if they really love each other," Aunt Althea sighed and made the swing sigh too.

My mother jumped up and said in the piercing chicken shriek she had when she forgot to "modulate" her voice, "Althea, you make me *sick*. You just make me sick with that mind of yours... tacky..." Her face was twisted and childish.

Aunt Althea made her remark about Southern women, which was usually touched off by such outbreaks from my mother. "We Southern women only do things for two reasons," she said while the swing creaked and Mother glared at her, "because we're in love and because we're not." I had heard her say it a hundred times.

That remark, which the family always said was "typical of Althea," reverberated and echoed down through the years of my growing up. It trained me to hypnotize myself with questioning. Incised with women's training in a world that dishonored and condemned it, I would long to be fair and would watch my dog self, salivating, waiting to know which bell had been hit. Such power to speak quite dumbly to the nerves gave Aunt Althea the kind of reputation for hard wit which drunks have, and which, out of some basic disappointment and an inborn knowledge of her rape muscles, she honed until it was as sharp as a knife—a circumcision knife. Still, Aunt Althea seemed unique to me; she was a woman in a place where most of the female sex went from a long, cute girlhood into tyrannous old age without an intervening period of responsive womanhood. Mother never spoke of her without a slight, teasing sneer.

Well, Mother couldn't buck the United States Army. After Johnny was drafted she shrank inside her frail body and treated the rest of us like strangers. All through the war she talked about "my son" as if she couldn't remember Johnny's name. She wrote him long, long letters to APO numbers I still remember, pouring out to him her pains of war and rationing.

She bore up beautifully. Those were my father's words. Then she treated me with a mixture of preoccupation, and sudden bursts of an affection strange to me, not affection as to a child, but as if she were leaning on my concern for strength. It was the only time in my life she demanded attention from me, a total adult concentration.

As for me, I stayed, as I always had, a few steps behind Johnny. I didn't know where he was; he was at APO. So I followed the war instead, every battle. I learned to identify enemy planes, I knew the names of generals, and I rolled acres of bandages for the Red Cross, all to be used in some corner of a foreign field, on Johnny.

But I was fourteen, and then fifteen, and sometimes I forgot. Once Candy and I raced through the house and Mother stood at the door, yelling, "You just don't *care!*" and calling my name over and over in a panic until we were out of earshot and safe.

Dinner was long, silent, and lonesome.

"Hey, Sissy, hey, Hannah," Johnny called, finished with his own thinking in the telephone booth. "God, it was strange, honey . . ." He had the door open for the river breeze. I could hear River Street. He was letting the middle of a memory come out in words.

"It was a huge black shadow. I saw it crawling against the glass . . . the big window. Huge."

"When?" God, when in time was he?

"Tonight, honey, we were in the ballroom. I saw this *giant shadow* across the glass front of the clubhouse. It was like the woods fighting back. It looked so free. I had to get out of the place. You know?"

"Sure." I had to know. He always said "you know," taking for granted that I did.

"I ran out. I left Linda's visitor on the dance floor. Hey, you know what it was? This skinny bastard was standing in front of a floodlight on the hill beyond the pool. Just as I got out he ran down the slope and started pushing chairs into the pool.

Christ, chairs and floats and crap. It was great. I didn't stop him. I wanted to help him.

"They heard the noise inside and old Spud ran out then. He was yelling, 'Hey there, hey there, man.'" Johnny imitated Spud's busy voice. "Bunch of fat phonies raced out after him..." I could see the fat phonies flapping across the terrace. It was a twelve-year-old word and we were for a minute twelve years old, the children of light jeering and mocking the awkward, ugly children of darkness. "God, it was great! The skinny guy got away, though. He just cut out through the woods and over the golf course like a coon."

I was helpless, laughing.

Johnny switched again; sober, casual. "You coming down when the quail season starts?"

"Maybe."

"Don't be that way. Remember that covey up at the hill farm above Beulah? We could go there. Hey..."

Oh, I remembered with quick tears. Johnny made me cry, there in my safe Manhattan hutch, but I didn't say a word to let him know. I didn't because his convenient drunken memory—his Saturday-night memory, not his Monday-morning one—had gone back to the hill farm as it had been when we first went there with Uncle Ephraim. He told us that it was the old Catlett place before they moved across the river to Lacey Creek because they didn't see eye to eye with the family about the Civil War. He said his grandfather told him all about it. All the way to the hill above Beulah, Uncle Ephraim never said another word. The fall woods were all the color of light, translucent red and orange and yellow that seemed to vibrate in the air. Up through the hollow where the creek curled over the rocks, up past the old Beulah graveyard of the early settlers, with its nameless stones, we climbed to the edge of the abandoned hill farm. It belonged to Beulah Collieries, but they had let it alone. In the distance a gaunt house sagged, a big square clapboard, weathered and unpainted, its windows hollow-eyed. It reminded me of a deserted mountain woman, weather-brown, watching blankly across the neglected fields as if she wouldn't let anything but God Almighty stop her empty vigil. Around it, like hungry children, the well, the outhouses, and the corncrib leaned. Old gnarled apple trees still carried neglected late-fall apples. The whole huge field smelled of apples and ripe wild harvest.

Uncle Ephraim went on ahead, motioning Johnny and me

to keep behind him. Away to each side the dogs quartered through the high weeds and the lespedeza.

"You have to keep up," Uncle Ephraim warned, low in his throat.

We kept up, watching the feather tails appear and disappear, flicking through the cover; from time to time the dogs tossed their heads up above the weeds to check back.

Then the whole field went still, or seemed to. Fan froze on point, and Jubal loped across and froze behind her. Uncle Ephraim ran without making a sound, with Johnny beside him. He motioned Johnny to stand still, then he walked in, and the covey whirred up ahead of him. Johnny shot, and I saw a bird flip over and plummet down. Jubal went after it and brought it back to Johnny. I saw him take the bird and put it to his mouth as if he were kissing it, but I knew he was biting its jugular vein. He'd told me that was what you had to do. When I got there he was kneeling in the weeds petting the dog. He threw me the bird to carry. Its feathers were silk-soft and it was still warm.

Ten years later we had gone back to the hill farm. We had walked up the slag-paved hollow without a word to each other, not like Uncle Ephraim's mountain silence to keep from scaring up the birds, but stupefied. The mill creek was black. It ran sullenly along a ditch beside the dirt road grimed with coal dust. Where the old graveyard had been, the side of the hill was blown away to widen the lane up to the hill farm. There was just a blank wall of cliff rock, with a few trees still above it, their roots exposed where the cut had eroded in the rain. I don't know why we went on but we did, following the deep truck ruts up toward the old plateau. Johnny's new dog Calhoun hung his sad hound face down and stayed at our heels even when Johnny tried to hie him on ahead.

At the top of the hill we stopped. The hill farm had been sliced off and thrown down into what was now a dirty gully. The topsoil, weeds, apple trees, the house, the corn rick were gone. As far as we could see, to the line of trees marking the opposite hollow, there was only a vast dead-gray table. Nothing grew, or could grow, there. The farm had been exposed down to the coal seam, and that had been peeled away, leaving only an expanse of bare, dirty bedrock; there was not a clue of life across the great, abandoned strip mine. Calhoun loped toward the line of trees across the blasted space. We followed on. By the time we reached the center of the rock table there seemed to be no direction, no purpose to it. The place was dead. Not even a weed could find soil to lodge in and grow to cast a hopeful small pool of shadow. The hill farm had at last been harvested, down to naked rock.

When we got home we told about it—or I did. Johnny didn't say a word. Mother said it was too bad, that the garden clubs were discussing it. Then, excited, she told us about the blasting. She said that when the dust cleared, several coffins, hard as rock, were jutting out beyond the cut. She said they must have been some of the founders of Beulah, and that two of the bodies had been scalped. Then she said, "The Collieries and the Colonial Dames had them reinterred near the family plot here at Canona. We couldn't put their names of course, so we just put up a plaque to the first settlement on the Canona River." Her voice had lilted solemnly.

Johnny and I didn't mention it again. On that Saturday night I realized that he had neatly stepped away from it in memory.

"Johnny, I don't want to come down there," I cried.

"Oh, for Christ's sake, Hannah, what the hell's the matter with you?" Johnny sounded fed up and tired. Then he added to himself, "Jesus, I can't even go to...I'm still in this damned monkey suit." He remembered me. "I need a drink. See you..."

He hung up. I found pajamas and put them on and went into the living room. Carlo was lying back on the sofa, looking at an unfinished abstract painting; he gazed at me as if he didn't know me, his eyes sullen. We both looked at the painting. Red streaks exploded apart, racing to protest against the confines of the canvas, escaping a dead black burn at the center. When I had spoken carefully about its vitality, Carlo had told me to shut up.

"He won't call back now," I apologized.

"I never know what's coming out of there," Carlo told me evenly without moving. I knew he had rehearsed everything he would say to me, and that it would be clever, because he was hurt. It had all happened so many times. "I just never know." He looked back at the huge, alive painting, swirling blood and coal and escape. "What do you hang on your walls for trophies down in God's country?" he asked.

Melinda had kept a fox head in the deep freeze until it leered sideways from being shoved against the game. She had it mounted anyway, and it grinned from the wall among the family photographs.

I went over to Carlo, hiding my face to keep from laughing, wanting him to touch me. I could feel him looking at me as if I were far away instead of right beside him.

"I never know whether it's going to be your rich good sport or your violated Southern virgin or your boy. In Brooklyn we call that incest. What do you call it down there?"

"Loyalty," I wanted to say, but what was the use? He wasn't a Southerner. I could have told him I had been trained like a dog to retrieve my brother from incest, its form the impotent seduction of the mother.

Instead, I just sat there beside him in my pajamas, still wanting to laugh. He looked so exposed, all bravely naked on someone else's sofa, safely hidden from his mama in Brooklyn, talking too easily and too much. "Oh, this time it's Tom Sawyer. Tom Sawyer in drag!" He took my shoulders and made me look at him. He didn't sound hurt. He had retreated into being objective, and I was the object, turned and inspected carefully. "This is the last time I'm going to paint your fucking fence."

He climbed slowly over me and disappeared into the bedroom. When he came back he was dressed. He leaned in the doorway for a minute. I thought he was going to speak, but he didn't. He just stared.

Then he said, "I'll come and get my stuff as soon as I find a place."

We could have quarreled. I could have teased him into playing Wop and hating me for a while for being what he called sometimes "a sleek American moneybag," but we were both too tired and we'd played that too often. I didn't answer or look at him. I heard him shut the door.

It was lonely. Outside, the street sounds had died down so I could hear the moan of the city. Carlo's painting died as I watched it—died from being looked at too long and from being there with the twisted wire sculpture from Nico and the tin-can montage from Lou and the plaster imitation of a Giacometti from I didn't give a fuck who. I thought of the language of Buber, how he said that the Zulus had one word they used as we use "far away"; it meant "there where someone cries out, 'O Mother I am lost.'"

I think I went to sleep. It was later—a space of time. I heard Johnny say "Hannah," as clearly as if he were in the room. I know these things aren't supposed to happen, but it did. For a second I thought he was there. In the bedroom the clock said four o'clock. I sat down on the bed, willing him to call back, cold with a fear I couldn't name, remembering the dream about the river and wondering if I'd had it again. I knew then what was tugging at my late-night mind's edge. Johnny's night was not yet finished. He had not reached the last call, the point of turning homeward, drunk to the sober point of defeat for another week.

The telephone was silent. Below the window of the apartment I thought I heard someone crying, but when I looked down at the street there was no one there. At five o'clock I called the airport.

There was no decision that morning. I just let loose, as if I'd been clinging too long to a rock to keep me grounded—let loose and let myself take off skyward.

The aircraft cruised at seven thousand feet as we came over the Potomac into Virginia with the morning sun behind us. Later I would know the country as if I had walked it from Alexandria through Fredericksburg and along the slow slow march on Braddock's road, or up the James beyond the fall line with Sal and Jonathan Lacey when they were pushed by circumstance past wild Kreggs Crossing that later was Albion on the James. Then the foothills of the Piedmont led to the endless mountains and beyond them opened to a West of hope and terror. But that Sunday morning I knew none of this. Oh, I knew London and Paris and New York better than I knew the land streaming by below me. I took that for granted. In the slang of 1960, America wasn't "in."

The tiny black shadow of the plane began to skim and dip over the rolling sun-green Piedmont. It was a glass-clear morning, so clear that I could see far ahead the faint backbone of the Blue Ridge. Virginia slid away, undulating green. We flirted nearer and nearer the mountain barrier. Over the foothills the plane's winged shadow danced. Here and there on the sky floor the white pattern of a nestled town passed, the long-drawn lines of rivers cutting east. Beyond the Piedmont we withdrew farther from the land, higher in the air; we climbed to ten thousand feet above the currents, which tossed the air as the land below had been tossed into hills aeons ago.

Johnny had told me the Royal Air Force pilots talked of height as angels. He had heard their voices calling, during the war, "Flying at ten angels." I could see the Blue Ridge rolling nearer, misty in the distance, as if their color reflected the bright morning sky. Patched with great blots, still waves of spruce and pine groves were night-blue on the gentle eastern slopes. The summer rhododendron made damp black pools.

The first ridge passed under us. As far as I could see, the mountains to the west were giant furrows plowed from north to south, row after row—a barrier backed by a barrier to the east which seemed endless. In between, little veins of rivers ran between the furrows to find stronger waterways to the eastern ocean. How empty Virginia looked that morning from the sky! We cruised over it with Blake's "confident insolence" of angels.

That was what Aunt Althea had finally said to Mother to calm her that day on the porch, the summer of Melinda's wedding, when we watched Johnny and Kitty Puss get into the car. They had had that confident insolence, Mother gazing after them, with romantic safe-money eyes, seeing what she wanted to see, screaming away Aunt Althea's sentimental intrusion she said was so "in-law" and tacky.

"They do look angelic," Aunt Althea had conceded. Then, her body senses always wiser than she ever allowed her conscious mind to be, she shuddered slightly. I could feel it through her dress as I sat beside her in the swing. She laughed and said, "Someone must be walking over my grave" —as if she were physically aware of something she thought it wiser not to tell.

The plane's shadow leaped the high backbone of the western watershed. Below, I could see the western mountains, steeper, narrow-ledged, limestone jutting from pools of dark where the sun had not yet filtered through the thick cover of the woods. Johnny and I called it the mean side of the mountains, grander, more aloof, more secret, with more dangerous steep divides than the gently rising, evocative Virginia slopes. No wonder the tall, walking Scots who settled there moved more easily in that stern, familiar place than the genteel from the rolling East, who either died, retreated into fantasy, or had to learn to walk too, grow longer, thinner, as jut-boned as the rock ledges and the harsh trees. There was no sign down in the narrow gullies that anyone had ever touched the mountains, much less lived in them. Far below, in the New River gorge, the sun reached the thin ribbon of flying water and made it shimmer. I could see the bald patches of the strip mines circling the ridges; from ten angels they looked as formal as ancient rock citadels. The valley widened and we lost altitude. Down the stabbed sides of the lowering hills, shale from the drift-mine entries flowed black. The river widened at the end of a still lake of water from the mountains. I could see Indian Rock, and then the falls throwing a veil over the rocks.

We began to be tossed by the air currents eddying from the prevailing wind that blew downriver. The plane tipped, and I saw the right wing dip toward Beulah Valley, lying way below us as if some small hand had pushed down the hills, its palm along the bend of the river, its fingers splayed to form the hollows. The raw rock table of the Beulah hill farm was dead gray in the sun, but that was the only sign of people from so high. Hidden in its morning shadow by the eastern hill, Beulah was bland and dark, as if it had never yet been found. The plane leveled. The whole of Beulah had been pinpointed for a few seconds at our speed, then was gone, as we turned south to make a wide arc for the Canona landing. My body begged the plane not to touch down in that wave after wave of western hills, not to commit itself to one point of dangerous ground.

Canona, long, narrow, on the right angle of its rivers, was below. I could see the new golf course, then the town's pattern and the exposed cemetery. The houses of the new suburb that had been naked on the raw ridges when they were built were already hidden by carefully tended trees.

At the airport the hills rushed up at us. I could have reached out and touched treetops as I felt the plane's wheels contact ground. The woman beside me, who had drowsed during the hour it took to cross Virginia and the mountains, jumped fully awake, seeing the woods, scared.

Across the flat tarmac the small airport was already black with people. It could, from the plane window, have been any modern terminal anywhere.

Johnny had let me go sometimes when he raced his car up the hill to the old airport with its wind sock and its shed hangars, to look at the girls perched on stools, waiting to be admired in the airport canteen. There Johnny and his friends picked up the town girls, who switched their shining hair and drew in their waists with wide belts we weren't allowed to wear. They sashayed through the canteen, their backs arched with promise, seeming so sure of themselves. Johnny had been secretly in love with Thelma Leftwich ever since the Decoration Day when he was fourteen. She was our cousin only because, as Mother said, her mother was Aunt Althea's sister and that was not kin, only a connection. When Mother and Melinda decided he ought to have a dance, she wasn't invited. Looking back, I see it as a first time that Johnny split his life into two worlds to keep the peace, but he gave in so easily that he must have already fallen into the habit. Maybe up to then I had been too young to notice. Whenever Johnny and I were alone in the house he talked to Thelma Leftwich for an hour on the telephone. I asked Mother why she didn't come to Johnny's dance and Mother said she wouldn't be happy. So Johnny met Thelma Leftwich in the airport canteen in the summer when he was sixteen and had his first car. They sipped Cokes, and listened to the jukebox, and hardly said a word while I sat beside them and watched the planes land.

He made up a game there. When the planes came into sight we would chant in whispers, "Old thin old Nobodaddy aloft, farted and belched and coughed," and beat one another's arms until one of us identified the plane, Eastern Airlines, American, United. Johnny had learned the rhyme his first year at Andover. He brought me Blake as he was later to bring me Yeats, tossing them to me and then forgetting them himself.

One time, as we drove down the hill, somebody in the back seat, I think it was Brandy, dared him to drive through Carver Street, where the women hung out the upstairs windows and called out to the boys. He just yelled, "Shut up! For Christ's sake, shut up in front of my sister!" Thelma Leftwich was in the seat beside him, but he said, "my sister." Already in our minds the lines were being drawn between city and sanctuary.

On the two-story wall of the new airport waiting room that Sunday morning there was a wall-size green, aerial view of the hills. In front of it someone had once put a plastic sign, *Prepare to Meet Thy God*, with a box of tracts. It was the same sign the people from the Church of God painted with whitewash on the cliffs by the road. The airlines got so many complaints that the plastic sign was changed to *Jesus Saves*. It was still there that morning when I walked through the waiting room to get a taxi.

I caught myself looking through the Sunday-morning crowd of mountain people who brought their children in jalopies to see the planes land. Even though no one knew I was coming, the child in me expected someone there, Johnny or my father, to meet me and let fall casually the temperature at home as we drove down toward the valley. They never knew they were doing it, but always by the time we had driven through the town and over the bridge I would know the state of home—what event, small or large, had tipped the scales off-balance a little, so that I was expected to walk carefully, aware and upright, for it was the unexpected that tipped Mother and Melinda, jarred the coiled tension they mistook for composure.

So I planned this time to slip in on Sunday morning when Johnny was asleep, Mother and Father gone to the spa, and Melinda and Spud to church, just to have the morning to myself and walk in the washed sun.

The taxi crawled through the clean crowds gathering at the cluster of churches in the tic-tac-toe made by Lee, Mosby, Carver, and Neill Streets. Godly, righteous, and sober, family squads trekked toward church. In a minute of panic I could see them surging over the taxi in that slow Sunday march, not even seeing it, just trampling it down. Plain George and Ann Randolph Potter crossed the street in front of me, George looking as if he'd had a hard night, Ann Randolph's lips folded for Sunday morning. I hoped they wouldn't look up and see me. Down the street the bells of the Catholic church rang out for Mass.

"Church makes me feel so good," Mother said on Sundays, when she came back bathed in the bland milk of an Episcopal God and flung down her white gloves. Then I wanted to pray, "If You'll forgive me, I will hereafter live a humble, sinful, exposed life to the honor and glory of Thy name," but I never said it. Through all those years, except in uneasy flashes, we were skimming people, leaving the taboos as intact as the unweathered gray stones of pseudo-Gothic All Saints, silent in public on matters better left unsaid.

Plain George turned at the corner as quickly as if I'd called to him and saw me. He ran over to the window. I thought he

said, "God, Sissy, I'm glad you're home," but I couldn't get
the window open in time and the taxi moved on. He stood
looking after it and waved sadly. I thought then it was
because of the hard, hot night he'd had and that he was
always glad to see me.

In the eighteen years since the twin Tudor houses had
been finished, the lush gardens had grown up around them
so that they looked almost as they were meant to, old,
ivy-covered, correct. The heavy, nearly ripe September leaves
of the trees on the drive whispered, and along the eastern
slope of Mother's lawn, the shrubs, in what she called her
Cruikshank curves, moved in the late-summer breeze. They
hid the garage that she insisted we use because cars ruined
the line of her garden. The trees that would later take over
the lawn were still small then, and cast pools of calculated
blue shade. England as a fashion had been replaced by
gardens, and the ridge land was rich green under the trees.
We drew up in front of Mother's house. Across the lawn I saw
that there was a strange car in front of Melinda's, parked by
the Sunbeam Alpine—a white Jaguar convertible. Spud's
Cadillac was gone.

I was relieved. They had gone to church, taking their
visitor to the beginning of the Christian Sunday: church,
drinks, golf, all the children buzzing like bees around the
pools. The hours stretched out ahead, formal, unthinking,
and Johnny slept upstairs, off-duty at church because our
parents were away.

Even so, I let myself in, as quiet as a cat, and stopped to
Indian-read the signs, by habit, as Johnny had taught me to
do, checking whether gloves were put away or flung across
the English refectory chest, whether the silver tray was filled
with unopened letters; or if the hall had the dark, deserted
atmosphere that sometimes my fingers could almost touch.

The morning sun caressed the polished floor. For a few
seconds I had the illusion, the waking dream of peace instead
of the destroying dream of the night's pit I always carried and
always rejected. Above the pine paneling of the hall the frigid
green walls were grotto-cool. Great-grandfather Neill's portrait dominated the wall over the card table from Beulah, as if
Mother announced ourselves at once to any stranger who
came beyond the brass eagle of the door knocker. She never
just pointed to it and told about it. Senator Neill and Great-
grandmother Melinda hung stated in the air of the house as

they hung in fact. The living room had, in Mother's phrase, been built around Great-grandmother Melinda, who had watched me coldly, so witch-beautiful with great black knowing eyes that seemed to move in the firelight at night. She made me feel as awkward as if she had been calling me down ever since I was a child from over the fireplace.

The Senator's portrait had really belonged to Uncle Dan Neill, but when he died, Mother pointed out that it ought to stay in the family.

We didn't see Aunt Althea much, after his death, except at funerals, that I remember. She would come dressed in left-over clothes from the twenties, no longer plump as I remembered her, but faded for me into anonymity. I simply didn't see her except as one of that row of dim Eumenides that Southern families have, who would file into the pew to haunt death with their presence. She had offered to sell the portrait to the state because she needed the money, but no one wanted it. Senator Neill had been forgotten except by Mother and her friends. Mother had me go with her to Aunt Althea's dark house. She said she simply couldn't face it alone. Johnny was still at war, and Melinda and Spud were hunting birds in Aiken. I sat while she laid down the law.

After two hours Aunt Althea had cried out, "For Christ's sake, take the son-of-a-bitch and leave me to hell alone."

Mother had told her calmly that she fully understood her grief, that she shared in it; she said all this as she marched across the Spanish room and lifted the portrait down herself, not even telling me to do it, clearing the way carefully over the plaster flamenco dancer and the china spaniel on the mantel. Uncle Dan had been dead a week.

On the way home she only said, "Of course it's so sad, but you have to be sensible. I couldn't just leave the Senator *there . . .*"

I didn't answer. I could see out of the corners of my eyes her white-gloved hands resting calmly on the steering wheel, and her soft fawn wool lap.

"Oh, Hannah, it's no use trying to make you understand the importance of family. You have to have roots," she muttered, as if there were a choice to be made.

I was too young to be quiet. I didn't yet know it was like shouting in a canyon. "She's family too," I began.

"How dare you talk to me that way when I'm still suffering

the death of my brother!" Mother's voice caught, strangled, tearless.

I stood for a minute in the hall that Sunday morning, looking again at the Senator's heavy face. He had sat, reared back and rooted, for his bad portrait with its false aging of a new Old Master. He was as stiff as his mind must have been by the time he had had himself appointed Senator, because he thought it good for the children to grow up in Washington. I searched for evidence in his face of the gambler he had been, but there was none. He looked, instead, like a satisfied Presbyterian elder, cheeks red, eyes small piercing dots over his patriarchal beard; in short, as Mother had explained in the small, awed tone she had for such matters, he looked very, very rich.

It was he who had provided both a fault and a strength in our family ore, that touch of protective aloofness that meant there had been money. In the crash of '98 he died, from what Mother called extending himself too far. I could see him then as a great wave, stretched long and longer over miles of hill land, until he broke and receded, losing his strength and leaving us, especially my mother, with one gold nugget of pride. The last extension he had made had turned out not to be the big safe deal he had staked his fortune on. Johnny said the Senator had at last been dealt a cold deck.

I thought how Carlo and his friends would have hated Mother's correct, cold, rejecting hall, with the portrait, the green walls, the two "good" small sofas from Beulah, the card table, the English chest; yet they, as rigid as Mother in their intelligent, brutal disdain, had for a minute more in common with her than with me. I was glad that none of them was here and that only Johnny was upstairs, flung across his bed, snoring as he did when he had drunk like that, in his room that was a jumble of clothes, letters, postcards stuck on the walls, photographs of a long history of girls that Mother would say proudly just ran after him like the girls had after her papa, his boots still in the corner from last hunting season, puddles of brightly colored golf tees and change catching the sun, an old jug he'd found with a skull and crossbones on it—a room suspended at twenty-two, where Johnny and I both seemed to have stopped, with a man of thirty-six lying in it. I wanted to slip past it upstairs, to where Mother kept my seventeen-year-old girl's room *virgo intacta* as she had planned it, but then, beyond the living-room door

I saw a pair of too thin legs, feet in brown-and-white shoes, quite still like a statue. The Tiffany lamp Mother would never get rid of, no matter how much Melinda hinted and teased, was still lit at the height of the sunny morning, as if the people in the room had not yet noticed it was day. The house was as cold with the sense of climax as it had been when Johnny dropped out of Princeton after the war—cold and clear with the precision of detail that shock points out.

"Who is it?" Melinda's voice was as sharp as a knife. She leaned on the doorframe, her face drained of its habitual decisiveness, looking as if she had been washed against the paneling. When she saw me, there was no passing of love or of relief across her deadened eyes—not even the tightening of hatred I had seen in them so often. Melinda stared at me as if she didn't want to be reminded I existed.

Her face without makeup was dry under her summer tan, her lips narrower than ever. She said, "How did *you* get here?" not even coldly, and then, not waiting for me to answer, "How did you find out?"

Seeing the sinewy legs beyond her, for one wild second I thought that Johnny had finally been shot down into their formal nest, and that she was facing the fact that he might marry with the same harshness she faced any fact of life. She and Mother for years had coaxed him to prove his love for them by marrying a copy of themselves. I had to wait for her to tell me. Loyalty to Johnny and years of secrecy were too strong for me to tell her he'd called me.

"I *knew* you had something to do with this," Melinda said and started to cry mildly, as if she'd cried before and this was the last of it.

"What's happened to Johnny?" In that dim house my yell hit against the upstairs wall and echoed down the stairwell.

The feet beyond us moved. Melinda turned her back on me and went into the living room. I could see her sagging spine stiffen under the fine baby-pink linen of her dress, as if she were calling all her training to help her.

"I believe you've met Katy," she mentioned vaguely. It was last year's widow by consent. She sat as if she had been hardened into a shell again. What seemed to be embarrassment at the atmosphere in the house, a flagrante delicto, chased over her face. She shifted her eyes across me when she nodded, saying nothing. She had the ruthless concentration of a woman riding a perpetual point-to-point. My family's wave of irresponsible affection for her had receded with trouble and left her stranded in her chair, with the party that would never happen ready in the living room and the year's best friend, Melinda, standing lost, twining and untwining her thin muscular hands.

"I just can't stand any more." Melinda tried to run out onto the terrace above the river, but the long white table Delilah had set for drinks after church was in the way. She stopped and clung to it, her knuckles white.

"If I've told Delilah once I've told her a thousand times—the silver julep cups have to be put in the icebox, not on the bar—in the *icebox*." She was sobbing.

Mother had bought the cups at Tiffany's and had them etched with the Kregg crest. They had long since become a part of the family silver "from Albion on the James." I concentrated on the cups as completely as Melinda did, knowing that I would have to break through a taboo against the truth as rigid as the forbidden name of God. It wasn't that she wouldn't tell. She couldn't. She had never learned the language. I took her hard broad shoulders and turned her toward me. For just a pause we clung together.

"What happened?" I asked her and held her until she answered.

"Oh, honey, Johnny fell. I guess he fell."

"Oh God! Into the water, about four o'clock?"

She heard my whisper. "No. Sissy, he hit his head. Spud's down there now. I called Ann Randolph and told her to call people not to come," she babbled. "I told her to tell Daisy to tell people not to come or call up, we needed the telephone free for the hospital."

My hands dug into her shoulders. Johnny was alive. "How bad hurt is he?" I, stripped to sorrow and hope, spoke like a mountain woman.

"The skull has been fractured over the ear." She retreated into hospital abstractions as if all concentration were on an anatomical head, not Johnny's.

"Hannah, you'll have to take Johnny's car and drive up to Egeria." Finding something to tell me to do made her voice gather strength again. "Mother can't be told over the telephone."

"I told you I'd do that." Katy's accent strode toward us from Nantucket.

"No. I think one of the family," Melinda told her. The woman looked as if her drained, aging, pale face had been slapped.

"Where is his car?"

"It's—oh, Hannah, the police have it." As if the last horror had been exposed, Melinda wailed, "What are we going to tell people?"

"I'll drive you down." Katy got up from the chair. I couldn't remember the last name she was using.

The telephone rang. Melinda grabbed it and listened, then said, "Oh, no, honey, we're trying to keep the phone clear." She hung up and looked at me as if she'd just seen me for the first time. "Oh, Hannah, why couldn't you and Johnny listen to me? Nothing like this would have happened." Melinda was right—nothing, good or bad, would ever, ever happen. We would have laid away our sex, our doubts, our lives, like toys to be outgrown. She wandered out of the room, through the door, toward her own house next door, forgetting us.

"Where's Spud?" I asked Katy, who was already striding toward her Jaguar.

"At the hospital," she flung over her shoulder.

"For God's sake, tell me what happened," I begged her.

"He wouldn't stay with us. He had to go wandering off somewhere. You people..." She made the engine roar. I could see more of the night. This woman's body had been begging then as easily as she rejected us now. She sat stiff with fury and defeat, revving the engine hard with her brown-and-white shoe, her hands gripping the wheel.

"Where did it happen?" I tried again, exhausted.

"In jail," she said coolly; the moving car had given her power back. She was ready again to travel. All the way back down the mile of winding road she never said another word. If she had been a man careening in that car down the road through the trees, between the manicured gardens, she would have been called psychopathic, but being a well-groomed, thin, rich American woman, she was as much a part of the road she ran on as a car ad—a social ideal for what Mother and Melinda sought, bought, and gave in to when they had a chance. Their hopes spun round such physically successful women, and she was now shrugging us off, without malice. She wouldn't have cared enough for that. It was simply that we were in the way of her light, fast, selfish road.

She drove on, almost physically jettisoning a burden of hope and choice. She had wanted Johnny for a little while, as she had wanted other men, men as hard and as easy as herself. Even the pathos I remembered, probably repeated at Johnny the night before so that he felt engulfed in it, was calculated so deeply that she had exuded a true momentary yawning need, but now that Johnny was out of the way, perhaps dying, she was dropping her pretense, putting us behind her.

I saw Melinda and Mother as so sickeningly innocent that they infuriated me—so vulnerable to any woman who fitted the parody of gallantry they called a lady, that cold irresponsible ease of privilege without responsibility that they could never understand but only copy.

"Where the devil is the place?" She swooped over Canona bridge. I pointed down Neill Street.

As I got out in front of the police station I leaned over toward her. She stared straight ahead, already bored and annoyed with my thanks.

"I want you to be gone by the time I get back," I told her quietly. She looked at me, unsurprised, all our language of understanding already spoken, then spurted the white car forward as if I had released her.

Five miles upriver from Canona she would forget us. She would shed her bodily fury by the time she took the four-lane ramp over Beulah at a neat sensuous sixty in that car. She would concentrate on the mountain curves, enjoying their feel under her fingers. East of the mountains she would fade toward Aiken or toward Middleburg. It didn't matter to her. She was one who obliterated her past, her crashes into contact, as she did the smooth miles behind her, unless within it there was something or someone she wanted enough to raise the stud fee.

Our exposure of organic grief had embarrassed and repulsed her as much as Aunt Althea's did Mother. Somewhere the reasons connected. We had shattered the American genteel rule of indifference, against diving deep, against tears, a rule most of us were prepared to protect with one another's lives.

The downtown empty Sunday street in front of the police

station was still littered with Saturday night. There was not a sound. There were not even any men sitting in white shirt-sleeves on the steps, leaning against its Greek municipal columns. I knew where to go. We all did, though we never admitted it. The dirty corridor to the sergeant's desk was as familiar as All Saints or the Club. The sergeant on duty sat with his chair tilted back and his feet up, talking to a black policeman. A row of half-empty bottles stood along the wall behind him, confiscated the night before. The sergeant saw me but let me wait for a minute, not unkindly; I was just another of that long line of women who come in on Sunday morning after a hot close Saturday night to bring bail or to question, sometimes to cry.

The black cop was going off duty. He lounged against the heavy radio stand, drinking a last cup of coffee.

"Me and Sadie was just settin' down to watch 'Perry Mason,'" the sergeant finished what he had been telling. "I come in off the porch and seen the temperature reading ninety degrees. I said to Sadie, 'I'm glad I ain't on duty. It's a fight night,' I told her. Heat lightning. We sat there drinking beer and watching 'Perry Mason.' Boy, I'm glad I wudn't on duty."

The black cop patted the radio. "This here never shut up from midnight on. One signal eight after another. Man, I tell you, two o'clock a call come in some guy was ridin' a horse in the post-office yard. There wasn't nobody but a signal eight, half on the sidewalk, half in the street. Them bastards," he said with the annoyed affection of a Carver Street mother. The big public face of the clock above his head said eleven-thirty. I had been home for less than an hour.

The sergeant lowered his feet and swung round to the window.

"I just got here," I told him. That wasn't what I meant to say. He waited, watching me.

"I have to pick up my brother's car," I explained, fast sliding toward tears under that impersonal warmth.

"Now take it easy. Who's your brother?" He humored me. His kindness, after the passion, the anger, the long night, probed with the efficiency of a nurse.

"J-Jonathan McKarkle," I told him and cried, "Nobody will tell me what happened." Somebody touched me on my shoulder. I told the hand, "They think they've told me but they haven't told me."

The black policeman said, "Now, Sissy, come in here and sit down for a minute. Everything's going to be all right."

"But it'll get rougher before it gets smoother." I wanted to tell him the answer that Johnny and I used. Then I recognized him. "Toey, I didn't know you," and reached for his hand as I had when we were children in the house on River Street.

He led me into the deserted, dirty courtroom. We sat down together on creaking flip chairs, still holding hands. I watched the empty judge's bench. The room was like some tawdry, abandoned flea pit of a movie. I said, "I didn't even recognize you, Toey."

"It's been a long time, Sissy." Toey's large brown hand was still on my shoulder to steady me—another brother, Johnny's boy shadow. Until they were fourteen, Toey and Johnny had disappeared on summer mornings down through the river-bank trees to raise their trotline in the dawn mist. On some mornings the night coal barges with their paddlewheeled boats had broken the line. On others, I watched while the little leaky johnboat they kept on the bank edged out through the river mist. Sometimes in the distance I could see them take a catfish off the line, but not often. The river was too dirty with chemical and coal waste for many fish to survive in it. But they kept on trying. Afterwards, Delilah gave us breakfast in the kitchen.

On fall nights when Johnny's mind and spirit were fighting the confines of school starting, they would sit on the back porch steps and Toey would hear Johnny's Latin.

"*Amo, amas, amat, amamus, amatis, amant.*" Their soft "a's" mingled in the dusk with the dry whispering of the fall leaves. I could hear them chanting from the upstairs window. Toey was an honor student.

Mother would say at the dinner table, "I think it's a shame that Toey isn't taught something useful. A good vocational school."

Johnny, struggling with dinner and Latin, never said a word.

Finally Mother said she had to put a stop to us eating together in the kitchen on school mornings. She said Toey would be happier. She started getting up early for the first time in years, and we had breakfast in the dining room. She said it was the least she could do, now that Johnny and Melinda had reached a certain age—but it was Johnny she was watching. Melinda had already been sent to Virginia to school.

I realized Toey had been talking. "If I'd've been here I

could've taken Johnny home," he was saying. "I heard the signal come in about two o'clock, 'Pick up somebody on the Boulevard.' The officer was laughin'. He said some guy was just dancin' down the street, hookin' an arm around the lampposts and then thankin' them, called them women's names . . ."

Toey's voice veered away. "We have to pick 'em up, Sissy. They git rolled or fall in the river. This jail here on Saturday nights is just a big nursery to protect drunks.

"I never knew it was Johnny 'til I come back and saw his name booked. I slipped out to call Mr. Cutright but I couldn't find him. I went up to the tank. It was dark in there, only a light from the toilet shinin' through the bars. Johnny was standin' by the iron bench at the back. I could see his face and the white dinner coat, catchin' the light from the toilet. He looked sober then, Sissy. I didn't want to see him in there. You know it ain't the first time. I tried to call to him without wakin' the others up. They was about forty of them in there by then. You don't like to stir 'em up. They's sleepin' all over each other. I whispered out—you know how you do— 'Johnny,' and he turned around and seen me. That floor full of men started to roll. Somebody hollered shut up and they started movin' awake, troubled.

"Johnny said, 'It's all right, Toey, quit tryin' to wipe my nose.' That hurt my feelin's. You know, it's funny. Lately he used to talk nigger to me when he was drunk. You know, 'Hey, boy.' He'd put his arm around my neck and talk nigger.

"Well, I come on back downstairs. Figured he was as well off there as anywhere 'til he dried out. They's bringin' this skinny fellah up. Lord, he was coming up them stairs just layin' down the law. Me and two other cops had to cool him down. We knocked him out a little bit, not so we'd hurt him, and throwed him in the tank. Johnny went on lookin' out the window, never even turned around.

"It was about an hour later, things had calmed down so's we was restin' a little. Saturday night hits a peak about one, two o'clock, then it begins to quiet down. We always know when it's going to be a fight night. Payday upriver—heat does it, makes the women feisty. They start hollerin' at the kids or git on some point and won't git off."

I glimpsed Johnny's night. I could see Melinda, on a point, flashing and flashing her demands. I could see cool Katy edging nearer and nearer. I could hear Mother in the Saturday-night corridors pacing until the whole house was a silent scream. On such nights the reins hung slack in the women's hands—even the downriver winds whispered against them, panicked them, aroused in the men a passion for freedom—just once—just a little freedom—just to have everybody shut up for once . . .

"These here Scotch-Irish mountain people, they hear enough hell-far preachin' and they take off—don't like nobody tellin' 'em what to do. Sometimes we have to do things down here I don't figure is necessary, but when the lid's off on a man full of fightin' whiskey . . ."

"It was about four o'clock"—I guided Toey to the dark cell again, with its racks full of men overflowing onto the concrete floor, sleeping like snakes in a cage—"I heard Johnny call me. Heard him call my name," I told Toey, knowing he wouldn't question that I had heard.

"About four o'clock," Toey went on, brought back to that night place, "we heard a ruckus. Near as we could piece together afterward, it had started when one of the drunks, old John Cockburn, he comes in and asks to stay because he don't like to go home to his wife and he's too dirty for a hotel to take him—he come and booked himself in. Long about three-thirty he woke up and started in to preachin'. Nobody don't listen to him usually. He thinks he's hollerin' but he don't do no more than a kind of singin' whisper. Only at night it gits penetratin' sometimes." Toey's soft voice went on, trying to conjure for me—a natural conjurer like his mother. They had both taught me to conjure, storytelling not in ideas but in colors and sounds.

"He tells Jesus he's a sinner and if he let him off this once he won't do it no more. He just plasters hisself against the wall so the devil can't come up behind him and whispers to Jesus he's sorry and he can see Him and he's saved and ain't never goin' to backslide no more. Nobody bothers him. They got right smart respect for each other's troubles up there. But last night he cut into the skinny guy's nightmares. I reckon he was dryin' out and it was hot and John's preachin' got on his nerves. Anyhow, next thing that happened was the preachin' woke up a colored man who was settin' on an upturned bucket. He said he saw Johnny still standin' there and offered him his seat. Johnny started to say somethin', and this skinny guy, he come out a-fightin'—took it out on Johnny because he told us later he couldn't shut a man up was talkin' to Jesus.

He swung on Johnny. He said Johnny said somethin' that made him fly red and he swung again. Johnny went down like a sack and hit his head on the corner of the iron bench. Then the skinny guy and the colored man got into it. We had to hose down the cell. They's forty men in there fightin' and pushin'.

"When we got things calmed down I waded through to where Johnny was still lyin' on the floor. The colored man was lookin' at him. He told me he'd stood right over top of him—kind of instinct—to keep him from gettin' tramped on.

"We took him to St. Stephen's and I reported the incident to your brother-in-law." Toey's voice was formal again. He had traveled with me from childhood back to his uniform and the empty courtroom.

"I been up there this mornin'. They told me he's still unconscious. They thought I was takin' evidence."

"Hey, Jack." The sergeant came to the door, awkward, trying to be of service. "Here's the keys to McKarkle's car. You follow the little lady up the hospital. See she gets there all right."

"Jack?" I looked at Toey, who had pulled me out of the water when Johnny dared me to swim and said he didn't want a little sister who didn't have the guts to swim the river. "Come on, old Hannah, get in and don't squawk." I could still hear Johnny teasing.

I had jumped in. Toey saw I couldn't swim and came in after me. Johnny was all sorrow and held his arm around me while Toey rowed the johnboat to shore, but I didn't squawk. Johnny said, "Look, Toey, she doesn't even cry. Not my old Hannah."

"My name is John Peregrine Lacey. I bet you never knew it," Toey said. "Your ma told Ma she couldn't get mixed up on Johnny and me havin' the same name. She called me Toey after my great-grandmother. You ma told me a lot about her. She thought Ma hadn't already told me who I was . . ."

I followed him out of the police station, back into the sun.

The day corridors of the hospitals are always light. Against that bright, impersonal, cheerful sun spread across the polished brown floor, the waiting visitors on benches huddled outside the ward, whispering to each other, the way people do in church. Sunday in St. Stephen's was the day whole families who were lucky enough to have someone to visit came, full of quiet excitement and careful manners, as to a celebration, bringing gifts of flowers, rambler roses, Shasta daisies, tiger lilies in tin cans or in wicker baskets with great hoops of handles. I heard the cult words, stroke, operation, the abstract stomach, the abstract heart, as if these, too, had been brought as Puritan sacrifices to the polished temple of the hospital. Against the walls women with bowed shoulders slumped in their own shadows, their feet splayed out with pleasure at the outing.

The corridor was long. I could hear my heels clicking fast along it, but I moved too slowly toward Johnny. I heard obsessive breathing above the quiet babble of voices. The breathing filled the hall, heavy, beyond snoring, a slow dragging in and out of groaning wind.

My brother-in-law, Spud, was standing at Johnny's door with Freddie, our doctor. He turned and saw me. His round, sad face looked no redder, no more bewildered, than it ever did. Spud seemed to have reached long ago the edge of surprise that his face muscles and his weak child's eyes could register. He couldn't show any more.

He and Freddie moved together, flanking me, shutting me out of the room by the instinct of men to protect the women they have shielded with their lives against any harshness, hiding from us the back rooms of the world where fact was, until the whole structure of their lives became a reassurance, and no one faced any fact at all.

"Now, Sissy . . . now, Sissy." Spud was rubbing his fat hand across my back.

"Can't I see him?" I asked Freddie Potter.

He, too, slipped formally into his role. "Hannah, now be prepared . . ."

"Don't go off the deep end," Spud muttered for some reason.

"It may not be as bad as it looks," Freddie told me. "Johnny's in a coma. It's just like being asleep. He's not feeling any pain."

I wanted to laugh at the old phrase about drunks—"he's not feeling any pain"—used to comfort me, as if it were an ideal end for a shallow life or a shallow party.

"Don't be surprised if he doesn't know you. We just have to wait. He may regain consciousness at any time."

Freddie and I locked eyes, forgetting Spud. Beyond the hurt look in the eyes of Johnny's friend reassuring Johnny's sister, I saw a man whose life had to be dedicated to fact. I understood then Freddie's preoccupied, watchful silence as he piloted a silly wife unobtrusively night after night, coming back to the hill from truth like this he couldn't share with any of us. Despite his careful helpfulness and trained lying, I knew that Johnny was going to die.

"Why did you tell me that?" I was furious, trying to get by him. Spud grabbed my arm harder.

"Let me talk to Sissy," Freddie told him.

"Okay, Freddie, you handle it."

We, frozen there, pulled against one another, exchanging child names we never had been allowed to outgrow, three more shadows in the corridor, better dressed, better fed, isolated from the others who were watching us with the patience of poor people used to waiting, watching with interest our impatience, knowing that it wouldn't do any good.

Spud walked back to the door, to the stertorous breathing that seemed to lift and settle in my head.

Freddie's hand dragged me to the window. "Don't lie to me, Freddie," I told him. "Lie to the others—they need it."

"Oh, Hannah . . ." I had forced him into silence but not into letting go of my arm.

Once when I was home Freddie, allowing himself to drink too much, had dragged me in a corner while the inevitable party passed and repassed in front of us. He kept trying to tell me something that I could hardly hear. People were touching my arm all through it and saying, "Hi, Sissy . . . hi, girl . . . hi, honey . . . hi . . . hi . . ."

"Goddammit, Hannah, did *you* ever try to tell anybody the truth?" I finally heard him say over the babble. "I can tell you who is on the road to dying here—too much mileage, drying up. I can see it . . . do you think I can tell them?"

"Hi, honey." Ann Randolph sailed by and winked at me.

"Hannah, why don't you persuade Johnny to get out of here? He's got more to him than this—nothing to use his mind on . . ."

He had touched on my hope. Johnny, across the room, was flanked by Mother, and Melinda. Mother was telling him something, leaning up to him, flirting. Johnny was watching her like a troubled nurse. I heard him say, "Let's go home," to her as if it were a sweet secret between them. She took his arm.

"Be back when I can, Sissy," Johnny whispered as he passed, his face dim.

"Genteel murder," Freddie had said that night to me, watching Johnny's back, "is the slowest form of murder. There's no law against it and no cure for it, and it leaves no sign of guilt."

"*Why don't you try?*" I begged his authority as a doctor, furious.

"Hannah, last spring a woman you and I both know came to me for the tenth time in a year with a frozen coccyx. She'd held in her goddam tail for so long it had stuck that way. I didn't have time to hold her hand or her tail or whatever she wanted. I had to get up to St. Stephen's—there was a woman dying of cancer. I didn't have *time*. So I told her the cure. I told her to get pregnant and the stretching and then her labor would cure her tail. She never spoke to me again. She's in this room and she has Nell and me to her parties. I go, pad along behind Nell. It keeps Nell happy. That woman won't speak to me tonight and she'll welcome the wall right above my head when I go to her house. *Try?* Oh, for Christ's sake, Sissy . . ."

"Where's Johnny?" Melinda swam by in the crowd.

"He took Mother home."

A shadow crossed her face, then she saw Spud and went after him.

"You can't tell anybody until it's too late and the dying has a name—*then* they beg. *Then* they want to know."

I could see his wife, little Nell Potter, plowing through the crowded room toward us, smiling to everyone she pushed out of the way, her still-pretty Irish girl's face fresh even from a distance. She was one of the women who had weathered, not aged. Fine dry lines were like a delicate veil. There was no record, in her skin or in her eyes, of choice or passion. Since the Episcopal Church told her to be, she was entirely faithful to Freddie, as she would have been to any other man of the "crowd," as long as he was patient, intelligent, convenient, and cynical enough to cope with her. She was known as "cute." She had a depraved view that passed for common sense, which would have done credit to a cathouse madam. She understood and talked a great deal about "affairs"—I had heard her ever since she and Melinda, growing up, talked about people on the porch swing, forgetting I was there. Of love she had a complete and clean horror, reducing it safely for herself to two manageable components—sex and secrecy. For those, people should be watched; if caught, punished; and through the years, in incident after incident, she helped without questioning. She bore down on us with her party look in her eyes. Later she would do a shimmy while Brandy played a heavy undergraduate piano, his repertoire stopping with the Princeton Triangle Show for 1940.

These two—sex and secrecy—were the only reasons on Nell's horizon a man and a woman should be talking and watching each other as earnestly as Freddie and I were.

She broke it up.

Because he'd let down his barrier for once, Freddie avoided me after that for five years until the morning, caught in the hospital corridor, when Johnny's dying had, at last, a name.

We leaned against the bench at the end of the hospital corridor that morning, and took up the old conversation where we had left off, took it up too late, as he had foreseen, with the sound of that breathing, that pulling of air into dying lungs.

"I won't lie to you, Hannah," he told me. "It's touch and go. Johnny may regain consciousness. He may go out this way. Somewhere deep inside him where we can't get to— can't help—he's working it out. If his body is strong enough to stand the strain he may make it, but Johnny's got a lot of mileage on him."

"Can I see him now?"

"Come on, honey." The door was the second from the end of the corridor; through the first open door an old woman in a pink bed jacket pecked at us with her eyes.

"I *have* tried, Hannah," Freddie apologized, whether for all the times he'd tried with all of us and been repulsed into the pleasant, hand-holding doctor he had become or for Johnny at that moment, I will never know.

When I walked into his room, I saw a separate, broken, self-used, unknown man, his blank face white and glossed with sweat, his mouth stretched catfish wide for air. He lay in the impersonal hospital bed, his arm strapped for glucose feeding, tapped like a tree. His left ear was bandaged, his face, in that deadly repose, only shaded darker under his left eye. Saliva channeled down a scar I didn't know about beside his mouth. He seemed in a perpetual pause. The only movement was his slow, loud sucking in of air, down his throat until his lungs could stand no more, then letting it out in a long, despairing sigh. An early, polite "Fall Arrangement" stood beside his bed, red and yellow daggers of gladioli, fat, fleshly-petaled, among the white enamel paraphernalia.

His eyes were open. He looked someplace else, like a bad portrait, never on me, as I moved toward his bed. He watched, meeting no demands, pure or impersonal, answering for once in his now ebbing tide no life, no lust, no wishes.

Then the person the man was, my brother Johnny, whom I carried as talisman-mentor in my mind, rushed into me and refocused my eyes. I saw his eternal boy's face. He became again the brother owned and demanded by my fixed heart.

I took his indifferent hand and begged him to live.

"Johnny," I whispered, trying by will to wake him for me. "Johnny, please. Oh, don't do that. Don't do that." My voice was petulant. I could hear it, involved with his hauling in of air.

"Sissy, honey, he can't hear you. Come on, come on now." Spud had slipped in behind me and now took my arm.

"I've tried, Sissy . . . God knows, I've tried," he whispered, echoing Freddie in the beginning of all the apologies we would make, in our ways, for Johnny. His hand was shaking on my arm. Shock had brought out the central wound. I knew what he would say because he always did, as if touching his heart could only touch one aware place in it.

"Sissy, you know I haven't had a cent from my father yet. I paid for the house Melinda wanted. Not anybody in town knows I paid for it." He hardly knew what he was saying. Everyone did know. He kept telling the open secret. He had for years. In the hospital corridor, that morning, it was not irrelevant at all.

The after-church visitors were walking through the shining halls as they had marched toward the churches, ladies stealing peeks into room after room for someone whose eye they could catch, recognize, and lightly cheer.

I could hear nothing but Johnny's loud breathing.

As I walked back out into the sunlight of the steps, two of Mother's friends pushed with great purpose through the crowd of ladies. I had known them all my life, and I realized with a jar that I couldn't remember either of their names.

They pinned my arms. Shock had cleared my eyes too much and I saw them.

"We wanted to see a member of the family," one said, gracefully, quietly, so the crowd couldn't hear and stare. "Oh, my dear, what a terrible thing. That dear boy..." Then, without a change of breath, bright curiosity took over her sad eyes and they glittered and probed at me. "What *really happened*?" She would never in her life believe that her consciously kind eyes could be that hard.

Under her soft, dry skin I saw something that Melinda and Mother feared and lied to. They had a right to fear it. It was naked curiosity for the lives of others, whipping, righteous curiosity.

Johnny was giving them, for the day, a holiday. They would take whatever words I stammered out, piece an "inside" story together, their unkissed mouths breathing the smell of cigarettes and coffee into their telephones, making little secretive sounds to each other. I remembered how small termite mandibles were, and how, if you lean close and pinpoint attention, you can hear them, how their combined tenacity can crush a building. These women were moving close to trouble, chewing at it because they had, that week, none of their own to feed the others with.

"We think," I spoke officially, "Johnny's going to be all right." Then I lied, as easy as breathing. "He stumbled and fell last night. One of those stupid accidents anybody could have." I even managed to laugh a little. Their knowing eyes seemed to meet each other's through my lying skull.

"We'll just *peek* in." They were away, up the steps.

"You can't. He can't have visitors..." I begged after them.

"Just a peek," one called back and smiled. "What a blessing it isn't too serious. My, we were upset."

I couldn't stop them. No one had ever stopped them in their lives.

Toey still waited, relaxed in the authoritative police car, elegant in his blue shirt and black peaked cap with the brass polished almost white, a man of great physical pride. He didn't turn his head, as if he knew I would come down toward him and lean into the open window.

"Jack," I said, to draw his head around. "He's still..."

He didn't turn, just went on watching the distance down

the tree-lined street. When he spoke, he only began aloud from someplace else, where he was thinking.

"Miss Leftwich ain't in there, is she?"

"No." We were murmuring.

"I seen her following him many a night along the street, seeing he didn't get into trouble. She never said nothing— just followed along. Every once in a while he'd turn and see her. When he did she'd stop, like an animal. She had a saint's face. She never moved 'til he went on. Then she'd follow him."

"Jack," I said, "why? Why didn't they . . ."

His mind jumped to the next place. "I don't know, Hannah." He still talked to the road. "Seems like everybody wiped Johnny's nose. It was there to be wiped and running. He never asked and he never thanked. He only thanked people he had to court. Melinda and your ma, the only ones he wasn't sure of."

"Jack . . ."

"We watched you-all. Just watched you. Every black person in this town knows what you are doing, and you can't even tell us apart. It's like you were always moving and acting in front of our black houses. Didn't even know we noticed, no more contact than through a glass. You just dancing around and what the hell."

"Jack, for God's sake, don't go nigger on me right now. I need you too much." I was so angry with him my voice rose and touched two mountain women. They stopped still to watch and listen, completely calm-faced. "I've got to go to Egeria."

"Honey, watch your pa."

I was surprised. No one had mentioned or thought of Father. "It's Mother . . ."

"Jesus, I hate that woman." Jack was completely at ease, telling me. "Have you ever been looked right through as if you wasn't there?"

"I just have . . ." I put my head down on the car window frame. My shoulders were heaving. "Jack, let me alone."

"I used to know Christmas was coming when her eyes started to focus on me. She stopped me believing in God. If there was a God she would have died when you and Johnny and poor little old Melinda were kids."

One of the mountain women came over and took my shoulders and held them, saying nothing. Her contact was the first impersonal blessed act that morning. When I straightened again, she turned away and walked toward the hospital door.

Jack was looking at me. I couldn't tell whether his eyes were bloodshot because he was black or because he'd been crying, but he wouldn't, or couldn't, stop his mouth.

"I tell you something. She *liked* Johnny's drinking like that. She *liked* it. That way he stayed guilty and he stayed home. When I'd take him home her face would melt with affection like butter and she'd take him over. It was obscene. If she could have carried him upstairs like a little baby she would have. Once she turned around under his shoulder and said, 'You have to understand, Toey, gentlemen act like this sometimes.' She didn't want no man. What she did want I don't know. Jesus, it was disgusting . . ."

"I've got to go," I told him.

"Sissy"—his thick black hand touched mine—"I'll be here. Wish I could go with you. Now drive careful."

"I've got to know *why*." I couldn't leave his hand. "Where's the man who did it?"

"We moved him over to the County. Charged him with malicious wounding, for now."

"Can I see him when I get back?"

"Sure. I don't know why, though." He watched me. "Okay, I know why. Now remember, go easy with your pa."

Without another word he started the motor and drove away, as if the car were part of him, down the Sunday street. The light on the top of the police car turned round and round, watchful as a lighthouse.

How could I "go easy" with my father—a man whom I had never seen separately, as you see another person, in a split second of love or death, in all my life? Christ, I knew a two-day lover then better than I knew my father.

Johnny's Porsche smelled of dogs. It drove too loosely. I had the same twinge of fear in handling it that I had of him, though until the shock of that morning I had hidden this all my life. The wheel swung as if it had been used recklessly. In the back seat was a check lead that had been there the year before. The Chipp straw hat had been flung down beside it; a few quarters had rolled out on the leather seat. When I stopped at Pagano's garage to have the car checked for the drive across the mountains to Egeria, Rose's brother, Steve Pagano, came out and touched the fender. His dark face was sad and veiled. I wanted him to speak, to give me a clue, as much as I had wanted the women to shut up, but he acted like he hardly recognized me.

He filled the tank and checked the oil without looking at me. I searched in the glove compartment for Johnny's credit card. The compartment was jammed to the brim with the secret life he carried within the turtle shell of the car: a map of Ohio, a package of condoms, an address book, matches from the Wayfaring Stranger and the Mountain View Motel, cigarettes, a dirty glass, a flask I had given him one glittering Christmas, a blank order book; hidden under them all, a prayer book. I couldn't find the credit card.

Steve put his hand into the car over my head and took it from the sun visor. "Sissy, honey, you be careful," he muttered. "I called Rose and Eph . . ."

I drove fast through the new valley road, lined all the way to Beulah with hot-dog stands, drive-ins, red-and-blue neon signs moving in the sunlight, rolling spirals for the motels, the beer joints. For the first twenty miles, marked by the deserted skeletons of the wildcat tipples bridged over the road to the river, past the chemical factories with their small towns of brick and iron and great silolike vats, I never glimpsed the river, a meadow's width away from the road.

Beulah's familiar hills swept past the slipstream of my concentrated vision. It was too late to stop and seek out the big house roof, too late even to slow down. The ramp swept me over it at sixty miles an hour. I caught a glimpse of deserted houses, the crests of trees, a few well-kept roofs, and at the top of the valley, on the little rise we knew as Old Fort Hill, the old red-brick church, Miss Leah's Chapel, with its sunken, neglected graves.

The sun fell slowly behind me. I drove east as if the whole river valley were in the way of my going. I read *Jesus is Coming—Are you ready?* whitewashed in a sprawl across the first cliff face near the foot of the mountain. Hung over it, the sumacs, the first ripeners, dropped their bright red leaves. My senses, trained to notice the coming of hunting time, of good scent, quickened and sang until they brought back Johnny, not condom-carrying salesman, genteel, small-town

man, but the escaped one. The woods up the first mountain
hollow vaulted over a rough nave where a creek flung itself
down against the stones and tunneled under the road.

I could not think of Johnny and still drive. I turned on the
car radio, forgetting it was Sunday in the mountains—McKarkle
country.

Thin voices sang a nasal song into the car—a single line
without harmonics.

"'I've reached the land of corn and wine,'" they whined,
echoing in some vault beyond the microphone. The car
passed under the last gaunt flayed tipple thrusting out from a
slag-dark hollow. "'And all its riches freely mine'"; the voices
began to fade professionally behind the homely cracker-barrel
intimacy of the radio preacher.

"This is WRIM. The Bible Hour is being brought to you
folks on this purty September Sunday by the courtesy of the
Cherokee Milling Company, God bless them. When you
make that Cherokee corn bread and eat those real, home-
made butter-soaked Cherokee biscuits I jest want you to
remember what day it is, folks. Hit's the day of the Lord, the
Sabbath. Drive careful."

The voices rose again, tinny in the fast car. I piloted around
the swooping mountain curves. The owner of WRIM drove a
Porsche too.

"'O Beulah land, sweet Beulah land, as on the highest
mount I stand, I look away across the sea, where mansions
are prepared for me . . .'"

A mouth that knew every nuance of the microphone swelled
through the car, arresting my speed. "Brothers and sisters, I
want to talk to you a little bit today about a little verse from
Isaiah 3." He was close, almost licking the microphone; he
stepped back and let his voice echo in the studio. The sound
blared through the car radio:

"'The mighty man, and the man of war, the judge, and the
prophet, and the prudent, and the ancient,

"'The captain of fifty, and the honourable man, and the
counsellor, and the cunning artificer, and the eloquent orator.

"'And I will give children *to be* their princes, and babes
shall rule over them.'"

He came back to the microphone as I drove past a sunken
dirty white-clapboard filling station perched on the mountain-
side. There were a few cabins sagging in the back, little
bigger than beds. A chipped paint sign read *Mountain View*

Motel. With what wild urge had Johnny driven up the
mountain, who beside him, to bury his need, secret and
ashamed, in that drab place?

Johnny, suspended in my mind, mingled with the obscene
courtship of the preacher's voice.

"Now, listen to that, children; we're all children. Listen to
that, little child.

"Did Jesus Christ have an education? Was Jesus Christ a
lawyer? Was Jesus Christ a captain and a mighty man? You
born-again Christians know the answer."

He stepped back again into the electric echo of his voice.
"NO! If you was goin' to put CHRIST on your payroll would
you keer what kind of education he had? If you git to lookin'
at one of the sinners and wonderin' if he's saved, do you git
him a good lawyer? NO. You don't give him nuthin' but Jesus
Christ to *face* his shame with.

"He don't wear no fancy clothes. He don't go to no fancy
hotels. He ain't got no money in the bank. He don't read no
dirty books. He don't drive no Cadillac.

"But He's here to save and judge us all. I seen a well-
dressed banker with tears a-rollin' down his cheeks. I seen
the owner of a three-car garage throw away them cigarettes
and lay aside that whiskey bottle, and I seen a good lawyer
forswear bad women and then a-kneelin' down in agony,
beggin' me never went past the fifth grade, clutchin' at my
pore pants they wouldn't put on their fancy legs and *a-beggin'*
me to save their souls from *Hell Far!*

"Jesus," he lapped the microphone, "come to them sinners
in their hour of need. All He asked for was their bad habits:
all He asked for was their fancy livin' and their dirty bodies..." I could hear him swallow spittle.

I managed to turn off the hate-filled ugly voice. Ahead of
me the indifferent mountains rolled. I knew I had to stop
shaking, get the perversion of that shameful, professional
envy in God's name out of my head, that terrible use of the
part to prove the whole. Johnny and I had heard the verses
from Isaiah before, more quietly used, but as wounding.

The preacher had not finished the prophet's words. My
Grandmother McKarkle had, and as much for her purpose as
he for his. Somehow, though hers had sounded more sancti-
fied, as she would have said, their motives seemed connected
by a tenuous wire of envy.

I had sat, huddled, licking my always scabbed six-year-old

knee and staring at my Grandmother McKarkle's heavy-booted feet. Johnny, an impatient Melinda, and I had been caught by her there on the sunny porch in Greenbrier on a cloud-shifty summer morning, just after we had listened to one of those muted quarrels the grownups seemed to think were ordinary conversation. When the whole family was there, words spat like the bacon in the thick iron skillet. Out beyond us the water in the limestone sink where Uncle Ephraim watered the cattle glittered as the sun came out, then went a sullen gray as the sun scudded behind a dark cloud.

My grandmother's face went dark like that as she turned to my mother at the farm-laden breakfast table.

"I don't see why people have to go and stay at some hotel when they got a perfectly good home to go to," she said over her head, then turned to my father as if she had asked him a question.

No one said anything. It was obviously the end of an old grownup argument we hadn't heard. As if the last word of the solid old woman at the end of the table eating a mound of spoon bread had pricked her, I saw my mother's controlled excitement, which she always showed when she went to Egeria, go flat. Her face hardened.

"I have to go get packed," she said and got up. She turned again at the door and looked past Grandmother's head. "Children," she said, all sweet with that ire I knew so well, "I'll pack all your things. Remember, the servants know who you are when they open your suitcases." She was gone.

"Servants!" my grandmother said to the spoon bread and attacked it again. "Don't ketch me let some nigger unpack my grip."

Then, as we waited for Mother to pack and Father and Uncle Ephraim wandered out by the old barn, Grandmother flipped open the Bible and leaned it between legs grown wide and relaxed with age as if they had shed all their taught shy woman ways and at last allowed her to set them aspraddle, as Uncle Ephraim called it. She read the same Isaiah as the thin-voiced preacher—but she went on to her own proving verses:

" '. . . and babes shall rule over them.

" 'And the people shall be oppressed, every one by another, and every one by his neighbour: the child shall behave himself proudly against the ancient, and the base against the honourable.' "

She leaned back and delivered herself of a sigh. I couldn't see her; the sunbonnet she had sewn herself and wore belligerently whenever Mother came, and never any other time, hid her cheek from me. The rest of the time she wore an old hat of Uncle Ephraim's.

Johnny exchanged glances with me and winked, but I didn't wink back. I firmly believed what she said. After all, she had taught me to dip in the Bible for the word of God and told me never to do it in front of my mother, who didn't know about such things, being a different "kind of people," as she called it.

Mother and Grandmother tilted for us in language. Mother called Grandmother's square brick house, built in 1860, set in the thick grazing grass of the limestone plateau, the "place" in Greenbrier. Grandmother said it was a farm, it had always been a farm, and so long as Ephraim had breath in his body it would be a farm. She said "places" were for people who didn't work their own land and bought up good pieces of property to spend coal money on living higher on the hog than their people had before them. All this was with a sharp glance at my father, who, she told us, had thrown away a perfectly good education to go into the coal business with "that Baseheart gang."

On Uncle Ephraim's vacations from Washington and Lee, he repaired the old snake fences and rode over the grass pastures among the cattle all day in an overseer's saddle with wooden stirrups, hardly saying a word, but letting Johnny and me ride after him, flop-legged and bareback. His seldom-heard laugh was as rich as good leather and amber whiskey. He had an acre-owning stride and when I heard him on the porch with the men after I had gone to my sun-scented sheets to huddle in the dusk and listen to the whippoorwills and wonder who was going to die, he'd sound as if he lived in an easy kind of joy I didn't know.

He would take Johnny hunting but not me then, but at night when they came back he would let me sit on his lap and even hold my head against his tobacco-and-man-smell chest and let me go nearly to sleep. He just didn't have a word to say in front of any grown woman. He said it wasn't any use. He said not to ever flush a covey until your gun was ready, or scatter chickens until you had something to give them to shut the damn things up again.

I knew what he meant, how words could start them. When

Mother made the mistake of telling us in front of Grandmother how, when Colonel McKarkle came home from the
War, there wasn't a soul left and he had to put his hand to the
plow himself, Grandmother laughed and said, not like an
oath but like a personal statement about God, "For the love
of the Lord, Sally Brandon, Gideon McKarkle would whirl in
his grave if he heard that. Sounds like he never did a lick of
work in his life before." Then she ignored Mother and told us
why Uncle Ephraim's grandfather named him Ephraim.

"Colonel McKarkle told me. He told me he'd had just
about enough." She looked at Ephraim. "Your grandfather
named you from the Bible because of Jehovah's promise after
trouble that Ephraim shall not envy Judah and Judah shall
not vex Ephraim. He said there been enough bloodshed
between brothers."

Johnny asked why Father wasn't named Judah then, and
Grandmother said she named him Preston after her side of
the family.

On that morning, after Mother had gathered us up and
stowed us in the Buick sedan, she went back onto the wood
porch where Grandmother rocked. I saw, from the flip-up
seat in the back, Mother lean stiffly down and plant a hard
kiss toward Grandmother's cheek. Grandmother never stopped
rocking. When Mother came back, those small tired tears she
never seemed to notice were swimming in her eyes.

On the way to Egeria Mother told us, biting at the
information and staring at the road to watch Father's driving,
that there were certain things we must not mention in front
of his mother—whiskey, cards, dancing, and the federal
income tax. She said every time she left us there she had to
come and pick up the pieces.

I wasn't paying much attention. I was remembering how
Grandmother let me watch while she sat wide on a tilted
stool and nuzzled her gray head into the big wall of the Jersey
she kept and milked herself. As the thick fingers pulled and
caressed at the heavy mottled udders and the fine streams of
milk whistled into the bucket, she gave me advice. There was
so much of it I couldn't remember what it was. I just
connected it with work, the cow she insisted on keeping as
her own, and strong disapproval of everything that wasn't
hard as a rock and as clean.

I saw my father smile slightly in the rearview mirror, but
Mother seemed frozen solemn with annoyance and a kind of

ashamed hurt she picked up as she entered the gate of Grandmother's farm and then shed two or three miles down the road toward Egeria Springs.

There, on the road to Egeria again, I saw my dead grandmother and recognized for the first time how she had always defeated my frailer mother. She bore a mark of suspicious, shy pride, her simplicity a rock-ribbed Methodist arrogance that trusted cows and children and Ephraim, but never what the wind blew in from downriver or across the eastern mountains to runnel her hard righteousness. Seeing her, I felt lightened, shed of her, and sensed in the tensile fault in Mother's ore a shame of joy that ran all the way through to a salesman's sex and made him keep condoms in the glove compartment of his car and sneak over dark mountains to cheap motels to act.

I had an absurd vision of John Wesley in his great testimonial anger traced down through a grandmother's envy to a mother's hurt to shame as a sterile Rexall condom hidden in a Porsche sports car in the Allegheny Mountains.

There is a time when even sorrow and wondering become unbearable and fade away for a while. I felt rested, as if the guy ropes of all the family burdens had been cast off to let me glimpse a freedom from the heavy love I bore them, just for a little while.

I twirled the radio knob to jazz and drove like a fugitive across the long mountain plateau toward the Greenbrier levels. I sped through Shiloh, Sunday-dead and mine-dead. The stores of the main street, catering to coal miners, were boarded, their windows grimy and empty. My body swayed to Sidney Bechet. Around the road through Zion Corner my knees loosened and I sensed the way of the machine. I passed the sign to Fairy Land Cave, the two-and-a-half-hour mark into the mountains of Canona. It was three o'clock.

Ahead, the levels of Greenbrier lay, a great natural savannah of grazing land with limestone rocks jutting above the green meadow, dented with pools and springs which disappeared into hollow caverns. Away to my right, its neat, elegant split-wood fences a mile from the main road, lay Uncle Ephraim's "place." It was now so classic it made me grin to see it.

In the year after my Grandmother McKarkle died, when Uncle Ephraim was fifty, after the first stunned months in which he saw no one and hardly said a word, his strength flowed back from where he had always found it, from the land. It spread and burst beyond the pastures and downriver to pick Steve Pagano's black-eyed, smooth-moving sister Rose for a wife and take her back to Greenbrier. All the secret caches of his pleasure opened, and he began to enjoy being a man as sanely as he judged horses, raised cattle, and hunted. Mother had a sick headache the day of his marriage, but as word began to come back from Greenbrier that he was what she called "remodeling" the house, which meant setting columns in front of a square farmhouse and taking the yellow-and-brown linoleum off the wide boards of the floor to please Rose Pagano, she began to let the McKarkles creep into a place in her careful conversation they had never had before.

It was from there that Johnny called on rare Saturday nights when he had flown that far. I would know from his voice at once where he was.

As I drove between the white columns at the entrance to Egeria Springs, I still felt the twinge of excitement I had known ever since I was a child and went there for the first time with my parents. In my memory, it was a place where everyone walked more easily through old quiet paths under the last virgin trees, or down muted high corridors that filled my child's eyes full of wonder and made my mother call me down, embarrassed at my staring. Voices were muffled there under the rotunda of the dining room, where not even the table silver made much noise. Egeria's smell, from the gate on into the rooms, a smell compounded of expensive secluded mountain air, hand-ironed linen, polish, huge, glossy, well-fed plants, and thick notepaper, I recognized later wherever I smelled it, and it brought me back to Egeria Springs. It was the clean, crisp smell of American money.

The avenue ran under trees around the near hill. Down in the valley below me, the sunken temple that covered a spring which had once been the center of Egeria stood under its painted Roman statue. Now it was a place we were taken to see once, to say we'd seen it. After that we raced past it, past faded, frail, disused cottages, to the Nile-green pool with its scarlet umbrellas or to the black tennis courts. Mother said that the temple still had its original wooden columns, but Uncle Ephraim told us they were about as original as Grandpa's ax, which had had five new handles and four new blades.

As I stopped Johnny's car I glanced up across the huge white Roman façade of the hotel, jutting out between the broad dining-room porch and its balancing twin that opened off the ballroom. The Chippendale railing, unchanged, quiet in the shade, held me suspended in the driveway. Johnny was back, his heavy breathing in my head, the danger which had been there so long with him and now was pinpointed on a hospital bed, as if, for a second to split the brain, all his roads had led to it. I remembered the expected beauty of the first dance I went to at Egeria.

We were in the bedroom of the Laurel Wing. It was night. Faintly, far away, I could hear music. Mother fussed behind my worried, frowning head, flicked the taffeta ruffles of my long dress. Under it my knees shook, and my feet hurt in new shoes. I was at that clear, exposed fifteen when a girl is first conscious of herself as moving awkwardly across endless alien floors, only knowing later that self-consciousness had its special grace. Every frightened walk down wide stairs to these first dances was an ecstasy of fear and hope, a dreamed-of meeting with some Sebastian-eyed boy whose hidden, nameless grief only one's self could cure, for in 1945 the ideal boy, the dreamboat, had a lost look about him.

So in front of the mirror I forgot what night it was, that it was all for Johnny, home at twenty-one from Europe, to celebrate his release from the service. Mother had planned it all because she said we had always been so happy at Egeria. Johnny watched us as if we moved on a screen in front of him, making no contact, even with me, his eyes as stony as a cat's with a dead anger I couldn't understand.

Mother was saying, fidgeting in the pink bedroom, as she had said over and over behind Johnny's back when he disappeared into the Wayfaring Stranger to sit with Charley who had been in his company, "I think the best thing is to treat Johnny as if nothing has happened. We'll make it just like it always was. I think that's the best. Just put it out of our minds."

Once I heard him stumbling up the stairs to his room in the middle of the night, crying. Once he screamed and woke the whole house, but in the morning he said he'd been asleep. I could hear Mother telling about it on the telephone. "He has these *awful* nightmares," she told Aunt Mamie, bright with excitement at her glimpse of war.

It was October. Outside the windows and along the walks, I could hear the bright leaves swishing as they were harvested by the wind.

There is only one time when the form of dancing and light comes as true as the dream, and that is the first time one sees it, as some fledgling might see the swallows swoop and know it needs only courage to follow, and falls all feet and wings from the nest, then either gives up to the dog's mouth or learns to learn; only one time when fear and beauty together meet and swirl through one's senses. For me, trained from the time I "dressed up" and smelled the musty, dry-grass smell of stored silk, and found my mother's old scuffed satin slippers in a trunk in the attic, it was my first grownup dance. Evasiveness and delight were, for a little while that night, instinctive.

The door into the ballroom was at the end of a long corridor covered with dark red flocked paper and lit dimly by electric candles in crystal sconces along the walls. I was literally borne through it. Ahead, under a glowing chandelier that had come from a castle in France, dancers whirled past the door, dresses swaying as if the fall wind had entered the ballroom and was swirling them like leaves. On the edge of it Mother and I stopped to watch. They all were strangers, swinging and whirling cloud skirts, kept from flying away by tall men in black tailcoats, with white ties and vests, a few still in uniform, tree-trunk colors. They played that year and that minute "Sentimental Journey."

I stood for those few minutes that stretched to hours, wanting to be taken into it—part of the ancient ceremony of women waiting. Then my father caught me and piloted me around the floor, in and out among the dancers. They took on their own faces, became familiar, and I was part of the whirling, the dresses, the heavy billowing of the red velvet curtains as the wind pushed in from the open porch. My father stopped to talk to Uncle Sugar by the bar, where a mass of men had gathered in a still center of the dancing, and I hung on to his arm, dancing inside and watching.

I wanted to find Johnny to tell him how beautiful it all was—to tell somebody about the excitement that pours into my eyes and ears, into the rhythm of my body, and surging through my veins. He wasn't there. Kitty Puss Wilson floated by, singing into Brandy Baseheart's ear; he looked pink with pleasure and handsome, for once, in naval uniform.

Then, out beyond the moving curtains, caught by the pale drifting light from the ballroom, no longer glittering but lying in soft fingers across the porch, I saw Johnny. He lounged against the white Chippendale railing, watching the dancers as calmly as if they performed for his judgment, drinking his drink. I could hear the ice tinkle in his glass as he jerked it down from his mouth, never stopping that cold stare.

Behind me Father was saying to Uncle Sugar, "We sure managed enough whiskey for the boys. Boy, it wasn't easy," as if the whole United States Navy floated on whiskey so they could have only a little, and that with guilty pleasure.

"We sure did that," Uncle Sugar told him as proudly as if they'd made it themselves.

I raced out to Johnny, forgetting the long dress. It made me move so slowly. I pulled it away from my legs and heard the skirt tear.

Johnny saw me coming but he didn't do anything. He just stood there, drinking and watching. I forgot what it was I was going to tell him. His face, now in profile in the pale light, looked worn and noble, just as it should. I hitched my bottom up onto the railing under the green taffeta, imitating him, trying to be as blasé, and watched the dancers, ashamed that my heart still thumped at all the movement under the blinding star shower from the chandelier.

"All those soft, fat, pretty shoulders," Johnny muttered. "It looks so goddam *fat.*" He put one hand up to my protruding shoulder and jerked at my taffeta ruffles.

"All that *crap,* Sissy . . ." He seemed to be talking to himself but accusing me at the same time. He wasn't even looking at my eyes but at my neck, under my hair. His fingers bit deep around my collarbone, just for a second, then he turned his back on me and threw his glass as hard as he could. I heard it crash against a tree.

He said, "It's like a bad dream when you wake up in the morning in the same place. It's the same place and it isn't because you have the bad dream inside you. It's behind your eyes, you know, so it can't be the same place . . ."

Johnny knew something I didn't and couldn't know then. He had the hard, unforgiving eyes of those whose bridges have been burned behind them by somebody else.

Then he said, quite calmly, looking at the dancers again, "Jesus, Hannah, it's just like it always was."

I didn't dare tell him that it was, after all, the way Mother had planned it.

Released from the pull of the dancers, one dark figure swayed in the doorway against a haloing light that made her face and her wide skirt a dark shadow, kept on swaying, trying to get her balance by grasping the lintel of the door.

Johnny sighed an exhausted sigh, then raised his voice. It soothed and flirted, faintly teasing. "Honey . . ."

Kitty Puss swayed from the lintel to Johnny. Her face was glossy, her teeth clenched.

"Honey," she mocked him, "come here and let me rehabilitate you." She leaned forward deliberately into his arms and slowly sank her teeth into the shoulder of his tailcoat. They were together, rigid. I could hear them breathing. I wanted to run. The party changed focus—was ugly, loud, too fast.

"Get back inside, Sissy," Johnny ordered over her shoulder, but he was looking at her hair. He twined his fingers in it and began to pull her head back.

"Hurry!" he whispered. "Hurry! Get back in there!"

His face was concentrated with a cold, hard joy. I had seen him look that way before, when he hit the boys on the shoulder playing airplanes, when he shot, deliberate. When he sensed my minding, it would make him tease, annoyed. "It's only a game, Sissy—have some sense of humor." I was crying, but they were locked together and couldn't see.

"You damn prince, hurry. Oh. God . . ." I heard Kitty Puss behind me whispering. "Where can we go? Where can we go in this goddam fish tank?" She sounded as if she hated him.

"Get the hell gone, Sissy," he whispered into her ear.

The floor was too bright to hide me. People clogged my way. I got through to the dim corridor, and Mother caught me there.

"For heaven's sake, Hannah, pull yourself together. Carrying on like this. Can't you appreciate what's done for you for one evening of your life? I knew better than to let you come. I *knew* better," she was muttering, half helping, half dragging me toward the elevator so no one would see.

I was sobbing too hard to look at her or answer anything she kept saying, but I could hear the band still playing "Sentimental Journey."

My father had seen us and come up behind us, just was there. "What the hell is the matter with Sissy?" he asked Mother.

"I don't know. I can't get anything out of her. Where's Johnny?" The elevator door opened, and I got away from her.

"Let her go," my father ordered as the door closed.

How much I cried, and even why I cried so, I didn't know

then, but at last in the darkness of the bedroom I drifted off to sleep. I woke to murmuring outside in the living room of our suite, the low, urgent quarreling of people who didn't want to be heard. I could tell by the dry taste in my mouth I had been asleep a long time.

Something had happened between Johnny and my father and mother; their voices were naked with each other, a sound so rare it made me go cold again with fear.

The voice of my father with that phrase he used at the end of long, long-built-up silences broke through the door. "I've had just about enough, Jonathan. Your mother and I have tried to be patient with you. God knows...no son of mine..."

I heard Johnny murmur.

"That will be enough out of you. We've spent over a thousand dollars to bring you up here. Your mother has sat and listened for her son to come home every night since you got back. You don't know what she's been through, waiting for her son to come home."

Mother interrupted; she was urgent with protection. "What right have you to talk? What right? *You* made a damn fool of yourself. He made a fool of himself," she begged Johnny.

Father turned even on her. "I don't care what he's been through, the boy's going to have to learn some respect for his mother and sister."

"Well, I just can't stand any more." I heard Mother's door slam.

As if their monitor had gone, the two men, for a minute, treated each other with as much politeness as if they were strangers, thinking no one heard.

"I'm sorry, son," Father said. "It's been too much for your mother." Johnny answered as gently and formally, "I'm sorry, Father."

"Son," Father told him, "I don't know what to say. Finding you in a car, using that sweet young girl I've known all her life like she was...I just want you to know I won't say a word. You can trust me. After all, *we can't disturb the women.*" He said it as if he were saying one of the Ten Commandments.

Johnny started to laugh. He pushed Father into silence with his laughter and went on laughing. I heard my parents' door shut, softly.

Then my door was being tried. A shaft of light followed Johnny inside. I saw his dark shape move over to the window.

He snapped on a small lamp, and the light made my eyes sting. He didn't turn to look at me. He watched himself in the black glass of the window. I could see the dark reflection as he stared at himself. Beyond the window a branch in the night wind slapped at his reflected face.

He knew I was awake. "For Christ's sake, Sissy," he asked his reflection, "you too? What do *you* want?"

I wanted to bury my face in the pillow, shut out that man who watched himself so coldly. I wanted to cry, "I want my brother," but there he was at last, standing in the muted light of the room that was all rich and pink with little roses on the dresser and all the polished mirrors, not off in some dark place I could only imagine, some lost place I had prayed every night for him to come back from.

Finally he sighed, the same way he had sighed before Kitty Puss had been aware that he noticed her. With a last look at his reflected face he turned, his shoulders sagging a little, and came over to sit beside me on the bed.

"Now look at that dress." He picked up a torn ruffle I'd slept on.

I began to feel warm and safe again. It was too soon. Johnny turned away and clasped his hands between his knees and looked beyond them at a space that was toward the floor, but he wasn't watching anything in that room. What he said rippled out then without stopping, some plug in his mind pulled by memory and trouble and whiskey and the night. He didn't seem to stop to breathe.

"I can't do it. Jesus, I can't do it. I'm too tired. You people don't know what it is to be tired all the way to your gut. You think you're tired when you go through a day and then go to bed. Pretty high-on-the-hog bed, out of a solid day into a solid night. I'm too *tired* for this." He was whispering and the wind outside joined him, whispering at the window, the tree branches scratched and tapped at the glass. "I've seen too many tears and wailing faces and cringing bodies and crazy heaps of dust and rubble and trash and dead things flung all the way across the damn continent until I am sick to death." He pounded the bed, once. "I am sick to death."

I watched all the pictures of him in the pier glass on the bathroom door, in the mirror over the pretty dresser, in the black window, his head now down, heard his voice muttering a litany. "God and Country and Virginity and Christmas and Dogs and Chocolate and Obedience and you don't fuck nice girls. I came back here, and the pretty girls with their thick round shoulders and their well-fed bodies make me sick. In Europe you could 'get engaged' for a few days for a bar of chocolate—same clean living room, same smiling mother. Here it costs more." He slapped my rump and laughed. "Look after it, Sissy," he told me. "It's worth a fortune."

I had a dim sense that Johnny hardly knew I was there, only that I was listening. After a silence he murmured, "*Wir haben nicht gewusst*," but when I asked him what it meant he wouldn't tell me. Years later I read that the citizens of Weimar whispered that when they were forced to walk through Buchenwald; by then it was too late to ask Johnny if he'd been there. He never talked about the war. In the new year Kitty Puss married Brandy Baseheart. She got on a laughing jag at the reception.

Was it the day I drove there in Johnny's Porsche, weighted with news, or yet another day in my abiding memory of Egeria? A man was standing beside my car, his soft hands on the rolled-down window, leaning a huge feminine body down almost as if he were bowling. He had the exaggerated politeness of Southerners who hate Jews and blacks and think women fools and yet have arrived at enough money to learn at least the commercial wisdom of silence.

"Lady," he said with great deference and patience, "would you mind moving your car out of the middle of the driveway?" His face was florid and veined, his eyes hard. On the lapel of his large madras jacket he wore a yellow-ribbon rosette, four inches across. In gilt letters at the middle of the flower were the words, "Fuel Association: J. P. Twilby."

I knew the formality of smiling an apology and letting him see a masculine, protective self in my eyes.

"Oh, I'm sorry," I said and tried to start the car.

He leaned, heavy on the window, assuming the expression for a dumb, pretty girl. "You want me to park it for you?"

I shook my head. He stepped back from the window and forgot me as I moved.

A bellow sounded over the car roof. "Why, Eldridge, you old son-of-a-gun," he was calling to someone on the marble veranda.

And always, step by step, I moved carefully at Egeria. Up the wide marble stairs between the great white dwarfing Federal columns and the huddles of men with yellow rosettes and pastel women, I walked onto the continuation of the templelike marble floor. Ahead, the double stairs curved out to make a bowl for a little forest of green tropical trees standing in pots in front of a mirror to the ceiling behind them, which doubled the plant forest and made an infinity of the foyer, reflecting the columns and the tree-studded sweep of the front lawn. I had forgotten how many mirrors there were at Egeria, as if the vain, more often the insecure, could check themselves forever, their walks, their greetings, their place in the green-and-marble world.

I can still see myself, as I was then, reflected among the glossy leaves like a wild thing in the ceiling-high mirror, in a scarlet shift I wore that summer, conscious of being conscious of the Douanier Rousseau. I see a slight, thin, easy-striding girl, note with the care of habit that the scarlet bag I am wearing in the reflection moves with a new self-conscious grace through the inhumanly high room, among the women in the last little waists and big skirts of the Eisenhower years, and I smooth my smooth hair with the checking, secretive dandyism we were trained to have.

At the top of the curving stair the huge lobby broke, gilt catching the faltering sun and swinging the space of the room so that the loud crowd of men seemed fishlike in movement under reflecting water. Was it that year or another year that I saw rosetted Brandy Baseheart coming toward me, his arms outstretched like a politician?

"Why, Cousin Hannah, baby!" He covered both sides of my hand with friendly paws. "Hey, Kitty honey," he yelled. He engulfed me, asked no questions, drew me into one of the clumps of rosetted people. The noise in the room was deafening. I floated in shade and noise.

Brandy had widened with the years; the questioning cheerfulness he had had as a boy had turned belligerent, as if he lived within a plastic bubble of good fellowship he guarded against breakage. Kitty Puss detached herself and turned toward me. She had grown muscular, the promise in her plump, pert girl's face fulfilled into the immobility of a woman who drank hard, played and thought hard, had learned secretiveness in her new smaller eyes against the constant buffeting of Brandy's good humor. She looked as if all caring had been burned out of her face. She had weathered brown in the sun that had covered her skin with a mask of lines. She simply had honed down, hardened, and survived.

"Sissy, come here and meet these people," she yelled back, casual and not caring. She had a cigarette clenched between small teeth and she grinned around it. "I don't know who they are." She had, through years, perfected a breezy carelessness that allowed her to be rude. She waved her drink around a little group of strangers.

One diffident man was embarrassed into speaking. "How do you do. I'm National Gas and Fuel," he told me earnestly as we shook hands. I smiled my way out of the clutches of the strangers already bored with one another in the four o'clock dullness of the Fuel Meeting that had gone on too long.

But I know it was that year that I moved among the women in their pink Hathaway shirts, some in bleeding madras Bermuda shorts, some in khaki skirts, older women sitting with their legs crossed in Davidow suits.

I was suddenly so incongruous there in my scarlet bag of a New York dress. I wore that dress, except for once, all the time I was there. I would catch a glimpse of bright scarlet in windows, in the glass doors of the hospital, and it flicked past the mirrors of the polished, hollow circle of the Egeria ballroom, deserted in the afternoon. By the elevators in the dark red corridor, I found a house phone to warn my father.

He let it ring once. I could hear anxiety in his quiet voice, naked on the telephone, when he could not hide his tone with the withdrawing gestures of his mouth.

"Father," I said once and stopped the urge to cry.

"Why, Sissy honey!" He sounded pleased and surprised. "Where are you?"

"Father, I'm downstairs."

The silence between us lasted too long.

"Why, honey." At last Father tried to breach it. "You better come right up." He paused again. "Knock on the living-room door, 1414. Your mother's asleep. She has a little headache. Oh, honey . . ." He was trying to tell me he was glad I was there, but he couldn't bring it out. "Come right on up here."

From the elevator to their rooms the corridor stretched on and on, muted, empty. I made no sound on the thick, soft gray carpet. The great labyrinthine acres of purple rhododendron that had once covered slopes of the wild mountains with its dark glossy leaves, that one day I would see as a maze of God to trap the first Hannah, had been imitated, sentimental and controlled, in patches of pale green leaves with huge blossoms of mild lavender over the walls and ceiling. Down the luxurious corridor, through arches of pastel mountain rhododendron, I walked to tell my parents about Johnny.

At the turn of the wing, far away, I saw my father already half gesturing for me to be quiet. Before he could hide it his mouth smiled, wide with pleasure, the kind of smile let loose rarely from a man who still wanted the love and approval of a boy but had learned to fold his mouth.

I was sickened by the pity I felt for him. The corridor seemed so long, what I had to say too heavy for me to do the thing my body urged—run toward him, comfort by being his daughter.

"Why, honey." He put his arm around my shoulders and whispered, then caught the tension as he touched me. His smile left and his mouth shot its tiny lines across his face as he asked, life gone from his question, "What's happened?"

"Oh, Father." I tried to crawl up his shoulder.

"Shhh! Honey, shhh! You'll wake your mother," he said, trying to stroke my shoulders as he led me inside the suite and eased the door shut behind him.

I stepped back from him. I stood as I was taught to and had to fight to do, on my own feet, halfway across the room.

"It's Johnny," I told him calmly.

"Oh, damn Johnny." All the memories of his annoyed disappointment went into the oath. "What's he done now?"

"He's had an accident. I drove up to tell you and Mother. Melinda didn't think you ought to just hear it by phone. He got knocked down."

"Is he dead?" Father shot at me, needing facts.

"No. He got knocked down. He's in the hospital." I had to get through his bland, stern wall of annoyance at the interruption, his disbelief in its importance. "He isn't expected to live."

Father turned his back on me. He walked to the window and looked, not out at the trees, but at his own reflection, as Johnny had so long ago. The shadow of his face betrayed a shadow of grief.

"How did it happen?"

I slapped at his back with the words. I couldn't stand any more retreating. "He was drunk. He got picked up. A perfect stranger hit him. He fell against an iron bench. He was just standing there. A perfect stranger."

A perfect stranger—that word for an unknown man, an absurd shadow with a fist to hit Johnny and nearly kill him for no reason—was between us in the room. The air conditioner hummed.

My father's shoulders began to sag, then bow. He was crying, not the tears of a woman with their evocative, demanding sound, but the completely silent tears of a man who had waited too long to cry, to tell, to ask one thing of us. He staggered into one of the pink chairs and hid his face. After a while he asked a question.

"Why, Hannah? Oh my God!" He knew there wasn't an answer that could be given all at once, for the answers between people are daily and are told in a lifetime of gestures. He put his head down again on his hand, hunched forward, shy. I had never heard him use the word "God" before, except at eleven o'clock in All Saints when he muttered responses, one among three hundred voices.

At last he straightened up. They were his last tears. He disappeared into the bathroom. I heard the toilet flushed, then water running. He was splashing cold water on his face.

"Hannah," he said, standing straight in the doorway again. "We have to be careful with your mother. You know she isn't well." He tiptoed toward the bedroom. "You know she's been through so much."

He put his head around the door. I could see the drawn curtains of the half-dark room beyond him.

"Sally Brandon..." He spoke softly, as if he were waking up a child. "Sally Brandon, Hannah's come to see us. Can we come in?" he cajoled.

"You can come in if you want to. I don't give a damn," my mother's sleepy, harsh voice came from the bed.

She lay, spraddled, with the abandonment of a child. As we tiptoed in, she heaved her body over, away from us. She belched and buried her head in the pink pillow, legs spread and body flaccid under the ruffled tester of one of Egeria's Confederate beds, her defenses shed like clothes.

"You know it doesn't happen often, Hannah," my father misread my shock and told me. "She gets these attacks when things get too much for her. Poor baby," he crooned, father-lover. She had used all the protective strength the man had.

There had been little left for us in that exhausted heart of his. "She just gives out."

"Oh, for Christ's sake, shut up, Mooney," my mother grumbled from the pillow; then she lay flat on her back, watching me.

"Hello, Miss Hannah, who asked you to come down here and tell us all where to get off? See the way she's looking at me, Mooney? It's your sainted damn mother coming out in her."

"Sally Brandon." Father leaned over her. "Now take it easy. This might be hard." He seemed to be sponging her with tenderness. She just lay there, sixty-six years old, staring up into his face without love, without hate, cringing in her dry white skin and looking like the wreck of a fifteen-year-old girl. She waited, hardly breathing, keeping her eyes on his face. When he didn't or couldn't say anything, she switched to anger, cold, but without moving, only sinking farther away from the head hanging over her.

"What's she done now? What have any of them ever done for me?" She pushed his shoulder and sat up, crouched back against the sleek mahogany, and looked at me as blankly as she had looked at Father.

"We sent you to Sweet Briar. What more did you want? Running off to Europe. Staying up there in New York not doing a damn thing. We've made great sacrifices. You know what privileges *I* had? You know what I learned?" The accusation was chased from her face by the new thought, melting and changing its lines. "I read poetry and I was pretty as a picture. Wasn't I, Preston? Wasn't I pretty as a picture? Papa said I was like a Rossetti." She grasped his hand without looking at it or letting him answer. "You know what I learned? I learned to hide." She pinned me, awkward and long-armed, in front of her. She seemed to read some judgment in my nearly blank, sucked-out mind.

"Who ever gave a tinker's damn?" she cried at the wall she saw in me.

She hunched there, her thin body jackknifed in the inevitable yellow georgette nightgown she always wore. Her short gray hair, brushed awry by the pillow, stood up from her gaunt white childish face. Her lips were so pale they were almost invisible, her skin as transparent, as lined and frail as fine broken bone china. She lashed out at me and "they" as if she were flinging words at a luckier sister. She had never shown the wound she carried as naked and bleeding as on that day—oh, unconsciously in her genteel protections and her barbed tiny spurts of envy, but never as flung back in time, reliving it. She was exposed, impaled on an irretrievable, unchangeable moment as if some longing hurt her and all the loving care in the world would not relieve one sharp barb of pain.

I would on that day have found this rift of blood in the brittle armor of her bodily dignity unbearable had I not faced it all through my growing-up. Once, in a hotel room in Paris, I had dreamed of her sitting alone on a straight chair, a thin, suppliant girl, her eyes moving to one after another of ignoring, noisy, faceless strangers, her sad, begging smile trying to connect with at least one indifferent passerby. It was the first time I had ever pitied her, and that was after a vivid dream, halfway across the world.

Suddenly, in a surprising spurt of sense, she looked up at Father and said quietly, "Preston, you better tell me."

"Honey!" He sat down on the bed beside her. They had forgotten me, he fathering her by old habit, she drawn back from him, afraid and starving.

He treated my mother as if he hadn't earned the right to be with her, or as if she honored and surprised him by letting him stay.

"It's Johnny," Father said at last. "Now he's been in an accident..."

Her face shrank as if he had hit her. "Is he dead?" She trusted him to tell her.

"No, honey. It isn't that bad. He...stumbled and fell on the stairs. It could happen to anybody. We think he's going to be all right." The lies caressed her without his even noticing what he said. "We better get packed and go on home."

"Not again. They're not going to do it again." Mother dissolved back onto the pillow. "They can't do it to me again." She didn't ask any more about Johnny.

"Now, honey...now, honey." Father stroked her damp gray hair until I thought she was asleep.

She opened her eyes. "Hannah," she said as soberly as if she had just waked from a nap, "get your mother some coffee, will you, dear?"

I ran to the telephone, and as I ordered I could see her pulling herself together, beginning with her voice. She began to take her own shape, hiding the woman again behind the lady.

"Get us some food, Hannah. Must eat something," Father told me, still watching her. It gave her a chance to react to a familiar sound.

"At a time like this . . ." she answered formally. But it made her lips purse and take on color. She pushed Father aside and eased her feet to the floor. She lurched toward the bathroom. We heard the bath running. She called with a quavering sigh through the shut door, "Hannah, you better help me."

In the bathroom Mother's frail naked body was an arc over the basin. Her legs were like crinkled paper, her hands talons, holding her up, her elbows trembling. I could hardly hear what she said. The water was rushing into the bathtub.

"I don't like anybody to see me like this," she begged me as she stared into the bathroom mirror at her sweating head. I wanted to reach through her old body to grasp the fifteen-year-old girl by the smooth arm, but when I touched her wrinkled seared elbow she jerked it away and climbed alone into the tub.

"You *know* I can't stand being touched," she muttered to herself.

She was preparing for the long, long exposed walk through the endless romantic corridors of Egeria Springs, and on and on beyond it.

I drove back blankly, fast toward Johnny, into lowering evening and then black night. After the tense heat of the valley the rain swooped down. I went through a black, shining tunnel of water, water swishing under the car wheels, pounding the padded top, night rain sluicing the roof, sweeping across the windshield. There was only the steady rhythm of the wipers. The path of my own lights reached ahead of me. Nearer Canona the neon signs in the wet night left long, glistening images in the stretched road, running with water like a river. In the small, powerful car, I left Father and Mother far behind me.

The visitors had all gone from the hospital. In the waiting room under the strident fluorescent light, a few of the truly vigilant sat exposed in their waiting. There was a silence so deep that when I stepped into the dark corridor to Johnny's room I picked up the slow, grating labor of his breathing as if it had never been absent from my brain. I tiptoed to keep my heels from sounding like shots on the dark floor. It was dark except for two muted lights in isolated pools, one over the nurse's desk, the other at the end of the hall over the wooden bench. I saw two vague figures sitting under the pale circle of the night bulb, one a bowed woman, the other leaning against her, comforting.

I must have appeared, in the edge of the dim light, like a ghost. One of the women lifted her dark head. It was Aunt Rose McKarkle, Uncle Ephraim's wife, who sat with her arm around a wan blond girl, her face like a young Pietà, as still as a stone virgin. Rose held hard to her shoulder as if she were trying to will life into her.

Rose said, unsurprised and not explaining, "There's been no change," as if she spoke of the whole world, unchanged by Johnny's decision to live or die. We stopped there, three muted women, attendant only on his breathing. Rose got up then and came and hugged me, and drew me down onto the bench. It was then I knew that I had gone too long and too far since morning and my body was parched for rest.

"Steve called back. He said he saw you at the gas station," I heard Rose say. "He said you were going to tell Sally and Preston, so Eph and I came straight here."

"Where are they?" The blond girl roused herself from her despair. She was much older than I had thought.

"They followed me. They'll be here in a few minutes," I told her, surprised at the shadow of panic I saw.

The girl stiffened, got up as quickly as a flushed bird. "I've got to go."

"Tel, stop it," Rose told her shoulders. She towered dark and strong over her. "You'll do no such thing. You have *some* rights . . ."

"Please take me home," Thelma Leftwich asked, not begging but stating.

To my shame, I could not remember having seen her since she and Johnny had sat together in the old airport canteen.

Rose looked at her for a long time. "Goddam their little souls to a small hell," she said, and took Tel's arm.

They turned to go down the corridor. Thelma Leftwich drew away from Rose and dragged herself back to stand in front of me. Her face was hallowed with forgiveness.

"If you need a place to come in all this . . ." Her eyes were great dark blots, sunk in grief far older than the night. "Rose knows where I live. You might . . ."

She turned to go without waiting for me to answer. Perhaps she saw I couldn't. In the blank eyes of that good woman's face, fed and nurtured on old sacrifice, was a condemnation of me and of us all beyond any hell that life-loving, strong Rose would ever know. At least, I thought so then. It was the condemnation of our indifference. Her face was gaunt with the kind of noble hunger that could only be sated by suffering.

They receded out of the light and disappeared from the unchanging world of waiting. The corridor was filled only with Johnny's breathing and my stretched, loose calm of fatigue.

Then Father and Mother tiptoed into the lights' periphery with Freddie. He must have been watching for them to come. He had one of Mother's arms, Father the other. Behind them came Father MacAndrews, tall, stooped, and moving awkwardly in time with the occasion. Mother was dressed in tragedy and black linen; she moved with the procession around her into Johnny's room. Her head was down and she was almost smiling, her face prepared through the long ride to love and help the son lodged safe in her mother-mind, waiting for her in the stark hospital room.

The night light showed obliquely on Johnny's face, caught in his blank eye pools and his gaping mouth, and softened the room around him with shadow. A nurse sat on watch beside the bed. When she saw us she rose and tried to fade back against the darkened wall, out of notice.

Then, just for a second, as I had, Mother saw the man in the bed. Her gaze sank and shifted; she looked at him as coldly as if he were a stranger. I saw the stranger fade from her eyes, the boy she needed replace him. I knew him by her voice as she walked, crooning with an element of humor called up to lighten what she said. As if she were waking him up in the morning at the boy-time of his life, she said, "Now, Johnny, come on. Come *on*, Johnny." I could hear, as if the boy answered, the voice I remembered from school mornings. "Oh, Mother, let me be. Let me *be*," and hear her seldom light laugh as he rolled over to sleep again. It was in the years that I, growing to ten, eleven, twelve, heard that lightness in her most often. She would say, proud and joking, "Johnny, you look just like a statue I saw once—a statue of an angel." Or, suddenly stopping whatever she was doing when he sauntered through the high, dark living room of the River Street house, she would pour her praise after him, letting him hear. "He'd make a wonderful hussar, wouldn't he, Hannah?"

Later, as he tipped over the balance of sexless beauty into his escape to manhood, she would follow him with disappointed glances whenever he would disappear from the house, as if one sad look could reel him back, caught on her lifeline like a fish. As the door behind him slammed she would say sadly, tinged with worry, "I *don't* know what happens." From time to time she would see flickers of what she had lost, see only that in him again, let her worry change to wonder, as she did when she found the Bible on his bedside table and told Aunt Althea in front of Johnny, "He's very religious..."

She touched the hand that lay along the brown hospital blanket. His body, aloof in its coma, rejected her; she let the limp white hand drop.

"He doesn't know me. He doesn't know me," she cried to Father. For once, he didn't notice her. He too was watching the impersonal face, his lips trembling. It was Father MacAndrews who took her shoulder and muttered, "Sally Brandon, do you want me to pray?" He was gruff with embarrassment, but when she nodded, dumbly, he laid his hand, as professional and strong as the nurse's had been, on Johnny's head, over his staring eyes. He knelt; Mother knelt beside him. I felt myself sinking down with them, and heard Father, behind me, sigh and creak as he got down to his knees. Only the nurse, ignoring us, went on watching Johnny's face and the instruments that were connected from his dying to the world, as if we were not there.

"O blessed Redeemer..." Father MacAndrews spoke softly into Johnny's unhearing, bandaged head. "Relieve, we beseech thee by thy indwelling power, the distress of this thy servant."

I, alone in my praying body, seeing darkness, heard my mother sigh.

"Release him from sin and drive away all pain of soul and body, that being restored to soundness of health..."

Were we praying for Johnny or for his fragmented reflection in each of our eyes, the need and dependence of each separate man that gaped and yawned in that night room? Could God have answered the corrupting demands we made

ther for son and heir of his way of living; mother for
y, conjured up innocent and dream-pure to her dicta-
or mirror-brother holding my hand, twin-flying, his
leg ee in the air before his fall? Did anyone pray for the
man who lay there, essential, unknown, unrecognized?

"That he may offer thee praise and thanksgiving; who livest
and reignest with the Father and the Holy Ghost, one God,
world without end."

We murmured Amen. Then there was only Johnny's breathing. We moved all at once, Mother like a blind child toward
me, the nearest in looks to him. Stripped of loyalty or
wisdom, she was wandering toward me as his replacement,
not for him, but for what he had been to her. Her head came
to my shoulder and lay there.

"I'll have to take her home," Father said and detached her
from me.

". . . in case he wants to tell me something. I'm sure he'll
tell me something." I could hear them as they left, Father
MacAndrews tensed beside them to catch their need. Father
said, "They'll let us know when he comes to. Now you sleep."

I heard Freddie say, "Would you like a sedative, Miss
Sally?"

"I'll sleep. I have faith," my mother told him, obedient.

Then between Freddie and the nurse Johnny became a sick
body and duty again. Freddie consulted the chart and gave
the nurse new orders. I sank into the armchair at the foot of
Johnny's bed out of the way of their work, in the dark. I
didn't know Freddie was leaving until he touched my hand.

"Hannah," he said, "why don't you get some sleep? There's
nothing you can do here." I shook my head without looking at
him and he was gone.

The night stretched on, as flat and dumb and cold as
Johnny, lying between the nurse and me, staring at the
ceiling, unseeing, disconnected from any of us, his incessant
drawing in of air like a huge gadfly caught between the walls.
Once he moaned, and the nurse and I both jumped up, but
the lamp was still reflected in his unwinking eyes. It was only
an animal moan.

In the language which is as deep as myth and does not lie,
"patients" do sink, and they are patient. Hour by hour I
watched Johnny sink, the blood ebbed from his face without
returning. His body flattened, heavier and heavier, sinking
into the bed, patient under the burden of dying. He no

longer fought for breath but allowed it in, faintly, delicately panting, not breathing enough to keep a bird alive.

I must have slept again, as I had only the night before, waiting for him to call. I remember hearing the clock on the Coal Banking and Trust Building strike four o'clock, hollow over the sleeping valley.

At seven o'clock Melinda was in the room, and the new sun drenched the sheets and her brisk dress. She ordered me home to bed. "We will let you know if there's any change for the worse," she said abstractedly, already slipping into hospital character.

As I went away I could hear her questioning the nurse about the state of Johnny's steadily ebbing body.

Later, I waited in my own bed without sleep and watched the flowered and latticed cage of the wallpaper. Far away a power mower ripped the Labor Day air. Mother had revived and was moving about downstairs, insisting that Delilah let her dust.

"I like to do it myself," I heard her say. "It takes my mind off things." Furniture rolled across the living-room floor. There was a dry tinkle of glass being put away. At eleven o'clock the telephone rang. Its shrill call shot through my waiting. At the top of the stairs I leaned down over the banister to hear what Mother said.

"Did he say anything?" she asked calmly and then crumbled in a little heap on the green hall rug, her dust rag still clutched in her hand.

It was late afternoon. I could hear the window blinds sucking and sighing against the upriver breeze. I opened my eyes. Oh, damn him, Johnny was dead somewhere, lying in the same flat way on an impersonal narrow cot, all tension gone, leaving me high and salt-dry. A fly had been buzzing, maddeningly, before I slept. Now it had escaped and the room was empty of its insistence. I remembered that I had lain across the bed, trancelike—that's all. I had been alone then. As I breathed awake I saw that there was a white hand with polished nails in front of my eyes. I looked up. Melinda sat on the bed edge. I had never seen her so still. She sat in a parody of the repose she had never known. We shared the dead blankness of the room and beyond it of the house, the unbearable, stolid brutishness of loss, anesthetized in it.

Nothing moved but the blinds. A howl began, tiny, and grew, but I made no sound. I was slapped awake as if I were newborn, into the alien hard air. I had been tricked by Johnny; that obscene, ludicrous death he served up, damned fool, unforgivable, shutting off so that he would not even be there to forgive, let live, let breathe. Damned Johnny, self-sufficient sufferer, dirty trickster, had left me nothing in the past to recall and face death with. He had served us with a final flippancy, a mute stranger, an inanimate iron bench to crush his delicacy of brain and leave his body to fade down, go out, leave a window blind sucking, a day like other days, damned with indifference, that most pure damning.

I could hear Mother in Johnny's room. A drawer thudded on the floor.

Melinda jumped up. "I told her not to. I told her she was supposed to stay in her room." She wandered over and snapped the window blind, letting in the late-afternoon sun.

"I'll go and see." I sat up, full of weight.

Melinda stopped me. "Wait a minute. I've got to talk to somebody."

I couldn't see her face, only the blind cord still swinging in her hand. She'd forgotten to drop it.

"Ann Randolph's answering the door. Maria's writing down people's names . . . close friends . . . Daisy's at Carver's." They had already formed their circle around Johnny dead, as they had in life. I realized then that the downstairs hummed with people, tiptoeing, whispering.

"We have to go down. Mother has to stay in her room. She shouldn't see people, except of course a few close friends."

"Have you made a guest list?" I was empty, drained of everything except disgust at the beginning of the inevitable formalities as they hid the body, the hopeless fragment of Johnny, and the rules for death took over. The guests of death in Canona moved slowly and lightly, those who wrote names at the door, those whom Father would take into the library for a drink, all permeated with the solemn embarrassment which was our way of mourning Johnny's soul.

And we would be watched to see how we were taking it, calm demanded; no embarrassing show of grief except in a still face where seemly feeling, controlled, could be read and commented on as the cars started outside; no one to disobey the rules and take our hurt hands.

"Oh, Jesus!" I got up. It might have been a cry of prayer, even dimmed as I was, but Melinda took it for swearing.

"Hannah, please, don't *do* anything." Melinda turned around. I saw that she was afraid and that her face was drenched in tears. She moved away from the window and sat holding her own hands hard, perched at my dressing table.

We could hear Mother shutting Johnny's closet door.

Melinda cried, "Make her stop!" Her tight fists crashed down among the old perfume bottles Mother kept there and called my collection. "Spud's down seeing to—he's down at the funeral home." Her mind leaped for safety, her voice scrabbled at it, clutched. ". . . Bess Everett is there with Daisy taking names. She's new but she's all right. They ride. They go to Aiken. They're nice. Business people go to the funeral home, and church people that you know in church but don't have much in common with . . ."

Finally I burst out of the stupor. "Melinda, shut up!" My mouth began to stretch.

"Hannah, there are people downstairs." Melinda's voice was sure. She didn't know how to deal with the words—she hadn't heard mine—she had heard only the tone, and that was too naked, too loud.

"Don't you want to know *why*?" I pulled at her arm.

"I don't want to know anything. I have to live here," she said calmly, the most honest words I ever heard her say. She smoothed her black dress and frowned. "It's a Trigère dress. Do you think it's too . . . ?" She submerged the neural touching of her grief and left the knowledge only in her small, fearing eyes.

Then I saw that the scarlet shift was gone. Hung on the bathroom door was a black dress I had never seen. It had a small waist, and a big acceptable Republican skirt.

"Ann Randolph brought it. I called her. You're about the same size," Melinda assured me. "Black shoes . . ."

"Melinda, where are my clothes?" I was too furious to raise my voice.

"I had Delilah wash that dress you'd been in for twenty-four hours. It's still wet." So neatly Melinda had had the foresight to strip me, leaving me only in my bra and pants.

She looked at the dress on the hanger, then at me. She began to cover the runnels of her tears with powder.

"I've worked so hard," she said to herself in the mirror. She waited for something. Sympathy? Approval? I couldn't say a word. She got up without looking at me and walked out of the room, shutting the door behind her.

In the hall I heard a woman's voice. "Somebody ought to sit with the mother."

"I think Mother would like to be alone for a little while," Melinda said coolly. Footsteps receded down the polished stairs. The woman had not been one of the tacit list who could be "brought in to speak to Mother," not in Melinda's book of rules. In her set nobody "sat with the mother," nobody "viewed the body," nobody cried, nobody got drunk, and nobody stayed over fifteen minutes. Nobody rocked the boat.

I put on the borrowed dress.

Melinda went into Johnny's room. What happened between them I don't know. The door reopened as I opened mine. Melinda was leading Mother toward her room. Mother was shuffling in a flat, calm doldrum to sit queenlike in her room with the beams of Canona's kind of mourning focused on her.

"I was only looking for something," she explained, her face and voice dry and matter-of-fact.

"We'll find it for you later." Melinda steered her firmly across the hall.

Mother balked at the door. "I don't want you. I want Althea," she told her and pushed at her body with tired flat hands.

Melinda's hard eyes weighed on Mother until she willed her to sit down on her flowered chaise longue. "There's nobody to go get Aunt Althea," she told her. "You'll have to see her later." Aunt Althea didn't fit into Melinda's mourning, not at all, and the tentative girl beneath my mother's skin who had asked for the comfort of the only woman alive she had known for nearly fifty years was a stranger to Melinda and, as such, unwelcome at such a time.

In the living room the wake went on and on, with little bursts of careful conversation, led by Melinda, obediently followed by the rest. She covered the silences by raising her voice, letting it flow, panicked, as she had in my room, telling the inevitable listener, Haley Potter, about a woman on a boat—she'd traveled on it and so had a woman whose friend she knew and the woman married a duke. No, they hadn't traveled at the same time, only on the same boat. The story reverberated among the women. What grief Melinda had I could not weight or touch; it had simply set off a chain reaction, as if she drew a possibility of life only in vague connections. I heard her behind me, starting the story again to a new woman about the friend of her friend who had married a duke and had traveled on the same boat—no, not at the same time. She seemed, as they say at such times, to find comfort in it.

When I turned I saw that the woman was Kitty Puss Baseheart. She watched Melinda, not listening. When she saw me she brushed Melinda aside.

"For God's sake, Hannah..." She didn't say any more. We stared at each other. The room was as poised as if a bomb were going off. Finally Kitty Puss said, trying to grin, "How's life in New York?" She sat down beside Haley on the sofa, who whispered so the whole room could hear, "Oh, Kitty Puss, can't you forget about sex at a time like this?"

Kitty Puss put a cigarette between her teeth. When she lit it I read *Mountain View Motel* on the dirty book of matches she threw down on the table beside her.

Dead silence honoring sex and bereavement filled the room. In the distance, upstairs, a toilet flushed in Johnny's bathroom. Mother had sneaked out again.

Melinda said to the ceiling, "I *told* her," and then, remembering where she was, muttered, "Excuse me a minute." She looked as if she had lost control of the day. On her way out of the door she asked Kitty Puss loudly and sternly if she could stand at the door and relieve Ann Randolph. Kitty Puss ground her cigarette into an ashtray and said, "Shit. Oh shit," a cry straight from the heart.

Melinda was willing the days to Johnny's funeral to be savagely correct to make up for the obscene manner of his dying; the manner of his dying was the only truth we had that was his own. I managed to get out of the room, but not before someone had grabbed my arm and squeezed it, hard, sincere body language. I looked at a mouth muttering something like, "Deeple sorr..." The woman cleared her throat and gave me another sincere arm squeeze.

I couldn't remember her name. I remembered that people said she was artistic because she was slightly crazy. Her house was filled with doo-doo-colored pottery. She got it for Christmas because she was artistic.

At the library door I heard Father say, "Thank you."

"Come on in, Hannah," Plain George called out softly. "Can I get you a drink, honey?" He led me over to where a small bar had been set like an altar on the library table. There were vaster patches of silence among the men. Silence had sustained them through all the labyrinthine training which had brought them to the library to swing ice in glasses over Johnny's memory.

It kept on sustaining them, except when Plain George spoke quietly to Uncle Sugar, "Do you know anything about the man?" His whisper carried through the room.

"Some redneck poor white," Uncle Sugar said. "Out-of-work miner . . ."

"He'll get ten years," Charlie Bland said at the bar.

"He'll get ten years," Spud said as if the words still didn't hang in the air.

I could find no whys there where none were asked. Only Jack had told me any truth.

I ran into the kitchen. Delilah sat huddled and crying, like any human being melted by grief and pity. I, starved and dry, watched her, jealous, not knowing then how to do that.

"Delilah, have you told Jack?" I held her shoulder.

"Toey," she corrected me gently, reminding me where we were.

I reached for the wall telephone and then stopped, cold with exposure. I didn't remember his last name. I looked mutely at Delilah; she answered what I was ashamed to ask.

"It's Lacey, Hannah."

"*My name is John Peregrine Lacey,*" Jack had said.

Mother had told me how they took anybody's name, usually the people they had belonged to. She had told it so often she had blotted the name out of my mind.

"Is he on duty?"

Delilah nodded.

"Jack . . ." I found his voice at last. "Do you know about Johnny?"

He was as hard as justice. "We've changed the charge. Involuntary manslaughter."

"What's the bail?"

"Ten thousand. He couldn't raise ten bucks."

"It's that high?"

"Lot of important people mad..."

"I'm coming down..."

"Don't."

"You made a promise."

He didn't answer for so long I thought he had hung up. Somebody, without listening, had started to dial a telephone someplace else in the house.

"You can come down," he said at last.

"I'll be there as soon as I can get away."

There was a little pop of an "oh." A woman had been listening.

Melinda was waiting for me in the hall, still holding the bridge against the untoward.

"Hannah," she whispered, "Kitty Puss picked up the phone and said you were making a *date*. She told *everybody*."

"Sure, Melinda," I whispered back to her, "there's nothing like a fuck at the funeral." Since both love and death in any undress were the only obscenities she knew, she shut up long enough for me to get out of the house.

It was five o'clock, silent tea time; the trees were yellow in the last warm daylight before blue evening, a calm time when people were in their houses or on their lawns and the neighborhood children caught the drift of the day ending and rode their bicycles quietly. Far down the drive at the end of the trees a boy balanced on one foot from his bicycle, staring up at our house, the evening paper folded in his hand, wondering how to deliver it where there was an unusually muted house front and a long line of cars, but no noise of a party. Finally he laid the paper reverently in the center of the driveway where the cars would run over it.

I found Johnny's car. I could not remember driving it home at first, then I remembered Melinda telling me to.

I sat for a minute to—what? Go all the way down to Johnny's death, touch bedrock, and then to start climbing again, just start, quite literally, for God's sake. From the house came the soft murmur of the dead burying their dead.

I knew that once I set out I would go on and on, that the road might be long, and that I would carry a sack of troubles packed by others, which was a fact that Paul Bunyan had conveniently forgotten to tell when Christian set out for the Celestial City.

My father clutched at the car window before I could maneuver from among the shining cars parked up the arc of our driveway. He said, using the words he'd found the last time he'd given me an order, when I was sixteen, "Young lady, you get yourself right back in this house."

I tried to shake him off. I reached out to push his hands away. He took the touch as something else, and patted my hand and went on patting.

I saw in his face the faint sad questions of an awkward boy that surfaced so seldom at odd tender times; only a glimpse, beneath the skin of that powerful man, of the boy they had called Mooney. He moved to open the car door and the hint was gone. He was himself again as I had always known him, a man who ran a mine and a law practice, wore good suits, shot in the low eighties, and who could, as he put it, "just pick up the phone."

But he seemed, slumped in the seat beside me, physically smaller.

"Do you think it's easy for any of us, Hannah?" He didn't look at me. He spoke seriously to the dashboard.

It was my time to say sorry, my time to carry through with the expected, asking nothing, making Johnny's death even more absurd and useless than it was already.

"Johnny's dead. I don't have to keep quiet any longer," I told, not my father, but myself.

"There are a lot of ins and outs, Hannah." He choked and cleared his throat. "Young people always expect..." He began again. "None of you women know what a man goes through..." I thought he was talking about Johnny, but he wasn't. He was talking about himself. "I tried to tell, but it wasn't a damn bit of use. Don't try. Don't be a fool." His face was harsh. He had turned away from me. I could hear Mother's voice, so long ago, in the corridor at Egeria: *He made a fool of himself*... As if, still trying to be heard at the point where he had been shut off, had paid with silence, Father said, "You always thought..." Then he sighed, gave up, as if it were finally too late to say any more. The hurt and disappointed boy's eyes were all that was left of what he couldn't tell me, in the face of the aging man.

"What can we do?" he asked finally.

Two ladies gave us a fragile white-gloved wave, and we watched them church-walk toward the door. Neither of us could speak.

Another pair of ladies church-walked out of the door, looked at us, waved, timid little mourning waves, and went toward their car with their heads down.

"Your mother and I . . . you and Johnny. I've seen your mother's heart break over and over . . ." He cleared his throat again and fumbled in his pocket for cigarettes.

"Your heart breaks only once. Once! Once! What you and Mother thought was heartbreak was disappointment. For most people disappointment and embarrassment are the strongest emotions they ever know." He forgot the cigarette.

He had led me into abstraction, the last stronghold against the buffeting of Johnny's death. "When you care—oh, not what we did, but . . ." I tried to draw him back.

"We . . . your mother's calling me!" Father's body was old that minute; he moved crabwise toward opening the car door.

Tears sheeted my face and my father's face. We put our heads down like two conspirators when the door opened to let out two more ladies.

I was in my father's arms. I'd thought he was a big man, but under his jacket I could feel his skinny body, his heart-beat and his breath-sighs that didn't move the hard bars of his ribs.

"Once you gave Johnny a present, not like a Christmas present or birthday, just a present he didn't expect. Once you did it, unexpected, and he called me in California to get me to thank you—just to thank you. I was in California. We didn't have any words—there I was in California on the run and he called me all the way there."

Father's hand moved over and over my bowed head. My tears flowed down his best charcoal suit and over his thin legs. I watched his shoes, waiting for him to give some small absolution. His body creaked when he sighed. I knew it would come. I knew it would come, like his hand on my head. "Oh, honey," he said, "somebody's going to *see* you."

I straightened up to wait for him to get out. He only looked exhausted and surprised.

"We, your mother and I . . . always gave you everything we wanted. To the best of our power, Hannah." He didn't hear his confession. He got out of the car so slowly, so defeated, life in him so too late, not wanting me to stir him ever again by begging or by trying to help. Slowly he was trying to get back into the only soft safety he knew, where things took care of themselves and families loved each other. I wiped my face on my sleeve.

"Father, I'm going down to the jail," I told him.

"You *can't*. A girl . . ." He tried to grasp some reins again and turned to forbid me.

"I'll be back soon. Nobody in there will notice," I reassured him. "Don't tell Melinda and Spud."

"All right, girl, find out. You go and find out." He tried to smile.

"Everything is going to work itself out," I said solemnly.

He wandered toward the house. He had the awful walk of a man growing old among demands he was literally dying to ignore.

So that was his blessing. When I revved up, and drove out of the driveway, I knew and still know that it was a blessing. Those were the only words for it in the language of the Deadfoot tribe to which I belonged.

So it was then that I set out to ask why, the traveling word, the dream-splitter. I drove slowly between the thick green planted lawns of our manicured hill and watched for the wet-haired children who, after swimming in back-yard pools, played and darted under the groomed trees before dinner, free of being organized for the little while of cocktail hour, to play the play of generations, loose and wandering, taking sides, touching, fighting, hurting.

A small boy squatted on the sidewalk, fastening his skates at the wrong time of their child year for skating, just to skate by himself through the amber time of evening. He stood up, found his balance, and looked around him as if the world had just been created.

I was setting out on a long trail of cleansing whys, beyond Johnny's death, beyond one small valley. I caught the child's wonder and rippled off, leaving death behind, flew by the houses on the hill citadel that I knew as well as my own, where the beds were too short for a man to stretch himself and the covering narrower than he could wrap himself in, where too many sons had died while they were still sons, not men, not fathers yet, not even old Adam, except in secret. There was not an envied ivied front with its safe rhododendron religion where some man did not have to change his face as he changed his shirt when he came home to dinner,

where sex sang no good way to love and live daily but
sneaked and whimpered on pipe dreams or hidden places.

I was off to find Johnny's faces before they all faded,
humdrummed out of our minds, because death too soon was
a serious business, a plague. The price per ton for our
standard of living was getting too high. How far the search
would lead me I didn't know then. It seemed at that point to
lead to the man in the jail if he would let me in.

Down at the hill point overlooking the bridge and the dark
river, I slowed to enter the town. After the small cluster of
hill homes it looked big, unknown, full of people whose lives
spewed all along the narrow banks, not knowing we existed.

I crossed the bridge where the western sun made the
water shine.

I knew what I would find in jail—a shirttail hill boy, slim
and mean as a rattlesnake, a Saturday-night hell-raiser, a
car-roller, nigger-hater, tire-stealer. I went to meet my feral
twin from the underbelly of the Republic, White Anglo-Saxon
Protestant, Quantrill raider, Indian killer, a Dalton Boy, a
bushwhacker, agate-eyed wildcat.

For the second time in my life I saw Jake Catlett—not that
I knew it. It would take years for me to recall a sixteen-year-
old boy, old Jake's least one, who looked, in his Sunday suit,
like Ichabod Crane.

At the jail that late afternoon I only saw the back of the
man who had murdered my brother, and I wanted, in a surge
of hate, to kill him, stamp him out. He was leaning on the jail
windowsill, watching downriver through the bars. When Jack
opened the cell door he didn't look around or speak, even
when Jack said, "Somebody to see you," and then, "Catlett,
you got a visitor." I saw his back arch as Jack walked toward
him.

"Let me talk to him by myself," I whispered. When I
heard his name I only connected it with the Catlett that my
mother said brought her papa downriver on a shutter.

He turned around. The man who stood there, watching
me, was tall and quiet. The grief in his black eyes under
heavy brows was so deep it could have been mistaken for
aloofness. His face was gaunt and made without fat, his black

hair fell long on his neck, the sideburns made his cheeks hollow. He needed a shave. He was spare-boned, straight, skinny as a rake; his head jutted forward as he took me in slowly, then Jack, and said, low, like a man not used to speaking, "I don't want to talk to nobody."

I was afraid Jack would say something to make the man retreat into the isolated mountain of himself.

"Can I stay for a minute, by myself?" I begged.

Jack knew when he was shut out. He made one last try. "Okay, Catlett, you're in enough trouble."

"I ain't gonna bother no lady," Jake Catlett told him.

We could hear the rattle of Jack's steps as he went across the iron floor and clanged the outside cell door, and sat down within hearing in case I raised my voice.

Like any other cage, the cell had bars; the sun drew them in great shadows across the sleeping face of a man in the next cell. The place smelled of urine and Lysol. We stood, watching each other. What had happened did not show with him. He was just waiting, shut away from the river; he kept on glancing at it, clenching and unclenching his long spare hands.

"You from the newspaper?" he finally asked.

"No." I sank down on the end of the rack, becoming small, obliterating anything that might rouse his distrust, because he had to tell me what he didn't know himself. I was in an agony of guile.

"What did you come for, then?" His voice came on strong. He was rooted out, ground-hog cornered.

"Catlett, shut up." The man in the next cell turned over and went to sleep again.

"Don't pay him no mind. He's full of sneaky pete." Jack Catlett stared at the man's scrap-bag back.

"It was my brother," I whispered.

He looked at me as he would look at a wounded or frightened animal. I, stone-cold, willed him to it harder, using everything I'd lady-learned.

"I never meant to," he muttered. "I never even knowed him. I never knowed he was your brother."

I watched him.

"Look, lady. I never meant it. Why, I'm thirty-eight years old. I never done nuthin' like takin' on to scrap like that since I was a boy. You . . ."

"Tell me!" I had to force him back to where it had to begin, the key, the point, the place.

Jake Catlett sank down on the rack beside me and put his gaunt head between strong hands that could work a coal face, hold a woman hard by the shoulders, or hit Johnny. The black hair on the sunburned back of his fist stood out. That hand was the source—one hand, clenched, one strike—from that one hand, all the questions, a life that would never be the same again, not for him, not for us. I couldn't stop watching it.

We sat so long that the outdoor sounds came in and surrounded us: the beep of a car horn, across the river the whistle of Number 6 as it drew into the station. We were getting used to the smell of each other. The time tightened into the insistence between two people dwelling in the same needs——he to tell, me to learn. I had a dim urge to take his hand.

I broke the tightening stillness. "I heard he said something."

When he did begin to speak his voice was gentle. He was thinking aloud. He seemed to have forgotten who I was. "I been settin' here figurin'—goin' over and over it. He was just standin' there, and that feller kept callin' on Jesus—I figured I had to shut him up, leave me time to think. Gawd knows, I needed it even if I had to get locked up. That old man kept on and on—*he's* just lookin' out through them bars. I seen his face and his clean white coat in the light from the toilet. That was over at the City before they moved me over to the County. This here is the County. I ain't never been to jail before . . . Gawd, when I think about Loretta and Maw and Paw . . ."

He stopped for a minute, then came back from his thinking. "I reckon I flew red. Couldn't nothin' be done to shut that old feller up. *He's* the only one I could see. I took and hit him one and he—you know, when you shoot, a bird seems to linger in the air for the longest time, only it ain't more than a second. I seen him standin' before he fell and he looked kind of surprised. Then he said, 'Thank you.' He said a real quiet thank you, and just sighed down on the floor and hit that iron rack. Jeez Christ, I hated him when he said that, that thank you, lording it over a goddamn drunk tank. I never hit him hard. Just blowed off the last of my steam. I figured he was makin' fun of the rest of us . . ."

"How long had you been standing there looking at Johnny

before you hit him?" It was such a curious question, not what I had meant to ask him. I wasn't seeking the power in one Saturday-night pint, but the power behind that.

"Just about all my life." He looked at me then.

I began to laugh. It insulted him. I managed to stop laughing.

"Y'ought to be ashamed of yourself. Settin' there laughin' with your brother not cold in his grave. I can sure see you two are brother and sister."

"That's the trouble with all you damned people who strike out blind. Your fist is packed for an enemy, so you hit the first person who looks like him." Disgust of the man beside me made me stand up to get away from him.

He looked up at me and studied me for a while as he must have studied Johnny. "You people make me sick. When you spit you hawk coal dust same as us." He was taking the bandage of wariness and grief and surprise from his eyes, and they showed clear, clean hate—lit up with it—something honest to deal with.

"What got you into it, Jake? What put the chip on your shoulder?" I questioned fast, before he could retreat again.

That curious tenderness of quiet men, even with the hate there, made him get up and put his hand on my shoulder. His grip was viselike.

"Now look here, lady. I'm goin' to tell you. It's too late not to, ain't it?"

"Yeah, it's too late not to." Our hands had the same shape. Behind us we could hear Number 6 pull out of the station, going west.

"I've about had enough. Here I end up with ten thousand dollars' bail and I ain't never had nuthin' since we sold the farm but a few acres of ridge land and Loretta's womb and Gawd knows ye cain't borry money on that. Looks like a man works hard all his damn life and things are goin' along all but Loretta's womb."

He sat down and folded his hands in his lap and told himself the story, as he seemed to have told it forever, over and over. "Loretta come to Jesus and took to gettin' sick along about the same time. She had fifteen operations, that purty little gal; she come from up around Beulah—Slavish people. Come here in the mines. Ever time she'd get in the hospital she'd get purty as she ever was. Then she'd come home and get drug down again and takin' to goin' to bear witness on

Wednesdays, gettin' up there in public tellin' how she had all them operations and come to Jesus and Maw fussin' and fumin' tell her that kind of carryin' on wasn't like no Jesus she ever knowed. They'd fight and argue about Jesus never shut up. Maw is Baptist, and that there womb of Loretta's must'a had a rock in it that couldn't nobody find start in to draggin' her down again, that thing must'a weighed a ton." He paused long enough to fetch a deep sigh. "Then this July the union ruled you couldn't have no Number 8 for the hospital, unemployed over a year. I been out of work one year last Saturday, that damn Number 8 was all we had worth a red cent. I was a good coal-face man. I been makin' coal up and down this here valley since I was fifteen years old." He remembered me and accused, "They ain't a damn thing, ain't even that dress on your back didn't come off the coal-face and don't forgit it. You people puttin' on to act high and mighty…"

From his own coal-face all the way down his life he was getting to Johnny. But his voice had dropped so low that what he had to say ran out toward the floor and I had to lean almost into his lap. He didn't even notice, for he was no longer talking to me.

"We're good people. Come from upriver, up around Lacey Creek. Sold out up there. We had to. Even Paw saw that. Automation come in and we read out to move. Ain't nary a thing left now. They done stripped it. We come down here and Paw bought a little piece of property. Old Carver place… I got me another job."

I could see the hill farm at Beulah, the neglected fall field rippling, the lespedeza, the orchard covey wurtling in the air, before it was all thrown away, stripped down to bedrock like the Catlett place on Lacey Creek, or this man's face, this distant cousin stranger. "You're Mr. Jake Catlett's son," I told him. "We're kin, a long way back." He didn't even hear me.

"Things were purty good." He sighed. "Didn't look to us like no end to it. I'se makin' a good livin'—workin' the farm when I come home. Them ridges around, wasn't no people to bother us'n. I whitewarshed the house. I don't know what happened. There wasn't nuthin' wrong with the coal. It was fetchin' a good price. We had some labor trouble. Last time we come out on strike, I was workin' for the Cornstalk Collieries then, last time we come out, the Cincinnati Company and the union got together and sold us out—put in one of them Joy loaders. I ain't never been much for machines, so

I got laid off. They was eighteen hundred men workin' for the mine. Now they got five hundred. They're runnin' more coal out of there than they ever done. We never knowed what hit us . . ."

"Shut up, Catlett." The man on the next rack turned over again. "You been talkin' to yourself for two days in thar."

Jake Catlett didn't pay any attention. He was figuring; I knew it was the same story, as he went through the facts, that he had told himself as he sat on his front stoop or tended his garden or waited for a squirrel to flit down a tree trunk, trying to find out what happened.

"Loretta's womb got turble. Five thousand dollars' worth of serious operations at the UMW hospital." He suddenly remembered I was listening and accused me of something I hadn't said. "You ask me why we don't pick up and move. We got no place to go. Now with Loretta sick like that and Maw won't move three feet down the road. She said she moved far enough. I tried to raise a mortgage on the place; they was a feller name of Potter wanted to buy it but Maw set her foot down. She thinks mortgages is something like the public works. He wasn't goin' to give nuthin' nohow. Figured we never knowed nuthin' about the value of property. Well, what little we saved up went. Maw said she'd wish she'd died before she ever seen the day we was on mollygrub. She and Paw'd just set there in the kitchen and Loretta give up. They'd set there watchin' the television waitin' fer me to do somethin'. Loretta got so she wasn' even keepin' the kids clean. What could a man do? I went to Dayton and I went to Akron and I rode a freight train to Detroit. They wasn't nuthin' there. Them folks don't want us nohow.

"I got to goin' down every day, walkin' five miles down to Slingsby Street and five miles back, actin' like I was some use in the world. Me and them others standin' around shiftin' nails in our pockets and goin' off to collect a relief check make a man ashamed of himself, a strong man. Wouldn't have been quite so bad but there didn't nobody else seemed to bother about it. Wasn't like when I was a boy and everybody was broke so there wasn't so much feeling like you didn't belong noplace. I'd stand there, watchin' them fancy cars and them lit-up store windows and readin' the paper over somebody's shoulder about how prosperous the country was under Eisenhower. It was like it was all around me and nobody couldn't see me—like I was a ghost."

He was wandering along Slingsby Street where the jukeboxes blared and the stores shone, among the neon lights and the traffic stream. I left him silent until he was ready to speak again. I'd seen and not seen Jake Catlett so often, driven past his country eyes that watched the town as if it were a show, taking no part in it.

"One time some woman come up in one of them cars—last Christmas—with a basket. Maw took and run her off the place. She squawked like an old chicken about us'n not apperciatin' nothin'. Run a tar-ridge right through my plowin'. Maw run her off all right. She run her off with a hoe.

"When you people come up and built that there golf club right in our faces, it was like them fancy cars was chasin' me right to my own doorstep. Not a covey on the place no more. Wouldn't even let us hunt squirrels on land we knowed every tree on. It wouldn't've been so bad if we didn't feel like we'd been plowed under like a bad crop. Even took the creek and put it down the other way. My kids was run off when they wanted to go a'wadin'."

Beyond the highest green, where the hills stretched away in the distance, there had seemed to be no one. Their houses were hidden along the creeks, nestled in the hollow heads, houses like lairs, where they looked out straight and still, saying nothing, trusting no one.

"We didn't know," I muttered. Jake's fist with its black hairs caught the late sun and I was cold as a stone.

Jake Catlett sighed again as if so much talk hurt. ". . . layin' under a tree like hawgs eatin' chestnuts and never look up to see whar they come from . . ." He straightened up as if part of the story had ended and he was a new man.

"It was Saturday night and thar wasn't nuthin' to do, so I got drunk. That's what I done. I took two dollars out of Loretta's relief money—twenty-five dollars a week. I took two dollars and bought me a pint, then when it got dark and I was damn sick and tired of listenin' to Maw and Paw and Loretta settin' there complainin' because the television broke and we didn't have no money to get it fixed and them snotty-nose kids was a-bawlin' around the place because the truck wouldn't go without no gas and I couldn't ride 'em downtown to see the sights. I took my bottle and I walked along the ridge. It was a black, hot night, but I knowed every foot. Only once I like to fell in one of them fool sand traps and purt near broke my pint. I was headin' for a tree I knowed—squirrel tree—I been settin' watchin' that tree since I don't know when. Knowed every mark on her—big sycamore . . ."

Like most silent men, Jake Catlett didn't stop once he started. He just went his own way in words, sometimes pacing up and down the cell, sometimes coming back to me and sitting with his chin on his fists, watching the river through the bars, letting his dark face bathe in the gold evening sun.

The old man in the next cell put his face against the bars to listen.

"I knowed where I was goin' all right. Done more figurin' there than anywheres else. I'd about got out of earshot of my own people and into about a quarter of a mile of dark and peace and quiet when I seen the sky lit up pink like a bowl ahead of me and I heard music. The light and the music was comin' from the clubhouse.

"I snuck up under my tree and just set there drinkin' my pint and watchin'. A floodlight out ahead of me lit up that big porch like a television show. They was just like butterflies all flutterin' around down there, different colors in the light. They had them candles on all the tables. Every once in a while they'd all go inside and you could see 'em just a-whirlin' around dancin' behind that big square glass front. I wished for a minute Loretta could see it. She used to be the purtiest little thing, didn't have no religion or nuthin'.

"I never done no figurin' or nothin', reckon I'se plumb figured out—jest a-settin' there under my own tree drinkin' my own pint. Down in front of me this big swimmin' pool was layin' quiet, all lit inside. I'se gittin' purty lit inside too. I must of been because I fergot everything and got to actin' like it really was a television. I got up and went and stood in front of the floodlight and my shadow stretched right down across the pool and along the porch. I had a giant shadow. I put my shadow hands up on both sides of that big square of glass and acted like I was turnin' it. I was big as a mountain stretched down there with my shadow playin' with that whole big glass front like it was a toy. Then I needed another drink. When I hunkered down again they wasn't but one left in my pint. I took it and rared back.

"Somethin' happened. They all come out in a bunch for a while. I seen they was settin' there drinkin' enough licker to keep us for a year and me up there under my own tree without even a drink left in my damn pint."

The man in the next cell laughed an old man's hee-hee-hee. His spit hit my shoulder, but I dared not move for fear of stopping Jake Catlett.

"I was beginnin' to get mad. When they all went inside again in a bunch . . ."

I could see Johnny, neat, handsome Johnny, leading Corn-stalk Collieries in, making sex manners for a Saturday night; from Jake Catlett's tree I could see them, small as pretty insects.

"I got up and went down in front of the floodlight again. I was lonesome. I wanted somebody to notice me. It wasn't nuthin' but that there. I knowed that land better'n they done and we was in the same place, only that glass wall between. I danced that shadow around didn't even nobody look up out the winder."

"Johnny did." I was crying. "Johnny saw you and wanted to . . ."

He didn't hear me. He sat and watched the window without seeing it. It was his Saturday night and I wasn't there.

"So I run down to the swimmin' pool and lit into thowin' them chairs and mattresses and stuff in the water. Just run around thowed 'em in and the water was splashin' and a hell of a racket. By Gawd, they noticed me then, and some of them fancy men didn't look like they could button their own pants come a-runnin' so I lit out through the woods. They wasn't a one of 'em could of follered me."

The old man coughed out, "Hee-hee-hee." I could hear him lying back down on his back.

"I come on down to Slingsby Street to look at the lights and wander around. Somethin' had broke loose in me and I didn't want to go home and didn't want to figure nor nuthin'. Just one night, please God, I wanted not to listen to nobody. I figured I'd lay out all night on account of Loretta. She don't hold with no licker. I hadn't backslid for so damn long—two, three years. I figured if they picked me up, if I done enough, Loretta and Maw and Paw could git on the D.P. and A. If they ain't no man it's the law." When he saw my face he added, "Hell, the state penitentiary's full of men, better for their families they went to jail, so they took and went. I knowed then it was go to jail or go home, one. So I found me a brick

and heaved it through the window of the Slingsby Hotel.
They wasn't nobody settin' behind it so I couldn't hurt
nobody.

"I put up a purty good fight when they tried to take me in.
I was stone-cold sober by then but I still couldn't take to
them layin' hands on me. A man's got his pride..."

He ran down and put his head back in his hands.

I tried to touch his arm, but he drew away.

"What are you after?" he muttered.

"Does Loretta know where you are?"

"No, she don't know. She'll figure I'm off lookin' for work.
Ain't no way to tell her nohow."

"I'll phone."

He smiled then, very slowly, and spoke as slowly, "Listen,
lady, you gwan back to that there gold cradle you're livin' in
and leave us alone. We ain't got no *phone!*" He began to think
again, shutting me out. "We had a phone, though. We had
one... Swear to God, Loretta never got off the damn thing..."

"I'll go up there." He was making me beg to help him and
I could feel the ire rise.

"What do you want? What the hell are you tryin' to do?"
He shook me away, unfolded slowly, and went to the window
again. This time he put both hands on the bars and seemed to
hang there until his knuckles were white. "What's the matter
with you people? It was your brother."

I jumped up and could feel my nails biting into my palms,
and I hoped I'd stay mad enough not to cry. He had blackmailed
me into suppliance.

"I'm sick and tired of my brother," I yelled at him. "You
talk about us not giving a damn. You people won't walk across
the hollow. Let people ride roughshod over you and you just
back a little further up your hills and whine because you
haven't real guts enough..."

We faced each other, the razorback bone of the country, me
stripped from the topsoil of training down to rock pride. If it
was kinship that held me there, stark-stiff with the whole
mess, the crisscross hatreds, if it was brothers, I had more of
them than a dog had fleas, a whole hard valley of brothers.

"We don't ask nuthin' of you." Jake Catlett tried to shut
away from me.

"You're damn right you don't. You'd rather hate. You'd
rather live on your rock-farm pride. You don't even love your
people enough to let me..."

"Love, Hannar? Go back to the damned picture show! I'm kneelin' down thankin' God I'm in jail for 'em, ain't I? What more do you want?"

Somebody down at the end of the cell block started clamoring at the bars. "Quit that hollerin'. . ."

Jack came running, yelling, "All right, Catlett, that's enough."

"He didn't do anything." I turned around and hollered at Jack.

"All right." Jake Catlett came and took my arm. "Go on up and see Loretta. She'd be mighty grateful to you." He was giving me permission to go and there was nothing to do but accept it.

Jack unlocked the cell to let me out. Jake Catlett stood straight as a man should, wherever he was, and he watched me from under the porch of his brows.

"You can find out one thing for me," he said as if it were doing me a kindness. "Find out if I can vote in here. I don't know what the law is on that, and I sure want to vote. I been a Democrat all my life but *this* time I'm gonna vote."

So Abraham Lincoln Andrew Jackson Catlett stood there stone-faced in the last place he could find in the valley to look after his family, behind the bars of the county jail, and I told him I'd find out.

Jack held my arm all the way down the iron-grill stairs. "Hannah," he told me when he put me in the car, "if you want to come over and sit with me and Irma, Ma'll tell you where we are."

The sun had gone downriver when I recrossed the bridge, avoiding the long road up to the isolated monoliths standing sentinel over the valley, dark against the evening sky—their windows blind. I turned instead up the south hollow road, the low road to the new Country Club, to find the Catletts, having no idea what I could tell them. I drove with the face of Johnny, stranger, the man who was killed for the cut of his jib; it was a treasure hunt, the treasure an answer to a ridiculous question of death and train wrecks and all accidents. I knew who had held his spirit. I'd grown up with that; now I knew who hated him for what he stood for; I wondered how many people hated him for what he was.

At the fork of Slingsby Creek a road turned left past the Country Club entrance and began to climb the eroded ribs of Carver Ridge among thin third-growth pines. It was dark under them. My lights put up a grouse ahead of me. I drove carefully up the winding dirt road through the woods.

At the top of the ridge I broke out of the trees; the back nine holes of the new golf course stretched across the ridge fingers, a dark lawn under the purple of early evening. Beyond the highest green I could glimpse the lights of a house, appearing and disappearing through an orchard of gnarled old trees. I drove along the flat top of the ridge where the meadow grass was dark bronze in the last light, and the stalks in the cornfield beyond it shivered a little, September dry.

I guess I knew it before I asked. The Catletts' cabin squatted at the side of the dirt road beyond an orchard and the long neat furrows of the fall garden. A pickup truck jutted halfway out of a corrugated-iron shack. A long grape arbor, heavy with grapes, led up to the side of a low stoop across the cabin front. Neatly in front of the house two old tires from the truck had been whitewashed and filled with geraniums. Inner tubes hung on a nail on the cabin wall. The logs were huge, gray with age; a single virgin trunk thirty feet long ran under the steep shake roof. In its aged grooves there were still traces of Jake's whitewash. Two small girls darted across the road in front of me, rolling a tire. I jammed on my brakes even though I was slowing down and heard a high wail from the stoop.

"You youngins watch whur you're a-goin'." A skinny woman ran out of the house, letting the screen door whang behind her. As I stopped the car and looked at her I saw that she was young enough to be the mother of the two girls, who now stood in front of the corrugated-iron shack and watched me without surprise, letting their tire bound off down the hollow. An old woman sat barefooted in a rocker on the stoop. She didn't stop fanning her great head with a huge arm and a Jesus fan—just watched. Beside her an old man had tipped a kitchen chair against the log wall. I saw that he had one leg. He was in his undershirt, but I noticed that his one shoe was highly polished and that he had a heavy watch chain across his neat pants. He wore an old Stetson hat as square on his head as if it were a uniform cap. His lips were covered by a large white mustache. He sat with his arms crossed on his thin chest, staring out over the hollow. I was surrounded by calm people watching and waiting for me to move.

"Is this the Catlett . . ." I was going to say more, something, I don't know what. Their calm was a solid wall.

"Yes. How do?" It had to be Loretta Catlett who eased herself down off the stoop and walked slowly toward the car. She waited without another word for me to get out of the car. When the two girls heard the door slam they spurted forward to inspect the fenders.

"You youngins git your dirty hands off there," she ordered them without interest. The smaller one grinned wide across a square Slav face. Her imp eyes darted up at me.

"I'm Hannah McKarkle," I told Loretta.

She waited, crossing her arms. I remembered that the old woman on the stoop had chased a woman like me off with a hoe.

"From up Beulah," I called beyond Loretta to her. She stopped fanning and rocking and began, not to smile, but to allow her face to take an interest.

"We're from up thar too, acrost the river. I wasn't from around there, though. I'm from down around Toey's Valley," she told me.

"My mother"—I was crashing through the watchers toward the stoop—"was a Neill."

The old man tipped his chair down and peered at me. Only his eyes were snap-black alive; the rest of his face was like the logs, grooved and dried out. "You Annie's girl?"

I remembered the language. "No, Sally Brandon's girl."

"Well, honey, come on up here and set down." Jake's mother opened the way to them without changing a muscle or line of her body. "I'm Essie Catlett, and this here's Jake and my boy's wife Loretta. You call me Ant Essie everbody else does, don't they?" she asked Jake, who I was sure everybody called Old Man Catlett. "Essie"—she raised her voice toward the little girls—"go git my shoes." The older girl sidled past me in a run, her sad eyes taking me in. She had the thin, high-boned, pale face of an Anglo-Saxon beauty, but I thought then that circumstances would carve her into an image of Loretta, not of me, though the child and I stood there in the evening in the high pass of the mountains and I thought then that the only thing that made us strangers was not a deep difference in blood, for we had a whole heritage of blood in common, but an accident, long past, of the inheritance of hill land and the inheritance of bottomland.

Ant Essie Catlett went on telling me, "I'se jest settin' here gatherin' my breath; me and Loretta put up thirty quarts of beans today." The thin girl knelt and put the shoes on her grandmother's feet with awkward pre-pubic grace. "Loretta, show Sally Brandon's girl what we done..."

"She was a right pretty little thing," the old man's memory interrupted.

"Who are you a-talkin' about?" Ant Essie didn't want to be interrupted.

"Little old Sally Brandon Neill, pretty as a picture. That was my cousin Perry's girl. I never did care for her. High-hat youngin..." He talked with the privilege of hard truth earned by his age.

"I know that," she agreed with him. They had forgotten us.

"I come down there the night Perry died. Brought him down from Beulah on a shutter. That girl froze up like to never come out of it. She married the McKarkle boy from up Greenbrier. He done right well for himself." Jake Catlett remembered me. "How's your maw?"

"I have to tell you..."

"Well, set down, honey." Ant Essie motioned to the second rocker and ordered me into it. I felt so small before the insistent calm of her great body that I wondered if my feet would touch the floor.

"Loretta, ain't there some coffee left? Git this gal somethin' to eat."

"I don't..." I tried to say.

But Loretta had disappeared into the cabin.   .

"Now lemme see. Your grandpa's maw and my paw was brother and sister. I lost my leg. Load of mine props fell on me." Jake Catlett looked out across the pass where the hills rolled in an infinite front yard. "Didn't have no pension in them days. But we had the farm on Lacey Creek. That was free and clear."

I tried to cross the spate of memories. "Your boy Jake..."

"He ain't here." Ant Essie wouldn't let me go on. "You knew young Jake? He never told us. He's our least one. Surprise. Born late. I'se forty-five years old. Young Jake ain't here. He's gone off to Ohio. He can't find no work. If I told him onct I told him a thousand times, there ain't no call to worry. Things gets bad and then times gets better. Just wait it

out. Didn't I?" She turned to the old man to demand that he
take her side, as she must have done in that incessant
pounding at their dinner table, Young Jake the least one,
sitting there, stony-faced as I had last seen him. Old Jake
Catlett was someplace of his own; the words "bad times" and
the thought of my mother putting him back to the reality of
Lacey Creek and Beulah and the old days.

I wondered if Noah's mother had looked like Ant Essie
Catlett, large, habitual, and immovable, telling Noah not to
worry about a little rain, that it was nothing to the rain they'd
once had, and had gone on sitting there quite calmly with the
flood up to her nose while Noah sneaked off to build the Ark
feeling guilty as hell. Those two, unmovable and stolid, had
been carved by the past for an unsurprising present, a soft
time, not like it was, never good or bad, like it was. I began
to see why young Jake Catlett got his Saturday-night pint.

Loretta was standing beside me, not saying a word. She
had a cup of coffee in one hand and a slab of corn bread in the
other.

We exchanged the burdens of the old woman's hospitality
like conspirators.

"You say Jake..." Loretta ventured.

"He's..."

As if she sensed that something was wrong and didn't want
to hear it until she was ready, Ant Essie laid the phrases she
was used to between us, cobwebbing over what I had to tell,
as she would have used cobwebs to staunch a wound.

"Who'd ye marry?" she demanded.

"I'm not," I fenced with her. What if I had said, "Johnny
and I marry? We've done everything but that"?

"That's too bad. You're gettin' on." I could almost hear the
laughter of the cool, refusing generation of my fast-moving
friends at the perpetual good-sport Rover Boy I'd made of
myself, turned on the spit by this enormous old censor of a
woman.

"What do you do? Schoolteacher?"

"No, ma'am." If I'd told that old woman what any of us did,
she'd have run me off with the hoe, too. I wondered which
kind friend of Mother's had been run off that way.

"We're kin through your grandpaw," Mr. Catlett entered in
from where his mind was. "Perry's maw Miss Liddy was my
paw's sister. Show her the pictures, Loretta."

"*She* don't want to see no pictures." Ant Essie didn't have to glare at him. She just stated word-law.

While they waited to see which way I'd jump, a whippoor-will called from the sycamore away down in the depths of the darkening hollow; another answered it. A hound dog crawled out from under the stoop and stretched along the walk.

"I'd like to," I said to Loretta. I thought if I could get her into the house I could tell her there.

She walked toward the door and I followed her, coffee, corn bread, and all.

"Show her the knife," Mr. Catlett called. "Come from up Beulah."

After the deep twilight the tiny living room was dark. I could see a shadow of a door to the other room, dividing the cabin in half. Loretta snapped on a light. Its pink satin shade cast a warm glow as if it had been lit in a cave, and turned the last of the daylight to night through the open door, where the evening star and one other lower, tiny one sprang out in the dark. The light cast the shadow of a large plaster Victory of Samothrace across the wall. The winged, headless figure looked like it had stopped in that alien room to rest on the way to someplace else. A lightning bug attached itself to the screen. There was not a word from outside. They were listening.

I set the coffee and the corn bread down on the tatted tablecloth, and when Loretta saw the unconscious gesture she snapped, "Don't ye want it? That's all we got." Her voice grated, bitter, too low for the proud old queen of the mountains outside to hear.

Loretta pointed from the light to the fireplace. She looked witchlike, bending over it and casting her shadow over the double brass bed covered with its crazy quilt and up the wall where the wallpaper had faded to a mild tan and had begun to curl away from the window, dried like the logs and the old man's face.

Two stern, faded daguerreotypes hung side by side in brown oval frames on jutting nails over a stone chimney that must have been built before the cabin. It was black inside with age. It stood like a great mud-and-stone altar, command-ing the tiny room. Lewis Catlett had a full beard. His eyes stared over it, unyielding. Sara Lacey Catlett, beside him, under the flyblown specks of age, looked straight at me, vague and dim, her head held high above her tight collar, her hair skinned back, making her ears jut out. She still looked scared, after all that time.

Mr. Catlett waited until he was sure I was as pinned by the pictures as I had been on the porch, by their stability and the squalid surprise of kinship having been found by way of a man-killing joke.

"That's my pa, Lewis Catlett. He and the rest of them never did see eye to eye. Ma was from east Virginny. Me and your grandpaw Perry got along fine. Loretta"—his voice changed to an order—"show her the knife."

Loretta met me with a glance of annoyed patience. "I wish Jake'd come on home," she muttered. "Them two never shuts up a minute. Them youngins won't do a thing I tell 'em and I ain't feelin' so good. I tell you, I'm just about at the end of my tether." In the pink satin light her hair was still soft and blond, a halo. For a second I could see the pretty girl. She knew I was looking, and it made her brush it back and nearly smile, then turn away, shy.

"I'll git the knife," she said.

"Air ye a-gittin' it?" Mr. Catlett called.

"I'm a-gittin' it." Loretta disappeared into the lean-to kitchen. She brought the knife back and laid it in my hands.

"Take it over't the light," Mr. Catlett called.

The Catlett family heirloom lay across my hands, its heavy silver handle nearly smooth with polishing. I could trace the chasing of a crest. As I brought it closer to see it, the knife overbalanced and nearly slid out of my hands. The carving blade didn't equal the weight of the handle. I saw that it had been soldered in. Mr. Catlett kept on calling from the porch. "It wasn't always a carvin' knife. I done that. I took and soldered it—t'wuz more like a whip, but that wore out." That was the first time I ever saw the haft of Ensign Cockburn's riding crop. Then it meant so little to me, if not to them.

"Loretta," I murmured to her, "I've got to tell you."

Our heads were together. She watched me, her eyes so close I could see myself in them.

"Jake sent me up here. Now wait a minute." Her body had begun to move downward. "He's all right. He's down in the county jail."

She moaned once.

"He and my brother Johnny got picked up Saturday night." Loretta began to rock. "Oh, Jesus, forgive him for backslidin' . . . oh, Jesus . . ."

"He hit Johnny. He didn't mean to. Johnny fell . . ."

ou two girls come right out here this minute!" Mrs.
...lett yelled at us, and we ran like children.

"Now what is all this?" She sat like a Buddha, four-square
on great hams. I could see her head etched by the light from
the door.

"Johnny hit his head on an iron rack. He died..." I was
moaning and thought it was Loretta until I realized she was
pulling me back into the rocker. Her hands fussed over me.

Mrs. Catlett's face went ash-white. I heard Mr. Catlett say,
"...hit Sally Brandon's boy..."

There was a pause as dead as Johnny on the stoop.

"I know Jake never meant nuthin'. He's a good boy," Mrs.
Catlett told herself.

Loretta was rocking my rocker back and forth. It was the
only way I knew she was there at all.

It was so still that I caught a false calm and let myself rock
in Loretta's hands. "No," I told the hollow, not caring if
anyone heard, "nobody ever means anything. But it happens.
Nobody ever stops to *mean something*. That, oh..." I let my
head fall back against the rim of the rocker; Loretta's hand
crawled like a mouse and ran over my hair in little darting
strokes. "That would take more caring than any of us give.
We're not lazy people. We just have lazy hearts..."

We sat there on the stoop as if we'd known each other
forever, letting the night fall over us. The first star hung in a
royal-purple sky, low in front of us. As the star was resurrected
every night for the Catletts to watch, a resurrection of care as
if Johnny had died to waken it was in me like my blood and I
had to nurture it and keep it alive. When our pretense was
stripped as mine had been by shock, it was the only nobility
we had.

Mr. Catlett got up and balanced himself on his crutches.
"I'm goin' over to get Eddie Lacey take me down to see about
Jake," he told Mrs. Catlett. She didn't answer.

He didn't say goodbye. He slung himself off the low porch
by his crutches and went down the ridge road in a long,
swinging glide, straight-backed, familiar with the impersonal
law and the bedrock of a world I'd never glimpsed before. I
had never earned the right to know it. Mr. Catlett swung
away into the night, a man in the way of the big grab, like the
topsoil in the way of the coal seam or the forgotten mansion at
Beulah in the path of the four-lane, high-speed ramp upriver,
a man who had learned to wait out change, who had to stay

on his own land like the trees, and when either was rooted out the land eroded, and the people eroded into Johnny and Loretta and Jake and me. No one moved to help him.

"That's where he's goin'." Loretta pointed down the hollow, where away in the night distance a tiny light twinkled that I had thought was a second star.

"I'll take him down," I begged them and started off the porch.

Ant Essie's voice came cold and exhausted behind me. "He wants Eddie Lacey to . . ."

There was nothing to do but go, not home, not anywhere, just off down the road by the now dark space of the golf course to plunge into the black corridor of the pines.

I forgot for a minute about following Johnny's Saturday. I just didn't want to go home, which was usually the reason for opening the peeled wood door on the riverbank almost under Canona bridge. Its neon sign read *The Wayfaring Stranger*, and a smaller sign on the door, "Athletic Club, Members Only." Johnny and I had always called it the Escape Hatch.

On the bank downriver from Canona bridge, wooden houses had once opened into the street and cast their waste down behind them into the water. There had been a town pier, a blacksmith shop and saddler with a life-size wooden horse at the door, huddled fronts of ex-saloons turned beer joints. All but one of the buildings had been torn down. I drove in beside the last of the wooden houses. Its side loomed up in the green fog lights of River Street, covered with layers of signs: Coca-Cola girls, a Chesterfield ad. The same long-legged girl that had hidden the Mansion at Beulah so long ago still lounged forgotten across the top of the little building, half elephants from an old circus sign were almost covered by a huge tin Royal Cola bottle, and a red plaque promised quick relief from neuralgia and rheumatism.

I parked between a souped-up two-toned blue-and-white Ford and an old Dodge convertible, its top patched with dirty white tape.

Beyond the peeled door a bell clanged to warn Charley as I walked in. It was only a dark hallway: Charley hadn't bothered to spend any money on the hall. I went past the steep wood stairs that led up to the bedrooms on the second floor that no one ever mentioned, past the door marked "Game Room" which had been the old parlor. Now its window on River Street, where women had once sat to watch life go by them, was boarded up, and a big shaded light shone down on the inevitable green baize-covered round table twenty-four hours a perpetual night. Beyond its closed door I heard the quiet murmuring of concentrated men.

Lucille, Charley's little hard-muscled waitress, flung open the back door of the hall to see who it was. She took me in without a word, just put her bony arms around me.

Behind the door, Charley had built a narrow screened-in porch overlooking the river. I suppose that now it has new walls covered with Daisy's macramé, with local soft sculpture, and acrylic paintings of the river, and bright museum lights in the ceiling, but then it was almost as dark as the night outside. On the few kitchen tables with their red-and-white-checked cloths Charley had put candles in small cups of dark red glass that made them look like votive candles. I sat down at the table where I had always sat, then slumped, as if I had, for a minute, come to some kind of home—the impersonal American home from home—all the way across the country.

Beyond the big doors to the bar in what had been the kitchen, that Charley kept open in the summertime, the Miller High Life sign shot its perpetual cross-country fireworks into the black square—a trick of firelight to watch, start to figure out, then keep on watching, not figuring, not anything, just watch as if peace depended on the fine thin spurt of red or green, arching, then disappearing. Over the bar, in a colored print as dark as an Old Master, General Custer took his never-ending last stand. The jukebox was turned low. It played "Honeycomb" over and over. Every time it stopped, waited with its breathing undulations of cheap electric color, a slim-hipped boy played the song again and then crawled back onto the bar stool and curled his denim legs around it. I saw him because the jukebox was beside the phone booth where at any minute I expected, peace-fooled as if it hadn't happened, for Johnny to turn from the shadowed end of the bar, hidden from me, and go into it to call me in New York. Time turned back only enough to take us both where we would never be again, to that indifference of the high-stepping, easy cutout.

Lucille set a drink down in front of me. I didn't want her to see my face, not yet, and she knew it. Her skinny hand retreated under my hidden eyes and I took the drink and leaned back against the screen and watched the overhead span of the bridge, its high steel structure arched across the night, its lights lining its graceful skeleton, as if it bridged a mile in the night sky over the timeless womb of the Wayfaring Stranger. I could hear the water suck and swish, almost at the foundations of the house, as a line of empty barges a city block long slid upriver, pushed by a sternwheel tug that churned the dark channel and cast a glow from its pilothouse across the water to the bank.

I hadn't even known Charley was sitting across from me until he said, "... didn't know anybody would be working on Labor Day." His head was turned away from me, his fat, sad, strong face following the barge, but he knew I was looking at him and he knew what I had come for. He added, "I could set here and watch them barges forever. I spent ten thousand dollars on lawyers so the city won't clean me out, so I can watch them barges pass. It's worth it. Lucille, get Sissy another drink."

She was leaning against the inner wall, just waiting. She said, "She don't want it," and folded her arms across her bony chest.

"He called from here," I told them, knowing they knew.

It had begun again, what I came for—the last following I would ever do along Johnny's Saturday-night dream ridge to pick up the pieces.

Any voice seemed to wake the Wayfaring Stranger. A redheaded boy in an old Eisenhower jacket, his hair in a greasy ducktail, his sideburns long, his pants tight, his speech a marriage of mountain and television, said to the boy playing the jukebox, as if it had been on his mind and now could be allowed out, "I'm cuttin' out."

"Whar ya goin'?"

"Dayton."

"Hell, Dayton. Ain't nuthin' in Dayton."

"Anyhow, I'm goin' to Dayton."

"You ain't goin' nowheres." The legs uncurled from the bar stool and "Honeycomb" began again.

Charley lurched up and switched off the jukebox. "You played that goddamn thing fifteen times. I'm tard of it," he told his two customers.

"One beer and three hours on the jukebox," he complained, coming back to the table to stand with his back to me, following the lights of the disappearing barge.

"Oh, let 'em alone, Charley. They ain't got nuthin' to do," Lucille told him.

"Hell, I'm lettin' 'em alone."

The boys had turned and were staring at me, with the same stone-wall faces that the men would have had for Jake Catlett if he'd walked into the bar of the Country Club on his fight night.

"I'm in love, I'm in love." The red-haired boy kissed the air without changing expression.

"Cool it," the other one muttered. Then, as if he'd caught it in the air, he went on, "I hear that rich son-of-a-bitch got hit the other night died."

There was a dead silence. The blank eye of the television set Johnny had gotten wholesale for Charley watched us all, reflected in it.

Lucille was between the boys without making a sound.

"Who's the pig?" one of them asked her.

"That's his sister," I heard her whisper.

"What the hell's she doin' in here?" They stared over her shoulder.

Lucille snapped the jukebox on, dug a dime from her pocket, and let it drop in.

The sound of "Honeycomb" parted us from the bar. Charley let himself down in the chair and we talked under it. "Sure, he was in here. Sissy..."

My glass turned slowly around in my hands, and caught the maroon reflection of the candle shade. "People hate us, don't they?" I asked Charley.

"No, honey, just ain't got time for you. That's all."

I had to settle it, there and then. There didn't seem to be anyplace else to run to. I agreed with the boy at the bar more than he could know—there wasn't nuthin' in Dayton, not there or anyplace left that wasn't around us and in us at the Wayfaring Stranger with the dark water lapping below. I could see Johnny's reflection, destroyed by the beer can, then the candle reflection destroyed, swimming and reshaping through my tears.

"He come in about one o'clock, all dressed..." Charley sighed and began.

"One of those parties, you know, the moon and the stars there," Lucille added.

"He said, 'Charley, what if you'd been asleep for fifteen years and woke up in a blue sateen bunny suit?' I'd go back to sleep, I told him . . ."

One of the boys at the bar snickered.

"Of course he couldn't go see Miss Leftwich, dressed like that . . ." I thought for a minute Charley meant the bunny suit.

"Leave her alone, Charley," Lucille muttered.

But Charley, vague in the distance across the table, great sad face gaping and swaying there, wasn't listening to her, or to me. He was burning out troubles of his own.

"How many times I'd hear you and him comin' in that door like you owned the place. Your voices stridin' ahead of you, just takin' us in for a while, then hightailin' off on somewheres, didn't even know we'z alive. Ever' time I'd go home my wife would ask me what you had on. I never knowed. Hell, she'd lay into me then, she'd say I bet it cost an arm and a leg. Yeah, I'd say, whose arm and whose leg? Whaddaya care . . .

"Like them youngins there—they'd watch him when he come in and he never noticed 'em except onct in a while layin' out to be friendly, imitatin' the way they talked, the son-of-a-bitch." Charley was just mumbling, but the undercurrents of his old patient rage danced to the surface like a slag-heap fire licking out its tongue and then fading away again in the darkness of what he had to say. Completely silent tears ran down his cheeks. He didn't notice them. "Wife studyin' your picture in the paper and them boys sashayin' around . . ."

He had begun it, a long series of reflections, the ending nowhere except back within the isolated self. They had watched and imitated us, as we had watched and imitated some vague pacesetter somewhere, now caught in the latest rich widow, now in a connecting fragment to a grander life, like Melinda's incessant voyage with an unknown woman which had kept her safe from grief in the afternoon with the mourning ladies. In an imitation of the oppressor as primitive as the cannibal who eats his enemy to gain his strength, it strengthened the frail armor of the dispossessed.

Charley's eyes were glistening. "I don't mean none of this, Sissy, I don't know what I'm goin' to do without Johnny. He changed...We'z together all through the war, only time I ever saw him free. I dunno, maybe all you folks is good for is dyin'. You sure as hell don't know how to live, unless you sneak off somewheres to do it."

Charley's tears were frank and healing. "Gawd, I'm sorry," he said, his head lolling on his bare arms. "I been with it so long, worryin' about Johnny." He looked up, his face working. "He'n that pore little old girl Tel Leftwich would come in here. Johnny'd take her upstairs like we wasn't even here, didn't even notice. She's a nice lady. She deserved better'n that—come from good people. He wouldn't even take her to your family's house—not in all those years. I'd go plumb wild, seein' 'em goin' upstairs. But I wouldn't say nothin'. This here was the only place Johnny had to do what he pleased."

I must have been grinning. I could feel it pulling at me, the grin. Lucille came over and held me hard by the shoulders. I began to tell him.

"Oh, no it wasn't, Charley. Johnny had the phone booth. He had Uncle Ephraim's place, and he had women; he had every place he asked for except the one place he couldn't have." I wasn't grinning; my mouth was gaping because I couldn't control it any more. "You don't know what it's like to have something expected of you and not know what it is except that it isn't ever what you do, it's what somebody else does or somebody else did. You know, don't you, Lucille?"

"No, honey. I ain't got time for that kind of stuff. I got six kids to raise." She slapped me sensible with her rock-hard wisdom. "Why don't you git out and grow up? You two! Gawd!" She slammed the door on my wail as efficiently as she would have cleared the table, pocketed her tip, or broken up a fight before it started. I could see Johnny and me and all of us through her eyes, our lives a long, sensitive, attractive, self-suffering wail down through the unchanging years, our flippant suffering a fashion of the time, children beating at a soft, evasive world with silver christening spoons.

"Now I'll git you a drink," she stated, having shut me up.

When she brought it back she said, "Charley, all that stuff about Miss Leftwich. You don't know a damn thing about women. She liked it. She's just another burden on that guy's back." She flopped in a chair between us. "Hell, I knowed that woman. She taught two of my kids."

The three of us sat and watched the river now in a more peaceful wake of Johnny's dying, letting the night heal. We sat there until we heard the bell in the front. Uncle Ephraim walked in and took the fourth chair. Behind his square ugly head the bridge arched as if he were holding it up. Rose had put him into a Tattersall's waistcoat, like all the disguises, but she, without realizing it, had only disguised him as himself. He wore his Tattersall's frankly, not giving a damn that it was more to her than a pretty vest.

"I been lookin' all over hell's half-acre for you, honey." He put a callused palm over my hand and held it. "Lucille, get me a drink, will you? I better call Preston." He wandered into the phone booth.

When we closed the door of the Wayfaring Stranger behind us he said, "Leave Johnny's car here and come for a little ride with me." He led me to his own car as if he'd just thought of it. I suspected that Uncle Ephraim in his slow, sure way was getting ready to say what he had to by telling a story, because he always had, a sort of earth-smelling parable. I had once seen him put a newborn calf to cow, and his hands and voice were as gentle and persuasive as a mother's were supposed to be. He didn't stuff the udder into the calf's mouth. He just gave the calf a chance to live and persuaded it softly that it was worth doing.

He drove me slowly up River Street, down Lacey Street with its same-after-same square houses with open front porches falling behind us, just driving easily, not talking. When we'd driven for twenty minutes and the calf was calm enough for the udder he said, "Sissy, I want to tell you a little story." Uncle Ephraim waited to see if I was listening, then went on driving and talking slowly. "Everybody had two dollars in the bank had to have a horse. You know all that, honey."

I remembered when Melinda and Haley Potter had discovered a new language, new ways to spend time. I had been surprised at Melinda, who had always neglected her animals and had had Spud's old dog shot one time when he went away for the weekend because it smelled.

"Well, I reckon this begins when Melinda called me up one day, three, four years ago now, and told me. She never asked anything, just told me she was sending the Potters up to Greenbrier to buy a horse.

"Rose and I had them for dinner and you never heard such going-on. You know Haley—she had taken up horses so damn hard a horse couldn't lay down and rest itself without her going on about casting—we'd go out toward the barn and she'd lay out to tell me about the conformation of every workhorse I had. You know how these women go on when they get onto a new thing.

"They had a pretty little youngin with them. Prettiest little thing you ever saw."

I didn't want to hear this story, but there was no way to stop Uncle Ephraim. He spoke so seldom that when he did talk, he usually had something so, to him, worth saying that he'd keep on its track through any interruption until it was finished. We turned slowly out toward the north hills.

"I never could figure out how two awkward-looking people like that big hulking brother of Plain George's and old Haley who looks like a dressed-up farmhand could breed such a delicate little gal, fine feet and hands, little pale heart-face, blond hair, good slim head. You can do it with animals, but it sure takes a hell of a sight more care than it does with humans.

"Anyhow, I knew what they wanted, just a mild-mannered little horse for the gal, not more than fifteen hands. I didn't have anything small enough. You know how big I breed. Hell, I don't want to sell a horse I can't ride—so I called up Lester Tolliver. He had a little gelding his boys had rode 'til they outgrew it—they're right good people. The boys and the animals both got good manners. I knew I couldn't turn Haley loose, not with that little youngin having to ride what somebody would maniac around and big-talk into unloading on her. Haley didn't know a damn thing she couldn't read in a book and never would.

"Well, we went over there to the Tollivers' farm. The youngest boy rode the gelding pretty as a picture. Lord, Haley was sashayin' around there, talkin' about teeth and withers and flanks, Lester and me trying to keep a straight face and say nothing. Dammit, I felt so safe with what we were doing. I knew once she and Melinda got their minds set on a thing nothing would stop them.

"They asked me once to come down and lay out a hunt. I thought they'd gone plumb wild and told them so. You can't do nuthin' but fox-chase in these hollows. They just got some feller from Ohio to come out and he took their money . . . I felt kind of sorry for them. I tell you, there was some mighty sore asses in this valley before they took up bridge again. They wasn't satisfied just to hack and pleasure themselves a little."

Uncle Ephraim was quiet, expecting me to follow. When he went on he was back at the Tollivers' farm.

"Looking back now, I see I should have stepped in. The little gal got up and she looked pretty as a picture, hands down, heels down—but, Hannah, she was scared. You could smell it. Then I realized she wasn't scared of the horse, she was scared of Haley. I could tell it. She watched that big hulking woman standing there, never even looked at the horse.

"Haley was judging her like she was a dog in training belonged to somebody else. She was talking, oh, something about the poor little youngin's seat and way of going, never even reached up a hand to touch the little gelding. Now the first thing somebody gives a damn about an animal will do, unconscious even, is touch it, touch its life.

"I borrowed a mount from Lester and took the little youngin at a walk around his horse field. I never said anything, just watched her relax, watched her begin to care about what she was riding. She'd been scared all right, oh, pushed too fast, handled without any idea of what she was like. On a nervous animal she would have been in real danger, but I knew the gelding, knew its breeding, sound, seen it come to maturity, seen it trained, even seen the boys jump it. By the time we'd gone around the field a few times that little youngin had some color and was going well. We trotted and we even cantered, and she was all right without her ma anywhere near."

Uncle Ephraim was taking me back to the long rides, the patience, the watching, that I hadn't known at the time was teaching from him, not hard, imposed form at first, but affection and ease, the caring from which form came naturally, to ride well out of pure spirit and pride. We were back in the barn, brushing and cooling out the little pony, never being told, always being led by that quiet man, Johnny finished first and sitting on the steps to the hayloft, Melinda uninterested, staring out of the barn door across the hill meadow.

"I didn't know any more about the thing; I remember Lester telling Haley not to feed the gelding too much grain, he'd get too spirited for the child, and wishing he hadn't told her that. I just didn't trust her. These big women around horses, they push too hard, push everything.

"Well, two summers ago they had to have a horse show and

they asked me and some woman from Kentucky, real hard-looking woman, to come out and judge. Me and Rose had to laugh. There was a big fight between Melinda and Haley who'd keep the judges. I was glad that we went to the Potters' house, partly because your mother and Melinda drive me to drink, always have. Seen Preston and Johnny both..."

His voice ran out and he drove on. I glanced at him, but he was thinking something he wasn't ready to say—not directly, perhaps not ever directly.

"I think I was partly glad too, when we got there, because of the little gal. I swear to God, Hannah, Haley had entered that youngin in an open jumper class for children. I just hoped to God the child hadn't had the spirit too knocked out of her to ride.

"That morning at breakfast the little gal came down turned out like one of the catalogues Haley had stacked nose-deep in the living room. She looked like a little princess, but when she slid into her chair for breakfast she couldn't touch her food, just shrunk against the chair back. Haley was going on about champion's nerves, how the youngin was always like that and then rode like a dream. "Don't you, honey?" She kept trying to get her to answer. I can still hear her saying it. Well, she got an egg and some orange juice down the child.

"I didn't like it, Hannah, I didn't like a thing about it. I've been around animals all my life and I can smell fear; anybody can who will let theirself. I was really scared if Haley went on talking the child would faint, but you know Haley. She has to win. She'd drag out every time anybody in the family ever watered a horse and you'd have thought it was the Whitney Stables instead of one little old youngin and a cross-bred Greenbrier gelding wasn't worth more than two hundred dollars.

"Then, by God, she said it. She said it's a matter of honor. 'You see you earn a ribbon from Uncle Ephraim here.' I was so mad I damn near disqualified the child, but I didn't have enough sense to.

"We got to the show. A lot of good coal money had gone into a right nice little stable and ring—good stalls, horses looked fine, pretty little tack room with all the ribbons pinned on one wall, them damn ribbons..." Uncle Ephraim was telling the story to himself now.

I had seen it. Melinda and Haley had made it as correct as

a whiskey ad: the pine paneling, a rustic "early American" cobbler's bench with a few copies of *The Huntsman* which nobody read, a neat row of racks for the saddles with their polished tack hooks above them, the shine and smell of saddle leather. Steel tack caught the light, and like cheap flowers bursting red, blue, and yellow, ribbons with their gilt lettering were carefully flung across one wall.

"We all went in and Haley started in on the child again. 'We want one of these,' she said to her. The youngin parked the orange juice and egg all over her mother's new brown-and-white pumps. Haley was trying to wipe it off with Kleenex and hollering about champion's nerves again because Melinda came in about that time to find us and Haley was embarrassed.

"I did try then. I said to Haley that I wondered if the child was too sick to ride and she looked at me like she was going to hit me. I know her, she told me, she always behaves like this. Youngin no more than nine years old didn't have no more business bein' pushed half scared to death into any show ring, but I couldn't make Haley see."

He sighed, and I watched his big hands slowly turn the car back toward the river. "Oh, Hannah, I still don't know why I come down. I wouldn't have judged at all if it hadn't been for Preston. I knew them women would get after him." Then he added, smiling peacefully for a second in the middle of his story, "It pleased Rose, too. Now, I like a little harness racing myself, but the sight of a poor bunch of hacks gingered up, rode by people don't care a thing about 'em, don't please me."

The streets were summer-quiet. Through open doors lights washed into the street. He was driving so slowly that I could hear a swing on a porch and the patter of people's voices dropping through the night as calm as sleepy birds. Uncle Ephraim's voice was as quiet as the night.

"It had gotten loose from Melinda and Haley outside. You get yourself a ring and you get you some hillbillies and you got yourself a fair. Come in all sorts of cars, kids running back and forth from a hot-dog stand. I knew the people, way they hollered when a sulky showed with a nice little trotter comin' around in a free-legged dash. It was a pretty sight. I've always been partial to trotters. Used to breed some... Anyhow, pretty soon a couple of fellers come out and set up the jumps, old Haley following them around, bossing—regular hunt course.

I could see three, four youngins walking their mounts out by the barn.

"The class was called and the Potter youngin was first. I wouldn't've known that little old country gelding. He'd sure been manicured, and when she cantered him in for the turn I could see she was holding him in hard—it was her own nerves, but it still looked good, too collected a canter, though. I could see that. I could see, too, that the little gelding had been grained to make him look good. I almost whistled the child out. She was glancing over where Haley was leaning against the fence. Later I remembered Haley's face. She wasn't nervous for the youngin or the horse. She just wanted to win.

"The little gal let the gelding out and he come toward the brush jump. The crowd went dead-still. We could all see that pale youngin, crouched up, just as perfect as training could make her. The gelding sailed over. I thought everything was all right, followed along to the next jump. She went over like a swallow—three-foot-six Aiken fence. The turn at the end was short. She come over the chicken coop sideways and faulted—the gelding's hind foot touched going over. I think it was that and the angle and seeing the ring fence loom up in front of her panicked her. She drew the gelding in and he must have caught her fear through her fingers. The next jump was a post-and-rail. He shied out and turned. She stayed on but I could tell he'd left her behind. She didn't collect him. She just clung on and the gelding whirled and come back toward the fence on his own and sprang. He went over like silk, cleared it by a foot easy. She was still on but her hat went and her hair streamed out behind her. The gelding turned and come up for the stone wall. I had gone over near it to watch her over the last jump. I can see her face in the air now, coming toward me, seeing nothing, but the gelding had been schooled to finish the course. Haley had seen to that. He gathered and jumped. I think her body gave up. She just couldn't take it any more. She came off on the rise, just sailed off. I can see her white face plunge like a shot bird against the jump. The crowd oohed like a big gust of wind. When I got to her she was dead—unmarked, just as if she'd fallen as a leaf falls. Her head fell back when Kregg Potter ran out and picked her up, not as big as a minute, her little slim neck had broken and made her head loll and her hair hang down."

He stopped—his point lost somewhere in his
and drove down the same tree-lined street we'd k
back to—Lacey Street, where Mother had once sa
of plain people lived who went to high school an   ......ers
college. I had retreated from him when he finally drew me
back.

"Later, when the crowd had almost gone—they went gently, Hannah, like people leave church—well, I went to the
tack room. The ambulance was waiting outside the barn.
Haley and Kregg Potter weren't anywhere around. When I
opened the tack-room door he had Haley's shoulders under
his hands. She was leaning against all the cheap ribbons,
crying. They heard me, and she turned around. Haley had
finally earned her ribbon. It had run like a damn red birth-
mark all down one side of her face."

He stopped the car in front of one of the blank square
houses on Lacey Street and sat there staring down the
jade-green arch where the street lights touched the leaves,
letting the evening peace come in and gather around us for a
minute. He gave me a cigarette. When I saw his face over the
flaming match, tears glistened in the deep sun-wrinkles under his eyes.

"A man," he told me carefully, so I knew he was touching
for me the nerve of what had happened, "he bred the fastest
harness horse ever bred in Greenbrier county. He told me
every champion had to reach beyond his breeding. A champion horse and a champion dog got more in common than
either one has with their breed. This quality—I dunno. I can
see it—can't tell about it. There's a place where you quit
training and let it take over—little neglect . . . a little trust . . . I
dunno.

"You can't make a champion, Hannah, you can only recognize it. That's what those strong-willed women don't know—a
little neglect works with animals, works with people. I don't
think Johnny ever had an unwatched minute . . ."

Uncle Ephraim was telling me his answer, but it wasn't
enough. Johnny was no scared child, or whipped dog, not
Johnny Escaper, Johnny Flirt. He could do what no animal
could. He could pretend to love and still remain untouched. I
shied away and let a question come. "What's mollygrub?" I
asked Uncle Ephraim. He relaxed against the seat and laughed.

"It's what you give folks to eat ain't got a job, honey—like
all you people live off the coal-face without putting anything

..ck. You live on high-grade mollygrub—damn high-grade, too."

He opened the door and eased his big body out of the car. Then he reached back in and turned off the headlights.

"Now you're going to come in here with me for a minute, honey. Rose's been here with Tel all day and it's just goddamn time one of Johnny's people showed up."

He came around to hand me out. His touch on my arm was a delicate pat of his big hand, explaining no more, leaving me to know where we were going.

"You were the lucky one . . . extra child . . . ran out of models . . . neglected . . ." This was more to himself than to me as he turned away.

I followed him up the stretch of concrete between the hard square of city grass toward the dull wooden porch of Tel Leftwich's house.

I didn't want to go in, didn't want Uncle Ephraim to make me face the blank humiliation of a woman whom I had ignored all my grownup life. To me she had been glimpsed only in fragments, a pretty child in mourning black, a shining girl at the old airport, a shadow following Johnny through the night streets, seen by Jack as he rode on patrol, a Pietà in a hospital corridor, who had drawn only indifference from Mother and Melinda, compassion from Charley to feed his sad hurt, and then a woman swept aside with the broom of Lucille's professional earthy scorn.

She cringed under a lamp in one of the overstuffed chairs, her frail hands folded in her lap in the square, dark room beyond the open window. Rose stood spraddle-legged over her, saying something with such strength that Tel Leftwich shrank from it as if a weight were pushing against her pale, delicate face, framed in blond hair which seemed to mourn down her cheeks in wings, softening her eyes, avid as she stared up at Rose.

Her eyes fed on what Rose was saying, waiting for some new expected blow as her body retreated. They gleamed with a kind of sacrificial lust I had sensed at the hospital. They should have changed. I knew they should have changed with Johnny's death, but they hadn't. They were used to being fed on pain and now they glowed as if what Rose was saying were a drug.

Rose and Tel were so intent on each other that they didn't hear Ephraim and me come in. I hung back in the shadows, fighting through the foreboding and the shock of the small living room Tel seemed hung in as if she would never move again. Rose's dark angry body was rooted, holding the room down. It was cultic in its reflection of my mother's house, forced into a Lacey Street oak square parlor. A gas fireplace with wooden columns, an inset beveled mirror above it, flyspecked with age, dominated Tel's chintz-and-glass attempts to lighten the room, defeated sternly the patches of Mother's colors—cool yellow, frigid blue-green.

The inevitable family pictures marched across the top of the dark oak bookcase under a high window edged with green-and-yellow strips of stained glass. Aunt Althea as a young girl—I had seen it before in her house—wore a lace guimpe and yearned toward the camera under an enormous puff of hair. Beside Aunt Althea, I guessed because Tel looked so like her, must have been her own mother, Mary Rose. She seemed to rise out of a cloud, faintly tinted, a 1925 movie actress, frail child face under frail marcelled hair. She was turned away from a young embarrassed-looking man in a high collar, looking toward him over her shoulder, pouting a little, as if he'd just hurt her feelings.

They were all in the same kinds of matching silver frames as in my mother's bedroom, and in the place of honor, as my mother had, Tel had placed the same enlarged snapshot of Johnny-wandering-boy, his head thrown back, laughing at a joke beyond the picture. He wore an old hunting cap and a dirty canvas coat. I sat beyond him on the fence, almost hidden by his body, a twin profile, laughing too. Uncle Ephraim had taken the picture; the joke flooded back, drowning my eyes—it was only that Johnny's dog was trying to charm us into going on when we stopped for a rest. I could see old Nelly running down the trail and back to us, barking.

"I told you, Tel, over and over..." Rose broke the spell, threw her head back, and sighed. "Thank God for Ephraim. Jesus, I hated Johnny." She turned and leaned against the mantel and the reflection of her dark shining head heaved in the mirror. "I wanted to kill him..." Her voice was muffled.

I longed to stroke Rose's back and comfort her, the strong one, and tell her that I hadn't understood until that minute that even in the dark corridor of that woman's body Johnny had wandered, ignoring everything but her sex and zest, visiting her body as he visited my mind, only when he needed to. Johnny and I had done the same thing, followed to break taboos, using with our charm the passion, ty, of the earthly born, giving nothing except a sex we didn't care much about, silencing anyone who loved us with our mild, wandering insistence, our cold arrogant kindness. Johnny, as usual, had escaped and left me to bear the knowledge that we had strip-mined every stranger who had let us in.

Johnny had had his final revenge on us. He was lodged in our minds as the man we had all demanded. Each in our way had let our love light on him and glow. I saw him, for a second, as dark within, gathering, reflecting our light back to us as what we wanted—a loved one. The ecstatic eyes of Tel had reflected on him and found recognition as in a mirror. I thought we would have stayed suspended there forever, with Johnny fragmented between us in death as he had been in life, had Uncle Ephraim not sensed the neural haunting and broken in by putting his arm around Rose, who turned from the mirror with a child's trust and rested her head against his cheek. He held her. Johnny had left her with him, and he had accepted her as he would have a good animal which had been brutally treated, knowing that there would be scars.

They were in an oasis for a minute that I saw was new to them both—a minute that radiated relief. Uncle Ephraim had forgotten me. He said, "I'll get us all a drink," and disappeared as quickly as such a big man could toward the kitchen, through the black hollow of a dining room.

Tel had seen nothing of this. She spoke out of her own staring. "He would have come to me if *they* hadn't . . ."

Rose picked up the tune; the broken record of hatred went round, turned down so Uncle Ephraim wouldn't hear, the forever mutual harrowing of women's "they."

I could hear Johnny's voice on the telephone, lighting another point in his wandering: "Hell, I don't know, Sissy. I've got on these damn clothes." Johnny had been dressed in the call-boy uniform of our private, ruthless world. It would have turned on Tel's patient, suffering condemnation of "they" like a tap.

He had had no place to go—no place the size of a man's rest. Perhaps he had never trusted anyone enough to ask for it.

"I know them, Tel. Christ, I've been through it. They're killers. Your ass would make them a face," Rose was saying as if she'd said it all before. "Johnny . . ."

"No," Tel said. She hypnotized herself with her soft voice and the nod-nodding of her haloed hair. "I can't listen, Rose. I knew him . . . what he was capable of . . . what hurt him."

"Who the hell didn't? He was as public as a damn privy," Rose yelled, but she didn't get through to Tel.

"No," Tel said again, and then, "Oh, no," and kept on shaking her head, undisturbed, refusing to give up her sacrifice—a burden of loyalty Johnny had not asked for or deserved. It made her virgin-looking, as if the renewal of it out of her loyalty, her shame, her soft hatred, had taken each day the concentration of a saint, with Johnny caught as her lost sheep. He had at last become complete, too late for anyone to love him. He had been sinned for, trapped by the righteous, and judged all his life. At least his death saved him from either of the final corruptions; he had not become his oppressors or his disguises.

I had sunk against one of the carved columns of the door when Tel finally looked up and saw me. Her face drained, seeing another picture of Johnny. Her eyes changed then. They softened with a kind of joy. She told me what that surviving, hard-working woman must have wanted to say for years.

"You get the hell out of here," she said sweetly.

Uncle Ephraim made a great noise, blundering through the dark dining room with the clattering glasses.

We all sat and had our drinks politely.

As we drove on down Lacey Street, Uncle Ephraim said, pleased, "I'm glad we did that, honey. It meant a lot to Tel."

We drove back toward the bridge through the dark spacious city between the small centers of Johnny's mourners. The clock on the Coal Banking and Trust Building began striking eleven as we passed above the roof of the Wayfaring Stranger, over the dark moving water; the sound faded behind us into a last faint knell as we wound up the snakelike hill road toward the tiny protected fortress of the hill houses. Their lights winked toward us among the dark trees. Up above us the indifferent, bright summer stars hung low in the black sky.

III

The Beginning
1960–1980

Once some potent event evokes before your eyes the invisible thing, there is no way to make yourself blind again.

JOSEPH CONRAD, *Lord Jim*

I MUST go back so carefully to that night twenty years ago. There is something hidden there that I have not yet found. At some point in that night I did, in the language of the forlorn hope at Naseby, "come to the shock" that thrust me into twenty years of work and to this time and this place, and it has to be lived again in order to cleanse my faulty vision. I have learned since neither to be impotent with anger at the polite brutalities of those nice people, their indifference, their knife-sharp manners, nor to be ashamed of my love for them. I must take this learning with me and go there again, step by step.

There is a time when all that we have done, or thought, or dreamed, meets in a moment that no matter how deeply buried in us is always in the present tense. It is more than a revelation. After that first fool's whirl of ecstasy comes the slow, hard trudge. The moment may be a shock, a spark, a detonator, but it is more, I see now. It is a veering toward direction, a taste of the inevitable. It defines itself, that moment, by a sense of rightness, a "this is what it has all been about." Ahead of it is a blank, a darkness, out of which a new vision may or may not come, but that is not our business at the time.

But behind it are all the divergencies, the detours, the cruelties, the shortcuts, the lies told and heard, the loves lost, the silliness, and even those brief foreglimpses that have been ignored or forgotten. There they converge, and there is a sense that nothing has been lost. It may be the first hint of

273

grace. It promises, but the fulfillment is one's own affair.
There is many a wreck on the road to Damascus.

The event of that moment may be only a glimpse of the
world at the corner of the eye or behind the door, always
appearing, not a whole vision. No. That is caught, if ever, in
the act of telling, of facing clear recall as I did without choice
when I let myself become a child again in the cemetery at
Beulah, memory distilled and made pure by time and forgiveness, unclouded by nostalgia, which is a backwards kind
of hope, and, as with hope, it clings, like those furry leaves
that stick to your fingers.

I must relive that night with the clarity that is the essence
of compassion for all of us, myself as well as the others.

The nice, attractive dangerous aging girl I was, of a generation to whom nothing had happened, untrained in disaster,
swinging hair, long legs, a virgin pacer, perfector of the art of
sadness, paying my way to knowledge with my body or my
money, and never looking back to see the damage I have
done, in short, this innocent, has raided the town as if it were
hiding the secret of Johnny's death to shake it out in one long
afternoon. He has died at eleven o'clock in the morning and
now it is eleven o'clock again and I am getting out of Uncle
Ephraim's car.

It is dark, and most of the cars are gone. The downriver
wind is sky-high in the trees. I can hear it, and see it touch
the shrubs in the light path from Melinda's living-room
window across the wide lawn. Melinda's Scottie is whimpering
at her French door, scratching the glass. Someone, Uncle
Ephraim, jogs my arm carefully as he would a sleepwalker. I
am aware of being very tired.

I am getting out of the car, and someone is standing in the
light of the open door; I can't see his face yet, but I know it is
my father, who has been watching the driveway. Behind him
the Senator watches, too. The Williamsburg replica lamp is
lit on the Duncan Phyfe card table from Beulah, as it is night
in night out until I think the bulb is immortal. It makes the
Senator look fat above it. His beard retreats into darkness
behind my father's head and I am almost swimming toward
him, lost in fatigue, no food, slightly drunk, piloted across
Johnny's undersea lawn, and the dark man says, "Hannah,
you'd think you'd have more respect..."

I am close, too close to his Mooney face, all brokenhearted
for the evening, and for twenty years I have forgotten it. I

don't—this is too hard—don't like what I see. He has expected this sorrow of himself. He has never liked Johnny. He has envied him for reasons I don't know yet, his social envy a mild version of Jake Catlett's fury. He has no right to look like that, not my coal-owner, corporation lawyer, Episcopal father with power in his walk.

He is taller than I have remembered him, and his face is runneled with the "worry" he takes such pride in, as if that were enough attention to pay us all out of the isolation of Mooney's ambition, of which we are all only a part. His mouth is deeply creased, that long ago in his photographs was sensuous and full, from too many years of being held in. But there are still his betraying eyes that have not changed, his terrible tentative eyes.

Uncle Ephraim says, "Preston, leave the girl alone."

My father does not look at me again. He goes into the library, where he is at home as in no place else in this house, and Uncle Ephraim pats my shoulder, and says, "You get right to bed, you hear?" and follows his brother.

At the door my father says, "Why can't they all . . . ?" What he is asking for I don't know. He has shut the door.

I am in the hall alone, as on the Sunday morning, but there is not even a deceptive peace, only the dullness of a death in the house. I hear a drift of voices on the terrace beyond the living room, no words, a monotone. The living room is bigger than it was in the daylight. All the women have left it. Now only Spud and Melinda sit there in the raw space of night, too far from each other.

Melinda has, for once, forgotten to turn on all the lamps and draw the curtains which she says you must do, even though only raccoons, and squirrels, and once in a while, still, a deer, could see into our lives, which move, at this eleven o'clock, muffled and slow. They sit like people who haven't said anything for too long, and have lost the will to begin.

But when Melinda sees me in the doorway, she finds words. "Where on earth have you been?" The words are so familiar I can hardly hear them. But the house has lost its familiarity and I feel shock at this as a physical tremor in my arm against the doorframe. The simple things I have been used to seem new. For the first time all the objects have their histories.

My young, sad, raven-haired Great-grandmother Melinda

yearns delicately at the rosebud in her too-long hand. The
chair by the fireplace is hollowed by years of my father's
body. I remember the insistence of Melinda that the rug be
pale blue-green because Daisy has told her it is right for the
room. Mother's Tiffany lamp sits on a small table beside one
of the sofas, unlit. Melinda doesn't like it. It is more than a
lamp. It is my mother's delicacy pitted against Melinda's
strength and Melinda always loses.

The English chintz on the twin sofas that face each other is
a shadowed expanse of muted flowers. "You *must* have two"
—I can hear tears in Melinda's voice—"*nobody* has one."
The coffee table in front of one of them has three copies of
Town and Country and three copies of *Antiques*, exactly
symmetrical on either side of an arrangement of new fall
flowers, the inevitable Cruickshank curve.

Melinda has taken out her form of mourning by straightening
the room, an old ritual that she knows nothing of, shaking the
ghost out of the house corners. Not an ashtray is out of place,
not a bloom sags on the alien florist's chrysanthemums that
fill almost every free space, a desert of condolences, a tomb. I
think we will stay this way forever, Spud in the reproductive
Chippendale, Melinda upright on a little straight chair that
Mother says is early American, refusing the comfort of the
sofas, me in the doorway, as if we are caught in this moment
of genteel despair.

I listen to the voices on the terrace.

"Some people just don't know when to leave," Melinda
says, loudly enough to be heard outside. She gets up at last
and adjusts her black dress. "I hinted but it didn't do any
good. You'd think people would have more respect."

But when Father MacAndrews hears her and comes in, she
puts on the low-church voice she commands for such times,
even though she is, I can see, ready to drop in her tracks.
Her lips look parched, and she is getting a cold sore.

Father MacAndrews says, "Honey, we couldn't leave without seeing you."

Impatience breaks through Melinda's taut politeness. "Don't
be too long, Hannah, Mother's been asking for you . . . We
can't get her to sleep."

Father MacAndrews is used to Melinda. "We won't be
long," he tells her, and ushers me, as if I were a visitor, onto
the terrace.

Far below us, lights have shaped the city streets into lines and clusters of fallen stars. Someone gets up from the glider and I feel, close to my body, another living body holding me, and the sweet comfort bursts my tears at last. It is Candy, who doesn't say a word, not yet, and neither does Father MacAndrews, until I have kicked off my shoes and huddled against her and the glider rocks with the faint creak of summer nights.

When Father MacAndrews does speak, it is to Candy, over my head, something that they have been discussing while they waited for me to come home to give me this time in the dark, this easeful closeness so alien to this house, this familiar love.

"Man..." he says. "You take man..." They have been arguing abstracts, their peculiar form of comfort.

I hear Candy, over my head, "Don't say 'man' say 'I.' You don't have any right to say anything but 'I'!" They are enjoying this. I think this has gone on for a long time, longer than this night.

"You don't talk 'man' when I bring my little hillbillies up to your planetarium at the children's museum. You name the stars. Save 'man' for your sermons." There is the deep impertinence between them almost of lovers, but they are not. They are people who are lonely for a language and who have known each other for a long time.

"All right, Candy—I." Father MacAndrews sounds young and unconsecrated. I hear him sit down. "I can use the balance and order I see in the stars as an excuse for indifference to other men. I can come out of that discipline, expecting and seeing some balance in the world. Or I can stay in that until the world refocuses so that I can't see my own feet. Hannah is in danger of that." He knocks his pipe on the chair arm, then there is silence. I hear him scraping the pipe bowl and a match flares, lighting his face. They have brought me down into their argument. I sense that much of this has been discussed already. They are using their privilege of love to rearrange me. It makes me sit up, distrusting them. I had seen the hands of this man, practical, square hands, serve the Eucharist, clean the altar afterwards with impatient house-wife gestures, his big feet in black shoes moving like a farmer's under his robes. Now he leans back. Beyond the window of the living room Melinda keeps glancing up as if she ought to come out and interrupt, but respect for the vicar stops her. She licks her sore lip and says something to Spud.

"Now you be quiet, Candy, I'm going to talk to Hannah about Johnny," John MacAndrews says. Candy adjusts her arm around my shoulders, and rocks the glider back and forth.

"No man was ever made but once, or like any other. That's a miracle... God in him if you care for that way of saying it, which I do. It's my job. Johnny turned his back on the miracle of himself every time he glimpsed it, turned his back or let himself that was himself fester, secret and ashamed. He did it partly out of training, partly out of despair, partly in order to sate every little demanding reflection he met. He chose it. Even in letting go, we choose. Oh, I know I'm not supposed to talk about the dead this way, but my concern now is with the living." He is still talking to Candy, not to me. "Hannah is a rebel." His voice is far away. I am adrift in a half-sleep lulled by the comfort of being the subject. That he is talking about me, not what he is saying, rocks and comforts like Candy's arm and her foot rocking the glider.

Away behind us, through the open door, I can hear Melinda's foot drumming the floor to keep away the silence which has settled like a pall within the house.

"This is not the way to be free. She could end up no more than a rebel for words—oh, causes maybe. It's cold comfort ...just another way to hate." Through the thin lids of my eyes his pipe glows and dims. He sits unmoved in his protected calm. "You don't see people you've christened and confirmed and run out of your yard and prayed for, *think*. You only..."

"Say 'I.' Say 'I'..." I sit up, confused, echoing Candy.

"I can only see the way they are going. That's all I can see..."

"Who ever saw Johnny until it was too late—if anyone ...you..." His stolid assurance has wakened me, I want to fend it off, get rid of him.

"Honey," he says, far away, "he did what you're doing now. I turn my collar backward and you're as suspicious as if I'd turned my feet backward to hide where I've been. He would only have thought I was doing my job. I am. You try it, Hannah. Take on a job...and do it...and *then* come back and talk to me.

"There was no way to get through Johnny's lightness. He wore it like a caul. He wouldn't—or couldn't—be born. You know, the second birth is very like the first, same pain, same sense of betrayal, same gasp of fear that lets the life air in, same flow of water. Then finally, so Johnny would not be born—hurt—he acted his parts. You saw him as a rebel because *that's what you wanted to see...*" He reaches across the dark space between us and taps my knee at each word.

"Is *that* all you give him?" I remember being careful with fury. "Today I saw him killed. All my life I've seen him killed. He died before any of us had the guts to let him live. This"—I drive it into John MacAndrews like a nail—"is a matter of life and death."

He retreats for a heart's pause into the protection of his pipe until his head is able to turn to me. We have forgotten Candy.

"Dear child..." He attacks quietly as if he is too angry to raise his voice. "Death always happens too soon. It always leaves fury, the 'if onlys,' a plea for one more minute. What would any of us have done with Johnny's one more minute? Nothing! We've been living that one more minute all our lives!" I am aware that Melinda's foot has stopped. She's listening, too.

He puts his head down in his hands. I have seen Methodist men pray that way, huddled on big-boned fists.

"I thought my failures would be tragic... I tried, honey. My failures have come from a barrier of nice women shutting my mouth with a million cucumber sandwiches. There was a woman in this town—she was in hell. Have you ever faced the dark night of the soul in Canona, West Virginia? She was a widow, not a very attractive one. After a while, people forgot to go and see her, even her daughter... Naked sorrow embarrasses nice people. I was on call, night after night. One night I was out with my telescope. I had the best view of Venus I have ever had, pink and glowing. The telephone rang and I didn't go in. I just didn't go in.

"That night she committed suicide. She left money to the church for a chapel of repose—I think where someone else sometime might find out what it was like to be alone without God's hand stretched out through any human touch."

He straightens up and leans back, looking into the dark. "When the chapel was dedicated the ladies who had helped kill her—and make no mistake about that, Hannah; the ladies served cucumber sandwiches and talked about that unattractive driven woman as if she were a saint. I even spoke about God moving in mysterious ways in order to put some damned furniture into one more room of All Saints Church. If I had said what was on my mind they would have run me out of town. I simply was not strong enough to bear their hatred... You see, they already knew. That's why they set a wall against my speaking."

It is Melinda who finds all this unbearable. But it is not why I am harrowing this night, not the moment when she can't stand it any longer, but it leads to it; and she bursts out onto the terrace and says, "What in the world have you done to Ann Randolph's dress? It looks like you've slept in it."

And her shrill voice is echoed, right over our heads from Johnny's room; the tone says, Can't you see I'm suffering. Can't you *hear* it; but my mother's words, frail over the terrace, are, "I can't find what I'm looking for."

Melinda can't wait any longer. "Hannah, go upstairs and *make* her *cry*. I can't stand any more of this." Spud looms behind her.

"Now, Melinda, honey, you just wait a minute." Father MacAndrews gets up, knocks out his pipe, puts it in his pocket, and commands by beginning to pray. He joins Melinda and me by his two hands, blessing our hair.

"The peace of God, which passeth all understanding, keep your heart and mind in the knowledge and love of God, and of his son Jesus Christ our Lord: And the blessing of God Almighty, the Father, the Son, and the Holy Ghost, be with you, and remain with you always. Amen. Hannah, your head's hot. Get to bed as soon as you can."

Melinda, of course, takes him to the door and I hear good night, good night, good night, and at last there is a moment with Candy, that may be what I am looking for.

Candy has always said that the first thing I said then was "I've been looking for Johnny," like a child. She has built a pathos around that through the years. But it is not what I said.

Now, I hear myself: "It's all so goddamned *thoughtless*." Everything, the flowers, the clothes, the faces, the questions, is lodged in that word; but that, too, could have been later.

Melinda, in the doorway, says, "Take off Ann Randolph's *dress*. Delilah is waiting for it." Has she, in that time, waked up Delilah? "Take it off," she orders and holds out her hand and snaps her fingers, and waits until I take it off and am in my white slip, of course, and white bra and pants, we wouldn't be caught dead in colored underwear, and am standing on the lawn. I can feel it, cool manicured grass, under my stockings. She is forcing Candy to leave. She has never liked her. She says they have nothing in common. What she means is that they don't go to the same small parties, only the same big ones—Nothing in common is Melinda's habit term of social rejection, followed, if she is being passionate, by "*Imagine.*" She tells her, stern as she used to be when it was dinnertime and we had played too long, "Hannah's mother wants her," and marches away with Ann Randolph's black dress like a trophy.

That is when Candy hugs me and whispers, "She sounds urgent. You're in shock. You should have expected Johnny's death for a long time—that brother of yours—" She says that as if she never liked him. "It's Johnny *in you* who's in danger now. I've been listening to them discussing you. They're gunning for you. See you tomorrow."

Melinda's dog is still whining and scratching at the door.

I am at the stairs when she catches me again. She holds on to my wrist as if she is trying to keep from falling. "I don't see why you have to talk to her"—she sounds lost. "Why can't you spend more time with your own family." She holds my wrist tighter. "I've been discussing things with Mother and Father."

The first hint is a sense of cold in my back.

"Adjustments. There have to be adjustments"—she sounds like she is going to cry.

Above us we hear a door shut. Our mother has been listening. Melinda has been snapped into weak tears by the sound.

"Oh God, she's still awake. She's been cleaning and cleaning Johnny's room ever since people left. Wouldn't even eat. I can't do a thing with her"—her inevitable sad cry.

"Hannah, you have to face the fact that Mother will need you now. We've discussed this . . ." I can hear their ranks closing. I am being thrust now toward what I have forgotten. Melinda is putting on her gloves to walk across the lawn. Does she know she is doing this?

"Come on, honey. Please come on home," Spud begs from the door.

She cries, "I haven't *finished* yet. There is so much to do!" Then, "Go to Mother," and again, "Make her *cry.*"

I kiss her. "Go to bed," I tell her. "You've had to cope with everything"—which, in the only world she will ever know, she has.

She says, "Why, honey," and rubs her cheek.

As I begin to climb the stairs I hear her let herself out of the front door. Spud must have been waiting for her. I hear her say, "I forgot to ask Hannah if she had a black hat..."

Spud answers far across the lawn, "Come to bed..."

I can hear the low hum of Father's and Uncle Ephraim's voices as they talk behind the closed library door. Outside, the cry of fall crickets is an undertone to the night. Melinda's dog stops whining. There is no other sound.

I would as lief climb these stairs again as go alone into a cave, step by step against a strong current of darkness, but somewhere in this night is a core, for leverage and balance, so strong that it has resisted any pull that could be brought to bear on it. It is called the dead man. This is how a dead man is made, a strong anchorage for mining or building. Take a good grip on the earth itself; make a slanted hole, a foundation for a block and tackle. The tenacity of the grounding will sustain any weight.

I must, after this time, find again the strength of the dead man that has sustained me for twenty years. So there I am, in my pretty slip (a little lace between the breasts) and stocking feet, tiptoeing, and all I am going to do is talk to my mother. That's all. So, once again, in my mind's eye, I seem to climb on and on, as in a dream, up the familiar stairs, avoiding the telltale creaks by instinct and long training. Johnny's door beyond the head of the stairs is open. The lamp beside his bed is lit. Mother has turned it on as she has done every night.

She has been busy all evening cleaning Johnny's death out of the house. His room is purged of everything he has left in it unnoticed in the last fifteen years—the hunting gear gone, the collection of photographs of eligible women, even the old photograph of Tel Leftwich, hidden in his top drawer among the golf tees and the match covers. Only the thirties "portrait" of Mother by Bachrach that she gave Johnny on his sixteenth birthday is left. It commands the room, dangerously lovable, her delicate face turned slightly away, her hair marcelled, her smile sweet. The sepia print of Michelangelo's Pietà that she brought from Rome hangs alone above the bed, the dawn-young face of the girl-mother gazing without sorrow or pain at the broken man in her lap. Across the bookshelf, now cleared of the golf trophies and the bottles, the shoe-cleaning kit, the silver cocktail shaker from Melinda's wedding, tiny painted tin hussars march in neat formation. There is anger in the strict regime. I have not seen them since Johnny swept them into his wastebasket and replaced them with model airplanes. They belonged to Mother's "Papa." The only other picture left in the room is a framed postcard of a German mechanical organ, all red paint and statues and baroque gilt, which Mother says Johnny loved so as a baby. Every object Johnny has outgrown or rejected has been returned.

Half of Tel Leftwich's face, one eye, watches me from the trash in the wastebasket. God knows what other marks of Johnny's life the woman waiting for me in the front room has destroyed. I have to scrabble among the little ruins, torn letters, broken bottles, and it is here, what I don't even know I am looking for, the black flint spearhead that he kept beside his bed, which is the only single thing I ever remember my father giving Johnny which was not one of the impersonal props for a respectable son of a respectable father. I think it is the only thing I will want of Johnny's. I take it carefully in the flat palm of my hand like a jewel, to my own room to hide it, by instinct, so my mother won't find it again.

Across the hall, my door is standing open too, frail, pretty, and waiting in the glow of ruffled white lamps. I stand there in the hall unable to move. The long corridor from the airport, through the jail, and the rhododendron-covered halls at Egeria, has led me now to this. There is no place to go. All the doors, Johnny's, mine, my mother's, lead to a safe and killing past, and I am more afraid than I have ever been in my life.

Something touches my body lightly, the filmy white curtain over the hall window, billowed out in the river breeze, ghost fingers against my arms. Down the hall, where her light stains the carpet outside of her closed door, I hear my mother call, weak and thin as the curtain. "Hannah, honey, is that you?"

"Yes, ma'am," I say to the curtain, caressing it back away

from my body. I put the spearhead in my handbag. Now there is nothing to do but open her door.

She lies propped up against her pillows, staring out of her window at the magnolia that has grown against it. Her face is stultified with calm. She looks up at me, and just for a second, she smiles a five-year-old child's shy smile.

"I heard somebody on the terrace," she says.

"It was Father MacAndrews, and Candy." Her calm is drawing me toward her. "Oh, that was sweet of them," she says and smiles again, her motherly Bachrach smile. "Oh, honey, thank God you're here. I don't know what I'd do without you."

I am across the bed, curled up against her, trying to burrow through to her, a honey-haired girl of thirty still trying to crawl for safety into that thin grill of ribs, that gate of bone, those wasted arms. She strokes and strokes my hair, and I stroke hers, and even now in my memory I feel her sensuous hair, her wondrous tent of hair where I can hide. But that night her hair was gray and little wire curls, and when I found the braid she saved when it was cut, curled there in tissue paper, it was thin and small. But for this time of this night, she is my city, my citadel, my seducer. She knows it. She is almost whispering. "Johnny was everything a mother would want in a son. Oh, I shut my eyes to things. You have to . . . but now . . . we will all have to make adjustments." She snaps out her bedside lamp and plunges us into the dark.

She has been listening all the time. She has caught Melinda's word, adjustments. She has already adjusted Johnny's room. Now she is ready to adjust me. Johnny has ceased to function for her; that function must be fulfilled again. He is, like a machine, irreparably broken and must be replaced, first by a nostalgia created in his room, and then by me. "I put his soldiers back. Did you see? He just loved those soldiers." Even her memory is a censored, self-serving lie. I am as frightened as I will ever be again.

I turn and lie on my back, as far from her as I can. "The man who hit him was Jake Catlett," I tell the ceiling.

"Old Jake Catlett!" Mother's face draws in and she is dead-white in the reality of moonlight. The branch of the magnolia taps at her window.

"He called Grandfather 'cousin'—it was his son."

"Oh, Hannah, I'm so tired." She is that dangerous little girl again. "Jake Catlett . . . you try so hard and you're right back where you started. Jake Catlett, oh Jesus, oh God, will he always be where our trouble is?"

I can hear the diesel grunt and the rattle of a long train of empty coal cars, going east up the valley. It reminds me of exits and possibilities, and hopes. Mother melts back into her sprigged sheets and starts, at last, to sob. It is not my news. It is the sound of the diesel that seems to break the water of her grief. I turn over, face down beside her, exhausted, not daring to touch her to save my soul. Her muttering dribbles, like her tears. "I just can't stand those damned diesels. They don't sound right . . . lonesome . . ." Her hand creeps out on its own to find mine.

I think, Jesus Christ, she's going to have one of her talking jags and I can't stand it after looking for Johnny all day; Johnny dead, the sack he came in, which had driven the bored women wild, refrigerating in a drawer the width of a child's trundle bed in the back of the Dodd mansion on River Street. A small brass plate reads CARVER'S FUNERAL HOME, lit discreetly all night long. All I have to do is raise my head to see it, a tiny bright dot in the distance, down the hill and across the river.

"So lonesome," Mother is crooning. Her hand touches mine and grips it. It feels dry and hard, cold even in the hot night wind that makes the magnolia scratch the window, brushes the organdy curtains, finds our bodies, and ripples over them.

"That night when I heard the whistle of Number 13 I knew right then it was too late. It passed on the other side of the river about eight o'clock in those days. Then all I could hear was the rumble of empty coal cars away over the night across the river. That awful October. Now it's all happening again. You think you get away but you don't get away . . ."

"That awful October" is Mother's touch point. I, who have heard it so often, shrink away from that repetitive recital I've been brought up on, when my grandfather, Peregrine Neill, had died—they never used the word "suicide"—at Beulah. The hot wind fingers my back. Mother's grip is tighter, as if she is trying to hold on, keep from swirling down into the old minute, sliding toward it, fighting away, losing, now an old woman lying in her bed, staring at the blowing curtains.

"I felt so cold that night. I couldn't shake that cold." She shivers. It shakes this summer bed.

"I remember leaning against the porch at the house on River Street, wondering why he didn't come back and keep his promise. I was cold under the sailor suit I hated so, when I should have been dressed in my Sunday best and right that minute going with Papa on the streetcar the way he had promised. I thought it would be different when we came downriver, but it wasn't. It was just as bad as Beulah."

She is lightly touching things which fit nowhere into the old Beulah dream. She is bringing me toward the sigh of dead leaves and the sting of cold on her cheeks, my grandfather for the first time a man and not a legend.

She pats my hand across the body-flattened frill of the bedspread. "If I ever knew a gentleman, it was your grandfather. Don't forget it." But it is too late for her to retreat from the devil she is letting loose in the night. "You couldn't *force* a word out of him when we wanted him to *do* something. He was a weakling, Hannah, or he wouldn't have gone and left me like he did. I hate weaklings."

This new truth makes me rouse up heavily on one elbow, push back my sweating hair, and stare at her.

"I just *hate* them all." She is ten years old. She cries little-girl words and tears. "Leave you high and dry. Just when you need them the most."

She whispers the words. I can hear her spittle. She lies there, her fine, loose, dust-white skin fallen back, leaving her mouth slack; her teeth are clenched, as if she were in pain. One white rootlike leg is thrust out beyond the sheet as if she wants to be caressed by the wind, if only that. My heart contracts at the sight of her and makes my hand move forward again to try to touch her, but the touch makes her twitch and draw away. She stares at me for a second, hating me too. "Don't look like that at me. I *hate* that hound-dog look. What do you care? Nobody cared a damn bit. Papa didn't. Just pretended to. He proved that, all right." Then she glances at me again as if she were afraid and turns away, watching the curtains, trancelike.

She begins to talk again, out of the depths of where she is. "They didn't care. Nobody did. He didn't care. He just wanted to keep that stubborn grip on Beulah, old, ugly, dead place. That's where he'd gone that day when he had no business up there any more. Beulah was gone. It didn't even belong to us, and I was glad."

She sighs as she must have sighed that night in 1908, when

she was fourteen, watching for her father from the porch on River Street, next door to where Johnny lies. She sounds hopeless, and smells of the hot milk Melinda has made her drink so she would go to sleep. "Well, even if he had just disappointed me to death it was too late to do anything about it after Number 13 had passed."

Where is she now? Somewhere beyond the nostalgic lies she has depended on for so long. They have at last and for this little while betrayed her.

She makes a little humph. "Broker Carver was holding forth in the dining room. He and Dan were drinking. I can still hear that loud hee-haw. You could have sent him to Princeton for twenty years and he still would have brayed like a jackass. Now you wouldn't know whether he was dead or alive."

I want to say, "No, you wouldn't would you, Mother? You wouldn't care if he was lying across another bed in a dirty hotel on Slingsby Street, crying out his scarecrow heart because Johnny is dead." But I don't. I am trying to listen her toward sleep for once, not goad her into waking up. But dammed-up talk is flowing from her, relevant and irrelevant together, as if she is at long last sluicing her mind.

"When he deigned to notice me at all, he called me colty. He looked like a big bay himself." She giggles. "Of course, Princeton in those days was the be-all and end-all. I could just see all those men in a gray-spired town, a Prince town like it said, full of lean, hard princes of the money blood."

She twists against her pillow to release her nightgown, drawn too tight over her flat breasts, and admits, still ashamed, that they had been sore that night under the camisole that she'd outgrown because she had what she called little buds that nobody had noticed enough to give her new underwear.

"I wanted Papa to come and just for once keep a promise. I was the one who'd been disappointed, but I didn't care. I just wanted cold words. I didn't want anybody to sweet-talk. Don't you get tired of that, honey?" she asks me but doesn't wait for an answer.

What the promise was she hasn't told me. Every time she mentions it she seems to veer away from it. "I just didn't want to be reminded," she says as if she is answering me. "I didn't want to think about the promise and I didn't want to go into the dining room. So I sat on the cold porch and gathered strength. I used to do it by practicing my gestures. Did you ever hear of anything so silly?" she says to her child self, amused and fond. "You know what my papa used to say about me?"

Oh yes, I know. She has always told it with a little air of surprise, as if she'd never told it before. "When I was fourteen," she says, and is fourteen again, "your grandfather told everybody that I reminded him of the 'Annunciation' of Dante Gabriel Rossetti." She had put on then the shutting-out, frightened gesture of the girl like a coat. It was the only joke Johnny ever allowed himself about Mother. When the temperature went down and she turned her head, suppliant and withdrawn, to show how moved she was, Johnny would make the word Rossetti with his mouth at me, and she would catch me grinning and punish me with her silence. She never saw him do it. It was a part of why beloved "Papa" was set in her mind as the mentor of all the culture she'd crammed into her young-girl head and left there like an old scrapbook she'd stopped adding to long ago but still used. She had a picture from him of the court at Dresden, and Paris and operas, and, in her words, all the important things of life. She would tell proudly, as if cruelty were a privilege of what she called "cultural things," how Grandfather used his memories to flog her brother Dan when he came to the table during what she called "one of his times." Once he yawned in the middle of one of her father's stories about Washington when the Senator was alive and she said her father told him to dine in the kitchen with the servants, and the awful thing was there weren't any servants and Dan's laugh was like a nightmare. Her father said "dine" in front of company and he drank in a courtly way.

"You know," she goes on and we are on the bed that we will never leave, sunk there in the constructed past, her moment of raw truth long since over. She is playing "Papa" like a comforting old song. "I just love that word 'dine.' Papa would say it in such a sardonic way. Nobody is sardonic any more. I guess they don't have the time. And it takes manners too."

She shuts her eyes, her face peaceful, and I think, after a few minutes of lying still, hardly breathing to keep from jarring her, that she has gone to sleep at last. I move inch by inch from the bed and tiptoe around to turn on the lamp on her night table, to be sure. When I look at her again her face is wrinkled and pink. She is crying like a weak child. I sit down beside her to catch and hold her until it is over.

She gathers herself in my pity for comfort and stammers through her tears, "Why didn't he take me? Why didn't he keep his promise? You think it didn't matter but it did matter." It is not the death of Johnny that reaches her at last. She is drawing from me the pity she has craved for so long. Her hands are flat against my breasts, demanding that I be her mother as I have tried to do to her who is so ill-fitted for it. "Don't you see?" she mutters against me. "It wouldn't have happened if Papa had done what he said. None of this would have happened. We wouldn't even have been there that awful night." Where is she? Where is she now? "We would have gone to Luna Park, like he promised, and I would have sat in front of the big gold-and-red mechanical organ and just let the music half drown me and watched the carved angels beat drums and blow trumpets and the ballet-girl statues dance around and around and the Hermes at the ends would be watching me under their grape hair and the music of *The Merry Widow* would be playing like it had that summer when Papa took me . . ."

"Never mind, never mind." I stroke her dry gray hair. "He couldn't help it, now, could he?"

"He could have found a way." She is curled against me, this sad little girl. "When I heard that music I could just feel the elegant hussars Papa told me about with their red coats and their kid pants so tight they put them on damp, all young and gay and ready to die in their purity."

Her face streams with tears as the music must once have streamed over her. For a second she looks blessed, with that unquestioning light in her face, by the thought of a mechanical organ. Then the light is gone. "All *I* had was Dapper Dan and Anderson Carver to tease me. I wanted to see Papa's face shine again like it had the year before. All the way home on the streetcar he told me about the court at Dresden and how the chandeliers glittered and the gold braid and the ladies' jewels. We sat close together and he held my hand while we pretended and we sang 'We're going to Maxim's' instead of plain old River Street, and kept time with our feet. Then he sighed and wouldn't sing any more, and I knew he was going through the disappointment of not seeing his way clear to send me abroad or East to school or at least to eastern Virginia. Several other nice people whose money had run out were going there to school. Nowadays, well!"

She turns away and plumps a pillow behind her and

wiggles into it, now a gossiping young girl, forgetting the tears before they are dry. "He made another promise that very night. He told me he'd take me to New York the next time he went. But we both knew he couldn't. I was embarrassed for him and looked out of the streetcar window and didn't talk to him any more. The shadow was back on his face and all the shine from the park was gone from him. He went to Philadelphia and New York a lot, but he always said he was going on business and I wouldn't like it. Dan said he wouldn't let anybody go with him because he spent all his time waiting in offices, trying to lease what little land there was left for the mineral rights. Northern men who came down and accepted our hospitality made him cool his heels and stay in cheap hotels. In those days a land-poor place like West Virginia had to go begging. Papa always said nobody cared who or what was on the land's surface. They had to dig down a little bit nearer hell to get what they wanted. He always said he would take me to stay at the Plaza Hotel." She sighs. "Think of the number of times we've stayed at the Plaza Hotel. Well, that doesn't settle a thing, does it?" She nestles in her pillow, almost contented.

"Turn out the light and stay with me while I go to sleep." Now she is a lady, an autocrat giving orders, and she watches me as I lean forward to touch the switch. She looks, for a second of the last light, cool and relieved. I feel my way around the bed in the dark and slump down again beside her.

The city lights far below us spring out beyond the wide window of the bedroom. The room itself seems suspended in black space, drifting in the air above the slow-flowing river moving west through the river valley, long before and long after us, too deep for any sound, after the arterial spurt away east in the mountains. The wind tugs at the shutters, and whips the magnolia against the house wall, tears at our nerves, makes my mother sigh. In light all the way from the valley, mirrored on the river and thrown back swimming on the ceiling, I see her sad, young virgin face.

She is muttering to herself, drifting into words I can hear. "I'll bet Jake Catlett hasn't entered my mind for thirty years. He said it was his duty to come back with Papa. I can still hear his new boots scrunch across the board floor, big old lace-up boots from the company store. He would come downriver and he and Papa would sit out on the front porch where everybody could see them and there were big spaces of quiet. They always did that whenever they got together, sit very quiet, before they started to talk about whatever it was on their minds. I guess Jake Catlett was the last person in the world to call my papa Dandy, like Yankee Doodle. Papa slipped into a different way of talking when he was with Jake. He seemed to change shape and size, and he had that way like he ruled the roost. Of course it was only habit. Poor Papa didn't have an ounce of authority left, but none of them seemed to pay a bit of attention to that. Of course Mama said Papa was never happier than when he was with the white trash. When he said they were his people she just laughed, one of those sharp bitten-off laughs. Mama said there wasn't a Catlett or a Lacey left to amount to a hill of beans, and she'd been named after the Laceys herself. Of course your Aunt Althea was a Lacey, but Mother said it was the wrong branch of the family.

"Papa just fell into that way of talking and rared back in that tacky comfortable way whenever he was with that awful bunch of Catletts and Hunkies and rednecks. In his last years he found a comfort in it he never found with us, God knows.

"Papa just never seemed to trust any of those new people. Good God Miss Agnes, what would he think now? It's everybody we know! He said Kitty Puss Wilson's daddy was like all those Confederate officers from eastern Virginia who hired out for pay and fought for the Khedive of Egypt and in South American revolutions because there was nothing for them at home any more. He said they could charm the gold out of your teeth and were as ruthless as panthers, coming out to make money in West Virginia west of the mountains, deal after deal on land they didn't care about. I always thought he sounded a little jealous. It was a lesson he never learned. When Papa talked about Toddy Wilson he usually ended up talking about money. It would remind him. I can hear him now, saying that word 'money' as if it were a curse, and telling me that nobody won the War but fat Mr. Money. He said defeat made the weak ruthless and killed the strong, and that there were things that a gentleman didn't do for money, but that men like Toddy Wilson didn't know that, that they did a sight more with their honey tongues to kill what we stood for than the North ever did.

"Mama would interrupt when he talked like that and say that ideals didn't fill the pot and that you couldn't borrow money on poor man's pride. But she was as proud as he was and still served dinner at noon and said luncheon at one-thirty, like the Carvers had, was new-rich, coal-baron tacky."

Mother heaves a deep sigh in the darkness. "All we brought down to River Street was pride and a few nice things, the Duncan Phyfe table, the portraits... I don't know. God knows Mother tried. But Papa. He just lost air, lost..."

In and out, fading, sometimes clear, sometimes disconnected in her voice or in my memory, I can hear her night voice: "... great big blobs of red flowers, damp-looking pools, twelve of them," and then her refrain: "I just *hated* that carpet, and that awful hooded parlor lamp, and the mossy old red velvet chairs, the masses of photographs of relatives and connections, the brackish-looking huge gilt mirror, the fleur-de-lis of dead baby's hair, and Grandmother Liddy's embroidered velvet picture of Leto holding her twins in her arms. I loved the portrait of Senator Neill that had been painted in Washington and which hung over the piano in the parlor.

"... oh, and I just loved the stuffed pheasants. They were in front of a real painted forest. But of course that was childish, not real taste, don't you know? Oh, honey, I just wanted nice things. I had a game I called playing house. You know I still do it, in other people's houses—you know, when they have oak instead of maple or mahogany in the wrong place because they don't know any better.

"I would sit and I would watch my Grandmother Melinda's portrait over the fireplace and I would promise her that someday I would have a room fit for her to hang in; oh, her straight slim nose, and her swan neck, and her white face and her night-black hair, and her delicate long hand holding that rosebud; she always had them in her bedroom at Albion on the James before the War, always buds. The minute they were full-blown she had them thrown away. Ant Toey told me that.

"Mother and the ladies would sit in the parlor on River Street just like there was still money and talk in those silk, low voices women used to have. Then Mama would look like Grandmother Melinda's daughter and I would study her movements. She never forgot them. I would copy them afterward, whenever I could find a way to be alone: her way of sitting and talking, the balance of her hands.

"We were what people used to call poorhouse Tory... Boardinghouse," she says, separately and carefully. "Oh, I'm so glad to have you to talk to..." and I can hear her hand scratching at the silk blanket cover to find mine again.

Is it that poor thing she has been trying to tell me so she can sleep at last? She touches the next depth of her memory with a murmur, buzzing through the summer night. It chills my back as I withdraw from its sound and her cold, seeking hand. Her mouth moans the sound, and she thrashes over on her side, so that her eyes stare, darker pools in the dark, a foot from my face. How old is she now? A terrible fourteen? "Money money money. *You* don't *know.* I sat in the parlor that night and I made it all better in my mind by playing house for Grandmother Melinda and Senator Neill. I've always had extremely good taste, you know that. There would be cream walls and a clean green rug and a stained-glass window, and I would have a Tiffany lamp with tiny electric lights like flowers—that was good taste in those days and I like it I don't care what Melinda says—and a Lalique vase with a single red rosebud in it always for Grandmother Melinda, and I would wear a taupe georgette dress that fell like a Tanagra figurine's when I moved. Of course I had never seen a Tanagra figurine but I had read about them. They were all the rage. Later I had a taupe georgette. It was the only visiting dress I owned that came from a store.

"Oh, I had big ideas. About half the time I was going to marry a sensitive genius who looked just like the angel on the mechanical organ. We just loved the poets then, Papa and I. It was all right then. Everybody did who was, well"—I hear the faint embarrassed sigh that has always gone with the word—"a lady. Papa read me Byron and the Lake Poets. Oh, I had big plans. Dear God!"

As if she has wandered into a cold place she can't escape from, I feel my mother's body twitch, then freeze. Her voice rises in pitch, high, thin, faster than I have ever heard her talk before. She catches my arm and thrusts me down with her into what she is seeing, caught, unable to move.

"The front door slammed. I heard Jake Catlett call out, 'Miss Lacey! Miss Lacey!' and then I heard him go to the dining-room door and call Dan. There seemed to be a lot of men in the hall.

"Then, honey, I just stood there.

"Nothing happened. They'd left the front door open. The cold draft hit me all the way through the hall and then stopped as if the door had been eased shut. I couldn't move a step. Do you believe that? I was afraid to move, even when I heard Mother dragging downstairs. Her feet sounded tired to death.

"I don't remember getting from the parlor to the back hall. I just know I was leaning against the wall, looking into the big dim mirror in the darkened downstairs bedroom, you remember that...

"Men rushed out of the dining room. I couldn't take my eyes off my frozen reflection in the dark mirror. I pinned myself to it for safety. There were running boots across the front porch. Men's voices were babbling over the scrape of wood. I watched my head in the mirror. It was thrown back against the dark wallpaper. I couldn't swallow. My throat hurt me.

"I heard boots shuffle toward the door. They brought Father in on a shutter from Beulah and laid him down in the front hall, Jake Catlett and men I didn't know and one no more than sixteen... Dan ran to the wall telephone and pumped it and pumped it and sobbed out, 'Oh, Jesus, oh, Jesus. Get Dr. Dodd quick. It's Father.' Jake Catlett and those men had brought him back downriver from Beulah on Number 13. Jake said they went over to Lacey Creek to get him because he was nearest to kin still upriver. Dr. Dodd's brother had a fine new house next door on River Street, the one who inherited the farm and opened the mine. I couldn't move. Dan yelled, 'He's shot himself,' as if it were Dr. Dodd's fault. He had Papa's little pearl-handled revolver in his hand. I saw my own mouth in the mirror. It was as thin as a blade. God damn you, God damn you, selfish, you're selfish to leave me alone in the grip of their hard charity, forever, cut off, cut off, hopeless!'"

She yells at the blowing curtains and the summer night, twisting and turning in the rebirth of the minute. We hear somebody fumbling to open the door. She shouts, "Go away. Don't come in here!" I hold her arms down until I feel her collapse and soften into sobs under my fingers. The sounds she makes are disconnected, then gradually draw together in her mind, first in flashes, then, more calmly, into words.

"...then I heard Mama's slow drag of feet on the stairs. That stopped all movement. Mama's voice was as hard as hate. She said, 'I might have known he'd leave me to cope with it all.' She held out her hand to Dan and said, 'Give me that gun.' Then she began to moan, 'Buboo, oh, Buboo,' to

Dan. She was calling for him by a name that hadn't ▮
for years. They walked past me into the dining roo▮
from Papa and the others, Dan holding her head aga▮
shoulder and the revolver held on her finger like a rin▮
kicked the door shut behind them without even seeing ▮▮. I
couldn't look. I couldn't look at anything but my face in the
mirror." Mother's sobs are quiet at last and she sighs, that
repetitive gasp against the rigid cage of her chest.

"Then, if somebody wasn't gripping my arms," she says,
"you know, hard. I hoped for one second it was your Uncle
Sugar, but it wasn't. It was a sixteen-year-old boy I didn't
know from Adam. He had come down from Beulah with Jake
Catlett. Wouldn't you just know it was Preston McKarkle,
your own father, who tried to steady me with his strength in
the dark hall? And you know I was still watching myself in
the mirror. When I turned my head a little I *did* look like the
girl in the 'Annunciation' of Dante Gabriel Rossetti. I *did*. It
was just like fate, like Papa passed me from his arms right
into your father's . . ." Mother smiles. "Of course I made him
court me for the longest time . . . I had to make up my mind."

Then she says, "They're all such babies . . . just little
boys . . . you can get them to do whatever you want, Hannah.
I've always worried a little about you. You never would
learn . . . you're so gullible . . . Now, Johnny would do anything in the world for me." And then, completely calm, she
says, "I just don't know who I'll have to depend on," and
reaches for my hand again and this time she finds it.

She knows. She has known all the time. In the very ice
wall of her calculated innocence there is something as cold as
evil. She will go on, keeping as a safe shrine—because the
dead are safe and they destroy no dream of them—a room for
a boy who has never existed, except in answer to her demand, as in all the years her father has existed exactly as she
wanted him to be, and all the time she will know that she is
doing it. To her people will be their function as her servants,
or their pictures censored and retouched in her mind, and
when they break, or she loses them, she will replace them, as
my father replaced "Papa," and Johnny, the sexless, pure
Chocolate Soldier, has been trained to replace them both,
and he is gone, and she sits up against her pillows, and her
voice rejects the disappointed girl she has let me see.

"Do you think," she murmurs to the light as she turns it on
again, "that they'll put it in the paper? All that business about

ake Catlett being a distant relative? After all, everybody has a less fortunate branch of the family..."

She is wide awake now, and she drops my hand as if she has no use for it at the moment. When she speaks, the autocrat I know so well is back. "Now, Hannah," she says, as if I had just come into her room. "I've been waiting to discuss matters with you. Now is as good a time as any." She smooths the lace that binds the silk blanket cover and keeps on smoothing it. She doesn't look at me.

"Your father and I have had to make decisions. Things"—she makes a little habit "humph" in her throat—"things have not been easy... the coal business... taxes... expenses... upkeep..." That is not what she means to say, and she begins again. "We have found it a strain to keep two establishments ... You have to consider..." She is still not saying it. These are fragments of a discussion I have not been a part of. "We all think it best that you give up your apartment in New York and come back home where you belong," and she repeats, as if she has lost the thread of her decision, but she hasn't, the thread is made of iron, "Come home where you are needed. There really is no reason for you not to. It isn't as if you were *married*..." Her fingers scrabble at the lace.

She is moving me into Johnny's place as if I were a piece of furniture or the regiment of tin soldiers. Now she folds the lace, and smooths it, and folds it again. "You have to face the fact that we can ill afford to go on keeping you in New York forever..."

Now she shares a little joke with me. "Delilah said the cutest thing the other day—" I know this mood. She has put her wishes into Delilah's mouth for years, making a "darky story." "You know how they are, far worse snobs than we are." She even giggles. "She said I wish Miss Hannah would come on home and marry that nice Mr. Charlie Bland... Wasn't that cute?" Already she has chosen a victim, everybody's dreamboat, Charlie Bland. Delilah has never called me "Miss" Hannah in my life, but mother is courting me, and there is no honor in it, only persuasion.

When I say nothing, she senses urgency. She sets her foot down, literally, moves around and puts it to the floor as if she needed traction. She keeps on patting that one bare foot, keeping time with her nerves. "Now you listen to me, young lady. Your father and I have made a decision and there's nothing you can do about it. You have to face facts. *We can'*

afford you anyplace but at home where you belong. And tha
is my last word."

I have been rearranged and there is nothing to say.

"It is after all"—she makes that little noise in her throat
again—"your rightful place. I shouldn't have to point this out
to you," she adds, a little sadly.

She has been stern with me, and she draws her legs back
up and clasps her hands around her knees. Now in another
Protean change she is seventeen, and she says, "Let's have a
cigarette." We are chums together smoking late at night.

"I've been lying here figuring it all out. I know"—she is
forgiving about this—"that our tastes aren't quite the same
and of course I want you to be happy here. We'll take yours
and Johnny's rooms and we'll have the best time redecorating
them—you can make a cute sitting room for yourself. Let's
see"—she loves to dream rooms. We are poised here in a
whole house that has been a dream, after all. "That sofa you
got at Bloomingdale's will fit, and the pretty coffee table. Oh,
I can just *see* it, can't you? I think blue-green walls. You'll
like that, you know you will . . . We'll be"—she dreams a
House and Garden TV commercial American dream—"like a
mother and daughter are supposed to be . . ."

The woman all playful on the bed is the descendant of
slave owners, and she knows no other way to survive. No
matter that the responsibility for great acres has shrunk to a
suburban house on a suburban hillside, no matter that
Johnny and Melinda and I are all that is left of ownership of
people. She takes this for granted and she has never in her
life been asked to question it. When my father finally does
open the door, she smiles at him and says, "I've told
Hannah. We've discussed it all . . ." She puts her cigarette
into an ashtray made of two white china hands, and holds
up her thin arms to be hugged as if I were not there. "I *told*
you," she speaks into his chest while he comforts her, "that
it would be all right."

I think that touching each other releases them. They are
both crying; sorrow drenches them. They are so still that my
mother's cigarette plumes smoke up into the lamplight in a
straight line. Nothing moves. Powerless, tender, and perpetually young, they cling together as if the house were surrounded
by quicksand. They are mourning, at last, the loss of their
only son, and when I, and Johnny in me, tiptoe from the
room, they don't know we have gone.

Now, after twenty years, between that moment and the recall of that moment, I can come to some kind of rest. I have thought all the years that it was Johnny, my uncompleted brother, I searched for, through his rejections and his acceptance. It has not been Johnny's death that has evaded me, it has been more; it was what was done with his death by all of us, not the event, but the release or the self-imprisonment afterwards; the substitutions, as if he were an object of desire and not a separate man. After the numbness, death is or can be a spur, an urgency, a surge among the living.

I have traced the moment of decision, the no, or the failed no from Johnny Church who refused to doff his hat, through the demands of politics and circumstances on Jonathan Lacey, then the turning back to defeat of Johnny Catlett, through the escape to death of Lily, and at last to the woman who stood in a girl's room at midnight on a hill in Canona, not knowing yet where to go or what to do or how to grasp as hallowed the choice of disinheritance.

But I would, through the years, have a genetic inheritance more powerful than money; slave, slave owner, slave in turn. I would trace the tap of my mother's bare foot back to poor little genteel Sal who carried with her over the mountains, imitation of an oppressor she did not know, a camouflage, and sent it as a current, a current of fear sometimes too strong to withstand, through Leah, through Ann Eldridge, through all the barricaded women, and to me, who had to fight it in myself to keep from making the sad incestuous choice that Johnny Catlett had, or Beverley Lacey, or my brother Johnny. And it was in me that night, the seduction of duty and comfort and compliance, the deep training of a place I had not asked for, earned, or prepared.

And I would carry, too, the other extreme, the impotent seduction of the rebels, the wild boys, the blood of poor anarchic Thompson, Doggo Cutright, Peregrine Lacey, Indian Killer, Big Dan O'Neill, or one moment of Jake Catlett's fury the feral edge of what has made us.

But most of all I would carry that itch for balance between them, a quality that quarrels with itself, poised between democrat and slave owner, a dilemma all the way to our founding, that seemed so often to have no place in the pragmatic surviving days of living, but yet had had a place, had built a country, fused dreams into cities, seeking always the illusive balance, sometimes almost imperceptible, but even then it had so often left behind a residue of spirit, like an old campfire, gone cold but potent with clues.

It would be the armature, an ambiguity of steel, on which I have built my book.

Then in that night room I didn't know this. I only knew, as stunned as those two people clinging together, that nothing would be the same. I put out the cigarette she had given me, and sat down on the bed, as if it were as far as I could go. I had no Johnny to cling to, to hide with behind his mild sacrifice, no occupied center. I had only the pale, watery reflection of some hero I called Johnny. I had yet to see him as he was, and recognize the gallantry, the lucky star, the birth wound, that had to be my own. If I sought the bird-free heart I would have to carry it myself on my search and find in all that time the people who reflected it, a shadow of honor, a hint of courage, the necessary beat of sustained commitment.

I lay down exhausted on the bed for a minute before I undressed, and was deep at once in a dream I have never forgotten, a key dream that I was Johnny and myself watching and following, too, and I as Johnny was in danger, the undefined danger of something unseen.

I was in the dark, dark so deep that it had its own space. Only the dead spongy punk clutched in my hand kept me from floating in a valley of blackness. I was in the hollow sycamore across the river where Johnny and I used to play. It was as I remembered it before the suburbs were built and the ancient grave below it was exposed. I was hiding, waiting as I had so often, to be found. Its aged angular roots bit against my skin so that I couldn't turn, pricked and held me. Something moved in the dry leaves; I waited for the snake to caress my thighs. My eyes were bound with blackness.

Beyond me in the steep hollow, through the whole valley, I knew that there was nothing, nothing to scream at, nothing to hear, not even any wind. I knew it was only a game we had been playing all the time, but Johnny was leaving me there after the sounds of hide-and-seek had long since died with day, the test of the tease, gestures and jokes, all the games dependent on—not a breaking—but an evasion of trust.

And when I found him he was a Gay Huzzar and I was a

Gay Huzzar and we licked each other's necks, two boys fusing into one boy safe for Mother, and we were going to make safe soft love and she was smiling approval of something at last we did with our pretty bodies and she was young, appallingly young and getting younger and she was Sally Brandon Neill fading and falling so pretty so lost still fearful and fearsome a monster carapaced child. Birds screamed. I woke up in my own bed still in my white slip, watching the two neoclassic Picasso prints Mother had chosen because, after long consultation with Melinda at Christmas, they decided I would like them. She had waited in the doorway for me to notice them.

"I always believe," she said shyly, "in breaking up the period of a room."

A yellow, still, breathless morning lay in the valley beyond my window. On my blue chaise longue Melinda had left a black Jackie Kennedy pillbox hat.

For a few minutes the air was as still and empty as my dream had been, as if the past were gone into that black space, and there was only the terrible freedom of the day.

In the hall Mother called out, "Melinda, I can't find it." Her voice was young.

"I *told* you, Mother." Melinda's footsteps pounded up the stairs. They disappeared into Mother's room and I heard the door slam.

Delilah sounded as if she were dragging herself up the stairs. She stood at the top to catch her breath loudly, then knocked on my door. "You got to eat something," she commanded, coming in with Ann Randolph's black dress, pressed, hanging across her fat arm. "You got to be more careful with this dress. It cost an arm and a leg," she told me, and she hung it carefully on the closet door.

The clock said nine o'clock.

"We got to be down there by ten-thirty." She stood waiting for me to get up off of the bed.

Mother, Melinda, and I sat in the breakfast room, not looking at each other, our white hands stark against black dresses, drinking coffee as black as coal. Melinda's silver spoon tinked lightly against her china cup, and I remembered Mother's weightless, secret giggle of the night before. They passed each other dry toast with their white hands, white hands crawling along polished mahogany. I could hear Mother chew, then little "humphs" as she tried to keep the toast quiet in her mouth.

"Do you know," I stabbed at the embarrassed silence, "that preachers are buried head first and everybody else feet first?"

Mother and Melinda avoided each other's eyes.

"So that when they are raised up on Judgment Day the preachers will face the people," I went on explaining.

The clock said nine-thirty.

We looked, in "good" black dresses and black hats, like three provincial ladies having tea at Mother's Plaza. Mother cleared her throat.

"Please God, help me to understand them," I prayed. To dress and empower us, to pay for our manners, our polite blue-green oases, the grabbers bit at the coal-face, the conveyors carried out coal and left the men unneeded. Johnny was dead so stupidly, Jake Catlett, the least one, wandering a wasted man in his own wasted corridors, two more men in the way of the big grab. Without land to till or people to care for, Johnny had been caught in a parody where the land had shrunk to a genteel suburban house he wasn't even needed to work for, and Jake had been caught by the inertia of change, both with the taproots of their women clinging to the defiled rock, making them stay.

So we sat, the women Johnny had let pull his heart and hamstrings until he was small enough to live with us, we the slave owners, who had inherited the punishment unto the third generation, that of having to rule, but having no one to rule but each other; need and training turned inward, slave and master one.

Mother sighed and mewed gently, watching my face. "You might try to see some of the nice things in life, for all our sakes. You think too much," she said sadly, and patted my arm and left her hand on Ann Randolph's black sleeve.

Melinda watched the hand. "Have you discussed things with Hannah?" She looked scared, embarrassed at the way the sister cat might jump. It was the only emotion she had left that would make her act.

The hand went on patting and patting. They watched me tentatively, hopefully, as they had watched Johnny for so long.

"Hannah will be staying at home for a while, won't you,

honey? We've already discussed it." Mother decided. She went on patting my arm, misreading my calm face. "She'll be just fine. Everybody watches you," she added vaguely.

All the way down the hill the valley held its breath. As we drove across the river the yellow air began to move; it made the trees sigh. No one said a word. Mother huddled between Melinda and Spud in the back seat, her face smaller than I had ever seen it. She saw no one. She only clutched at Melinda's arm. Beside me, Father watched straight ahead as we passed our old house on River Street and the funeral home that had once been the Dodd mansion.

Along the street by All Saints Church, paper bags had been put on the parking meters. They had the word FUNERAL printed on them. It seemed to have nothing to do with us.

At the side entrance of All Saints a strange, thin young man stood, watching for us. As we got out of the car he came forward and touched Father's arm. "Would the family come this way, Mr. McKarkle?" He was almost whispering, as if any noise might wake the dead.

We followed him in a straggly line into the Chapel of Repose, all looking at the floor.

"Some of the family is already present," he explained to Father. I wondered if he laid out corpses, if he'd defiled Johnny with his long manicured fingers, or if he was just the front man. He tiptoed like a Third Avenue antique dealer. I wondered if he had dressed Johnny in the Argyle socks he'd paid for with his life.

Inside the Chapel of Repose the first member of the family to arrive sat, clean and upright, his watch chain glittering on his shiny black suit, looking straight ahead as if he were carved in stone. It was Mr. Catlett, with his crutches beside him. When he saw Mother he struggled out of the pew. The man beside him, his narrow face rock-solemn because he was in church, didn't look around.

Mr. Catlett swung himself over to Mother. "Sally Brandon, honey, I ain't seen you for over twenty years, ever since that day at Miss Leah's Chapel. Eddie Lacey brung me. I wouldn't of had it no other way." He leaned his old gray face down to look at her.

Mother's eyes were glazed with aloofness, that look which had become poetic in our lazy eyes. I saw for the first time how cruel and innocent it was, a trained, unquestioning gaze.

"Why, I'm Jake Catlett," the old man went on to explain.

Mother gave her arm to Father and let her [...]
away, leaving him stranded on his crutches. He s[...]
aisle, watching her as she went into the first pew a[...]
say prayers to whatever God had trained her to be so cruel.

"Mr. Catlett"—I held his arm—"thank you for coming."

"Eddie Lacey brung me." He looked around at the other
stone figure.

The funeral director waltzed up the aisle, sensing trouble.

"I told this fellow," Mr. Catlett whispered, "I wanted to
pay my respects."

"I explained to him," the young man said, copying Mother's aloofness, "the people of this congregation don't usually
view the departed."

I steered Mr. Catlett back into his seat and knelt beside
him to hide my face in shame.

"Oh, Johnny, get me through this," I prayed.

Mr. Catlett whispered to me when I'd sat up again, blank-
faced, "You folks Catholic? They ain't nobody in the family..."

"No, Episcopalian," I whispered, not softly enough.

Melinda looked around, willing me to drop dead.

"Oh, I thought 'twas Catholic." Mr. Catlett subsided.

Someone's hand touched my shoulder. It was Aunt Althea
Neill. I had not seen her for ten years. Whatever plumpness
I remembered had gone. She had begun to shrink into age
and she had stopped dyeing her hair. I could see a tide line of
white below her inevitable "off-the-face" hat. Perversely, it
made her look like a young girl made up badly to look old.
"Honey," she whispered and clutched my shoulder to strength-
en me. Then she looked beyond me.

"Why, Jake Catlett!" She leaned over and took his hand
and held it. Tears swam in her eyes.

"Awe, Miss Althea," he said, shy and pleased.

Aunt Althea slid with infinite care into the pew beside me.
Beyond her head, the brass plaque dedicating the Chapel of
Repose shone brightly, polished by the altar guild:

IN MEMORIAM
ELIZA CARVER WILSON
REQUIESCAT IN PACE

Mother had said, "I don't know what's happened to Eliza.
She's just let herself go. After she got Kitty Puss married and

:n Toddy Wilson died and she rattled around that big
ouse alone..."

Father MacAndrews leaned down and whispered to Father.
It was time.

We followed an usher into the church. I saw Johnny's
pallbearers sitting in a front pew—Charlie Bland, Wingo
Cutright, Luddy Wilson, Charley Carver, Brandy Baseheart,
Plain George Potter, and a man I'd met once before in a
downtown bar, Johnny's boss, who was in white goods and
television.

In front of us the empty "family" pew yawned, beyond it a
vague faceless crowd. I looked down, trying to pretend they
weren't there, hoping for a second of training as rigid as
Melinda's that there would be no writing of grief on my face
for them to read. I helped Mr. Catlett into the pew beside
me. Eddie Lacey followed us.

We sat in a savage, long black row to wait for Johnny.

There was a rush of people standing up, like wind coming
nearer, pulling us to our feet.

I heard Father MacAndrews, far away, intoning, "'I am the
resurrection and the life, saith the Lord: he that believeth in
me, though he were dead, yet shall he live...'"

There was a whir of little wheels behind us.

Father caught a glimpse of the crucifer carrying the cross
high above his head, and the genuflection ran from him,
caught by us, until it got to Mr. Catlett, who had not risen.

"'I know that my Redeemer liveth...'" I could hear
Father MacAndrews; the cross swam and sparkled in my
eyes.

Johnny, hidden as he had been in the midst of life, lay at
the foot of the altar steps, his iron-gray steel casket the only
reminder of the corruption of his protected body. The casket
was covered, as if the church were trying to overlay and hide
it in hope, with a huge crossed pall.

Father MacAndrews said, "'We brought nothing into this
world, and it is certain we can carry nothing out...'" Uncle
Ephraim stood nearest the casket, the tears running unchecked
down his face. Someone sobbed. Melinda glanced over, her
face blue under her makeup, to see who it was.

Father MacAndrews clumped up the altar steps beyond the
casket, his eyes set on the back wall of the church, and began
to chant the De Profundis, the words as impersonal as all
dying, a thousand years of the naked moment, when the

church demands, even of nice people, that they face, for once, an unavoidable mystery.

"'Out of the deep have I called unto thee, O Lord: Lord, hear my voice...'"

The response rumbled beyond us and filled the church. "'O let thine ears consider well: the voice of my complaint...

"'If thou, Lord, wilt be extreme to mark what is done amiss: O Lord, who may abide it?'" Light ebbed away from the altar. The new stained-glass window went dark. The answering chant was drowned in thunder.

It began to rain, pelting, rolling down the valley, harrowing the church roof. Even so near the altar I could barely hear Father MacAndrews read the lesson.

"Cloudburst," Mr. Catlett said to himself. He looked straight ahead still, as if he hadn't realized that he spoke aloud.

The rain steadied its pounding. Behind us, mingled with it, the tentative singing of people unused to church except at weddings or at funerals struggled with the old and blood-stained hymn.

"'When wounded sore the stricken hart lies bleeding and unbound'" sounded as thin as wind or grass under the roof studded by rain.

"'The Lord be with you,'" Father MacAndrews told us.

And we answered, sighing through the rain, "'... and with thy spirit.'"

"Let us pray," he said, and the crowd behind us rustled to its knees. Father helped Mother down. We were at last able to hide our faces for grief or embarrassment or whatever moved the black family pew of strangers. Or perhaps it was guilt, that old cross-bred feeling between a hell-fire gospel and the tentative manners of the perpetually changing American.

Father MacAndrews motioned to the pallbearers, who shuffled to either side of Johnny's casket. I could see its bronze handles, eighteenth-century good taste, peep out from under the pall. No one touched them. They walked beside them, while the correct attendant rose carefully on his toes and began to wheel Johnny out, following Father MacAndrews and the crucifer. He might have been wheeling a baby carriage.

The rain stopped. The stained-glass windows began to blush and the church was filled with their prisms, rods of blue, squares of red and yellow light, flung through them by the washed morning sun. My heart leaped at the bright color as hearts leap, unprepared always, when being alive unexpectedly lightens the world, seen as the boy on skates had seen it, free for a second, and new.

We drove to the cemetery through yellow water. It roared down the ditches, carrying clay from the scarred hillsides. I could see the hearse ahead splatter and part great sheets of hill-laden water that overflowed the ditches and burst across the blacktop, making it shine in the sun. The sleek black body plowed on, its rear curtains drawn thoughtfully so we would not see where Johnny lay, the corpus delicti for so many hidden in death as in life by lazy, easing custom.

I had been "helped" into the front seat beside Father. In the back seat, as if they were playing the quick march to ease them away from stupefied sorrow, Mother and Melinda muttered the kind of talk Southern women keep on exuding when they think their mouths are closed, a dripping tap of remarks unmatched by their dim, drained faces. As unthinking as the water that rushed unstopped, unchanneled, and rilled down the rocks of Cemetery Ridge, they reconstructed Johnny.

"He would have appreciated . . ."

"He would have liked . . ."

"He would have laughed . . ."

Melinda said proudly, ". . . the church was crowded."

Mother sounded worried. ". . . there were a lot of people there I didn't know."

I hadn't seen either of them look up.

Melinda explained that they were business people. "You know, a man . . ."

"Oh," Mother said.

In a little silence the motor purred on and the hill water splashed under the wheels.

"I always thought it was 'heart,' you know, inside—not *a* hart . . ." Melinda's voice began to ripple again.

"Isn't it? That changes *everything*."

"No, it's a hart, like a deer."

"Oh, I don't like that half as much." Mother began to chant in her voice for poetry and for God. "When *woon*ded sore, the *strick*en heart. No, the broken heart is more apropos."

"Mother. It's a *hart*, like a deer." Melinda had the last word.

Mother began to hum, as she did when she was nervous, or when the subject was closed. She hummed faster and faster and drummed her fingers on the windowsill in an incessant woodpecker noise. I thought she was going to fall into talking about God's love, which she usually did on our trips to the cemetery, but she said nothing, only went on humming and tapping.

We turned in at the cemetery gate. The narrow ribbon of road curled and twisted around the family plots and the acres of planted stone in the golf-course green sod of the "perpetual care" section. We passed the Carver mausoleum with its heavy Greek pediment, passed the newer Potter plot, where a flat stone, isolated from the shiny, mottled marble monuments, marked Sally Bee's grave. She had been the first casualty of our "age group," as Melinda called it, in the new convertible Ann Randolph had given her the year the highway was opened.

We wound up the hill. Far ahead of us I could see the hearse. The casket was being carried to a rain canopy just visible over the Grecian urn of my great-great-grandfather and -mother Catlett's vault, moved to Canona from Miss Leah's Chapel at Beulah when the ramp was built. Away above it against the sky were spread stone wings that looked from a distance like a triumphant angel. The road was tortuous on the steep hillside. We wound past the monument of rough-hewn native stone over the grave of Colonel Peregrine Lacey, who had died at Beulah in 1833. I could not forget it. Once on a dare from Johnny I had let myself be there until darkness came, my back pressed hard against the bronze plaque put on the stone by the DAR. It was a bas-relief of a cabin with Colonel Lacey's revolutionary titles under it. When Mother saw it, she laughed and said the Colonial Dames never would have made such a mistake as to put one of the old Lacey family in a log cabin.

The car had stopped. Then I saw Mother's face, mute and played on as a tree in rain. When Father reached for her hand she shrank back and turned her head away into a dark calm of her own so that the hard, etched curve from her thin shoulder to her chin was all I could see. Father and Melinda crooned and helped her from the car as if she were the only one with the ritual right to mourn.

Away down the road behind us, cars had stopped and small huddles of people wandered in and out through the tombstones of our family plot. In a long line beside the nearly black fluted pedestal with its Grecian urn, where a weed was growing, the rest of the bodies moved from Beulah lay under neat gray marble markers. They were washed clean by the rain, the dates ludicrous on the new stones. Our black heels sank in the wet grass.

Someone took my arm and I realized the family had walked on. It was Uncle Ephraim. I glanced at him, but as he walked me nearer the presence of people, quiet but not so quiet as death, I watched again the eagle on the top of Senator Neill's monument, flying against the sky, frozen in the air. The life-size figures of Minerva and Justice still mourned against the ten-foot-high black marble column. The draped stone American flag clutched in the eagle's claw was dark against the bright sky.

Uncle Ephraim made me go toward Johnny's grave. There was none. There was not even any soil to cover Johnny. His casket lay on the surface of the ground, its pall turned greenish by the light from the canopy. Then I saw beyond the canopy's shade a mound covered with bright green fake grass, so that we would not be offended by naked earth.

I could not take my eyes off of a corner of dull steel that was not covered by the pall. It seemed the only substance there that was itself.

Father MacAndrews began to murmur, "'. . . man that is born of a woman hath but a short time to live.'" I looked away toward the valley. At the other end of the casket from Father MacAndrews, Broker Carver stood, like an aged, unemployed guardian angel in Johnny's cad check suit, standing out from the black around him. He was drunk, his runneled face suffused with peace. The suit and his frayed collar were clean. "Amen, Johnny, amen, old Johnny boy," he kept muttering. Johnny's boss, who had a fat, serious face, red from mowing his lawn, kept jogging Broker with his elbow and sneaking side looks through the prayer with his little silencing eyes, but Broker had been jogged by life far more harshly than that soft man could ever do. He didn't even feel it, just went on muttering with his pebbly voice, "Amen, Johnny, amen, old Johnny boy . . ."

"'In the midst of life we are in death . . .'" Father MacAndrews raised his voice, sensing the interruption. Broker caught my eye and winked and wiggled his bony shoulders.

Uncle Ephraim stood on the other side of Broker, looking past me up the hill. Rose was beside him; she clutched at Tel Leftwich's frail arm. Tel looked hypnotized with grief. From the way Rose gazed across the casket at Mother's drooped head and held on to Tel, I knew she'd forced her to come. Steve Pagano stood by her, too, not taking his eyes off the pall, his hat flattened against his stomach. But it was Mother Rose was hating with her stare; she was using Tel as a naked weapon.

Father MacAndrews put his hand back toward the funeral director, who was watching us all so closely for anything out of order he seemed to be counting heads. I could see Delilah and Jack, in his uniform, away behind him by a clump of yew trees, as solid as if they too had roots. Both their faces glistened with rain or tears.

"'. . . and we commit his body to the ground; earth to earth, ashes to ashes, dust to dust; in sure and certain hope of the Resurrection unto eternal life . . .'" Fine grains of clean white sand fell like salt from a silver vial in Father MacAndrews's hand, making no burial sound, planting Brother Jonathan, Johnny Reb, the old sly boy, in sterile play sand where nothing could grow.

Then Father MacAndrews, forgetting us as Uncle Ephraim had forgotten us, looked out across the wide valley, through the blue air. "'I heard a voice from heaven,'" he called against the space, as if he had had enough of our smallness measuring the terrible miracle of another useless death, "'saying unto me, Write, from henceforth blessed are the dead who die in the Lord'"—his voice echoed among the stones and hollows—"'even so saith the Spirit; for they rest from their labors.'"

The air paused around us. Someone sobbed. Far down the green slope I heard a bobwhite from the graveyard covey. Father MacAndrews began to pray.

"'Christ have mercy upon us,'" our voices sighed weakly in the space.

Neither the dead nor the living were with me. I was alone. But I knew I stood as politely as the rest, the well-pressed skirt of my borrowed black dress scudding a little in a new hilltop breeze.

It was over, and we were being led away from the awning,

and Johnny had not yet been buried. I looked back. Only Father MacAndrews and the crucifer, his small cross shining out from the shadows, were left under the canopy. The funeral director had backed away with two strange black workmen. Delilah and Jack still stood against the yew tree. On the near side, safe among the Catlett graves, Mr. Catlett leaned on his crutches, with Aunt Althea beside him. Eddie Lacey waited behind them.

I tried to pull away from Melinda. She turned and saw Aunt Althea.

"What is she doing?" she muttered.

"I'm going back," I told her.

"You're going to do nothing of the kind . . . You're going to do what everybody else does!" she whispered at me. Melinda had finally said the prayer that was nearest her heart. Her hand was like a vise. People walked in a wide arc around the two mourning sisters leaning together in their sad time.

I twisted my arm out of her grasp. She looked up to see if anyone was watching. "Never do anything the way . . ." I heard her mutter as she shrugged away.

It was Melinda's epitaph for me, as cold as if it were etched on one of the stones.

As I wandered back to see Johnny buried, Mr. Catlett came to me, moving fast enough for Eddie Lacey to take long hill strides beside him.

He looked down at me. I had not realized he was a tall man. "Goodbye, Miss Hannar," he said and took my hand. His cheeks, since the night before, had shrunk even more. The white mustaches went down below his chin in a horse-shoe. I remembered for the first time that day that only his ingrained hill manners made him hide that he, old and dispossessed, had troubles of his own.

Behind me I could hear a machine begin to hum as I watched Mr. Catlett and Aunt Althea going off to Eddie Lacey's pickup truck parked away from the road, almost in front of Colonel Peregrine Lacey's tomb. All the way out of sight over the hill's edge the dead lay in the last green grass before the suburbs on the southern side of the river. The valley spread out below, covered with roofs of red and brown and gray, its spires tiny against the space. I wondered if meadows had gone down to the river, or if the dense forest had hidden it. There was no sight of the scars, the stabbed hills, only an innocent town, lying deceptively safe between the hills in the sweet curved valley, hiding its wounded land, its unneeded men.

When I turned again, Johnny's casket had been lowered halfway into the grave. The winch sighed and squeaked as the young man turned it with his pretty fingers. The fake grass cover had been removed, and the earth to cover Johnny lay in the sun, sodden with wet—not earth at all, not even dust, a mixture of clay and shale, which was what we had left on the eroded, naked hill.

The boy holding the crucifix kept it steady, the staff between his eyes, like a cadet on parade, while the workmen threw the heavy clay against the casket, grunting slightly in unison at its weight. The clay rumbled, loose pebbles danced, beginning to dirty the clean pall.

Father MacAndrews watched until the grave was nearly full, he away from me, I away from him.

"Now, Hannah," he finally said, sounding as down-to-earth as the workmen's grunting and the thunk of the wet clay, "I'm going to take you home." He came around the grave.

"We'll take her, Father," Jack said behind me. I hadn't known that he and Delilah were still there.

"Well, anyway, walk a little with me." Father MacAndrews led me down among the neat squares of marble. He sighed by Jonathan Catlett, his work with us not yet done.

"Why are you a preacher?" I asked him by Leah Catlett's headstone—Leah born Cutright, my great-great-grandmother from Cincinnati. What had she brought us besides cobwebs of kin and old pride? How far back could the unknown scars go? How deep was the anger behind Jake Catlett's fist? Father MacAndrews turned up the hill for me to follow him, but I was caught among the graves of those who had left their lost gestures somewhere in mine and Jake Catlett's blood. I knew then that to find Johnny's death, or any man's death, was more than the work of one spoiled girl in a few days of being touched and formed for once in her life.

Father MacAndrews had turned and stood below the eagle, waiting for me. As I followed I saw his hand reach for his pipe, forgetting he was in his cassock. He sat down on the wide, damp base of Senator Neill's tomb, flanked by Minerva and Justice. Away over his head the eagle soared. He looked so awkward sitting there, with his big shoes and his uncreased pants' legs jutting out from his skirt, that it drew me to him and I huddled under Justice, watching him, and took off the black hat.

"Hard to tell, honey. It runs in my family," he told me after I had forgotten what I'd asked him. "At least," he added, "it's a duty to your own people that you can't run a road through or strip the top from or run down the river like topsoil."

Away in the valley, from far down the river, came a fine call of a noon whistle.

"My plane leaves in an hour," I told myself and Father MacAndrews and Senator Daniel Neill—"Whose unweeping devotion and unselfish service" I read over Father MacAndrews's head.

"You're needed at home," he told me, shocked.

"Don't fool me, Father, just don't fool me." I picked at the grass.

"Do you want to leave?"

"Whoever wants to leave home?" I asked the grass. I wanted to tell him that we were made of people who for three hundred years had left home because they had to, and who had had to carry with them that sense of loss, all the way to the American soul, a bleak, tentative place in the spirit.

"After all," he told me as if just for that minute we had the same mind, "our country was made by people who had no place else to go . . ."

Not because Johnny had died, but that his death had no meaning that I knew yet; that was the loss—the revulsion against waste, as I was revolted by slag heaps, the dead water, the stripped hills.

"I'm going to find . . ." The grass was tattered in my fingers.

"You better find some of the solid guts that were bred into you," he muttered softly, afraid of hurting me.

"Why did Johnny . . . ?"

"I don't know why. Find out."

"I'll find out," I promised him.

Delilah sat, shy in her grief and her Sunday clothes, in the back seat of Jack's car. He helped me in beside her. All the way down the hill and across the valley we clung together in our silence.

They let me off by the Wayfaring Stranger to pick up Johnny's car. Delilah looked at the closed door. "You come right straight home, you hear?" She was stern as she had been, saying the same words, ever since I could remember.

"I will," I said, and turned away to keep from crying.

When I had almost reached the house I remembered that I had left Melinda's Jackie Kennedy hat on the stone as a small correct offering to Wisdom or Justice, or Senator Neill.

In the living room there was a babble of voices. Ice tinkled in glasses. A sense of relief that it was over permeated the house. Delilah and Jack went into the kitchen and I tiptoed up the stairs, to change and get my handbag, which was all I had brought home.

When I went into the living room, my scarlet dress harsh against the dull green and the black, my father walked away and Mother looked up and smiled as if I were a stranger. The event had drawn them into life for a little while, and, finding it naked and unbearable, they were retreating, trying to find their safe, dry place again. The ice was familiar in their glasses, their eyes begged for habit, for me to shut up, not make enough noise to wake the dead. Rilke had said that there was evidence that the prodigal returned, but there was no evidence that he stayed. For me, the language of staying had been washed clean from my mind. I had to be born, and the doors to the past were as closed as my mother's womb. There was, simply, no place to go back to, and no more to say.

Melinda didn't speak. Like the prodigal's older brother, she sulked, her face heavy with a kind of perpetual disappointment, shutting me away from the duty she clutched as she clutched her drink.

Uncle Ephraim and Rose, Uncle Sugar, Brandy and Kitty Puss and Spud, as "family," were gathered around the drink table which was across the French windows, covered with its white cloth, with the silver goblets, the ice, the bourbon, and because it was still summer, vodka, gin, and tonic water and limes sliced on a silver plate, just as it had been on Sunday morning. It was time for the next act of the day, when the family are to be left alone to get on each other's nerves, ritually, and go on drinking, ritually, until the ritual night falls and the next morning the last of death is swept and shaken out of the house.

Mother's smile stayed for a pause after she saw how I was dressed. Then she sensed that something was wrong. "You're going," she stated quite calmly.

"Yes. I have to. My plane leaves in an hour." There could have been no one else in the room.

"You won't get another goddamn cent out of us if you do this. I'll see to it." She was still very quiet.

"I can work," I told her.

"You!" She started to laugh. The sound of it scared my father and he almost ran across the room to her and stumbled on the edge of the coffee table.

"What's the matter, honey?" He knelt on one knee to hug her.

"Oh for Christ's sake let me alone." She pushed him away.

"Hannah, what have you said to your mother?" He was tall over me. "Today of all days."

"Today's as good a day as any." I knew I was being insolent, but, looking back, I see why I needed that defense. I was afraid. It was not only that those two people, poised there forever in my mind on the muted flowers of the sofa, took for granted they had the right to make decisions for other human beings, but that I had to fight my way out of the sin of taking it for granted, too. I know now that there is only one dictatorship about which we can do nothing—the dictatorship of the dead, left in the minds of the living, too late for any change, for they are the only ones who have had their last word.

And so still they pause, long dead, she sitting very straight with her hands on her lap, he half bending over her, and I say, once again, "I have to," but don't yet know why, I only know that I have to, to save my soul.

And now it is Uncle Ephraim who comes close behind me and speaks to his brother Preston over my shoulder. "What's the trouble here?"

My mother answers him. "Hannah has decided that she is going back—right now—she can't even stay a few days to comfort her mother." She speaks of herself as somebody she doesn't know very well. "She has to go back to that bunch of riffraff she runs around with on our money."

"Now, honey," my father says, "Hannah knows things have changed." Now he straightens up. "Your mother has had enough. Go back upstairs at once. Now is not the time..." But now never has been the time with him.

There is nobody to take me to the airport. The rest of the family are gathered close to the bar, watching this. I have my back to them, but I sense them and that none of them will have any part of what is happening.

All but Uncle Ephraim and Rose, who comes over and puts her arm around my shoulder. I can see now, not the white-haired lady she became, but skin tanned by summer, a mouth that can laugh and spit out hate, smudged shadows around her eyes, and raven hair.

"What are they trying to do to you?" she says, but not to me. That is to my mother, who stares at her and doesn't answer.

"They are trying to starve me into staying here," I tell her carefully, and as carefully, "Even if I wanted to stay . . . you can't let people do that to you, you see that, don't you?"

"How much money do you have, honey?" she asks me.

"A hundred and ten dollars." I try to figure. I have always, as my mother says, spent up to the hilt of my allowance.

"I'm going to call Steve," she tells Uncle Ephraim over my head. "He'll buy Johnny's car. You give her a check for a thousand dollars."

I find a voice. "I'll pay you back . . ."

My mother has not moved, even her eyes. She seems to stare through us. My father doesn't know what to do. But obviously, as it always has, whatever decision he makes, a blessing or donation, is to him, through the medium of money. "You don't need to do that, Eph. She's going to stay right here for a few days while we work things out . . ."

Oh, I am tired of this; I am tired of the diminishment. I go to ask Rose to take me to the airport. She is hanging up the phone. "Wait a minute." She brushes past me. "Where's the title?" I hear her ask. No one answers for a minute.

Then I hear Melinda say, "What right have you . . . ?" and Kitty Puss say, "Oh, shut up, Melinda."

"I wouldn't want to go off like this myself," Uncle Ephraim says, as if there were no quarrel at all. "But there's not a damned bit of use trying to hold somebody hell-bent for election . . ."

"You don't need to aid and abet her by lending her *money*." My father has found the voice to say the magic word.

"*You* stayed with your mother!" Mother must have been accusing Uncle Ephraim of this.

"Hell's bells, Sally Brandon. I had a two-thousand-acre farm to run . . ."

"Oh, I'll find it myself. Come on. Hannah . . ."

"Jesus," Rose says when she sees Johnny's virgin room. Then she goes to the drawer of the little desk Mother chose for him when he was twelve. "He always used to... here it is." She knows this bedroom. She has lived in it, when the family has gone away, when Johnny has had the house to himself and she could play at the marriage he never considered. I wonder if she and Tel have known each other's playacting of dreams.

Now she guides me back downstairs. "Steve is giving you five hundred cash and a check for a thousand. That's enough to give you a chance..." She stops in the middle of the stairs. "That's all you can ever do to help anybody. Papa always told me that—a railroad ticket, a suit of clothes, and a hundred dollars. That's all a man needs. He told me that, over and over."

I don't know why she is doing this, and she doesn't tell me any more.

"You stay here. Don't go in there again. Eph," she calls, "did you write the check?" There is such a silence in the living room that I can hear the pen moving and the tear of paper.

"I'll take her..." That is Uncle Ephraim.

"No, you stay here. Don't worry about me." She turns and smiles, no, grins. "He treats me like a soft-boiled egg." She puts her arm around me and guides me to the door. "I'm pregnant as a bitch. God knows you need some Wop in the family."

I think it is the opening of the front door that pushes my mother up off the sofa at last. I hear her run to the door when I am nearly to Johnny's car, and hear her call, "Come right back here, young lady!" and fainter and fainter, "... selfish ... inconsiderate... selfish," and then, a cry, "... nothing but a damned fool."

And she still cries fool, and will cry it forever in my mind, and my father will say as he did then, "Honey, honey, it will be all right, honey," like a lost soul.

IV

Epilogue
January 1980

NOW, having gone to the mild and personal source, I have come to the point which is always present, the coign of vantage, the center of a circle of time and circumstance.

There has been a tracing of change in where and what home is. For Johnny Church it was a calm future by a fireside that he had no chance to find. For Jonathan Lacey it was a plot of land, an interior city. For Johnny Catlett, a past that seduced him back to defeat. For Lily, a trap of domesticity, sex, and place that clipped her wings.

I see it now as all of these. How many of us call the place we live in home? There is in the word the pull of past, the hope of future, the plot of land, the trap, and if we come full circle, perhaps a place to leave without guilt and return to without regret, and there the seeking ends. At that point there is no longer the sense of loss that can be played on, inherited from an army of people who for three hundred years were forced to leave their birth-home.

Much of what happened in the twenty years between is of my own newfound land, and when there were returns to that city which no longer needed me, they were only a pause in a life, touch points in a search for direction, for definition.

So in the fall of 1960, with twenty-six hundred and ten dollars, I set out into the void of books I didn't know yet would exist. It took a long time for me to realize that, compared to what most people start with, I had a lot of money. At the time I thought I had been plunged into a limbo of poverty. I didn't know then that people like me are never poor. Is there any image more ludicrous than a tall, elegant, arrogantly structured Anglo-Saxon woman totally without money? I went to those doors that are opened to women like me: a job at Saks, at *Harper's Bazaar*.

I couldn't help the way I looked, but I could help my own direction. New York is the easiest place in the world to change your life in. It is as simple as not giving the next party. I don't think I have seen the people I left on that Labor Day weekend in 1960 more than a few times in the last twenty years.

The bar closed, I gave up the apartment, the friendships died. Carlo had returned in the three days I was gone. He took his paintings, my hi-fi, my electric skillet, and my address book full of unlisted numbers. It didn't seem to matter, and is hard to remember. I do remember that he left his key centered on the white cover of the *Paris Review*, Summer, 1960, and the magazine squared on my glass coffee table. It was the first thing I saw, that, and living-room blinds still drawn for a night that seemed a long time ago.

I don't know where the money came from to sustain this work. I only know that it did, just enough to lead me to the next clue. I can point to one year or another and know that this was from part-time teaching, that was a fellowship. Some way I got to England. There was only one time of faltering—that false return to Canona in 1965. It was the only place in years, including a time on the dole in England, where I went hungry.

I see now that I wanted to give them all another chance to let the Johnny within me go free. I sought a blessing. It was a quest for what I know now is only an image reflected outside of an occupied center within a pulse of being. What was worked on then was a Pavlovian constriction of the throat at the possibility of love. I went back to forgive them, and to do so I had to let them act on me, not knowing yet that forgiveness comes only when the facts are faced, all the way to the font of tears and hope.

It was then that I tried for the first time to set down Johnny's death in words. It was too soon. I failed then because I knew too little of the past. The vision was a lie. It lacked distance and empathy. I had not yet seen my father, Mooney, as a tentative boy, or the killing pride of Captain Dan Neill. I had not caught Lily's blind yearning, or seen the child, my mother, in the speckled mirror, become her isolated self.

But worse than all of this, I still saw Johnny and myself as victims. In short, I was afraid—afraid of losing the beam in my own eye, on which I depended for innocence, nostalgia, impotence.

I do know that I could not marry until that third return was freely chosen and the third exile completed—for the first exile was of a childlike rebel, the second to save a life I didn't yet know I was going to lead, to follow the star that old Solomon McKarkle said was a star in the head, and the third—the third time was the charm, for after that expulsion I carried my sense of home within me, protected, like a Bedouin, and recognized it when I finally found it. For a while it was the worst exile because it was the most hopeless, the recognition of what I had to face—that this is the way it was and is and will be. Of course I tried to avoid the facts of life in stages as classic, sometimes as fashionable as the events of given years, the crack-up, the impulse to suicide, the popular gray intelligent views, all the cowardice and the faithless eloquence of despair.

Then, in a churchyard in England, I found the wall where Johnny Church and Thankful Perkins had been shot for what I took for granted, and the foolish hearts of the well-fed Gentiles afraid of the post-war twentieth-century dark shrank to the pathos of perpetual children crying comfort me with charge cards, stay me with mirrors, while cities go mad, and the young are destroyed again, for I am sick of—what? A search for love?

I have been back once more to Canona—two months ago. This time it was not to harrow memories, turn over rocks, read time-scapes, revive what had been forgotten. I have done that now. No, it was to keep a promise I hadn't made.

When Tel Leftwich called me in Virginia, I had to think for a minute who she was, God help me. She sensed that. Her voice wavered, with age and resentment. "I'm making the calls," she said.

I could see her then, not this aggrieved-sounding woman, running down a duty list, but the last time I had seen her, at Johnny's grave.

"Aunt Althea passed away," she said as if she had said it many times, "in her sleep," she added, and then, "...a blessing."

I didn't say a word.

"She always told me she wanted you here," the voice went

on, impersonal duty, no reaching out for personal connection. I was a name on a list, a call she didn't want to make. "The funeral is at four o'clock tomorrow."

"I'll come," I told her. "I suppose it's at All Saints."

I heard Tel Leftwich's faraway and hollow electric laughter. "Good Lord no," she said. "Aunt Althea said she wouldn't be caught dead there, she told me that a hundred times. It's at Carver's Funeral Home." She hung up.

When you've struck out, pulled up stakes, put your roots down someplace else, as I have done, the life you've left behind goes on, faded out of your mind. You are only told about the disasters, the deaths—the rest is not your business. It is the one reason for a long-distance call. So it all seems like a perpetual dying, as if that were the only event. I asked George not to come with me. It was my birthplace, not his, and like all of us, he has had his own American struggle to be weaned. He didn't want me to go. He feared the frailty of my vision. He says that I have still been too brutal, as one in love and trying to leave is brutal to survive.

In a way, he is right. It is alive as no place else to me. But it is not a present life. I have no part of that. I meet myself there, as I did that day. I walked up the steps of Carver's Funeral Home on Canona Boulevard and toward Martha and Jim Dodd's hall, the last Lancelot hallway, unchanged, toward the sounds of the house as I knew it, listening from my bed next door when I was ten to glamorous, grownup people, the sounds of sophistication. Martha Dodd had been beautiful to me, and she had given me silk stockings.

At the time when you face the first dirty trick of God, that you are condemned to be yourself, not someone more reflective of your dreams, I wanted to be Martha Dodd. My mother envied her, and so she saw her as a small-town Lynn Fontanne, but to me she had grace, a slightly awkward poise. She was the only window I knew then to some freer world where there was more laughter and people wore clothes like Noel Coward plays and stayed up late. That was the laughter I could hear at night in my bed, from their living room across a narrow strip of lawn. As people know their right place in a familiar room, she stands for me against the bookshelves with their mullioned windows, in that dark room paneled like a castle, throws back her head and laughs and turns toward Jim Dodd, who leans against the carved fireplace, and makes some secret proud sign, and I can see her long neck and her Spanish bun of hair.

But on that late-November day, where there had been the scent of polish, bourbon, leather books, I walked instead into a cloying smell of roses, aerosol cans of rose scent heavy in the air, and the sound of organ music, a faint, discreet, respectful moan.

Someone touched my arm. It was the floorwalker from Johnny's funeral, heavier now, his face still as unlined, finely powdered. Behind him, through the half-opened door to the Dodds' living room, I heard the soft sound of voices, respectful, before a service.

No one looked around in that small clot of people. They sat, waiting, their backs to me.

The paneled walls had been painted a comforting mild green. Where the fireplace had been there was a small altar. The light from the old stained-glass windows made a pattern of prisms on its white cloth. In front of it where I remembered Jim Dodd standing, rared back and proud, Aunt Althea lay in her casket, her head exposed for viewing. Two wreaths lay on the mahogany-painted steel, somewhere near where her stomach and feet must be. I could just see her face, smooth, pink, and tiny on a pink satin pillow. I sat down on one of the folding chairs so I wouldn't have to look at it. There were only five other people in a room with forty chairs. I suppose they were what she called the poor-mouth Leftwiches, one broad back of a man, and four of women. They had already "paid their respects." I looked around, hoping for Candy, but she wasn't there.

It looked like a bored, dutiful funeral by rote for a woman who had stayed too long, outlived too many, no debt of love or tears or pity left to pay, a necessary rounding out.

I half listened to the fruity voice getting through it as quickly as he could. Boredom hummed in me and I thought of all the things I had to do. I considered losing weight, what the triumph of the fathers had meant in the election, wondered how soon Eisenhower waists would be back in style, sat fearing the dictatorial future, the systaltic choice we had made so late in the century of apologetic, sodden-eyed old men in love with war, the Hamiltonian young who courted them. The day was the color of cold, the river black, the trees bare under an infinite space of white winter sky outside the window. I kicked myself for the sentimental waste of time, and the fact that there was anything left in my soul to blackmail me into coming back at all. The funeral director glanced at the window where people were gathering on the porch in the cold for the next death. On the other side of the hall, where Martha Dodd's "studio" had been, and where she and Ann Randolph had taught eurythmic dancing, I could hear faint funeral music through the soundproofing of the door. I glanced around. Our door had been closed. It was covered with discreet black punched leather, like a loony bin for the dead.

It was all so thin, so without awe or sorrow. I sat empty seats away from the huddle of strangers and watched the cars speed by on the Boulevard and hoped I'd make the plane East and felt like a fool for coming and was lulled almost to near-sleep that sees the wrong things and hears the wrong sounds, and could, just could, find the wrong answers.

It was over. It had lasted, by my watch, just fifteen minutes. Two attendants closed Aunt Althea's casket window and wheeled her away on rubber wheels from her last attention by anybody on earth.

I had gotten up to go and call a taxi when the man turned around. It was as if he had crashed into me and in the midst of death I was in life and nothing was neat and nothing was put away and I wanted to run like hell with my answers *virgo intacta* and my judgments safe. I was being robbed by his look. The lid was off, the room alive. Jake Catlett, twenty years older, twenty pounds heavier, stood there watching me with unashamed tears of true silent grief sheeting his face, and called me, quite calmly, as if the tears were in his mind and not his voice, by name.

"Hannar," and came up and took me by the hand, and led me out onto the porch into the November wind that brought the only tears I could shed, and the last scudding brown leaves.

"Come all this way, Loretta," he said to the woman who followed us. She took a clean handkerchief and wiped his face. "Of course she did, honey," she told him and stuffed the handkerchief back in his breast pocket and gave it a last little tweak.

She had, as Jake had told me that night in jail, been purty in her girlhood, and now it had come on her again. She looked plump, and fragile, not the old fragility of neglect, but that of a woman who had been cared for and had gotten used to it again. She had had her hair teased for the funeral and she had a nice plump bottom in sky-blue Dacron, machine washable, but scented with wind and sun, like the old church odor of Methodist gingham. Over it she wore a mink coat.

Tel Leftwich had not fared as well. She had dried into what she had prepared for herself; old stringy mutton from sacrificial lamb. We stood there with our arms folded against the cold, not liking what either of us saw. We were herded aside for the crowd that had filled the door, going to the next funeral.

She got straight to the point as we walked toward the porch steps. We split the line of strangers, passing around us.

"I didn't think you'd come."

Loretta said, "You remember my girls. Estelle graduated from the university and Lily got married. She wouldn't have it no other way." She presented a pregnant woman, who had been the dark Slavic-looking child. Estelle was blond and slim; she still had an elegance about her she had shown at ten or eleven. She was dressed as if she knew exactly how she looked and liked it. Her hair was so shiny it looked damp, cut close to her small head. She touched the arms of her sister and her mother. She seemed to want to assure them she was there.

"Estelle's up at the State House." Her mother looked up, pleased.

Tel interrupted. She hadn't said it all and she wanted to get it over. "Aunt Althea left you her chifforobe. She always said it belonged to her sister Lily. The rest is mine. I'd like to get it out of the house. If you'll leave your address . . ."

A latecomer to the next funeral said "Excuse me," and he and Tel did a little dance to get out of each other's way.

The hearse backed out of the Dodds' driveway.

Jake took my arm again. "Now, Hannar, you come on with me and Loretta. You girls go with Miss Leftwich." He guided me down the steps as if I were slightly blind. He felt big and solid, but his face was little changed. Faces like his don't. There isn't any flesh to sag, and there are no pity lines, just deep runnels from squinting in the sun. The heavy eyebrows over his sunken eyes were as black as ever. He wore a Stetson hat four-square on his head. His ears stuck out under the brim. His shirt collar was too tight. Loretta had obviously picked out his jacket. He was disguised in a blue plaid jacket under a vicuña overcoat. He looked uncomfortable, shy, and dignified.

We stopped beside a new Buick, the size and color my father would have chosen. "Loretta, you get on in the back. I want Hannar up here with me."

There was only a procession of two cars for a forgotten woman following the hearse, up the same road, now passing new house after new house, their lawns naked in winter, all the way to the cemetery gates. Loretta didn't stop. She talked on and on about the girls, and Jake, and herself. I wasn't listening. I only heard Jake's low voice when he said, "Loretta, honey, you cut your motor off. I got things to say."

Loretta was dead-silent, leaning her arms over the back seat.

"Now I know what you're after." He didn't look at me, just went on driving, slowly. Cars on the way to the airport were backed up behind us. Aunt Althea was getting her long procession, the sign of affluence and respect in Canona. You could read the life the dead trailed behind them by the number and kinds of cars. Aunt Althea was being laid to rest by a long line of impatient hire-cars and taxis.

"They're just going to have to wait." Jake looked at the rearview mirror.

Loretta told him to quit hauling at his collar.

He told her the damned thing was too tight.

"I tole you to come with me." Loretta craned her neck toward the back window. "People got no respect," she told the taxi driver behind us.

I wasn't after anything. It was so strange to be there with that dressed-up well-upholstered hillbilly in his Buick, who I had last seen caged behind bars in the county jail, desperate and skinny, that I could only take it all for granted.

Jake got right down to what he had to say. "She wouldn't never let me tell you, she said it wasn't none of your business," he started. "Your Aunt Althea come down there on the Wednesday morning, come right down there." I knew where he was, in the county jail twenty years younger. "I seen her and Pa settin' there together when they brung me down for the rainment. Nobody else, just them."

"She come up to us the night before," Loretta added from the back seat. "She only had one light on that Hupmobile, prit near scared us to death. We thought it was the police."

"Shut up, Loretta. She was settin' there. The judge set the

charge, involuntary manslaughter, and then he agreed to the bail for ten thousand dollars.

"Well, I knew I was a goner. I couldn't of put my hands on ten cents." He would have said "knowed" twenty years ago, but it wasn't twenty years ago in the new Buick. He was caught again, his jaw clenched, his hands pale on the wheel, the hands I'd stared at, the black hairs jutting out as they had then.

"She marched right on up there, little skinny woman, I never even knew her, and she posted my bond and I walked out between her and Pa, out on bail. I remember standing there in the sun in front of the courthouse and I never knew which way to turn.

"All she said was, 'This has gone far enough.' And she just stood there too, staring at the street along with me, little skinny woman looked like a young girl 'til ye got right up to her. My pa said, 'I helped raise you girls,' to her.

"And she smiled then and she said, like I wasn't there, 'You sure did that. You ought to of told me.'

"'Now, Miss Althea'—he looked at her right through me— 'you know I couldn't take on to do nuthin' like that.'

"'Men!' she said and handed me her car keys. 'The car's in the lot,' she said, 'old black Hupmobile.' My God I never seen one of them for twenty years. So I went over there and I got it and she never even batted an eye, why I coulda got in that thing and chunked across the state line and just lit out. I thought about it, too, instinct to run. We all got it in us. She and Pa knew I wouldn't do that."

We turned in at the cemetery gates. Aunt Althea's drafted funeral train speeded up, leaving us.

"We come on up there to the house. By God, she'd even stopped and boughten a poke of groceries. Some people know what to do, and some people are big-talkee and little-dooey, ain't that the truth?"

We wound around the narrow road between the quiet stretches of grass, a fairway dotted with tombs, a dead city.

"She took over, didn't she, Loretta? Yes, ma'am, we all consider that your Aunt Althea hung the moon."

Loretta didn't answer. I looked back. She wasn't sulking. She was reliving the story, too.

"Why, she had put up her house for me. Put up her house to go my bond. She had one little piece of property left in her name up around Lacey Creek, and while we was driving,

here I was, driving that old Hupmobile, it was just a-chunkin'
and a-strainin' up that back road, she told me she needed
some feller start a little gopher-mine on shares. She said
she'd thought it all out. She said she didn't have a pot to pee
in and she said she had need of some feller. She made it
sound like I's doing her a favor.

"I never knew until later why, but the charge was dropped.
I never served another day. Later, a long time later, she told
me she just went and stood right acrost from your paw's desk
and stood there and said, 'Mooney, you pick up that goddamn
phone,' she said. 'This has gone far enough,' and she made
him pick up the phone. She took me down to Sears and we
bought tires for the pickup. She said a company had to have a
truck." He grinned. "So we started out with an old Hupmobile
and a Ford pickup. They wasn't no Buick cars then, I'll tell
the world. I like to worked myself to death. Now! God
almighty, we got three coal trucks cost 17,000 dollars apiece,
and a earthmover and a grabber, and we don't rent nuthin'.
You ought to see what we done up on Lacey Creek. Put in a
good high-wall, all green. You ought to see it. Of course," he
had to admit, "the govment made us do it. I don't hold with
the old shoot-and-shove though. I think we learned our
lesson. You put back. By God, you put back."

"Don't cuss," Loretta said.

"I ain't cussin', I'm statin' a fact."

But I had seen it. I said so. "I took Aunt Althea up there
and she never said a word." Gulfs of things I didn't know
shook me. I had been fooled by silence and a past I hadn't
shared.

"Right purty job. The govment come up and taken pictures."

"Took," Loretta muttered from the back seat.

He didn't wait for me to talk about stripping. He answered
anyway. "Listen here, I started up there with a fourteen-inch
seam of coal. I hauled that wagon out with a strap and me
a-crawling. I ain't puttin' no man underground in the dark on
a fourteen-inch seam ever again don't care what you ladies
think." He leaned back and drove his new Buick with his
arms straight out. "What the govment ought to do is the
govment ought to passel out farmland on that there new
flat-top fill, they ain't much place left for people to live
around here. Contoors," he said with sour disgust. "Hell's
far."

Loretta said, "You cussed again."

He stopped the car behind Tel's and sat and watched his girls get out. "I'm mighty proud of my girls," he said, and then, "There's lots of things…" but he wasn't finished. "Hannar, you can't never see but from where you stand. She wasn't about to tell you nothing."

"Why?"

"She didn't want to."

That was all the explanation I had. All the digging, all the questioning, all the past I'd harrowed ended in that valley where it had begun.

I didn't for that minute know enough to get out of the car.

He unfolded himself from the car and came around to open my door. "She said they wasn't a bit of use in it," Loretta said from the back seat.

So we straggled through the manicured graves of the family plot, around a fiction of stones. Mother had seen to that when Father died. She had "remodeled" the forty-by-forty-foot square nearer to her heart's desire. The heavy vault was gone. The only thing unchanged, uncensored, was the Senator's tomb. The eagle still flew over an Irish son-of-a-bitch, clutching the stone American flag in its claws as if it were going to eat it. The statues had been sand-blasted. Wisdom's round breast was as white and obscene as when it was carved. For the rest, she had reconstructed and landscaped a past. The old DAR cabin on rough stone that had been Peregrine Lacey's monument was gone. In its place on smooth marble, the plaque showed a Tara-like house, and his epitaph "Died that we might have life, liberty, and the pursuit of happiness. Colonial Dames." There were five neat rows of flat stones, as if some game could be played on them, hop from stone to stone; I knew the game, throw pebbles, ten points, hop, lean, pickup, win, triumph of children in the sun.

Mother had, at last, constructed her new tableland. "I think"—I could hear her and hear her tap her foot to help her decide—"there ought to be yew trees flanking the Senator and along the borders. So apropos"—and hear her begin to hum her favorite hymn.

She had done what had always been done, carved a space within her own control out of what she saw as a wilderness. It was, after all, only the scale of the American dream that had changed.

We stood around Althea's last piece of property, under a green awning. The breeze tugged at Estelle's pretty hair and deep, deep, from under our skins, the cold drew blood to our faces. A jet flew over us low, on its landing path to the airport. It drowned out what the funeral director was saying. Its giant shadow covered us. We, under air, diminished into silence. I saw Jake look around, and smiled a shy, private smile.

There, up on the hill, hurrying, came Uncle Ephraim and Rose and their two boys.

Uncle Ephraim hugged me and whispered, "We went to All Saints..."

"She said to hell with it," I whispered back. It was my epitaph for Aunt Althea.

I had thought I was among the dead, but I was not. The two boys stood between their father and mother. Eddie, who had been born in 1961, was so like his grandfather, Eduardo Pagano, that I found myself staring at him. Under the shadowed darkness against the winter light he stared back until I had to look down. John stood beside him, a tall, shy boy, pure McKarkle. Aunt Althea was being winched down into her last rest. The winch creaked. Somebody sighed. Jake tried to loosen his shirt collar.

There was a silence as heavy as the cold. Finally, the funeral director had to say it. "She said to say this." He got out a small piece of paper from his pocket. "You understand," he told the unfilled grave, "that this is not the usual practice." He read, "I don't know who's up here in this fool place but let me tender you a piece of advice. When you want something done in this world, don't trust a Christian who goes to church on Sunday and buys himself a Joy loader on Monday. That's all."

Jake Catlett let out one bark of a laugh and Loretta whispered, "Quit that."

"I couldn't help it," he whispered back.

The funeral director cleared his throat. "She said no prayers. Would—uh—anybody like to say a few words?"

Nobody spoke. I saw young Eddie grin at Estelle.

Finally, in the embarrassed silence, and the shadow of the awning, and the smell of earth and dry November leaves, after a sigh and a last attempt to loosen his collar, Jake Catlett stepped so near the grave that one of his Hush Puppies was hanging over the edge. He looked down.

"I reckon she wouldn't mind if I asked the Lord to give her a little peace." He muttered.

Behind him Loretta said, "After the perils of this wicked world."

We all said a ragged "Amen," and the workmen waited for us to move. Jake leaned over the mound covered with false grass and flipped it back like a sheet. He picked up a handful of dirt. "Ain't nobody else gonna do it," he said to the hand that had hit Johnny.

He threw it down. It clattered on Aunt Althea's coffin.

"Hard pan," he said, disgusted, and began to walk away. It broke up the funeral. We backed into the white day, a babble of voices tuning up. Rose hugged me. "I *told* Eph you'd be here." She hugged me again.

Tel Leftwich took my arm. "Where do I send the chifforobe?" She sounded panicked. "I've *got* to *know*."

I found something to write on in my handbag. It was a bill from Altman's.

"C.O.D.?" she asked me.

We had spread out like a disturbed covey of birds. Up among the pure rectangles, Jake Catlett held his daughters by their arms and his voice, conjuring in the distance, was all I could hear. "Now them there are your Great-great-grandma and-grandpa Peregrine Catlett and Miss Leah. She was the one built the chapel. My pa tole me that when they opened the vault at Beulah to move the graves down here when the road come through..." A jet drowned his voice. Dog on point I went softly, stepping around Lacey Kregg Neill beloved wife 1860–1937, nearer to Peregrine Catlett, 1795–1860, "Death be not proud." Mother had been at the anthology for that one. They stood by Leah Cutright Catlett, 1800–1875. None of the women got a separate fiction from Mother. They were just beloved.

Jake had stopped to wait for the jet to pass.

"My pa told me he said Mr. Catlett would be let's see, his grandpa; he was laying there on one of them stone shelves, nothing but a skeleton, and he said he looked like he'd busted out of his coffin. Wudn't nothin' left. He's laying there, one bone leg over the side, and he said his hair was real thick—and his tie was still tied real nice. Her"—he pointed over to Leah—"her. She was still like the day they put her down there. She was wearing a ruby ring he said come down through the family." He saw me then, and I held up my hand. "There it is, girls, right there, the ruby ring, and he said your Grandmother Lacey Neill looked at that same ring and laughed and he said that laughter just sounded turble and she said, 'So that's what happened. My mother-in-law always said she put it on her mother's finger to bury it with her. Bury the past, she said.'" He turned to his girls again. "Perry, that's what they called him, that was your grandpa's first cousin, he said hell if you want it take it and she just looked at him and never said a word. Anyway, that's what he told me."

Mountain conjure man, teller of tales, he guided them down to the next line of stones and counted them off. "That there was Grandpa Lewis's brother Johnny." He pointed to Jonathan Peregrine Catlett, Fourth Virginia Cavalry, Manassas, 1831–1861. Mother had done herself proud, in brass, "Died for a dream." I could hear her voice lilt. "Him and your great-grandpa never saw eye to eye over the war," Jake Catlett told his daughters. He pushed them past Lydia Catlett Neill beloved wife and Lacey Kregg Neill. He didn't even look down. He stopped over Peregrine Lacey Neill, 1858–1908. Mother's story was in Shakespearean brass, "Whose solid virtue the shot of accident nor dart of chance could neither graze nor pierce." Jake read it slowly. "Now ain't that purty?" he asked nobody. "He blowed his brains out when the bottom dropped out of the coal business. Your grandpa like to had a fit. He brung him all the way down from Beulah on a shutter. Never quit harpin' on it. They had a fondness for one another."

We looked at each other. "Estelle here is running for the legislature." He patted her arm. "Endorsed by the UMW and all." He looked so proud that it gave me hope that beyond the systole of reaction there is and always has been a diastole, an iambic public pulse between Uncle Sam and Brother Jonathan. But he looked beyond me at the last row of stones, and said, "Oh, Hannar, honey, they's things in the past you can't do nuthin' about. I just don't like to think about that year." I knew he was seeing my brother Johnny's grave beyond my shoulder.

"Settin' up there in that shack like a bump on a log waiting for somebody to wipe my nose." He wasn't thinking about Johnny at all. With that apology, if it could be called one, he guided the two girls over toward the others and left me alone.

I could hear their voices come together when I turned around to look at Johnny's grave, all the Johnnys' graves to me in that one flat carpet of grass, each the size of a single bed. What I wanted to feel I did not feel. It was one of those moments when the reality that crouches behind circumstance reached out and shook me awake. I wanted to laugh. Mother's voice in brass said, "When wounded sore the stricken heart." That, as she had said, was the way she always heard it. Beside him she rested, no beloved wife for herself, but under her favorite hymn, "And view the shining glory shore, my heaven, my home forever more:"

She had willed me *O Beulah Land*. It was from her, murmured in Miss Leah's Chapel, hummed in the mornings when she forgot her fictions. I heard her singing, keeping away panic, "The angels come and walk with me, and pure communion here have we, the angels take me by the hand and show me heaven's tableland." The tears ran down my face. Land-hungry, frightened, blindly running, dragging pride as a weapon and a disguise, we met at last, and Uncle Ephraim took me by the arm and led me away.

And by the touch of his blessing, misunderstood. "I forgot you hadn't been up here since your parents passed away, honey." I had been in England at my mother's death, in France at my father's. Melinda and Spud had not sent for me. They had, Melinda wrote, too many things to settle, including moving to Aiken on Melinda's inheritance and J. D. Cutright's coal holdings.

Uncle Ephraim waited for me.

So I made my own fictions. For Johnny I wrote, in best funereal brass, "Prometheus when drunk, Epimetheus when sober." I moved to Mother, "*Sic semper tyrannis*," and for Father beside her where she had written, "Greater love hath no man," I wrote the same motto of the Virginia flag where a female "Freedom" stands on a recumbent male tyrant, the secret translation of *Sic semper tyrannis*, for poor old Mooney, for his mother and his wife and maybe, too, his daughters, "Get your foot off my neck."

Uncle Ephraim walked me down to where the others stood; new people, to something I had not seen before, parents taking pride in their children under the cold afternoon sun. One of the boys, young Eddie, was talking with Estelle. "I'm coming back and go into politics, too," I heard him say.

"You are?" Rose asked. She sounded surprised. Something had happened to her face. She had caught youth again from her children.

Eddie grinned at her. "Ma, you haven't got a chance. I'm going to law school at Morgantown. No, Ma, not Harvard." He turned again to talk to Estelle.

Rose looked at me as if she didn't want a chance. I was watching a new breed of child, maybe as mistaken as we had been, but at least unafraid of the fathers. Beyond the long knives of the sixties revolution, these children of the next decade had been granted adulthood as a right. It is the only lasting result of revolution I know, when a dream of one generation becomes a right of the next.

"There goes my vote," Uncle Ephraim said.

But nobody minded. No mouths folded. And nobody in that circle had room for the dead any more. It might not be better, but I knew there was something between them I hadn't ever known. Only Tel Leftwich still looked locked in anger, wrinkled as a prune.

Uncle Ephraim caught me looking at my watch.

"Come on down to Tel's?"

"No. I can't. My plane leaves in an hour," echoed all the way back to my parents' living room after Johnny's funeral.

"I'll take her to the airport," he told the others. Loretta and Rose walked on ahead. They seemed to have known each other in a long time that I had missed.

Jake shook my hand and held it for a minute. Then he walked away, back toward the coal business.

Neither Uncle Ephraim nor I said a word on the way to the airport. There simply wasn't anything to say. We were in the same car on entirely different roads.

When the car stopped and I got out, he leaned toward the window. "Now don't forget us, honey." He looked somewhere near my hands, not at my face, and then the habit phrase covered the silence: "You come on down see us, you hear?"

It was my turn to watch a car until it disappeared down the hill. I hadn't meant it to end like this, stranded and cut down to size in an airport. Busy strangers with briefcases eddied around me, unseeing, hailing taxis to the latest coal boom. I brought always a past they were doing their best to forget, even the men calling their taxis. They brought a present I had no part in. As every wanderer knows, the ones who are left turn away, back to the day, as soon as the door is shut, or the plane takes off, or the grave is filled, or Cassandra, an eminently sensible girl, the first novelist, makes her warning based on past, habits, and the end so easily seen when the means are known.

The jet rose over the tiny white dots in the cemetery below us. Its shadow flowed over green patches, bare trees, and stones. I could not pick out our family plot of land, all that was ours. The plane turned in its flight path. I thought I saw the twin roofs of Mother's and Melinda's houses, both long sold. Even that land had been exchanged into stocks and gilt-edged securities of paper in the Coal Banking and Trust Building. Spud administered a territory that was the size of two steel drawers.

We flew higher until the river was a thin line. The raw hills rolled bluer and bluer in the distance, their scars shining like battlements, their gashes black runnels down to the rivers, their new man-made tablelands pale among the skeletal winter trees. Below us, on mile after mile of mountains, the sun beat like a gong. We climbed higher, and it was all blue, as it had been when it was found by the lost people who bred us—people more lost, more frightened, more unneeded than we would ever be. It looked, so far away, like a new earth under a new heaven, where the former things could always pass away. Except in tiny spots distance hid where the exploited ground had turned to overlay us like a sleeping giant, clay and shale thrown over our wasteful faces. Once, we had cut down its trees, and the water had poured down its naked gullies and swept itself clean. Once, we had stabbed too hard, and in those places it had shrunk back, baring its rock teeth. Arrogance and lack of care toward its riches had grown into arrogance and lack of care for each other. The crash of the grabber at the coal-face had exploited, grabbed, as we had grabbed.

We had left a residue of carelessness through the blind days of our building, and the generation of our children had been born to clean it away. Our ruins still glistened in the tiny black scars below me, ignored by the miles of trees. We had forgotten our frontier, the same frontier that we had always found, a frontier of indifference, whether of trees or men.

I could see patches of green where someone, not us, had already begun the reclaiming of the land, men like Jake, who had "learned their lesson." It was theirs now, to build or to defile, and I had no place in it.

But I carried with me, after all the searching, from all the people that I had conjured up and brought to life again, a thing deeper than land. It was stratum on stratum of connection, neither by blood nor by conviction, but by one minute, sometime, of refusal, whether it was Johnny Church's to doff his hat, or even Jake's fist that had struck out and carried with it all the pent-up fury against "the way things are."

It was the choice to choose, to be singular, burn bridges, begin again, whether in a new country or a new way of seeing or a new question, which was as ancient as wandering itself.

Finally I knew that I had joined the wanderers, from Johnny Church, through the old Hannah, lost in the woods below, Jonathan Lacey who had brought us there, Johnny Catlett, Carlo Michele, Eduardo Pagano, and Lily; all of those who have set out alone, perhaps self-deluded by necessity. But it was the wanderers who had given us a country, and left the scars behind. Deep within us there had been instilled an itch, a discontent, an unfulfilled promise, perpetually demanding that it be kept. Johnny and Thankful, and all of us, would always fail and always win, and eternal vigilance and our sense of loss, of being unblessed, were the price of freedom.

I was nearly asleep. The last thing I remembered seeing as we banked northeast was the faint white bandage of the ramp over Beulah. Slowly, under our leaping shadow, the small wasteland of the hill farm turned like a dead bird nestled in a gray winter sea.

I slept between promise and hard pan as we always have and in my dream I saw a reconstructed town with authentic Jenny Lind houses and ladies dressed in authentic costumes with Mrs. Escew's apron moving dream-slow explaining it all to tourists in blue Dacron, "named for Jenny Lind the Swedish singer and here we mined moonstones but we stopped because moonstones are unlucky, except for witches," and the mine mouth and the ladies were as small, as diminished as fairies. They all wore authentic sneakers and followed each other under the hill, and I was twenty and there was only Thankful Perkins to tell it to.

ABOUT THE AUTHOR

MARY LEE SETTLE was awarded a Guggenheim fellowship for her work on the Beulah cycle. She now divides her time between her home in Virginia and Bard College.

THE WORLD FANTASY AWARD-WINNING NOVEL

"AMBITIOUS, DAZZLING, STRANGELY MOVING, A MARVELOUS MAGIC-REALIST FAMILY CHRONICLE."
—*Book World (The Washington Post)*

Little, Big

by *John Crowley*

Somewhere beyond the city, at the edge of a wildwood, sits a house on the border between reality and fantasy, a place where the lives of faeries and mortals intertwine. Sometime in our age, a young man in love comes here to be wed, and enters a family whose Tale reaches backward and forward a hundred years, from the sunlit hours of a gentler time, to the last, dark days of this century—and beyond to a new dawn.

Sensual, exuberant, witty, and wise, LITTLE, BIG is a true masterpiece, a tale of wonder you will take to your heart and treasure for years to come. It is on sale September 15, 1983, wherever Bantam paperbacks are sold, or you can use this handy coupon for ordering:

Bantam Books, Inc., Dept. LB1, 414 East Golf Road, Des Plaines, Ill. 60016

Please send me _____ copies of LITTLE, BIG (23337-8 • $3.95). I am enclosing $_____ (please add $1.25 to cover postage and handling. Send check or money order—no cash or C.O.D.'s please).

Mr/Ms _____

Address _____

City/State _____ Zip _____

LB1—9/83

Please allow four to six weeks for delivery. This offer expires 3/84.

New from
BANTAM WINDSTONE BOOKS

☐ THE HOUSE ON PRAGUE STREET by Hana Demetz
   (20184-0 • $2.95)

The haunting novel of a young girl's world, forever
shattered by the war—a tale of tragic innocence and
terrible devastation, of lost love, and ultimately, of
survival. "A lovely, poignant jewel."

—Chaim Potok

☐ LUNAR ATTRACTIONS by Clark Blaise
   (13402-7 • $3.95)

A sharply ironic, richly textured weave of the innocence
and cruelty of childhood, of the brutality and tenderness
of love. "The most ferocious and astonishing scene of
adolescent sexual first contact ever written."

—*The National Review*

☐ THE KILLING GROUND by Mary Lee Settle
   (23439-0 • $3.95)

The compelling story of author Hannah McCarkle; her
relentless search for the truth behind her brother's
mysterious death, and her fierce struggle for freedom
from her own past. By the National Book Award-Winner.
"[A] world so rich and so tough it is impossible not
to believe in." —*Saturday Review*

Buy these books at your local bookstore or use this handy
coupon for ordering:

Bantam Books, Inc., Dept. WD15, 414 East Golf Road, Des Plaines, Ill. 60016

Please send me the books I have checked above. I am enclosing $_____
(please add $1.25 to cover postage and handling, send check or money
order—no cash or C.O.D.'s please).

Mr/Ms _____

Address _____

City/State _____ Zip _____

WD15—8/83

Please allow four to six weeks for delivery. This offer expires 4/84.
Price and availability subject to change without notice.

The Most Important Voices of Our Age

WINDSTONE BOOKS

This new line of books from Bantam brings you the most important voices and established writers of our age. Windstone. The name evokes the strong, enduring qualities of the air and the earth. The imprint represents the same qualities in literature—boldness of vision and enduring power, importance and originality of concept and statement. Windstone brings you contemporary masterpieces at affordable prices.

Windstone Books from Bantam bring you the most important voices and established writers of our age. They evoke the strong, enduring qualities of the air and the earth. Here are more Windstone titles with that same quality.

]	23439	**THE KILLING GROUND** Mary Lee Settle	$3.95
]	20184	**THE HOUSE ON PRAGUE STREET** Hana Demetz	$3.50
]	23197	**AN UNKNOWN WOMAN: A JOURNEY TO SELF-DISCOVERY** Alice Koller	$3.95
]	22604	**THE DIVINERS** M. Laurence	$3.95
]	20850	**THE GOLDEN NOTEBOOK** D. Lessing	$4.95
]	22817	**MEMOIRS OF A SURVIVOR** D. Lessing	$3.95
]	20848	**AT PLAY IN THE FIELDS OF THE LORD** P. Matthiessen	$3.50
]	20847	**FAR TORTUGA** P. Matthiessen	$3.95
]	20665	**THE SNOW LEOPARD** P. Matthiessen	$3.95
]	13441	**ONE DAY IN THE LIFE OF IVAN DENISOVICH** Alexander Solzhenitsyn	$2.50
]	20647	**DELTA OF VENUS** Anais Nin	$3.50
]	22969	**A SPY IN THE HOUSE OF LOVE** Anais Nin	$2.95
]	13402	**LUNAR ATTRACTIONS** Clark Blaise	$3.95

Prices and availability subject to change without notice.

Bantam Books, Inc., Dept. WD6, 414 East Golf Road, Des Plaines, Ill. 60016

Please send me the books I have checked above. I am enclosing $_____
(please add $1.25 to cover postage and handling). Send check or money
order—no cash or C.O.D.'s please.

Mr/Mrs/Miss_____

Address _____

City_____State/Zip_____

WD6—10/83

Please allow four to six weeks for delivery. This offer expires 4/84.